NATIVE STRANGER

Book Three of the Lazare Family Saga

ELIZABETH BELL

Claire-Voie Books

NATIVE STRANGER (Lazare Family Saga, Book Three)

Print cover design by James T. Egan, www.bookflydesign.com

This is a work of historical fiction. Names, characters, organizations, places, events, and incidents are either products of the author's imagination or are used fictitiously. The opinions expressed are those of the characters and should not be confused with the author's.

Subjects: 1. Charleston (S.C.)—Social life and customs—19th century—Fiction. 2. First loves—Fiction. 3. Family secrets—Fiction. 4. Slavery—United States—Fiction. 5. Culture conflict—Fiction. 6. Identity (Psychology)—Fiction. 7. Racially mixed people—Fiction. 8. Passing (Identity)—Fiction. 9. Physicians—Fiction. 10. Love stories.

ISBN 978-1-7331676-5-9 (ebook)
ISBN 978-1-7331676-4-2 (paperback)
ISBN 978-1-7370374-3-9 (hardcover)
ISBN 978-1-7370374-8-4 (audiobook)

 Created with Vellum

For the outsiders

CONTENTS

PROLOGUE

NEBRASKA TERRITORY
NOVEMBER 1859

I love to roam over the prairies. There I feel free and happy, but when we settle down we grow pale and die.
— Kiowa Chief Set-t'ainte (White Bear), in a speech before the Treaty of Medicine Lodge Creek, October 1867

Ésh stared sullenly at the retreating landscape of his life. He and Lieutenant Gates, the bluecoat taking him East, travelled throughout the day and into the night. They stopped at ugly little "stations" made of mud only long enough to change horses and choke down food. At least these *veho* claimed it was food.

Every station took Ésh farther and farther from the Zizistas, from his family, from the land that he loved. Did the Sun play across the Earth anywhere else as he did here? Ésh fingered the rabbit skin that said *David McAllister* and *Charleston*—the words from the cave on Independence Rock, where Ésh's mother and grandfather had found him abandoned as a baby.

Ésh wanted to make them proud. He wanted to bring back to

the Zizistas the secrets of the *veho*'s powerful medicine. He also wanted to understand why his white family, these McAllisters, had left him behind. But he wondered if he would ever be able to find his way home again. Were these his last sights of the mountains and prairies?

Ésh hated riding in this *veho* contraption, like a child bumping along in a pony drag instead of a man united with a horse. The *veho* called it a "stagecoach." Its reddish-brown shape was a mockery of a buffalo. Its top was even humped with buffalo robes. Ésh sat inside the belly of this strange beast, facing West with his back to the six horses. Lieutenant Gates sat next to him, and two other *veho* slumbered across from them.

The unnatural beast swayed and jerked with every turn and dip and bump. Often Ésh was thrown against Gates, who glared at him as if Ésh had done it on purpose, when Ésh was clinging to the side of the beast with all his might.

For a while, a thunderstorm raged outside, and the *veho* secured the leather flaps to cover the windows. Ésh would have preferred to let the cold rain soak him. He felt as if he were trapped inside that underground cell at Fort Laramie again, this time in the middle of an earthquake. Or perhaps he was inside a rattle shaken by a malevolent medicine man. His last meal climbed his throat more than once.

Finally, the thunderstorm passed. Ésh tied up the leather covering so he could lean his head out the window to inhale the clean scents of sagebrush and Earth.

Am I going toward something, Ésh asked himself as he stared at the land disappearing behind him, *or am I simply running away like a coward?* He had so many reasons to run away. Méanév, the woman he had loved since he was a child, had married his brother instead.

His brother who was a real Zizistas. Ésh couldn't even blame Méanév. He'd tried so hard to be a good hunter and warrior. But the longer the Zizistas fought the *veho* for control of this land, the more they looked at Ésh and saw only another *veho*. Another white man.

Then, movement drew Ésh's gaze from the far-off mountains.

Much closer, keeping pace with the stagecoach, disappearing and reappearing with each hill that passed between them, a black wolf ran alongside him. Ésh's eyes widened in wonder.

This was the spirit he had seen as a boy, whose black fur Ésh carried in the medicine pouch around his neck. This black wolf had given him his formal name: Mo'ohtáwo'neh. This wolf had come to him again just last moon and led him to the *veho*. This spirit had appeared with the girl whose voice and hair were like honey, and she had told him in English: "The wolf will show you the way."

The Sacred Powers were giving him another sign—they had not forgotten him! The wolf was running eastward, just ahead of him now, showing Ésh where to go.

If he followed, he would find this Charleston and this David, Ésh knew. He would find the girl with the voice and hair like honey. He would understand what had happened eighteen summers ago at his birth.

PART I
IN HER WAKE

1851-1853

CHARLESTON, SOUTH CAROLINA

Then, there is a kind of contempt of the landscape felt by him who has just lost by death a dear friend. The sky is less grand as it shuts down over less worth in the population.

— Ralph Waldo Emerson, *Nature* (1836)

CHAPTER 1

EIGHT YEARS EARLIER
NOVEMBER 1851
STRATFORD-ON-ASHLEY PLANTATION

Love is strong as death, jealousy as hard as hell.
— Canticle of Canticles 8:6

As her foster-son, David was horrified by what Edward Stratford had done to his wife. As a scientist, he was fascinated.

Tessa had perished—violently—nearly a month ago, yet Edward behaved as if his wife might start awake and tap frantically on the coffin window at any moment. In life, he had abused and neglected Tessa. In death, his devotion was relentless. Edward sobbed and stared by turns, his clothes perpetually rumpled from sleeping night after night on the parlor settee beside her catafalque. David had had to watch for this opportunity to be alone with Tessa, the woman who had been his foster-mother for a decade, half of his life.

Ostensibly, Edward was waiting for the masons and sculptors to complete his wife's tomb in the plantation's cemetery. But as the days became weeks, as each vigil candle and hothouse lily was discarded and replaced, David wondered if his foster-father ever planned to relinquish Tessa's body. Perhaps Edward intended to keep his wife on display forever, like the quail under glass on the bric-à-brac shelf in the corner.

David had seen the advertisements—John C. Calhoun's body had been exhibited in one of these coffins only last year—but the sketch in the newspapers did not quite prepare you. *"Fisk's Patent Metallic Burial Cases: Air tight and indestructible, for preserving the mortal remains of the departed for an indefinite period of time above or under ground..."* Edward was certainly putting Fisk's claims to the test.

Worthy of a pharaoh's wife, at once exquisite and grotesque, the metal coffin followed the contours of Tessa's body like the wrappings of a mummy. The billowing folds and decorated hem of a shroud were cast right into the black iron. A carnation was also stamped into the metal, on the bulge for her feet. One bud drooped and the other bloomed, acknowledging death but promising resurrection. Two weeping angels flanked the brass name-plate over her chest, which read simply:

Teresa Stratford
1816-1851

If David leaned too close, he saw his own reflection in the oval window above her face. The undertaker had disguised Tessa's wounds well, and Edward had set the damaged side of her toward the wall. In the candlelight, her features appeared unchanged: the beautiful face in the shape of a heart, cheeks adorned by the fringe of closed eyelashes, delicate nose, generous lips, hair rippling down her shoulders. At first glance, she seemed only to slumber.

But in life, Tessa's skin had glowed like alabaster, her floor-length tresses as luminous as honey in sunlight. Now, her face was waxen, her hair drab. Like the dulled wings of a pinned butterfly, the colors were not quite as David remembered them. The longer he gazed down at her, the more he saw this for what it was: a mockery rather than a memorial.

Still he wished he'd been present for the embalming. The process was so expensive, only planters like Edward could afford it. David imagined the solution contained alcohol, arsenic, perhaps sodium nitrate... Vermilion or carmine dye, to make up for the blood she'd lost?

The embalming surgeon knew other secrets too: the nature and location of Tessa's injuries. The clues that might reveal whether she'd stumbled and fallen down the stairs or *leapt* from the balcony of this plantation house.

Saint Alphonsus warned against the dangers of curiosity. In this case, David conceded his wisdom. Father Lynch had accepted Tessa's death as an accident and approved a Christian burial. David's inquiries could accomplish nothing now—they would not bring her back—and they might do a great deal of harm.

David couldn't believe Tessa had taken her own life, but neither had he ever witnessed such despair. Tessa had endured thirteen years in a miserable marriage; and then, when she'd gathered the courage to elope with her lover, he'd refused her.

David felt a presence in the parlor behind him. He tensed, expecting Edward. Instead, as if David's thoughts had conjured him, Uncle Joseph appeared. His steps were heavy, his eyes red-rimmed as he stopped beside David and stared down at the face of his lover beneath the glass.

"She looks like an Incorruptible," his uncle murmured.

David returned his attention to Tessa and nodded. He'd never seen an Incorruptible, but his uncle had as a seminarian in Rome. Joseph had described them: saints whose purity in life persisted after death, whose corpses reposed in reliquaries of metal and glass for all to see. As a sign of their holiness, the bodies of Incorruptibles did not decay; they remained pliant and often emitted a sweet scent. Some bled or opened their eyes centuries after their souls had departed.

David found himself watching Tessa's eyelashes for movement. But to the Church, she was anything but pure. She was the worst of sinners: she'd committed adultery with a Priest and quite possibly committed suicide.

Joseph seemed to read his thoughts. "She *was* pure, David." Remorse thickened his voice. "The way she loved—it was holy, selfless and bottomless…"

And Joseph had thrown it away, because he couldn't stop being a Priest. David would have eloped with Tessa, if she'd asked him. But to her, David remained the ten-year-old boy she'd taken as her ward, not a twenty-year-old man who would have protected her with his life.

"You!"

David started and turned; but like Tessa, Edward saw only Joseph.

"How *dare* you come here!" Dull brown hair in greasy disarray, unshaven, eyes bloodshot, collar undone, Edward slammed his empty liquor glass on the nearest table. "That one is bad enough!" He motioned toward David, but his glare remained fixed on Joseph.

Joseph retreated from the coffin, stammering an apology. David followed.

"My wife is dead because of *you*." Edward pitched toward them, jabbing his finger at Joseph. "If you had kept your damned filthy hands off her, she would still be alive!"

David held his breath. Edward knew about Joseph and Tessa. He *knew*.

Edward staggered and caught himself on the coffin, staring through the window as if Joseph and David might have interfered with Tessa in his absence. Even amidst the scent of the hothouse lilies, Edward reeked of whiskey and unwashed skin.

The blood had drained from Joseph's face. "Mrs. Stratford was like a sister to me, and that is—"

"Like a sister?" Edward laughed bitterly. "Did you make a habit of fucking your sisters, Father?"

Joseph flinched and averted his eyes from the other man's glare. "I—*never*… We never…"

"That's what *she* said. You're *liars*; you're both *liars*…" Edward hid his face in his hand and moaned. "She was thinking of *you*. Always *you*."

Joseph waited for a lull in Edward's sobs. "I know I have no right to ask this, Mr. Stratford—no right to ask you for anything. But if you will allow me to assist at the Requiem—"

Edward turned back to him, clenching his fists. "Admit what you did first!"

Joseph's gaze settled on Tessa's coffin. "I loved your wife, and she is dead because of me."

"Damn right," Edward spat.

"But the last thing either of us wants is a scandal, and I remain your curate. How would I explain to Father Lynch why I cannot assist him in the burial rites?"

"You're a practiced liar—think of something!" Edward stumbled again, swaying dangerously close to one of the vigil candles. David stepped forward to catch it, but Edward misinterpreted the gesture. "Get the Hell away from her!"

David complied.

"Damned Lazares," Edward muttered, returning to the coffin and bracing his forearm on the lid.

For the first ten years of his life, David had been a McAllister; that was his father's name. But when David became Edward's ward, the man had insisted David use his mother's maiden name, Lazare. In Charleston, French names implied pedigree. Since Lazare was also Joseph's name, Edward must regret his decision.

Joseph remained undeterred. "Mr. Cromwell wrote us that the tomb is nearly finished. Father Lynch has set the Requiem Mass for Friday. Do I have your permission to assist him?"

Edward didn't take his eyes from Tessa's face. "What do I care if he comes? He can't have you again. He can't *ever* have you again. There is *that*." His voice slurred, then became incomprehensible. His body convulsed over the coffin, and he made a sort of choking sound. David feared the man would vomit. Instead, Edward began blubbering again.

Joseph seemed to take Edward's words as permission and left the parlor. David came with him. In the hall, his uncle asked in a low voice: "How is Clare?"

"About as you'd expect." David had resumed living under

Edward's roof so he could comfort Tessa's daughter. Clare had no one else, and David knew what it was like to be motherless.

He and his uncle found the eight-year-old girl where David had left her: asleep on a bench on the veranda outside her bedchamber, overlooking the garden, just around the corner from the staircase where Tessa had ended her life. Clare clutched David's handkerchief and a collection of fairy stories. Her hair was so like her mother's, the color of dark honey, but done up in girlish curls.

Edward's widowed eldest sister, Mrs. Hortense Fernande, had also taken up residence at Stratford-on-Ashley since Tessa's death. Hortense had given up on making her brother presentable to visitors offering condolences, but she'd imposed her unwanted attentions on her niece, insisting that Clare be properly dressed and coiffed every day despite her grief. Whatever she wore, the girl refused to relinquish her favorite bracelet, a turquoise ouroboros.

David knew his uncle had had a long ride from Charleston to the plantation—nearly three hours' travel for a few moments' hostile conversation with Edward. David whispered: "Should I wake Clare before you go?"

Joseph shook his head. "Let her rest. If she ever wishes to see me…" He sighed. His last attempt to comfort the girl had not been well received. "I will come at once. But I don't have any answers. Not anymore."

When his uncle had gone, David resumed his place on the bench beside Clare. Careful not to disturb the girl's uneasy slumber, hoping his touch might console her, he ran his fingers lightly over her hair. He made sure to brush the two little nevi on her left cheekbone, beneath the corner of her eye. A layman would call the spots moles, and Clare's Aunt Hortense always obscured them with powder. David found them endearing. He saw with satisfaction that his fingertips and Clare's own perspiration had restored the brown spots to their natural color. As he withdrew his hand, the girl whimpered in her sleep, but she did not wake.

The French called such birthmarks *envies*, which also meant "desires." Even in English, he'd heard them called "longing marks," from the belief that a mother's desire for a child stamped its skin in her womb. After six miscarriages, few mothers had longed for a child as fervently as Tessa had Clare—and yet, in the end, she'd deserted her daughter.

David knew Clare's father and aunt resented his presence here because of David's resemblance to his "Papist" uncle. A year ago, Edward had ejected David, who technically lived with his grandparents now. But David would not abandon his foster-sister like he'd abandoned his baby brother at Independence Rock.

Clare was part of his Penance: David atoned for his fratricide by being a brother to her. David entertained and distracted his foster-sister as much as he could, but mostly he served as her anchor now. He would let the girl sob against him or simply cling to him. She seemed to fear that if she let go, he would leave her as her mother had.

Often, David read to Clare: fairy stories and the tales of Indian life she liked so much. Sometimes an event in one of her books would remind the girl of her mother, and then the weary little voice would interject: "Do you remember when Mama…?" David would smile through his own sadness and help the girl conjure Tessa's shadow. It always slipped away again, even as her body lingered in the parlor.

When she stirred, Clare inched closer to him. She wanted David to read from her collection of German fairy tales. At eight years old, she could read them herself, but his voice seemed to soothe her.

Clare rested her head against his shoulder and listened raptly to the story of Snow White, who could not resist temptation. A single bite of poisoned apple proved her undoing. But she remained so beautiful, Snow White's friends the dwarves could not bear to lay her beneath the earth. They built her a glass coffin and watched over her night and day. Then a prince saw the dead girl who seemed only to be sleeping. He begged to take Snow White to his castle. As the prince's servants lifted the coffin, the piece of apple dislodged from her throat, and she revived.

Clare sat up. "All they had to do was lift the coffin?"

"The apple was enchanted," David explained. "You know there aren't enchantments in real life."

Clare frowned at the book, her small fingers caressing the page. Finally, she understood: "It wouldn't work with Mama."

"I'd bring her back if I could, *souris*." David stroked her head, using his nickname for her, a word that meant both *mouse* and *smile* in French.

Clare was not smiling now. But as she looked up at him, her curls danced, a jarring contrast to her mournful face.

"It will be easier after the funeral, don't you think?"

The girl stared toward the parlor. "She'll be all *alone*."

David stroked Clare's shoulder in reassurance. "Your Mama isn't lonely. She's with her father. She's with my aunt Hélène, who was her best friend." Yet if they believed in Heaven, didn't they also have to believe that Tessa would be shut out of it, for what she'd done? David longed for the simple justice of Clare's fairy stories. "She's with my sister Sophie, who was her daughter before she had you."

"But *I'm* alone."

"No; you have me."

The girl's head drooped. "You're going away to Paris for school."

"Not for two years yet."

Clare looked up again. "You said you were leaving next year."

He was becoming a doctor to help people; and the person who needed his help most was sitting right here beside him. If only heartbreak could be cured with a few blue pills. "I can stay another year. Would you like me to?"

Clare nodded vehemently.

CHAPTER 2

I carry away with me the regret of not having been yours!
— François-René de Chateaubriand, *Atala; or the Love and Constancy of Two Savages in the Desert* (1801)

The morning of the funeral, David woke—or at least gave up trying to sleep—just after dawn. He slipped from his bed, careful not to wake Tessa's brother Liam who lay on the trundle-bed. Tessa's four brothers and their mother had travelled from New York for her burial. Quietly David pulled on a fresh shirt, black trousers, and braces. He pushed his feet into slippers and gathered up his shaving things, which he took onto the upper veranda. Beyond its Tuscan columns, fog devoured all but the nearest branches of the live oaks.

After he'd trimmed his mustache and shaved, David returned to find Liam sitting up and rubbing his eyes. Still in his nightshirt, the Irishman watched David don his waistcoat and tie his cravat. Finally, Liam spoke: "David, do you think…?" He broke off, sounding uncertain.

David turned. "Yes?"

Liam handed David his boots but avoided his eyes. "I know your grandparents loved Tessa like a daughter, and that your uncle loved her like… I know they're grieving too, and I want very much to share a bit of *good* news, only I don't know if they'll see it that way. They may see it as infidelity…"

David looked up and frowned. "Infidelity?"

"Toward Hélène I mean." She was David's aunt, Uncle Joseph's youngest sister, who'd died because of a breast tumor nine years before. "But Agnes has lost someone too, and she has a little boy who needs a father, and…"

Now David smiled, guessing the truth. "Agnes?"

Liam was nearly forty, and still he blushed. That florid Irish complexion concealed nothing. "The widow who has consented to marry me."

David did up the last of his buttons. "Of course my uncle and grandparents won't see it as infidelity. They will be pleased, Liam— relieved!" He stood. "My grandmother will see this as an answer to prayer—as long as this Agnes is a good Catholic girl."

"She is." Liam gave a great sigh to release his apprehension. "Then I will tell them."

David nodded in approval and pulled on his coat.

"I didn't think it was possible, to love twice," Liam murmured, half to himself, as he checked his pocket watch. "I won't say 'tis the same—how could it be? Hélène and Agnes are different people. *I'm* different. But they are both miracles."

"I'll leave you to dress." David crossed the hall and knocked gently on Clare's bedchamber door.

The girl's grandmother answered. Mrs. Conley was a kind woman, but she had been devastated by the loss of her only daughter, and she was a near stranger to Clare. Mrs. Conley said she herself wasn't ready yet, but Clare could go ahead with David. The girl emerged in her grey dress, keeping her eyes on the rug. She still wore her ouroboros bracelet, the turquoise snake swallowing its own tail. David hoped the symbol was true: that nothing died without being reborn.

He stooped down to Clare and attempted a smile. "Good morning, *souris*."

"No it isn't." The words were not hostile, only resigned. She still took his hand and walked with him down the stairs.

In the parlor, they heard voices: Edward and his English-born secretary, Lucas Cromwell. Since Tessa's death, Cromwell had become Edward's steward as well, managing his plantations while Edward wallowed in mourning. Cromwell had also overseen all the funeral preparations. Edward trusted the young Englishman completely, treating Cromwell more like a son than he ever had David. Not that David begrudged Cromwell such a father.

"Don't make me put her in the ground, Lucas," Edward whined as if he were a child.

"It is a *temple*, sir. I showed you the drawings."

"Once we close that window, I will *never* see her face again…" Edward blubbered. "You don't know what it's like, Lucas: to have held something so precious and watch it slip through your fingers. If I could go back, start again… Where did I go wrong, Lucas?"

You married a woman for her beauty, and you never even tried to understand her, David supplied in his head. *You won't even be a father to her daughter —your daughter—when Clare needs you most.*

Tessa's four brothers and their mother descended the stairs next. The Conleys' dark looks toward the parlor showed they agreed with David about Edward. The man behaved as if he had a monopoly on grief.

Hoofs and wheels crunched the oyster shells of the drive. A slave opened the front door, revealing its mourning wreath of crape and yew. Outside, four sable horses mouthed their bits, their heads crowned with black ostrich plumes. They drew an elegant hearse of ebony, silver, and glass. The driver was a mulatto—free colored, David guessed. In addition to his dusky skin and black suit, the man wore a black sash trailing from the brim of his top hat.

Two other coaches followed. One contained Uncle Joseph and their tall, bespectacled pastor, Father Lynch. His black biretta concealed his receding hair, though he was not yet thirty-five—five years younger than his curate. Both Priests were vested in layers of black upon white: black soutanes falling to their black shoes, white surplices falling past their knees, and black stoles hanging from their necks. As the celebrant, Father Lynch also wore an imposing black cope.

The second coach held David's Grandfather René and Grandmother Anne. Since Edward was in no condition to carry his wife's coffin, Grandfather had volunteered as a bearer. He'd just completed his sixty-second year, but the combination of a strong constitution and his own doctoring skills kept him fit for such duty.

In the parlor, Cromwell reminded Edward that the funeral rites would be lengthy, that it would be hours yet before Tessa reached her tomb. Edward allowed them to screw on the face-plate. Father Lynch blessed the coffin with holy water and intoned the first Psalm: "'If Thou shouldst retain in memory our offenses, O Lord, who would have the strength to bear it?'"

David returned Clare to her grandmother. He, Grandfather, and Tessa's four brothers surrounded her iron coffin and gripped the handles adorned with cherubs. In unison, they lifted her from the catafalque. David grimaced at the weight, and he heard even the burly Irishmen grunting. Tessa had been slender, and David had carried her once, when she'd sprained her ankle. Even distributed among five other bearers, this was different. Fisk's Patent Metallic Burial Case more than doubled her weight.

David, Grandfather, and Tessa's brothers maneuvered their burden into the entry hall, through the front door, across the veranda, and down the steps. Behind them, Cromwell led Edward as if the man were ancient and crippled. Grandmother did her best to comfort Mrs. Conley without words.

Finally, they slid the iron coffin inside the hearse. Liam latched the glass-and-ebony doors. Against the plush cream interior draped with curtains and tassels, the black coffin seemed to shrink.

The day remained appropriately overcast. Furred with resurrection ferns, shrouded in Spanish moss, and veiled by fog, the great spreading branches of the live oaks seemed as insubstantial as gossamer. Father Lynch began the procession down the oak allée. The driver gave a low call to his plumed horses, and the hearse shifted into motion, followed by the mourners carrying their candles. In her small grey dress, Clare was conspicuous among their uniform black—as if a child's pain were somehow less than theirs, when surely the opposite was true.

David, Joseph, and the others chanted the Miserére, King David's prayer of repentance after he lay with Bathsheba: "'Be merciful to me, O God... For I acknowledge my transgressions, and my sin is ever before me...'"

David watched his uncle struggling to remain stoic as he followed his lover's remains. Again and again, Joseph's voice caught and his face tightened with grief and guilt. David hoped Father Lynch did not realize how closely Joseph's sin echoed the Biblical David's.

At the wrought iron gates, the procession paused. They blew out their candles and climbed into the waiting coaches, which the drivers had brought ahead. On the way to the Cathedral of St. John and St. Finbar in Charleston, they recited the Psalms for the Dead, repeating after each one: "'Eternal rest grant unto her, O Lord. And let perpetual light shine upon her.'"

Clare sat close to David. Her voice trembled as they read the words: "'Forsake not, O Lord, the work of Thy hands...'"

At the cathedral, David and the other bearers carried Tessa's coffin inside. With her feet pointing toward the altar, they set her on a bier surrounded by candles. Joseph and Father Lynch blessed her coffin with holy water and incense. They said the Requiem Mass and the Office for the Dead: "'O God, humbly we beseech thee on behalf of thy handmaid, Teresa Stratford... Deliver not her soul into the hands of the enemy...'"

The prayers seemed never to end. David allowed Clare the use of his handkerchief and his pocket watch. It was a skeleton watch, so the gears were visible. She watched them ticking and turning as the Priests pleaded: "'Forget her not forever...'"

Finally David and the other bearers were called upon a third time, to transfer Tessa's coffin back to the hearse. They returned along the Ashley River to Edward's plantation. David's empty stomach reminded him that it was now afternoon.

At the front gate, everyone but Tessa's driver climbed from their coaches and relit their candles. Led by Father Lynch, they approached the white-columned mansion draped with black crape, then continued around its back. David forced his eyes not to linger on the semicircle of stairs where Tessa had begun the journey she completed today. The horses' hoofs and the hearse's wheels smashed the acorns fallen from the live oaks. The procession wound through the garden paths toward the cemetery on a hill overlooking the river.

Several negroes fell in behind them, the women carrying flower garlands and the men pine torches. The slaves looked genuinely mournful, unlike Edward's sister Hortense and the other members of his family who had deigned to attend Tessa's funeral. They'd never approved of Edward's Papist wife.

Most of the garden was slumbering, but beside Tessa's shrine to the Holy Family, a red camellia shed petals like tears of blood across their path. Further on, marble statues of Diana and Cupid stood aloof on their pedestals, indifferent to the affairs of mortals.

At last the hearse and its cortège reached the Stratfords' family cemetery. They passed the six bare dogwoods that marked the graves of the children Tessa had lost before they were born. She was joining them at last, in the Earth if not in Heaven.

Her white marble monument stood in startling contrast to the other memorials, not only for its size but also for its style. Like Tessa's coffin, her tomb was Egyptian Revival—hardly appropriate for a devout Catholic. There was no pyramid or sphinx, thank God, but the overall effect was a palace on the Nile.

Two enormous columns resembling bundled aquatic plants flanked the tapered entrance and supported a rolled cornice. In the frieze above the columns, a winged hourglass lamented life's brevity. A sun disk, a pair of cobras, and another pair of wings ornamented the cast iron gates. These symbolized rebirth, death, and protection, if David remembered correctly.

The driver halted the hearse at the tomb's open maw. Beyond the columns and gates, a staircase disappeared into the Earth. Father Lynch descended fearlessly, chanting: "'From the gates of Hell...'" His voice echoed back to them from the depths.

"'Deliver her soul, O Lord,'" Joseph completed, his lashes damp with tears.

David stared down the marble stairs into the shadows below. His arm ached, and guilt sliced through him as he realized how much he dreaded carrying Tessa down such a steep path.

When Liam opened the doors at the back of the hearse, Clare dropped her candle and buried her face in David's coat. She clung so fiercely, even her grandmother couldn't dislodge her.

David glanced apologetically toward the other bearers, who were waiting for him. "*Souris*, I need to…"

Cromwell saw his predicament. "Perhaps you would allow me to take your place, Mr. Lazare?"

David nodded gratefully. The steward joined Tessa's brothers and David's grandfather, who pulled the iron coffin from the hearse and struggled very slowly down the stairs to the crypt.

David moved to follow, but Clare remained as rooted as an oak. She clutched his coat and stared into the tomb as if it might swallow her, fresh tears marring her cheeks.

"It's all right, *souris*," David whispered.

She shook her head. Of course it wasn't all right.

David lowered himself to one knee and gazed up at the girl's distraught face. "Mr. Cromwell told me there's an angel inside, large as life. Wouldn't you like to see it?"

Clare only shook her head again.

David decided to carry her, and the girl did not resist. She even agreed to hold his candle, clinging to him with the other arm and both knees. As the Latin prayers drifted up from below, David navigated the steps carefully, allowing his eyes to adjust to the candlelight.

At the far end of the crypt, he saw the arches of the great marble wings. Grandfather, Grandmother, Joseph, Father Lynch, Tessa's mother and brothers, Cromwell, Edward, and his family members crowded closer together to make space for David and Clare. The negroes remained on the stairs: there wasn't enough room.

Except in the vault below the floor. Tessa's coffin perched on two long planks, suspended over the stone-lined pit, which yawned wide enough to admit a second body. David imagined Edward planned to join his wife here on his death.

When David tried to set her down, Clare whimpered in protest, and he capitulated. He directed her attention past Tessa's coffin to the angel.

On the displaced lid of the vault, she knelt weeping over a marble sarcophagus. The angel's slender neck bent downward, her hair drawn back into a dishevelled chignon. Her head was cradled on one crooked arm, her face hidden, while the other hand stretched over the sarcophagus with an offering of marble lilies. Even her great wings seemed to sag in grief, their tips brushing the floor. Sandals adorned the angel's feet, peeking from the chiton draping her body. The candlelight created a chiaroscuro of each marble pleat and feather.

The angel nearly obscured the much smaller statue in the niche on the far side of the tomb. Flanked by votive candles, the Blessed Virgin stood with her hands open in welcome. Carved in relief on either side of her niche, a pair of inverted torches burned eternal marble flames, assuring them that the soul survived death.

Father Lynch continued the rites: "'We beseech thee, O Lord… that she who aspired to do Thy will may not receive punishment in recompense for her deeds…'"

Joseph hid his face in his hand and wept audibly now. But Edward's wails drowned even those of Tessa's mother.

Into the prayers and the sobs crept another sound, like the aching of timbers inside a ship's hull. David frowned, and he felt Clare tense to listen. The only wood in the tomb was—

"It's the boards under the coffin!" Grandfather shouted before David could.

Father Lynch broke off and crossed himself. Clare buried her face in David's chest. His eyes remained transfixed on her mother. Hanging over the pit, the planks groaned beneath the weight of the iron coffin.

Tessa's brothers snatched up half the ropes that had been threaded through the handles and under the coffin; but on the left side, the ropes had slithered down into the vault, where they lay useless to break Tessa's fall.

Edward tried to fling himself at his wife, as if his weight would do anything but hasten the disaster; but Cromwell threw out an arm to restrain him. Then, the steward braced himself on the edge and dropped into the pit between the groaning planks. He snatched up the dangling ropes and tossed them to Joseph and Grandfather— just as the board beneath Tessa's shoulders splintered in two beside him.

Cromwell darted to safety. Everyone gasped or cried out as the coffin plummeted downwards. Tessa's brothers, Joseph, and Grandfather pulled the ropes taut and almost broke her fall, but they all heard the head of the coffin smack the floor of the vault.

Clare sobbed. Cradling her between them on the ropes, the bearers settled Tessa's feet against the floor while Cromwell cleared away the wood.

Edward leapt into the pit like some privileged Laertes. "Give me the screw-driver!" he commanded, thrusting an open hand toward his steward.

Reluctantly, Cromwell produced it.

Edward exchanged his candle for the screw-driver and jammed the tool into the screw below the face-plate. Then he shoved aside the cover, took back his candle, and peered desperately through the window.

What is he checking for? David wondered. Fresh injuries hardly mattered now. Perhaps Edward knew the tale of Snow White. Clare leaned forward eagerly.

Edward released his breath, his shoulders sagging. "There's no change," he muttered, throwing down the screw-driver.

David wasn't sure if he sounded relieved or disappointed.

Dripping tears and mucus onto the coffin, Edward stroked the glass. "I'm so sorry, Tessie!" The rest of it was unintelligible.

Cromwell retrieved the screw-driver from the floor of the vault. He reached out to swing the face-plate closed, but Edward shouted: "Leave it open!"

The steward hesitated.

"Leave it open or leave my employ, God damn you!"

Father Lynch grimaced but said nothing. Cromwell retreated. Tessa's brothers helped lift him, and finally Edward, from the vault. No one pulled the ropes from beneath Tessa's coffin; they remained coiled on the floor of the pit like a nest of snakes.

The slave women filed down the stairs to toss their garlands over their late mistress. Edward's sister Hortense and the rest of his family returned to the world of the living without a backward glance. At the top of the steps, sunlight promised resurrection; but inside this crypt, it seemed impossibly far away.

Like the rigging of a ship, two systems of ropes and pulleys hooked into the ceiling above their heads and into the base of the vault lid, on either side of the sarcophagus and angel. Four strong negroes pulled the sculpture into the air, and Cromwell and Tessa's brothers helped them maneuver it over the vault.

When the great marble lid thumped into place, the reverberation was more terrible than the plank splintering or the coffin striking the floor. Clare screamed as though a gun had exploded, as though she were trapped inside the vault with her mother. David shuddered too and bent his head over hers.

"*Requiéscat in pace*," Father Lynch concluded.

"Amen," they all answered. *Rest in peace.*

Beside David, Joseph whispered hoarsely in Latin: "'Woe is me, that my sojourning is prolonged.'"

CHAPTER 3

She fell like a dead bird...
— Mary Eastman, *Dahcotah: Life and Legends of the Sioux* (1849)

As if Tessa were Persephone, winter seemed to descend all at once in her wake. In the chill of the next morning, David bid farewell to her mother and brothers. One of Tessa's sisters-in-law was expecting a child any day. Life went on relentlessly.

When they'd gone, David folded himself into a wing chair in the library. He decided on the chair that kept his back to Tessa's portrait. To see her gazing down at him like a ghost raised goose-flesh on the back of his neck.

He was considering ringing for a slave to light a fire in the massive hearth when Mignon came to warm him. First the old black-and-white cat perched on David's open book, but they soon found a mutually beneficial arrangement.

Morning sunlight flooded through the windows, across the scarlet brocade of the upholstery and silky black cat fur to the cream-colored pages of *In Memoriam.* David should be keeping up on the medical literature, since he was missing lectures at the

Medical College in Charleston. But Clare had a habit of appearing and asking what he was reading, and treatises on uterine polyps proved awkward. Instead, David tried to find comfort, or commiseration, in Tennyson.

Through the wall, he heard the clock in the dining room chime. David glanced up to see Clare hovering on the other side of the Oriental rug, her face nearly the shade of her grey dress. In her blue slippers, she padded to the sofa beside him, crawled into its embrace, and tucked herself against its arm. David sighed in sympathy and transferred his hand from Mignon's head to hers. The cat opened one green eye in disapproval, then returned to his nap.

"What are you reading?" Clare asked right on cue.

"*In Memoriam*." They'd already read through it together.

"Which part?"

David read aloud:

"'Tis held that sorrow makes us wise;
Yet how much wisdom sleeps with thee..."

"Clare? Where are you, child?"

At the sound of her aunt's voice in the hall, the girl gasped and sprang up. Her wide brown eyes locked onto David's. "Hide me!"

Clare's panic infected him. David deposited his book and the cat on the sofa. He glanced around the library for some place the girl might hide.

Clare found a solution herself. "Help me!" she called in a fierce whisper, struggling to shift the heavy screen blocking the maw of the fireplace. The screen was a brass peacock with its plumage unfurled like a fan.

Clare's Aunt Hortense called again, much closer this time.

Clare darted inside the firebox and shoved the empty grate to one side so she could crouch beside it. David replaced the fire screen and then flung himself onto the sofa, beside the annoyed Mignon. David took up *In Memoriam* with renewed interest and as much nonchalance as he could muster.

Hortense's boots tapped the floorboards and softened on the rug. "Mr. Lazare, have you seen my niece?"

David did not glance up, afraid his expression might betray him. "Not since breakfast."

"I heard your voice. Don't tell me you were reading aloud to the *cat*."

"Poetry should always be read aloud." To demonstrate his point, he resumed:

"There lives more faith in honest doubt,
Believe me, than in half the creeds."

Hortense narrowed her eyes in suspicion. She paced the room and yanked aside one of the scarlet curtains. David was certain he could hear Clare panting with fear inside the fireplace, so he read Tennyson even louder. Finally the girl's aunt glared at him and resigned herself to defeat. Hortense raised her voice above David's recitation: "If you see Clare, tell her I await her in the music room."

He bowed his head in acknowledgement but did not cease *In Memoriam*. Hortense lifted her chin and strode from the room.

David finished the Canto and then fell silent, listening for footsteps. Hearing nothing, he set down the book and rose cautiously. He crossed to the door and peered into the hall, making sure they were safe. Then he hurried back to the fireplace.

"The coast is clear," he whispered. He pulled aside the brass peacock to find Clare sitting against one wall of the firebox with her legs folded underneath her, staring upwards. He frowned when he saw the ashes smeared on her white stockings and pantalettes. "Are you playing Cinderella?"

Clare shook her head and did not look at him. "I'm Wenona, from Mrs. Eastman's book. Is this what it's like inside a tipi?"

David sighed. Clare was always asking him about the months he'd spent in the West, months he would rather forget. No one but Uncle Joseph knew David had abandoned his baby brother at Independence Rock, and the Seal of Confession meant no one else ever would. Maybe someday, David would tell Clare about his half-Sioux ancestor who'd been sold into slavery in the West Indies, where he'd fallen in love with an African slave. It was exactly the sort of story that would fascinate Clare—but she was still too young to understand that in a city like Charleston, such secrets could ruin a man's life.

David hesitated, then pulled out the grate and stooped into the firebox. The grey bricks felt hard and cool against his steadying fingers and left a film of ash on his skin. He grimaced but settled across from Clare, sitting Indian-style to match her and following her gaze upward. No wonder he had been cold: someone had forgotten to close the damper, and they could see up the flue all the way to the pale December sky.

"It's a little like a tipi." He remembered that Mrs. Eastman had been the wife of a post commander at a fort in Minnesota. She'd recorded the Indians' stories and published them as *Dahcotah: Life and Legends of the Sioux.* David had read the book to Clare, but he'd read her so many; he couldn't recall the details. "Why Wenona?"

Clare did not take her eyes from the sky. "She was in love with a warrior, and he loved her. But her family wanted her to marry someone else. 'With him she loved, life would have been all happiness—without him, all misery.'"

David swallowed. He thought he remembered the story now. Still he asked: "Did Wenona run away with him?"

Clare shook her head. "She threw herself from a cliff."

Against the cold bricks of the firebox, David shivered. How much did Clare understand, about her mother and his uncle?

Hortense, of all people, rescued him. Clare's aunt reappeared beyond the fire screen and exclaimed: "I *knew* you were concealing her!" She pried Clare from the fireplace and launched into a tirade, plucking at the girl's ash-smeared clothes. "*What* have you let her do to herself?" While David climbed out of the fireplace, Hortense tugged on the bell pull. "You have proven my point quite soundly, young man."

David frowned. "What point?"

"That you are a pernicious influence, Mr. Lazare. I have spoken to my brother, and we agree that it is time you returned to your grandfather's."

"No!" Clare cried, attaching herself to David.

Her aunt yanked her away so hard, Clare shrieked in pain. David tried to reason with the woman, but a maid appeared, and Hortense shoved the girl at her. "Clean her up," Clare's aunt commanded the negress, who bobbed her head and towed the sobbing child from the room.

"Clare is in mourning!" David objected.

"All the more reason for her to cease these ridiculous games and frivolous reading."

"She is eight years old! Every child needs—"

"You are in no position to say what she does or does not need, Mr. Lazare. You are not her father. You are not even her brother."

"I am her *friend*."

"She will make new friends."

"They won't share Clare's memories—they won't have known Tessa."

"I think that is for the best."

David frowned. "*What* is for the best?"

"That Miss Stratford puts the past behind her. That she forges a life independent of her late mother."

David stared at the woman. "You *want* Clare to forget her mother."

"Children are resilient. Miss Stratford's prospects need not be hindered by my brother's youthful *mésalliance*."

Teresa Conley was worth a thousand of you Stratfords! David wanted to shout. Instead, he argued: "You are not a Catholic, Mrs. Fernande. We *remember* our dead. To forget a parent is a mortal sin against the Fourth Commandment. Not to attend Mass is a mortal sin against the Third Commandment. Who will take Clare to Mass when I am gone?"

Hortense sputtered.

"As her closest Catholic relation, wouldn't you agree that it is appropriate for me to take her?"

"I am sure my brother has no intention of remaining a Papist, or of allowing his daughter to—"

"When your brother married Clare's mother, he promised to bring up their children in our Church. Does Mr. Stratford intend to break his promise?"

"I—I shall speak to my brother."

"Shall I ask Father Lynch to explain the obligation?"

"That will not be necessary!"

David smiled to himself. He'd found his trump card. The Lynches were proof that even in South Carolina, a family could be simultaneously wealthy, powerful, and Catholic. Staunchly Protestant though she might be, Hortense would not dare offend them.

Much as it pained him to leave Clare at the mercy of such a harpy, David vacated the Stratford household that afternoon. The next day, he received word that he would be permitted to escort Clare to Mass. By Christmas, David was able to extend this weekly visit into a full day together. Edward did not seem to care what his daughter did, as long as she kept out of his sight.

That was all Clare wanted: someone to distract her from her grief and keep her company without making demands on her like her aunt did. It was a small sacrifice. It was a pleasure. Clare reminded David of his sister Sophie, before stranger's fever had taken her, before she'd stopped loving him. Clare was his chance to prove he was more than that one heartless decision at Independence Rock.

David and Clare spent most of their visits outside, roaming the plantation's gardens and woods. Often they rode, Clare on her pony and David on his uncle's grey. During these expeditions, she safeguarded her ouroboros bracelet and her mourning locket in her jewelry box. Clare enjoyed wearing pretty things and playing with dolls, but she also possessed a tomboy's fascination with the natural world. Unlike the instinct to conquer a little brother might have shown, his foster-sister wished only to nurture and to learn. As her mother had loved plants, Clare loved animals.

So David helped her make houses for the wrens and chickadees that winter. In the kitchen, they mixed nuts and dried fruits into suet. Clare's favorite part was smearing this avian feast on the trunks and branches of the live oaks. The girl was always bursting to tell him what had happened during their week apart, like the great horned owl chicks she had spotted through her field glasses.

Clare's child's-eye view of the world always entertained him. Their days together were the highlight of David's week too, a stark contrast to the way he spent most of his time: dismembering corpses in the dead house at the medical college. If he caught a fatal disease from a cadaver or a patient, David could rest assured that his life had not been in vain: he had brought joy to a friendless little girl. For years, David had told himself he *must* love his foster-sister, as a Penance. But he had grown to love Clare for herself: for her compassion, her ebullience, and her fearlessness.

Few creatures frightened her—not even a Hercules beetle longer than her hand, if you counted the horns. Clare saw beauty even in toads. From the Charleston Library Society, David brought her the works of Audubon, Bachman, and Catesby. The latter had been donated by David's own great-great-great-granduncle, Thierry Lazare; his inscription was still on the flyleaf.

When the College of Charleston reopened their natural history museum, David took Clare to visit Thierry's butterfly specimens. The blue Morpho was her favorite: "It's the same color as your eyes, David!" Thierry's butterflies resided amongst thousands of other specimens: birds, fish, shells, minerals, fossils, herbariums, and a stuffed anaconda. Clare gaped at each glass case and read every sign. Even the mummy of an Egyptian child intrigued her more than it repulsed her. She lingered at the black wolf and the Indian spears.

But paleontology became her new obsession. For weeks, Clare strapped a shovel on her pony and dug holes all over the plantation. She was convinced she would discover a fossil bed containing an entirely new species of dinosaur, that one of the museum's exhibits would soon bear *her name*. Mary Anning had done it in England; why couldn't she?

"Mary Anning was a working-class spinster!" Hortense shrieked when she saw her niece covered in dirt. "You are supposedly a young lady!"

They reached a compromise: young Titus from the stables would do the actual digging, while Clare directed him and Hortense hovered nearby. On Sundays, David assisted. He became as hopeful as Clare that the ground might relinquish some prehistoric treasure.

They found only a stone arrowhead, likely made by the Edisto tribe, who had perished from smallpox a century before. Clare was too delighted to surrender her prize to the museum.

She longed for undiscovered country, to travel westward as David had done. She longed to see the Great Plains thick with buffalo and dotted with tipis. She longed to meet a live Indian.

David could not conjure his Dakota great-great-great-grandmother. But buffalo robes could be bought even in Charleston. Men of Edward's class considered them fit only for slaves, but David knew Clare would feel differently. The second Christmas after Tessa's death, David gifted her daughter with the finest buffalo robe he could find. Clare wrapped it around herself and squealed with happiness.

Her gift to him was a silver medal depicting the twin saints Cosmas and Damian, the patrons of doctors. As David thanked her and fastened the chain around his neck, Clare explained shyly: "I asked Father Joseph who could protect you best." Her relationship with David's uncle was mending but still cautious. "He said either Luke or Cosmas and Damian—and we decided two saints are better than one."

David smiled back. "Did Father Joseph tell you about any of Cosmas and Damian's miracles?"

Clare nodded. "He said they performed surgery even after they were dead! There was this deacon at their church in Rome, and his leg had a cancer. One night, the deacon dreamt that Cosmas and Damian took away his bad leg and replaced it with the leg of a dead Moor. When the deacon woke, his leg was healthy, but it was black!"

Since he was part African himself, the Miracle of the Black Leg had always fascinated David. Why had Cosmas and Damian used a *negro's* leg? These surgeon-saints could return to Earth two centuries after their martyrdom, yet they chose a mismatched part? Did the brothers think skin color didn't matter?

It was fortunate that Cosmas and Damian had not visited their peculiar services on nineteenth-century Charleston. To David, the Black Leg seemed an imperfect miracle, a tale that belonged in *Frankenstein*, not a hagiography. But the medal was from Clare, so he wore it fondly.

A FEW DAYS before he boarded his steamship for Paris, the girl came running to David, distraught over a ringneck snake hatchling. She'd found it trapped in a spider's web in the garden of her father's Church Street house. As insubstantial as a ribbon, the tiny black snake with the distinctive gold ring banding its neck had become hopelessly tangled. Spider silk bound up its tail and cinched its middle, rendering it helpless. His foster-sister couldn't simply pull away the web—that only made it tighter.

First, David smiled at the Clare-ness of this emergency. How he would miss her. Then, he retrieved his medical satchel. He chose his most delicate scissors and forceps. With these, he and Clare slowly freed their tiny patient.

The ringneck stretched its muscles in gleeful relief. The little snake twirled around Clare's finger like the rod of Asclepius, as if it were thanking her. Sometimes she would keep the creatures she found for a day or two, to study and play with them. But she gave the ringneck a final caress, set her hand on the ground, and watched the wisp of snake slip away beneath her mother's rosebushes. Clare remained crouching there for a moment before she whispered: "I wish *you* didn't have to go."

David returned his forceps to his medical bag and sat down beside her on the piazza steps. "So do I, *souris*. But Paris has the best medical schools in the world, and I want to be the best doctor I can be."

"You'll be gone for *years*." Her face still turned away from him, as if the little snake might return, she drew in a ragged breath. "You'll forget me."

"I could never—"

"And I'll forget you." She clutched her gold locket, which contained Tessa's hair. The girl's voice became thick and tremulous. "I've already forgotten so much about Mama."

"I'll help you remember."

She tossed a glare at him. "Not if you're in Paris!"

"I'll write to you. I promise."

Clare looked back, her expression hopeful even as the first tears overflowed. "Every day?"

David smiled. "How about every week?"

She averted her eyes again, and her chin trembled in disappointment. "I wish I could go with you."

"I'll be holed up in some garret with my books." Or up to his wrists in gore. "I won't be very good company."

Clare retrieved his surgical scissors from the pocket of her pinafore. "Could— Could I keep some of your hair? To put in my locket beside Mama's?"

"If you like."

The girl lost no time. She pulled a fine handkerchief from her pocket and unfolded it. She draped it over his shoulder and clipped several black curls. "'Hair is at once the most delicate and last of our materials and survives us like love.' That's from *Godey's Lady's Book*."

"I'm crossing the Atlantic Ocean, *souris*—not the River Styx."

"I know." But Clare's face was somber as she closed her handkerchief around his black curls, as if they were gold dust.

"What will you make with them?" From her mother's hair, she'd fashioned delicate gold-brown flowers for her locket.

"I haven't decided yet."

IN THE FIRST LETTER she sent David in Paris, Clare told him she'd created tiny feathers from his hair. *To commemorate our bird walks, and so you'll fly home*, she explained in the letter. Clare placed David's feathers behind glass in her mourning locket, across from her mother's flowers. *You and Mama are my Cosmas and Damian*, she wrote, *my protectors.* But Tessa had abandoned her daughter, and David could do very little to protect his foster-sister from four thousand miles away.

CHAPTER 4

In the first place, I am a girl, and not a young fellow, and would be shut up in a mad-house, if I did half the things that I have a mind to.

— Sir Walter Scott, *Rob Roy* (1817)

The day after David's departure, the weather echoed Clare's mood. She sat on the chaise longue beneath her bedroom window and stared at the rain coursing down the panes. Who would take her to the Charleston Museum now? Who would catch salamanders and fireflies with her? She clutched her knees to her chest and willed herself not to cry. What good would it do, with no one here to comfort her except the cat?

"*Clare.*"

She started and turned her head to see her father framed in her bedroom doorway, his hands clasped behind his back. He sounded irritated, as if he'd said her name more than once and she hadn't responded. Then again, her father usually sounded irritated when he spoke to her, as if she was hardly worth the effort.

"I have indulged you since your mother"—his voice caught and he hesitated—"left us, but you are nearly eleven years old.

You will soon be a young lady, and it is inappropriate for a young lady to keep worms in her bedchamber." He glared at her dressing table, where half a dozen Monarch caterpillars feasted on milkweed inside the fine mesh cages David had helped her fashion.

This was her Aunt Hortense speaking, Clare knew it—the woman had visited just that morning. She was always going on about what was and wasn't proper. Aunt Hortense's favorite sentence was *"What would people think?"* Clare planted her slippered feet on the floor and gripped the seat of her chaise longue. "They are *caterpillars*, not—"

Her father didn't allow her to finish. "As soon as the rain stops, you will dispose of those foul little creatures *and* their cages. I do not want to see them again—any of them. Animals belong outside, and ladies belong inside."

Clare's attention darted to the bed, where her black-and-white cat lay curled, his ears tilting back at the rising sounds of their voices. "W-What about Mignon? He's like an old man, and he can't—"

"You may keep the cat," her father muttered. "The worms and the rest of your menagerie *go*. Today."

Clare stood. "But the caterpillars are still eating, and they need—"

"You will dispose of them or I will!"

Clare started and winced. Her father rarely shouted at her anymore; but when he did, he still frightened her.

"I have also asked Mr. Cromwell to find a maid for you. She will report anything you attempt to conceal in here, so do not think you can deceive me, Clare." He whirled and strode away.

The traitorous rain was already lifting. As Clare crossed to her dressing table, the only sounds were her own ragged breathing and the Monarch caterpillars' happy chewing. How could her father hate them so much? You only had to stop and really *look* and you'd fall in love with them. With the way cheery stripes of white, black, and yellow ringed them from head to rump. The way they curled into plump circles when they felt threatened. The way their stocky little bodies transformed into delicate, majestic butterflies in barely a week.

One caterpillar was crawling up the side of the cage right now, her body rippling from back to front, her busy spinnerets creating a trail of silk to aid her climb. She was searching for a place to make her chrysalis. These next few days, she'd be so vulnerable, as she built a pad of silk, anchored herself, hung upside down, shed her skin, reattached and reformed herself—but Clare's father didn't care if the "worm" never became a butterfly.

"It's not fair!" Clare cried to the caterpillars, who bobbed their heads in unison, their floppy black filaments waving.

She doubted her father would make good on his threat himself —if she didn't "dispose" of her creatures, he'd send his manservant to do it. Richmond might not injure the caterpillars maliciously, but he'd probably do so accidentally. He would dump them far away from any milkweed, their only food source. To give her Monarchs their best chance, Clare had no choice but to release them herself.

With a heavy heart, she carried her little charges to the garden plot where Father Joseph had helped her plant milkweed. The leaves were still damp with rain. The next storm might throw the caterpillars to the ground. They were defenseless and nearly blind, and they had so many predators: lizards, spiders, beetles, ants, wasps, flies… Out here, she couldn't keep them safe. No caterpillar should have to die before it grew wings.

Two of the Monarchs had already made their chrysalises, jade pendants dewed with gold. Very carefully, Clare grasped the cremaster at the top of each one and pulled the chrysalises away from the mesh where they'd anchored themselves with silk pads. In obedience to her father's decree, she discarded the cages.

Then she pierced each silk pad with a pin and pressed the pins into one of the posts at the head of her bed. Since the weather was still warm, there was no headboard, to allow air to flow over her while she slept. But the mosquito netting draped around her bed would help conceal the chrysalises from prying eyes.

She still had Diana to contend with. She wasn't a mammy like other children had mammies. Diana wasn't even Clare's own maid;

the negress had many other duties besides minding Clare's chamber. But she worried like Clare's mother would have, when Clare pretended to feel poorly so she could remain in bed near her charges.

Diana asked lots of questions and felt Clare's forehead. She placed one hand on her hip and narrowed her eyes. Finally Clare pinched her lip between her teeth and pulled back her pillow to expose the Monarch chrysalises. Diana's eyes widened.

"Please don't tell Father," Clare whispered.

Diana smiled and winked. "I ain't seen nothing."

BY THE FOLLOWING NIGHT, both chrysalises had become transparent, revealing the tiny orange wings and fat black bodies packed tightly inside. Lying on her stomach in her nightdress, Clare tried to read, but she finished barely a page, afraid she'd miss the miracle.

Finally, one chrysalis split open, the little legs pushing till they created a hatch. Breathless, Clare watched the plump abdomen drop from the chrysalis, followed by the tiny wings. The Monarch butterfly tested his new parts, holding onto the chrysalis with his long legs and unfurling his proboscis, the spiral tongue he'd use to drink nectar. He stretched out his orange-and-black wings, which grew and grew while his abdomen slimmed, till they hung supple as freshly washed mittens.

"Clare!" called her father through her bedchamber door.

Clare's heart leapt into her throat.

"I've told you I don't want you reading so late. Blow out your lamp—*now*."

"Yes, Father." Clare obeyed, and the newborn butterfly vanished into darkness.

She could hardly sleep for worrying about her Monarchs. But the mosquito netting would keep the butterflies in like it kept the mosquitoes out, as if she were sleeping inside a great cage.

In the morning, Clare woke to *two* butterflies fanning their wings on the netting beside her, one boy and one girl. Strong yet delicate, glowing with sunlight, their orange-and-black wings resembled panes of stained glass. She could hardly bear to open the netting and release the Monarchs, knowing they would be her last.

For now—only for now, Clare reminded herself. When David returned from Paris, he would take her away from here. Then, they would live happy ever afterward with as many caterpillars and butterflies as she wanted.

PART II
LIFE IN SHADOW

1853-1855

POWHATAN COUNTY, VIRGINIA AND
CHARLESTON, SOUTH CAROLINA

A man is changed into a chattel—a person is withered into a thing
—a soul is shrunk into merchandise. Say, Sir, in your madness, that
you own the sun, the stars, the moon; but do not say that you own a
man, endowed with a soul that shall live immortal, when sun, and
moon, and stars have passed away.

— Charles Sumner, "On the Barbarism of Slavery,"
June 4, 1860 speech to the U.S. Senate

CHAPTER 5

American Slavery is not only not a sin, but especially commanded by God... Our slaves are the happiest three millions of human beings on whom the sun shines.

— James Henry Hammond, *Letter on Southern Slavery* (1845)

Master Lem was dead, Missus Claudia was going to live with her sister, and they were all going to be sold.

Hercules led them with his fiddle, as if they were going to a dance. They were even chained to partners and then chained in a long line, but everyone in Easter's line was a woman or girl. The men walked ahead in their own line, so Easter could glimpse her big brother Pompey only when they were marching around a turn and there weren't too many trees in the way. Easter's mother was chained just behind her, and her sister Verily was beside Easter.

She was thirteen years old now and Verily was ten, so they could walk on their own. But Easter had never walked so far in one day. By noon, her feet were throbbing, even though she had shoes, unlike some of the field slaves. With every step, the chains jingled, the collar rubbed against her neck, and her bundle got heavier. She was shivering, and the shawl around her wasn't enough. She'd let Verily wear their good blanket.

"Keep up!" the traders ordered as they rode alongside, raising their whips and narrowing their eyes. "Stand up straight! Smile!" The traders were usually yelling. When they spotted a white traveller approaching, the traders made them all sing. The rest of the time, Hercules just played.

"What if I tell a story to pass the time?" called Sukey, who was chained next to Mama. "Would that be all right, Massa?"

"I suppose," grumbled the trader riding beside them. "As long as it ain't about Brer Rabbit."

"It's about the Pied Piper. Any of you heard of him?"

The other women murmured no, their breath escaping in clouds from their lips.

"Well, there was this village that had a problem with rats. They was everywhere, eating all the food. The Pied Piper came and said he could trick all the rats into leaving the village."

"He could trick them with his pies?" Easter's sister asked.

Sukey laughed. "No, with his pipe—the kind you play, like a flute. His pipe was magic. He didn't have any pies."

"Then why is he called the 'Pied Piper'?" Verily pressed.

"I don't know. It's a buckra story. Hush and let me tell it." Sukey continued: "The Piper wanted a lot of money to get rid of the rats. The men of the village promised to pay him ten bags of gold, so the Piper began to play his flute. The rats came out of the houses, and they followed his music to the river. The Piper waded into the river, and the rats drowned.

"But now there were no more rats, the village men thought it over and decided they didn't want to pay the Piper so much. They offered him five bags of gold, half what they'd agreed. He refused to take it. 'You promised,' he said. 'Then you will have nothing,' the men said. But the Piper's flute had another magic. He played a different tune, and this time, all the children came out of the houses and followed him. He led them up a mountain into a cave, and they disappeared forever."

Verily gasped. "Where did they go?"

"Nobody knows. Some say they went straight to Heaven."

The trader beside them snorted. "The way I heard it, the children went into the river just like the rats, and they drowned."

Verily cried out and covered her mouth with her hand.

"Either way," Sukey concluded, "those village men learned their lesson: 'When you make a promise, you'd better keep it.'"

Verily whimpered.

"It's just a story," Easter and Mama assured her at the same time.

"I think the lesson is: 'Don't be trusting strangers,'" decided Abby, who was chained behind Sukey and Mama.

"But some strangers are good," Verily murmured. She stroked her skirt, where Mama had sewn her a hidden pocket. Inside, Easter knew, there was a card with an angel on it.

She kissed her sister's head and whispered: "Yes. Some strangers are good."

Maybe Hercules and his fiddle weren't taking them straight to Heaven, but this sale might be good too. They might end up with a kind Missus, who let her slaves name their own children. Maybe when their new Master got angry, he'd be satisfied with a few lashes, instead of whipping his slaves so hard that he'd killed Easter's father.

Better days might be coming. All they had to do was survive this march.

THAT SPRING, a few weeks after Master Lem killed Papa, a peddler had come to their plantation selling ribbons, spoons, and such things. Missus Claudia had one of her headaches, and Master Lem was in the north tobacco field. But Easter, Verily, and the other children had run out to see what the man had in his pack.

The peddler spoke with an accent unlike any they'd ever heard

—he said he was from England—and he was kind. He'd given each of them a card with a prayer on the back and a picture on the front. He said: "Do you know God loves you, children? Pray to Him and He will send His angels to protect you."

"Who is it?" Verily had asked, breathless, about the blond-haired man on the card. He had wings, and he stood on top of an ugly man with horns who lay on the ground. The winged blond man held a long blade, and his clothes were made of metal. "What's he wearing?"

"That is Saint Michael," the peddler explained.

Verily and Easter gasped and looked at each other, because their father's name had been Michael.

"He is wearing armor, because he is God's warrior. The creature he's killed, that's Satan. This is God's promise to us: Evil *will* perish. Your bondage will not last forever."

Easter liked her card too. It had a picture of God's mother, Mary. But when Missus Claudia found out about the cards, she was angry because of the prayers on the back. Even though none of the slaves could read them, Missus thought they were trying, so she ordered all the cards to be burned.

But Verily had hidden hers, and she always kept it with her. She often prayed to the blond angel. She'd asked Mama, who said there really were such things as angels.

Sometimes Easter wondered if the peddler had been an angel. He was like no other white man she'd ever met, the way he'd talked, the way he'd given them the cards and expected nothing in return.

"I THINK IT'S TIME for another song!" shouted one of the traders, startling Easter from her thoughts. "I want to hear 'Old Virginia Never Tire' again!"

Easter and the others tried not to groan. They knew protesting would only earn them blows. This was the traders' favorite song. Hercules provided the tune. Easter swallowed hard and sang with the rest:

"The fiddle sing, the banjo ding, Virginia never tire:
To laugh and sing is just the thing we darkies admire.
Oh, happy is the darkey's life…"

THAT NIGHT, Mama kept Easter and Verily as close to her as she could with their chains. Verily fell asleep right away. She'd always been able to do that.

The traders stood guard with guns, smoking cigars that glowed red in the darkness. One of the red cigars approached them, and Mama clutched Easter so hard it hurt. The cigar passed them by, and the trader ground it out in the dirt. He crouched down and spoke a low command. A woman whimpered. Easter thought it was Abby.

"I'm increasing your worth, girl," the trader hissed as he crawled on top of her. "Probably giving your new master a piccaninny free of charge."

Then Easter heard other sounds, grunts and—

"Don't listen, baby," Mama whispered. "Try not to listen."

Easter found the place in her sister's skirt where the angel card was hidden and squeezed it. Then she covered her ears instead.

THE NEXT DAY, they reached a road made of metal and wood—Sukey called it a "train track"—and followed it until they came to the "cars." As Easter walked with the others alongside the cars, she saw white women with furry shawls and white men with furry coats inside. Their children, especially the boys, pointed and stared. Some even made faces through the windows. It was more white people than Easter had ever seen together at once. But then, she had never been off Master Lem's plantation before.

The traders forced them all into the car closest to the huge smoking engine. The floor of the car was stained with dark shapes. The lingering smell of dung made Easter realize that this car had last held cattle. The traders didn't unlock anyone's chains; they only slid the door shut with a great creak and sealed everyone inside.

Unlike the cars for the white people, this car did not have any benches or even any windows, only slatted sides. There was nothing to keep them warm except each other and the blankets they'd carried from the plantation.

When the train started, Easter felt like she was trapped inside a baby's rattle. Soot blew inside with the cold, making her cough. Worse, there was no way to empty the slop buckets—and no way to use them in private.

Easter's mother spoke softly beside her. The motion of the train had made her sister sick, though they'd eaten only a little parched corn on the march, so she didn't have much to throw up. Now, their mother was rocking Verily to a different rhythm. She rubbed her back and murmured: "At least we're still together. At least we're still a family."

Easter looked to the other side of the car, where the men had settled. Amidst the sunlight and shadows that darted in and out of the train, she found her brother. Pompey sat against the side of the car with his arms crossed, but he smiled a little when she caught his eye.

Easter listened to her mother's calm, almost happy voice. "Where they're taking us, this Charleston, it's a *city*, Verily," Mama cooed. Her face was tight, and there were tears in her eyes; but with her head in Mama's lap, Verily couldn't see them. "You ain't never been to a city, but I have. When I was just a little girl, even younger than you, Master Lem bought me and my mama in Richmond. There's always something to see in a city. If you don't like what's in front of you, all you have to do is take a few steps, and it changes."

Easter thought Verily was already asleep, but their Mama kept talking, her tears falling fast now: "Maybe we'll get to live in Charleston. It's on the ocean. I've always wanted to see the ocean…"

Her chains clinking, Easter crawled closer and rested her head on her mother's shoulder. Mama put her arm around her, and Easter closed her eyes.

She must have fallen asleep, because she dreamed that their new Master looked like the blond angel. He gave Easter's family their own cabin near a beach. He let them have not only Sunday but also Saturday to themselves, and he never made them go to bed hungry.

CHAPTER 6

Everybody, in the south, wants the privilege of whipping somebody else.

— Frederick Douglass, *My Bondage and My Freedom* (1855)

It was warmer in Charleston, but not by much. When the train arrived, the traders marched Easter, her family, and the others deeper into the city. Mama had been right: no matter which way Easter looked, there was something new to see. As they walked, the fields got fewer and the gardens smaller, the churches and houses closer together. Wagons carrying pigs and chickens gave way to fancy carriages. Horses and people swirled around them, coming and going from every direction.

Half the people were colored, slaves walking a step behind their Master or Missus. Mostly the slaves glanced at Easter and then looked away quickly. The eyes of a few lingered on her face or the faces of the people chained to her, necks straining and expressions full of hope as if they were searching for someone.

Some of the lighter-skinned colored people were dressed as fancy as the whites and did not seem to be following any Masters.

Only one of them looked at Easter. His chin lifted in disgust, as if it were her own fault she was a slave.

They reached a high brick wall with two red banners hanging on either side of a tall iron gate. The traders drove them inside, where an ugly structure of wood and brick waited. It looked like two or three buildings squashed together, and its windows had bars on them. The men staring out of the windows were white. The traders took Easter and the others behind the building, where colored faces peered from white tents.

After they were unchained, Easter, her mother, and her sister hurried to Pompey. New white men came with pencils and little books to ask them questions: "What are you called? What can you do? Anything wrong with you?"

The traders frowned at Mama's grey hairs. They gave her black grease to rub into her head. It could have been worse: Easter saw that the older men were forced to shave their heads and beards. Then the traders murmured amongst themselves and decided what new ages to write down.

When they got to Pompey, one of the traders said to another: "Ain't that a fine buck?" Then, to Easter's brother himself: "Take off those clothes, boy."

Her brother was a boxer; he could lay any of these men on the ground with a single blow. Yet Pompey clenched his jaw and obeyed the traders. He let them examine his back, squeeze his arms, pull back his lips, and stick their fingers in his mouth.

The traders made the women undress too. Mama did not argue for her own sake; but when one of the men told Easter to unbutton her dress, her mother begged: "Please, sir—my Easter is just thirteen. She doesn't have any scars, and—"

"Then what do you have to hide?" the trader insisted.

Easter shivered with shame as the white men turned her around and made notes in their little books.

The men behind the barred windows whistled and taunted. "Well, Merry Christmas to *me*!"

Was it already Christmas? Easter had lost track of the days.

"Send her up here, won't ya?" cried the loudest man. "In the spirit of Christmas? 'It is more blessed to give than to receive'!"

"Like I'd waste a virgin on scum like you," one trader shouted back.

The traders let them wash—made them wash—and gave them all brightly-colored new clothing, then yelled at them to keep clean. They burned the clothes Easter's family had worn on the march, though they let Easter keep her wool shawl and the Sunday dress in her bundle. Her new shoes didn't have any holes, but they were too big.

At least they got plenty of food: rice and grits and even bacon. Easter's brother had met a young man named Ned who'd been in the yard when they arrived. Pompey asked him to join their family for supper. Ned was from right here in Charleston. He said this place was the city jail, that it was thieves and murderers staring down at them from the windows.

Verily clung closer than ever to Mama.

Ned lifted his spoon but kept talking. "You know where these grits are ground? The Work House." He nodded over the wall, where a building with towers loomed. Around the top of the towers and walls, the building seemed to have teeth.

"Looks like a castle, don't it? Like they're trying to keep people from getting in? *Nobody* wants in the Work House—that fancy building is to keep people from getting *out*. That's where slaves go for being 'uppity.' It's there for any Master or Missus who wants their slave punished but doesn't want to bloody their pretty white hands. Buckra can choose whipping or the treadmills. I bet you seen a man whipped, but you ain't seen nothing till you've seen a man's leg ripped—"

"Thank you, Ned—that is quite enough!" Mama cried.

Ned shrugged. "That's where these grits are ground—the treadmills."

Easter stared down at her bowl as if there might be blood in the grits.

"Why ain't you eating?" a trader shouted next to her ear, making her jump. "Nobody wants a skinny piccaninny!"

Easter forced herself to pick up her spoon and swallow.

THEY AWOKE TO SCREAMS from the Work House. The traders carried on like the moaning and crying was birds singing. Here in the jail yard, the white men carried not whips but paddles, which hurt but didn't break the skin. Ned explained that the traders didn't want any fresh wounds on their "merchandise."

They pinned numbers to each person's new clothing and ordered them to separate walls inside the jail yard. The men to the right, the women and their babies to the left; and in the middle, the children who were not old enough to stand with the adults, but not young enough to stay with their mothers. Children like Easter and her sister.

They stood lined up shortest to tallest with their backs to the wall. Swarms of white men came to stare and poke as they pleased. The men consulted booklets of papers and asked question after question. They squeezed Easter's breasts (even though there wasn't much there) and asked if she'd started bleeding yet (she hadn't). Some of the men made Easter run around the yard or do cartwheels, and then at least she could pass near her mother or her brother. She tried to tell the buyers about the rest of her family, but most of them weren't interested.

In her head, Easter talked to God and Papa and Saint Michael, begging them to help.

Night was better, with her whole family around her in the darkness of the tent. The straw didn't smell *too* bad. Pompey told stories that Easter had heard a hundred times, but she didn't mind hearing them again. Mama prayed a lot.

In the morning, it all started over again: new white men poking and prodding. Verily wouldn't stop crying. She wanted to go home. First, the traders tried to tempt her to behave with sticks of candy. When that didn't work, they forced corn liquor down her throat, till she stood against the wall in a daze.

That evening, Verily cried: "I saw him! I saw the angel! Did he talk to you too?"

Easter frowned. "What do you mean?"

"While another man was asking you questions, a man came and asked me questions. He sounded just like the peddler who gave me the picture card, but he *looked* like the angel!" Verily's breath still smelled like liquor, so Easter wasn't sure *what* her sister had seen or heard, how much she'd imagined.

Verily pulled out the picture card and petted it. "He'll protect us. You'll see."

Two days later, the traders ordered the men to line up—only the men. Pompey hugged Easter and Verily and Mama all at the same time. The traders started yelling at them, so finally Pompey joined the other men.

As the traders shackled the men together, one of the white prisoners jiggled the bars in his window and begged mockingly, "Take me too, broker!"

The traders drove the men out through the iron gate, and they would not let anyone else follow. Pompey looked over his shoulder just before he disappeared on the other side of the wall.

Mama staggered toward their tent and fell to her knees just outside. When Easter knelt next to her, her mother squeezed her hand hard. Tears dripped from her face, but she said nothing.

Easter waited and waited, but night fell, and none of the men returned. Verily asked when Pompey was coming back. Easter said the men had gone on ahead and the women and children would join them later. She wanted so much for that to be true. But she knew Pompey could be anywhere by now.

This wasn't supposed to happen. They were a family—they were supposed to stay together! Where was the angel when they needed him?

In the morning, Easter opened her eyes to see her mother's face. Easter had always found it a comforting sight. Now, she saw only grief in Mama's expression.

"Will you promise me something, Easter?"

She sat up. "Of course, Mama."

"Look after your sister for me?" Mama stroked Verily's braids as she stirred. "Protect her, best you can?"

Before Easter could answer, she heard the white men shouting outside their tent: "Come on, wenches! Line up!"

Verily rubbed her eyes. "Mama?"

"I love you, babies," she said in a choked voice, kissing both their heads. "Wherever I am, I'll still be loving you. Never forget that."

One of the traders poked his head into their tent and nudged their mother with his paddle. "Hurry up!"

Mama looked back at Easter. "Promise me you'll look after your sister?" The man cursed and grabbed their mama by the shoulders to drag her from the tent.

"I promise," Easter sobbed.

"*Mama!*" Verily scrambled to her feet, but Easter held her back. Her sister beat at her with her small fists and screamed for both of them.

Before long, one of the traders came back, raised his paddle, and yelled at her sister to stop crying. Verily cowered against Easter but obeyed at last; she only whimpered now and again. Easter held her sister and tried to remember one of Mama's songs. She sang it even though her voice was shaking:

"No more rain fall for wet you, Hallelujah,
No more sun shine for burn you,
There's no hard trials
There's no whips a-crackin'
No evil-doers in the kingdom
All is gladness in the kingdom…"

When Easter looked up, she saw other children at the entrance of the tent, listening too. She was the oldest one left.

That evening, only Rinah returned, an old woman who'd been

in the jail yard when they arrived. Verily ran to Rinah and clutched her dress, pleading, "Where's Mama?"

As she set a curled hand on Verily's shoulder, Rinah's voice was heavy with pity. "She's going to New Orleans, honey."

"New *what?*"

"She got on a ship, your mama."

Easter had never seen a ship, not a real one. But she had seen a painting in her Master's house, of towering waves and crooked slashes of lightning.

THE NEXT MORNING, Easter saw that her sister had thrown her angel card in the straw. Easter picked it up and tucked it into her own pocket. She didn't know why God and His angels had allowed Mama and Pompey to be sold away from them, but it wouldn't do any good to anger the angel now.

Today it was Easter and Verily's turn to be chained together with the other girls. They carried their bundles of extra clothing. Riding their horses again, the traders led and pushed the girls from the jail yard down the street. Church bells began to toll the hour, and Easter counted the steeples she could see over the roofs. She got to six before she spotted something else poking into view ahead of them: the masts of ships.

Verily saw them too. "Mama! We're going with Mama!"

The other girls started to chatter in excitement. Maybe they *would* be returned to their mothers.

"Shut pan!" yelled one of the traders, jerking the chain between their necks to get their attention. "Damned piccaninnies!"

The men turned them right, down a wider street lined with fine houses, and Easter caught the sparkle of water where the city ended. Ship after ship crowded close, flags flapping in the wind. Some had sails higher than buildings, and others belched smoke. One of them was sailing away. Easter wondered if her mother was on that ship.

Around her and the other girls, the murmur of voices swelled, and the crowd of people grew tighter. She turned her attention from the ships to see a grand building ahead: fancy white-framed windows, tan walls, and a round, open tower on top. Before the building waited a wooden platform. On it stood a bright red flag, a white man in checkered trousers, and a trembling little black boy.

Next to the platform, the traders halted beside a spiky tree and dismounted. A mass of white men watched while the traders unchained Easter, Verily, and the other girls.

"Where's Mama?" Verily demanded. She asked it more than once, but Easter was listening to the auctioneer:

"This boy is sold for no fault, gentlemen, and he is warrantied! Ain't no better investment than a likely nigger! This here is a *bargain*, gentlemen!"

Easter closed her eyes for a moment, only a moment; but when she opened them again, Verily was gone.

Glancing around her in panic, Easter caught a glimpse of her sister's blue kerchief disappearing into the crowd, in the direction of the ships. Easter did not hesitate—she dropped her bundle and followed her sister.

Angry male voices exploded behind her: "You! Stop! Right now! Come back here!" Women in their big dresses cried out too as she passed, creating a whirlwind of shouts around her. Easter wished her shoes fit better. She was gaining on Verily, but behind her she heard horse hoofs gaining on her.

They would never make it onto a ship. Easter knew that. But if they were caught together, maybe she could convince the trader to beat her instead of Verily.

As her sister tripped on the bumpy stones of the street and tumbled forward, Easter gritted her own teeth. Behind her, the trader was still cursing, but he yelled "Whoa!" to his horse. She glanced back at him as she reached Verily, and saw that even though he was jumping down from the saddle, his riding crop was raised. Easter threw her own body over her sister's and squeezed her eyes shut.

But the blow didn't come. Instead she heard a new voice, angry too but not aimed at her: "You damage them, and I'll strike you back, I swear it!"

Easter gasped. The voice sounded like the peddler's—his accent was the same. She peeked up to see that the white man standing between her and the trader's whip *sounded* like the peddler, but he *looked* like the angel. His blond hair was shorter, and he wasn't wearing armor, but Easter could see it—Verily hadn't imagined him.

"What the Hell business is this of yours?" demanded the trader.

"These girls are for sale, are they not?" asked the blond man with the peddler's accent.

"Yes…"

"I intend to buy them," declared the blond man. "Hence, this is very much my business. Now will you kindly cease and desist?"

Finally the trader grunted and lowered his whip. "You have to bid like everybody else."

"Of course." The blond man helped Easter and Verily to their feet. "Are you all right?" he asked.

Verily had scraped her hand, but she nodded. The blond man wiped away the grit and tied his handkerchief around the wound. The man's clothes were fancier than any of the traders' and even fancier than their old Master's. He was young—more than twenty, but not more than twenty-five.

As they walked back toward the auction, her hand in her sister's, Easter tried to keep her head down. She knew she wasn't supposed to stare at white people. Still, she watched the blond man from the corners of her eyes. Had he meant it, that he would buy them? *Both* of them? They'd stay together?

"Let me see if I remember: your name is Verily and your sister is Easter," said the blond man, looking through a booklet of papers. "Is that right?"

Verily nodded.

"Did I tell you my name yesterday?"

Verily shook her head and wiped her nose on her sleeve.

"I am Mr. Cromwell. Would you like me to purchase you and your sister?"

Verily looked up at him and narrowed her eyes. "Will you take us to New Orleans?"

Mr. Cromwell laughed, a warm and not a mocking laugh. "Why? What do you want to see in New Orleans?"

Easter decided to tell him the truth: "That's where our Mama's gone."

"Ah," said Mr. Cromwell, and his smile faded. "I'm afraid New Orleans is beyond my abilities. But I know another little girl right here in Charleston who also lost her mother, and she could very much use a friend. Do you think you could help her, Verily?"

She was looking back over her shoulder toward the ships and did not respond.

"Would you like to stay with your sister?" Mr. Cromwell pressed.

Easter felt her heart beating faster. She'd been right, about God sending him. "Yes, sir," she answered for Verily. "Very much, sir."

"And you'll do what I ask, if I buy you both?"

"Yes, sir. We will, sir."

CHAPTER 7

My mistress was…a kind and tender-hearted woman; and in the simplicity of her soul she commenced, when I first went to live with her, to treat me as she supposed one human being ought to treat another. … Slavery soon proved its ability to divest her of these heavenly qualities.
— *Narrative of the Life of Frederick Douglass, an American Slave, Written by Himself* (1845)

The trader pushed Easter forward, onto the platform with the red flag, and the auctioneer began to shout about her virtues: "Thirteen years old, gentlemen! In a couple of years, this little nigger will be prime breeding stock!"

"Is she *intact*?" called a man with greasy hair combed over his bald head.

"And free of disease!" the auctioneer assured him.

Easter shuddered, clutched her bundle of clothes, and tried not to listen. She gripped the angel card in her pocket and found the young blond man in the crowd. Mr. Cromwell stood watching with arms crossed and face blank. But when she caught his eye, he smiled. Except for the peddler, no white man had ever spoken to her and Verily the way Mr. Cromwell had—like they were just children. She imagined him wearing armor and raising a shining sword.

Everything would be all right, Easter told herself. God had heard their prayers at last and sent them a protector. Maybe Mr. Cromwell could find Mama and Pompey and buy them too. Maybe he'd even free them!

Easter's price climbed higher and higher—but Mr. Cromwell wasn't bidding. Desperately, Easter tried to catch his eye again, but he was making notes in his booklet. Finally, when the auctioneer was closing the sale, Mr. Cromwell spoke up, offering so much that the other men just groaned.

Easter breathed again, but only for a moment: Verily was next.

Master Cromwell kept his word and purchased her too. Easter and her sister were safe.

MASTER CROMWELL TOOK THEM to a wagon driven by a black man. The man looked well-fed. That was a good sign. But when Master Cromwell mounted his white horse and they started forward, Verily began crying again.

"Shh," Easter hissed. "We mustn't give Master Cromwell any reason to change his mind."

"Your new Master has a house on Church Street, but he and his daughter are at his Ashley River plantation till Race Week," Master Cromwell explained. "His name is Edward Stratford, and his daughter, your new Mistress, is Miss Clare."

Easter's shoulders drooped. Mr. Cromwell *wasn't* their new Master.

"I am Mr. Stratford's steward. That means I oversee overseers," he explained with a smile. "In addition to the rice plantation, which has been in his family for generations, Mr. Stratford has a cotton plantation—they keep us quite busy."

What if Master Edward doesn't want TWO girls? Easter worried. *What if he sends my sister to one of his plantations and me to the other?* She tried again to calm Verily, while her own stomach twisted in knots.

· · ·

MR. CROMWELL LED THEM up a drive of giant oak trees to a grand house with white columns all the way around the outside. A black man was trimming the bushes. Like the wagon driver, he appeared tidy and healthy.

While Mr. Cromwell was dismounting, Easter wiped her sister's nose with her own skirt and whispered that Verily had better keep her injured hand hidden inside her pocket. They must make a good impression on their new Master. Their future depended on it.

Mr. Cromwell took Easter and her sister inside, up the staircase, and down the hall to Master Edward's office. He was intent on his papers and barely looked up. Their new Master was maybe forty years old, with hair the color of brown leaves and a beard around his mouth but not on his cheeks. Mr. Cromwell was almost the opposite, with neat strips of gold hair on his cheeks and the rest of his face shaved.

"Easter has experience in the kitchen," Mr. Cromwell told the Master, "so I thought I'd assign her to Phoebe and let Verily serve as Clare's maid."

"Whatever you think best, Lucas," Master Edward said as he used something like a saltshaker to sprinkle white powder on his paper. Then he really looked at Verily. "She's rather young."

Easter's heart froze. Master Edward was going to send her sister back!

"Have you dressed a lady before?"

His voice wasn't mean, but it must have frightened Verily. She burst into tears again.

"Yes, sir, Master, sir," Easter answered quickly on her sister's behalf. "Mama was teaching Verily how to care for our Missus' clothes and her hair."

"Very well." Master Edward returned his attention to his papers. "If she doesn't suit, we'll simply have to make other arrangements."

He wanted to separate them already! "We'll do anything, Master!" Easter jumped in.

Master Edward ignored her. "Thank you, Lucas."

Mr. Cromwell took them back to the hall. Easter tried to calm Verily, but she wanted to cry herself. They still weren't safe from the traders. At least her sister was keeping her injured hand in her pocket. Easter glanced up to see how Mr. Cromwell was taking Verily's sobbing, but her eyes went past him to the little white girl peering around a door down the hall.

The girl looked about Verily's age. She had light brown hair done up in curls and a pretty green dress. She opened the door wider and came toward them. "I heard someone crying."

Mr. Cromwell introduced them. "Miss Stratford, this is your new maid, Verily, and her sister, Easter. Easter, Verily, this is your new mistress, Miss Clare Stratford."

Miss Clare frowned at Verily. "What's the matter?"

Easter didn't want to sound unhappy or ungrateful, but she couldn't think of a convincing lie. "She misses our Mama and our brother Pompey, Miss."

"Where are they?"

"Mama's in New Orleans by now," Verily sobbed. "I don't even know where my brother is!"

Miss Clare scowled up at Mr. Cromwell. "Why didn't you buy all of them?"

"That isn't always possible, Miss Stratford."

"Go away," the girl ordered Mr. Cromwell. "Come with me," she told Verily, taking hold of her good hand. "You too, Easter!"

Mr. Cromwell opened his mouth to protest, but nothing came out. He let Miss Clare take Verily and Easter into her room and shut the door behind them.

Their new mistress opened the drawer of the small table beside her bed and pulled out a handkerchief, which she gave to Verily for her nose. The girl also withdrew a tin and pried off the lid to reveal flat little cookies spotted with seeds. She offered them to Easter and Verily.

They hesitated. Was this a trick? White people didn't give slaves food from their own plates. Were tins different?

"They're benne wafers!" Miss Clare told them. "They're good luck. At least that's what Phoebe says." The girl popped one into her mouth and made satisfied crunching sounds.

Slowly, Easter accepted a cookie and bit it in half to make it last.

The wafer tasted nutty and sweet as caramel. Verily was still crying, but she nibbled one too.

Miss Clare offered them more. "Were you born on Easter?"

Easter took another benne wafer and nodded.

"And your name is Verity?"

Easter's sister shook her head. "Verily."

"I've never known anyone called Verily before."

"Our old Missus named us," Easter explained. "For Verily, she got out her Bible, closed her eyes, and pointed to a page. Her finger landed on the word 'Verily.' Missus liked it 'cause the rest of the verse was: 'Verily, verily, I say unto you, "The servant is not greater than his lord."' Missus said it was a good name 'cause it would keep Verily in her place."

Miss Clare frowned.

Easter didn't want to talk about Missus Claudia anymore, so she asked about the animal hide at the end of Miss Clare's bed. "Is that from a bear, Miss?"

The girl shook her head and grinned. "It's a buffalo!"

"What's that?" Verily mumbled, her mouth full of cookie.

"They're like big shaggy cattle that live out West. I'm going to see them one day." Miss Clare stroked the dark brown fur.

Easter wondered if it was soft. It looked soft.

"Touch it!" Miss Clare urged, as if it were natural for slaves to touch their mistress's things. The only time Easter had ever touched Missus Claudia's belongings, she'd been cleaning them, and Missus *still* struck Easter for not putting her vases back at the right angles.

Verily still had a benne wafer in her good hand, so she stroked the buffalo hide with her injured hand.

Miss Clare saw her bandage. "What happened?"

"I fell," Verily whimpered.

"It ain't bad, Miss," Easter answered quickly.

"May I see it?"

Reluctantly, Verily held out her injured hand. Her blood had oozed through Mr. Cromwell's handkerchief, which was coming loose. Miss Clare led Verily to her washstand and poured fresh water from the pitcher. Gently she pulled off the handkerchief and washed Verily's hand. "It's not deep. You'll be all right." From her bedside table, the girl produced cotton bandaging. "If my brother were here, he'd take care of it properly," Miss Clare explained as she wrapped the bandage. "But he taught me some simple things."

"You have a brother, Miss?" Easter asked, worried that they'd have *another* new Master to please.

"Well…not really. He's my father's ward. His name is David, and he's studying medicine in Paris." Miss Clare grinned. "Do you want to see what he sent me for Christmas?" Without waiting for an answer, she sprang to her dressing table, where there was a wooden box with beautiful decorations on the lid. Miss Clare opened it to reveal its insides: a golden rolling pin with bumps all over it; a silver comb; and three golden circles with— "See how the bell hammers are butterflies? It plays waltzes and polkas and Irish airs and opera overtures! Turn the key!" Miss Clare urged Verily.

Easter's sister obeyed, and something amazing happened. The rolling pin turned, the comb rippled like water, and beautiful music flowed from the box. The only good thing about Missus Claudia was that she'd played the piano and the harp. This little box sounded like both at once, delicate but rich as buttermilk. Easter and Verily both gaped.

Miss Clare invited them to sit on her buffalo robe and suggested they close their eyes. "Imagine you're sitting in an opera house, watching a ballerina dance with her beloved…"

Easter had no idea what an opera house looked like or what a ballerina was. But listening to that magical box, she felt hopeful.

When the music stopped, Verily leapt up to wind the key again; but instead she cried out: "Easter! She has picture cards!" Easter saw them now, lined up along the bottom of the girl's dressing mirror.

"You mean my prayer cards?" Miss Clare joined her and named each saint: Teresa and Mary and Luke, even one named Clare. "Do you have one?"

Verily hung her head. "We used to."

"I remembered it, Verily," Easter said, though she knew her sister had thrown away the angel card on purpose. Easter retrieved it from her pocket and returned it to Verily. Her sister held the card against her chest and almost smiled.

"Saint Michael is one of my favorites too," Miss Clare said. "He's the Prince of the Angels!"

Easter started at a knock on the door, followed by Mr. Cromwell's voice: "Miss Stratford?" Either he'd gone away and come back, or he'd been waiting outside all this time. "I imagine Easter and Verily are ready for supper."

Miss Clare pouted. "You'll come back tomorrow?"

"Yes, Miss." Verily tucked her angel card in her pocket.

Mr. Cromwell led Easter and Verily out the back of the house and down one of the curved stairs. Behind the Big House stood two smaller buildings facing each other. On the inner sides, they each had columns and porches—they looked almost as fine as Master Lem's home, only half the size.

Mr. Cromwell pointed to the door on the ground floor as they passed it. "That's the kitchen. I'll ask Phoebe to warm some supper for you." He climbed the stairs and took Easter and Verily through the door at the top. "This is your room."

Easter gaped at the window, the fireplace, the two chairs, the washstand, the little bureau, and the rope bed with a plump mattress, a pillow, a quilt, and real sheets. At their old plantation, she'd slept under a single blanket on a cornhusk mattress on the floor of the kitchen loft, alongside Verily, the cook, the cook's wife, and their three sons. All of them snored. Easter's parents had slept on pallets in the Big House, so they'd be nearby if Master or Missus wanted something in the night, and Pompey had slept in a cabin with other single men. Easter looked up at Mr. Cromwell in disbelief. "This is ours?"

"*Yours*, at least. Verily may stay with you for a night or two—but as soon as her hand is better, she'll sleep in Miss Clare's room."

Easter might have guessed that. But Verily wouldn't be far. They were still together.

· · ·

OVER CORNBREAD AND HAM SCRAPS in the kitchen, Easter asked Phoebe about Master Edward and Mr. Cromwell. "They're better than most, I expect," the cook said as she pressed dough into pans. Phoebe was making peach tarts for the house. "They'll have the overseer whip you all right, if'n they think you've crossed them. But Master Edward and Mr. Cromwell ain't the sort to beat you just because they can. Sometimes, they're even fair. And they leave us women alone, thank the Lord. Pay attention, and you'll learn their ways soon enough—learn how to make them *think* you're obeying, even when you ain't." Phoebe uncorked a bottle of sliced peaches and poured them into a bowl. Then she forked slices onto Easter and Verily's plates and winked.

THAT NIGHT, Easter held her sister in their bed and watched the fire.
"Will we *ever* see them again?" Verily sniffled.
"I don't know," Easter admitted. "I hope so." She wondered where Mama and Pompey were tonight. Easter's throat grew tight, but she knew it wouldn't do any good to cry. "This place isn't so bad, is it?"
"I guess not."
"I think Miss Clare will be kind to you."
Verily nodded and begged Easter to sing one of their mama's lullabies.
When her sister was asleep, Easter thanked God and the blond angel for Mr. Cromwell and Miss Clare. If Easter and her sister could prove themselves to Master Edward, they just might be content here. It wasn't freedom and it wasn't happiness, but she was finally starting to feel safe.

ONE WARM AFTERNOON a week after she and Verily arrived, Easter was helping Phoebe in the kitchen garden. As she listened, learning what was ready to harvest and what needed caring for, Easter also watched Miss Clare teaching Verily. Nearby, they were playing a game called graces.

With two crossed sticks, the young mistress held up a ribboned hoop. She drew the sticks apart quickly, sending the hoop flying toward Verily, the ribbons fluttering. Easter's sister caught it with her own sticks and tried to send it back. First she couldn't get the hoop off the sticks, and then she sent it plummeting sideways, far from Miss Clare. The young mistress didn't insult Verily or strike her; she simply ran to help, patiently showing Verily how to hold the sticks.

Easter found herself wondering about Miss Clare's mother. Missus Teresa must have been very different from Missus Claudia. Easter wished she was here still. Verily had said there was a painting of Missus Teresa in the library, and that the young mistress looked just like her mother, with eyes and hair the color of hazelnuts.

Easter asked Phoebe: "Was she a kind mistress, Miss Clare's mama?"

"She tried to be." The cook didn't look up but kept at her work, wrapping brown paper around the stalks of the leeks to blanch them. She nodded toward the twine Easter held.

Easter leaned in to tie the brown paper in place.

"Miss Teresa made some good changes, like getting us more rations and getting us women more time to rest after our babies come. Once, she stopped a family from being separated. We knew we could go to her, and she'd fight for us as best she could. But the last year or so before she died, Miss Teresa got so caught up in her own troubles, she couldn't see anybody else's."

Miss Clare's giggle drifted over to them. Easter looked up to see that Verily was tossing the hoop easily now. She even seemed to be smiling. Miss Clare was grinning at her success and encouraging her.

"It'll happen to her too," Phoebe sighed. "Miss Clare will grow up and forget us. Every white person who's kind to you, they make you think: 'Maybe this one will be different.' Sooner or later, they always prove you wrong."

CHAPTER 8

She will become prematurely knowing in evil things… If God has bestowed beauty upon her, it will prove her greatest curse. That which commands admiration in the white woman only hastens the degradation of the female slave.
— Harriet Jacobs, *Incidents in the Life of a Slave Girl, Written by Herself* (1861)

The first night Verily began sleeping in Miss Clare's chamber, Easter returned to her own room to find stacks of clothing on her bed. Mr. Cromwell had mentioned that she and her sister should have some new clothes, and Easter knew Verily was getting a few of Miss Clare's old things. But these had belonged to a woman.

In awe, Easter lifted each garment: day dresses and frilly underthings that must have clothed a fine lady—Miss Teresa, Easter guessed. There were linen drawers with the most beautiful lace around the bottom of each leg. Easter had never even worn drawers before, let alone anything so lovely. All the garments were too large, but she could fix that. Whoever had left the clothing also gave her a splendid new sewing kit.

The alterations filled any time she had after Phoebe's dismissal and before bed, the pretty patterns distracting Easter at least a little from missing her sister. Phoebe's chatting kept her thoughts occupied during the day.

Easter saw Verily mostly on Sundays, when her sister always had a great deal to tell her about her adventures with Miss Clare. The young mistress was teaching Verily about all the animals on the plantation and about the saints. Easter's sister was fortunate to serve such a mistress. But Easter was lonely without Verily.

Worse came: Easter learned that her sister would accompany Miss Clare and Master Edward to Charleston for Race Week, which involved not only horses but parties. Easter would remain on the plantation.

She'd attend a dance of her own, she decided. Surely there'd be one in the quarters while the Master was away. She'd find a friend, maybe even a sweetheart.

It was hard to know where she fit here. Mama and Papa had both been mulattos. Her sister had the same dark eyes and the same corkscrew curls, though their white blood showed more clearly in Easter's skin. So she was lighter than most of the field hands but darker than most of the house slaves. The nearly-white butler and maids considered her beneath them, while the field hands envied her.

Easter envied them right back. She might get cast-off clothing from the Missus and leavings from the Master's table, but the field slaves had more freedom. She might not have to wade through the rice fields under the blazing sun, but the field hands worked on the task system. As soon as they hoed the half-acre or sowed the three-quarter-acre Mr. Cromwell had assigned them, the rest of the day was their own. The field hands had time to tend their own chickens and cows and garden patches.

The house slaves didn't even have time to tend window-boxes. Their lives were dictated by the little bells on the back veranda. Even on Sundays and holidays, they always had to do something and they might be called to do anything. Though Easter spent most of her time helping Phoebe in the kitchen, if one of the maids spotted her, she might become their extra hands too.

Master Edward and Miss Clare being away slowed the pace a little, but there was plenty of work to finish before their return. Today was wash day. After Easter helped Sibbe and Rachel with the bedding from the Big House, she washed her own under-things. The clothes-lines were full, so Easter had to walk out of sight of the kitchen and the other slaves to find new bushes where she could drape her clothes to dry.

"How are you liking your new garments, Easter?"

She started. The voice was Mr. Cromwell's. Squinting into the sun, she saw him approaching on his white horse. "They're very fine, sir; I like them very much." She was wearing one of the gowns now, a red wool, beneath her pinafore. "Did they belong to Miss Teresa?"

"They did." Mr. Cromwell looked back toward the outbuildings, but no one else was in sight. "Edward keeps Tessa's room preserved like a shrine; he was reluctant to part with even a few pieces." Mr. Cromwell looked back at her and smiled. "But I think it was worth the persuading."

"Yes, sir. Thank you for the sewing kit too, sir."

"You're not afraid of ghosts, are you, Easter?"

She frowned. Was he asking because she was wearing a dead woman's clothes? "Not especially."

"Good. When Clare showed you around the grounds, did she point out her mother's tomb?"

"Yes, sir."

"Excellent. Meet me there tonight, just after full dark. I'll leave it unlocked and leave a lantern in your room. Don't let anyone see you, and do *not* change your clothes."

"Sir?"

Mr. Cromwell did not explain; he only turned his horse. "You know I am Master here, while Edward is in Charleston?"

"Yes…Master," Easter called to his back as he dug in his spurs.

What was she to make of such a conversation? Did the tomb need cleaning? Why after dark, then, and why must Easter wear Miss Teresa's clothes?

Perhaps Mr. Cromwell intended to conjure her spirit. Easter

shivered. Just last week, Phoebe had been telling her that séances were becoming fashionable among white people, who wanted to converse with their dead relatives. But Mr. Cromwell was no relation to Miss Teresa.

She'd know his reasons soon enough, Easter told herself as she scrubbed pots, churned butter, and collected her under-things from the bushes. She had no need to worry. Hadn't Mr. Cromwell proved himself kind? She was *wearing* that proof. If he wanted her to meet him in a tomb, she would meet him in a tomb.

STILL EASTER PAUSED at the edge of the graveyard. Her lantern left so much of it in darkness. Her brother Pompey had always avoided Master Lem's family cemetery on their old plantation. Pompey said that since slaveholders were damned, their troubled spirits must haunt their graves, wailing as the demons flogged them, chopped off their toes, cat-hauled them, and subjected them to every torture they'd inflicted on their slaves. Pompey had never explained how dead whites could haunt their graves and writhe in Hell at the same time.

Miss Teresa had been a kind mistress, Easter reminded herself. She wouldn't trouble anyone from beyond the grave.

Easter swallowed her fear and strode between the gravestones to the entrance of Miss Teresa's fanciful tomb. The columns looked like bundled plants, and the cast iron gates were decorated with wings and snakes. The doors opened when Easter pulled at them, as Mr. Cromwell had promised.

She was glad she still wore her pinafore and that she'd brought her wool shawl. Spring was coming on fast, but the tomb seemed to breathe cold. Easter tugged down her head wrap to cover more of her ears.

As she descended the steep stairs, lantern light and shadows bounced off the walls and everything around her. At first, the angel statue seemed to tremble. Even up close, she looked so real: every fold of her dress, every strand of her hair, every feather of her wings. Even the fingernails on her hands, one of them offering stone lilies to the stone coffin.

The angel hid her face in her other arm and brought back a memory. When Verily had asked Mama about angels, she'd said some of them had many wings, and Mama had taught Easter and Verily a song that began:

I want two wings to veil my face,
I want two wings to fly away...

There were leaves and flowers carved all over the marble coffin. Words too. Easter ran her fingers over the deep markings, cool to the touch, and wished she knew what they said about Miss Teresa. With her lantern, Easter lit up the flames carved on the wall. She wondered why the stone torches were upside-down.

Between the torches stood a smaller statue: the Blessed Virgin Mary, as Miss Clare called her. She was white like the angel. Everything in the tomb was white. Mary held her arms open as if she were inviting Easter to embrace her. Easter liked the idea of a religion with a mother at its center, someone you could talk to when—

"What do you think of it? Tessa's tomb?"

For the second time that day, Mr. Cromwell startled her. Easter turned sharply toward the stairs, where he was seated in his grey suit and tall black boots, beside his own lantern. Easter wondered how long he'd been there.

"Do you like it?" Mr. Cromwell asked. By the way his eyes roamed over the tomb, she could tell *he* admired it.

Easter looked back to the angel and the Blessed Virgin. "It's a sad place...but lovely and peaceful too."

"It's my doing." His arms were draped across his spread thighs, fingers interlaced, thumbs restless. "Edward was useless for *weeks* after Tessa died. The design, the contracts—he left almost all of it to me. So I created a monument to unhappy wives and unrequited lust." Mr. Cromwell stood and descended the last step, his boots making shushing sounds across the stone floor.

Instinctively, Easter backed away from him, but she only

bumped up against the wall beside the Virgin. She shifted her shawl and pretended she was leaning there on purpose.

Mr. Cromwell stopped at the marble coffin and placed his hand on its corner, his eyes on the writing. "Are you wearing her drawers, too?"

Goose pimples tingled on Easter's skin, and they had nothing to do with the chill of the tomb. "P-Pardon?"

"Her drawers. I can see you're wearing her dress, probably her chemise, and at least one of her petticoats—but are you wearing her drawers too?"

"Y-Yes, sir."

"*Perfect*," he smiled, drawing out the word like he'd just tasted a peach for the first time.

This wasn't right. This was very, very wrong. "Sir?"

Mr. Cromwell began to circle the stone coffin. "I told you to call me Master, didn't I?"

"Yes, Master." Easter's eyes went to the stairs. He was crossing behind the angel; it would take him a few seconds to follow her if—

"You love your sister very much, don't you, Easter?"

Easter had already stepped forward. Now she stopped, though he came closer with every breath. "Y-Yes, Master."

"You'd do anything to protect her from harm, wouldn't you?"

"Yes, Master." Easter felt as if she were rooted where she stood. She couldn't leave without knowing why he was talking about Verily —about *harming* Verily.

"That's very good to hear, Easter." Mr. Cromwell was standing beside her now. "Because from this moment on, Verily's happiness is in *your* hands."

Easter broke the rules. She glanced up at him, into his eyes. His irises must be pale blue. In the shadows of the tomb, they looked grey. He still didn't look cruel. But she dropped her gaze again, to the buttons of his waistcoat that were even with her eyes.

"I am going to make a bargain with you, Easter. I promise you your sister's happiness, her safety." Mr. Cromwell took the lantern from her hand and set it next to the Blessed Virgin. "*I am in control here, even more than Master Edward. So I have the* power to make that promise, and to keep it. You have my word that Verily will never be harmed, by myself or the overseer or anyone else." Mr. Cromwell reached toward her and unknotted her shawl.

Easter said nothing and did nothing as it fell to the floor. She must make him think she was submitting.

"In exchange, you will reveal to no one anything I say to you or anything I do to you."

Easter sucked in a breath and darted toward the stairs, but he anticipated her flight and blocked her. She doubled back quickly, dashing around the marble coffin. But that side of the tomb was in shadow now. She tripped over the sandaled foot of the kneeling angel and crashed to her knees.

Mr. Cromwell didn't chase Easter. Instead, when she scrambled back to her feet, she saw he was standing at the bottom of the staircase now, one hand braced against each wall, barring her escape. Easter gripped the wing of the angel as if it might carry her through the ceiling.

Mr. Cromwell kept talking while her heart pounded with dread in her ears. "Most of all, you will do everything in your power to prevent *Edward* from learning about our arrangement."

There is no arrangement! Easter wanted to scream.

"The man lives like a monk, you see, and he expects the rest of us to do the same. Only a few weeks ago, he made me dismiss an overseer for 'interfering' with a woman in the quarters. I've had more than three years to make myself indispensable here. I imagine Edward would retain me as his steward were he to discover that I am, in fact, human. But I doubt he would still welcome me as his son-in-law." Spanning the entire stairwell was awkward; Mr. Cromwell dropped one of his arms.

It was something. She must keep him talking, keep him occupied. Easter prompted: "S-Son-in-law, Master?"

"Once Clare is my wife, you may say whatever you like."

Miss Clare was eleven years old. No—Easter mustn't think about that; she must *plan*!

"I anticipate it will take five years, perhaps, for Clare to ripen and for her father to grant his permission." Mr. Cromwell shrugged off his coat—and moved away from the staircase.

Easter ran. She bolted up the stairs. The darkness didn't matter; the darkness was her friend; all she had to do was— She slammed into the iron gates and nearly toppled backwards down the stairs. She was expecting the gates to open, to free her.

They shuddered, but they did not give. He'd locked them. He'd locked the gates from the inside.

"Have you been listening, Easter?" Mr. Cromwell loomed behind her on the stairs. "This is very important: No one else must ever know what happens when we are alone. Five years of your silence in exchange for your sister's safety. That is the bargain. Do you understand?"

Easter pressed her face beneath the iron snakes and the iron wings on the gates.

I want two wings to veil my face,
I want two wings to fly away...

She began to sob.

"Don't do that," Mr. Cromwell sighed. "I will probably tire of you in a year or two—but even when this ends, as long as you keep your mouth shut, I will continue to protect your sister. I will even protect *you* from other men. Do you understand?"

Easter gripped the gates and shook them as if she could rip them from their hinges.

"Where would you go, Easter? Who would you tell? From the moment you drew your first breath in a slave cabin, *this* moment was inevitable."

Easter kept pressing her forehead into the iron, but her hands fell limp at her sides.

She felt his fingers at her back, snatching open the bow at the waist of her pinafore. Roughly he tugged it from her shoulders and threw it to one side of the steps. As if she weighed no more than a doll, he picked her up with one arm around her waist and carried her back into the tomb. "It will hurt less if you don't fight it." He set her feet down on the raised base below the marble coffin, facing the angel.

Easter swayed and caught herself on the end of the coffin. Her tears dripped onto the marble. Behind her, she heard clothes rustling. Not hers. Not yet.

Maybe this would be unpleasant instead of horrible. Even after she'd tried to defy him, Mr. Cromwell hadn't lost his temper. If she submitted now, maybe he would be gentle. It could be so much worse. Mr. Cromwell wasn't ugly or slovenly. He was refined and polite. He had the face of an angel. Miss Clare might well fall in love with him when she was older. Easter could pretend to be in love with him too.

His hands burrowed inside Easter's clothing—inside Miss Teresa's clothing. Bunching up the skirts of her dress, her petticoats, and her chemise. Parting the two halves of her drawers, exposing her private skin to the sharp cold of the tomb. Easter's tears began anew. She'd imagined her first time so differently, face to face with a man whose skin was the color of midnight...

Mr. Cromwell was murmuring low, delighted words. He spread her legs apart and pushed his hand through the gap in the drawers. She started at the unwelcome prod of his fingers. "Those traders weren't lying!" He sounded pleased.

He withdrew his fingers only a little, creating a sort of inverted V, a gateway he filled in an instant with a sudden, hot bulk. Easter flinched and tried to steady herself at the end of the marble coffin. He pushed harder and harder at her, gripping her waist with one hand to keep her in place.

She couldn't pretend anymore. She didn't like this *at all*. It pinched. It *burned*. Short forceful cries were coming up out of her, but she didn't think Mr. Cromwell heard them; he was too busy grunting and—

Some part of her ripped open, and her cries became one long scream.

Easter grappled at the coffin, trying desperately to pull herself over it and away from him. Both his hands locked her hips where he wanted them, and he forced the brand deeper. Easter kicked and kicked but she hit mostly air. All her writhing only twisted each burning jab inside her, only spiralled the agony upward till she tasted bile. He was grinding her into the coffin's harsh corners and carved flowers, but they were smooth and calm and kind compared to him.

Through the tears blurring everything Easter still saw the stone angel, who just knelt there across from her in the lantern light and kept offering her lilies, kept hiding her face in her crooked arm. Why didn't she *move*, why didn't she raise her head and lift her great wings? Why didn't the angel strike down this demon and carry Easter away?

The Virgin Mary watched too. She stood there with open arms and did nothing. She did nothing.

By the time Cromwell released her, Easter had gone limp and screamed herself hoarse. She hung there on the stone coffin, shoes dangling over the floor of the tomb, staring at the Blessed Virgin while Cromwell's slime and her own blood dribbled down her legs.

He was still talking to himself, celebrating. The word "memorable" penetrated her haze of pain, then a matter-of-fact command directed at her: "Show me you can get up."

Easter didn't move. She couldn't move. She would never move again. Every breath hurt, pulling on the rawness of the wound he'd left.

Cromwell sighed as if she'd disappointed him. "Easter, Easter— your name *means* resurrection." He stepped closer and grasped her hips again.

Her body jolted, trying to renew the fight before agony locked her muscles. But Cromwell did not renew his assault. Almost gently now, he drew her away from the stone coffin till her shoes touched the floor again. Her legs shrieked; they wouldn't hold her. So Cromwell guided her slowly onto the floor, till she lay flat on her back and he crouched over her head. Easter clamped her eyes shut so she wouldn't see him.

Cromwell did not touch her again. "The pain you're feeling right now—imagine your sister feeling it. Imagine *her* lying bloody on the floor of this tomb. It doesn't have to happen, Easter. You can stop it. All you have to do is keep your mouth shut." He pressed something into her hand and left her.

It felt like a single handkerchief. A thousand would not be enough. Easter opened her eyes and stared at the ceiling, light and shadows chasing over its surface through her tears. Cromwell had left her lantern.

It didn't matter. If she didn't move, she could die right here in this tomb, from the blood and the shame and the cold. It would be so easy. All she had to do was wait.

Verily…she was abandoning Verily. Easter closed her eyes anyway.

CHAPTER 9

What use me tell him no? He have strength to make me.
— Sophy, enslaved on St. Byrons Island, in Frances Anne
Kemble's *Journal of a Residence on a Georgian Plantation in 1838-1839*

"*Look after your sister for me?*" Mama begged in Easter's head. "*Protect her, best you can? Promise me?*"

Perhaps the cold seeping from the floor of the tomb dulled the pain, or Easter simply became more accustomed to it. When she opened her eyes again, the lantern light had gone dim. The wick had burned too low. Some deep instinct took over, the training as a maid she had had all her life. Easter swallowed hard to prepare herself and rolled carefully onto her side. It hurt, badly, but she could bear it.

She sat up slowly and dragged herself to the lantern to turn up the wick. She braced herself against the wall, drew in a shuddering breath, and raised the hems of her skirts to see her stockings. The insides were stained red. Her frilly drawers must be too. Some of the blood and the—*him* had puddled on the floor. She sank to her knees and rubbed at it with his handkerchief, gritting her teeth with every painful movement. She stared back at the angel.

I want two wings to veil my face,
I want two wings to fly away...

Easter would keep her mouth shut till Verily returned from Charleston, and then they would run. Slaves did it all the time. They didn't have to make it to Canada; they just had to make it to the swamps. Phoebe had whispered that there were whole communities of runaways there, "maroons" who'd banded together and managed to avoid the patrollers.

Phoebe had also said the maroons were nearly all men. Verily was a ten-year-old girl. She would never survive in a swamp. They'd be devoured by alligators, or they'd end up right back where they started with dog bites on their legs and stripes on their backs for their trouble. Easter could not leave Verily behind—she could not even kill herself—or Cromwell would punish Verily in her place.

This must never, ever happen to her sister.

The tears returned. Easter hated Verily, for being helpless, for being her sister, for being Cromwell's bargaining piece. She hated Miss Clare and Miss Teresa, for being pretty, for making Cromwell crazy with lust. She hated Master Edward, for being so stupid he couldn't see what Cromwell wanted. But most of all, she hated the demon who looked like an angel.

SHE HAD ALL NIGHT to drag herself from the cemetery. She needed it. She forced herself up the stairs to find the gates unlocked.

But Easter knew the demon had been right: from the moment she'd been born, the gates had *always* been locked. Even after losing Papa and Mama and Pompey, some shred of her had still believed in kindness and mercy—still believed strangers could be good. All that had died in Miss Teresa's tomb.

Easter staggered from gravestone to gravestone, tree to tree, till she reached her room behind the Big House. Her new sewing kit greeted her atop the bureau full of Miss Teresa's clothing. Easter snatched up a spool of thread and hurled it across the room. It struck a wall and rolled back toward her, unravelling its crimson thread along the floor.

She tore off her dress and her underclothes. With trembling fingers, she cleaned herself as best she could with the pitcher of water and the towel on the washstand. She lit a lucifer and touched it to the wood in her fireplace. She threw Cromwell's handkerchief, her stockings, and Miss Teresa's drawers onto the flames.

Her mother had made those stockings. Easter had been so proud to own the frilly drawers. She lay on her bed and watched the cloth smoking for the rest of the night, till there was nothing left but grey ashes.

In THE MORNING, Phoebe noticed her absence and knocked on Easter's door. When Easter didn't answer, the cook let herself in. "You feeling poorly, child?"

Easter's hands tightened on her quilt. She didn't answer.

Phoebe spotted her bloody chamber pot. "Oh, you having your monthly! This your first time, child?"

Easter managed a jerky nod. It was an accurate lie, she supposed.

"I'll ask if Mr. Cromwell will let you rest. With Master Edward and Miss Clare gone, I bet he'll approve it."

Apparently he did. Phoebe brought Easter clean rags and rice pie with mutton. The cook tidied the thread Easter had "dropped," emptied her chamber pot and water basin, and refilled her pitcher.

The next day, Easter remained in her bed. Phoebe fussed. This was so kind of Mr. Cromwell, to allow this, but she advised Easter not to try for a third day.

In the morning, Easter found she could rise and reach the washstand. She returned to the kitchen, keeping her eyes down and hurrying so she wouldn't see Cromwell and he wouldn't see her. Easter settled in to peel potatoes and said almost nothing. She only pretended to listen while Phoebe prattled.

· · ·

TWO DAYS LATER, as Easter was carrying water from the creek, Cromwell was suddenly behind her, whispering hotly in her ear to come to the tomb again that night. He was gone almost as quickly. Easter sank to the ground and sobbed, letting her buckets overturn.

She did not go. She was keeping her half of the "bargain," Easter told herself—he wanted her silence. He had it. He would not have *her* again if she could help it. If she could avoid him till Master Edward returned, perhaps she'd be safe for a while, perhaps Cromwell wouldn't dare then...

Only the next morning, she was making her way back to the trap-door at the top of the attic stairs, through all the odds and ends of trunks and furniture. She turned the corner around a spare wardrobe, and Cromwell was there in front of her. Easter jumped and strangled a cry. The Madeira she was fetching would have smashed on the floor if Cromwell hadn't caught it.

She tried to flee. But the attic was a maze, and before she'd taken ten steps, he had her trapped between a wall and an old cradle. "Please— Please don't..."

"Look at me, Easter."

She couldn't. She was looking for an escape. She saw none. She wished she hadn't dropped the Madeira bottle; she might have used it as a weapon.

Instead, Cromwell held the bottle, as casually as if he were inviting her on a picnic. "I'm not going to fuck you here."

She didn't believe him. At least his voice was calm instead of angry. But he'd been calm in the tomb, too...

"Look at me, Easter."

When she wouldn't, he tried to take her chin in one hand. She wouldn't let him, turning her head sharply and recoiling as far as she could.

"It won't hurt so badly the next time." Cromwell sighed. "Didn't your mother teach you anything?" He caught her chin and forcibly turned her face to him.

She whimpered and refused to meet his eyes.

"I can be gentle, if you earn it. It's been a long time since I had a virgin, and those *drawers*..." His grip on her chin tightened. "I also had to make you understand what I *will* do to Verily if you ever disobey me. And then, you disobeyed me." He rubbed his thumb over her lips. "Tell me it won't happen again, Easter."

Her mouth opened, but only ragged breaths came out. Though the attic was warm, her teeth chattered. She imagined biting off his thumb. She imagined him bleeding and screaming.

"Do you remember what you said to me before the auction? You promised to do what I asked if I bought you and your sister." Cromwell released her and shoved the bottle of Madeira back into her hands. "You will come to the tomb tonight, or there will be consequences."

Easter slid to the floor, clutching the bottle as if it were a child.

Cromwell was already striding for the trap-door. He called back: "As long as you obey me, Easter, you have no need to fear me."

SO SHE OBEYED. She became Cromwell's whore. He'd been telling the truth, more or less: the first time was the worst, and he could feign gentleness. But it never stopped hurting. And he never stopped talking.

Cromwell rambled on about anything that came to his mind, mostly complaints: about his succession of courtesans in Charleston; his struggles to manage the other slaves; the overseer's stupidity; the few times Master Edward surprised him with a good idea about the plantations; the vicissitudes of the weather; the idiots in Columbia or Washington. Cromwell thought most people were idiots, apart from himself.

He had everything planned. If Phoebe or anyone else ever saw Easter slipping away at night, she was to "confess" that she was meeting a sweetheart from another plantation. After Easter's monthlies truly did start, Cromwell introduced her to the pessary and the female syringe.

Even though the vinegar stung, Easter was happy to wash his leavings out of her body afterward. She didn't want Cromwell's bastard any more than he did. But inserting the little rubber cap *before* their meetings felt wrong as well as uncomfortable, as if such preparation meant she was giving him her permission.

"You put in the pessary?" he'd asked the next time they met in the tomb.

"No, Master."

Cromwell stopped unbuttoning his trousers and scowled. "What are you waiting for?"

I am waiting for you to change your mind, Easter thought, fingering the drawstring bag he'd given her to hold the pessary. Refusing to do this one thing was the only way she had left to defy him, to delay what she could not prevent.

"I showed you how to use it—it isn't complicated."

And somehow, that tiny victory made her bold. "Lordy, Massa," Easter drawled, "I is jes' an ignorant nigger—cain't tell one hole from t'other."

Instead of striking Easter for her insolence—he had, in fact, never struck her—Cromwell burst out laughing. "I knew there was a reason I chose you, Easter." And he seemed quite content to insert the little cap himself.

The pessary became almost a game with them: he always asked if it was in place; she always pretended she'd forgotten; he always chuckled and snatched the bag from her hand. "The last thing this world needs is another bastard," Cromwell would say. For a moment, he'd seem reasonable, even indulgent. Then, his rough finger would shove the rubber cap up inside her, and worse would follow.

Afterward, she would wish she could inject her ears with the vinegar, to burn away the echo of his voice and the memory of what he'd done to her.

THE MONTHS MASTER EDWARD RESIDED on the plantation, Cromwell left her alone most nights. And in the sickly summer season, Cromwell too fled to the coast, daring only brief visits to make sure the overseer and the driver were working the slaves hard enough. Sometimes Easter would be free of Cromwell for weeks.

It was during the summer that she missed her first monthly. Cromwell had told her the pessary and the syringe might not be enough. He had told her to inform him immediately if she was late, so he could bring her something to start the blood again—some medicine. But she had no way to reach him while he was away from the plantation. While Easter waited for his return and tried not to panic, she remembered overhearing Phoebe talking to Rachel a few weeks before. Sometimes women were late even when there wasn't a baby, they'd said.

Sure enough, the blood returned before Cromwell did. Easter decided not to tell him about her scare. Or the next one. Sometimes she even missed two months, but the blood would always start up again. She learned not to worry. At least, not about a baby.

In Cromwell's absences, Easter would dream that the last time had been the *last time*, that he would tire of her. But he never did. The "venue," as he called it, wasn't always Miss Teresa's tomb: more and more, Cromwell wanted to fuck Easter in Miss Clare's bed.

Wherever Miss Clare went—the plantation, Charleston, or Sullivan's Island—Verily would accompany her. Easter did not really miss her sister when they were apart. It hurt Easter too much to watch Verily laughing with Miss Clare, to know what that happiness was costing her.

ONE RAINY SUNDAY, Easter sat on the porch of the kitchen house, mending a skirt her sister had torn climbing trees with Miss Clare. Verily pranced back and forth in a pair of shoes the young mistress had given her, talking on and on about Miss Clare's secret pets—the ones Verily was helping her hide from Master Edward.

Her sister's voice blended into the patter of rain on the roof—till Verily stamped her foot and cried: "Easter!"

She did not look up from her needle. "What?"

"Are you even *listening*?"

"Is it important?"

"You *never* listen to me anymore! And you're always so gloomy, even when it's not raining!"

Easter glanced up for only a moment—long enough to glare at her sister.

Verily's shoulders slumped, and she sighed. "I haven't forgotten Mama or Pompey. But wherever they are, us being miserable isn't going to make it better. Don't you think they'd want us to be happy? We can be, Easter. Ending up here—you and me, we got *lucky*."

Easter answered in her head: *No, Verily—you got lucky*.

Easter hated lying to her sister, so she just stopped talking to her much at all. But she did not stop protecting her.

PART III
AN EDUCATION

1853-1859

South Carolina and
Paris, France

A *little Learning* is a dang'rous Thing;
Drink deep, or taste not the *Pierian* Spring

— Alexander Pope,
An Essay on Criticism (1711)

CHAPTER 10

We have been taught more concerning the structure of the earth, the laws of the heavenly bodies, the habits and formation of plants…than concerning the structure of the human frame…
— Catharine Beecher, "The Profession of a Woman" (1847)

Clare *wanted* to learn. She wanted to draw as well as David, and she wanted to play piano as well as Mama. But she didn't want to attend school so far away from Charleston and Stratford-on-Ashley. Since Mama died, Clare had been taking lessons from Aunt Hortense and tutors. She didn't understand why that couldn't continue, or why she couldn't go to a school in Charleston.

But her father and Aunt Hortense said the best girls attended the South Carolina Female Collegiate Institute in Barhamville, all the way past Columbia. They did not admit it in so many words, but Clare knew her father and aunt were also banishing her from the stables, ponds, and climbing trees on the plantation.

If she *had* to go to school far away, why couldn't she go to Paris?

"A twelve-year-old girl alone in Europe?" her father scoffed. "Don't be ridiculous."

"But I *wouldn't* be alone! I could live with David!"

"Are you *determined* to become a doxy?"

"What's a doxy?"

"You will go to Barhamville!" her father commanded, "and that is the end of it!"

"Can't we at least *visit* David? Maybe next summer?"

"I said: 'That is the end of it!'" Her father clenched his fist.

Clare shrunk back and fell silent.

For her twelfth birthday, Aunt Hortense had given Clare *How to Be a Lady: A Book for Girls, Containing Useful Hints on the Formation of Character*. Clare knew she wouldn't like it. For one thing, it had been written by a man. The author said the instructions of her father were like the voice of God, and disobedience—or even reluctant obedience—made her a monster instead of a girl. "Obedience is a woman's first duty," as Aunt Hortense was always chiding her.

Because she had no other choice, Clare would obey—she would go to this school far from everything and everyone she loved—but she refused to do so cheerfully. Her father wouldn't even let her take Verily. He said Clare was too fond of her already. What he meant was: *"I bought you a maid so I could spy on you, and instead you befriend her! How dare you!"*

Clare had never thought of Verily as only a maid. Her new friend had been frightened of them at first, but Verily had grown to appreciate cicadas and bullfrogs almost as much as Clare did. She'd learned to ride so she could accompany Clare on her own pony. When Clare graduated to a horse who threw her, Verily saw her through her convalescence.

Verily had also been there when Clare discovered that sweet old Mignon had died in his sleep. David was thousands of miles away, and no one else cared about the cat. Clare didn't know what she would have done without Verily's shoulder to cry on. A funeral wasn't a funeral with only one mourner.

"WE CAN'T EVEN WRITE to each other while I'm away at school!" Clare muttered, sitting disconsolately on the low chair at her dressing table while Verily tucked fresh bedclothes around Clare's mattress. "If you could write, you could tell me how many pups the otters have and..." Clare's eyes widened with an idea, and she turned to her friend. "We've months yet before I have to go—I could *teach* you to read and write!"

Verily looked up at once, and Clare saw she was interested. Then, her friend shook her head as if to shake the desire loose and returned her attention to the counterpane. "It's against the law, Miss."

Clare glanced toward the door. She'd closed it earlier, but she lowered her voice nonetheless. "It would be our secret!"

"I couldn't send you any letters, and I couldn't receive any, or everyone would find out."

Clare sighed. "I don't know who decided slaves can't read. It's a stupid rule! In France, colored men *write* books!"

Verily's eyebrows bunched in surprise. "They do?"

"Remember *The Three Musketeers*?" Clare often read aloud while her friend did her hair or tidied her room, and they'd shared the novel a few weeks ago.

"That was written by a colored man?"

Clare nodded. "Alexandre Dumas. I didn't know it till after we finished, but Father Joseph told me. His father was born a slave in Haiti—Saint-Domingue, it was called then. Yet Dumas's father became a great general who commanded thousands of white men. His enemies called him 'the Black Devil'—but he saved France. His son wrote about it in his memoirs."

"I'd love to read those..." Verily reached for Clare's buffalo robe, which she'd folded atop the chest at the foot of Clare's bed.

"Dumas based parts of *The Count of Monte Cristo* on his father. That's an even better story than *The Three Musketeers*."

Her friend worried one corner of the buffalo robe. "Even if we can't write to each other... If I'm careful and keep them hidden, maybe I could read some of your books while you're gone?"

"You could," Clare smiled.

Verily caught her lower lip between her teeth in excitement. "You'd really teach me, Miss? And keep it a secret?"

"Of course."

"Then...I want to learn."

ONE OF THE FIRST THINGS Verily wanted to know was what her own name looked like. Clare remembered that there were lots of examples in the Bible. Christ often said it twice in a row; it was practically His favorite word. They figured out that the verse "Verily, verily, I say unto you, The servant is not greater than his lord" wasn't really about slaves and masters but about how everyone should be humble. Christ Himself had washed His disciples' feet.

Clare didn't much like the thought of washing Verily's feet—or emptying *her* chamber pot. But in another of the "Verily" verses, Christ told His disciples: "Verily I say unto you, That a rich man shall hardly enter into the kingdom of heaven... It is easier for a camel to pass through the eye of a needle." Clare had never seen a camel except in a book, but she knew it was a large animal, and she'd seen plenty of needle eyes. Not even a baby snake could pass through that. Clare had trouble getting thread through.

She supposed that if a rich man couldn't enter Heaven, then a rich girl couldn't either. Her family wasn't as rich as the Middletons or the Pinckneys, but they were rich compared to Verily or even David's family. What could Clare do? She knew her father and Aunt Hortense would never let her sell all she had and give the money to the poor; they'd replace Clare's fine clothes and baubles at once.

She couldn't ask Father Joseph about this: he'd been assigned to Beaufort and its missions, days away. Clare decided to ask Grand-père René and Grand-mère Anne. Despite her father's grumblings, Clare still attended Mass whenever she was in Charleston. David's grandparents took her. Clare thought of them as her honorary grandparents, since her mother's mother lived in New York and her father's parents were both dead.

During their Sundays together, Clare enjoyed practicing her French with René and learning signs with Anne, who had been Clare's sponsor at her Confirmation. Being with them made Clare feel closer to David, and they told her their memories of Mama.

Together, René and Anne explained that Christ didn't mean it was impossible for a rich man—or a rich girl—to be saved. Instead, Christ was saying that it was more difficult for rich people to remember that a person's true worth came not from the things she owned but from the way she treated other people.

Clare must have looked worried still, because Anne continued: 'Often a person's time and company are the greatest gifts she can give.'

René translated the signs Clare didn't understand, then added with a grin: 'Like the way you spend your Sundays with us old fogeys.'

"But I love our Sundays!" Clare blurted, then remembered to sign. 'I'll miss them when I'm at school!'

'We'll miss you too, Clare.' Anne smiled, though her eyes were sad. 'Your company has meant so much to us, with David in Paris and Joseph in Beaufort.'

'And now *I'm* leaving you too!' Clare said with her voice and her hands. Who would converse with Anne once Clare was at school? She placed her fists against her heart to show she was sorry before the tears started. Then Clare forgot all her signs, so she hugged Anne instead.

"There's nothing wrong with your conscience, *souris*," René assured Clare. "You'll pass through the eye of that needle just fine."

WHILE SHE PACKED HER TRUNKS for the school in Barhamville, Clare realized just how many fine things she owned. With regret, she decided to leave her music box behind. She was afraid it might be damaged on the journey, and she'd learned she would have to share a room with other girls. What if the opera overtures and Irish airs annoyed them?

She had other things to remind her of David: the drawings he'd sent her from Paris, the locket with Mama and David's hair, her ouroboros bracelet. All of these she kept with her, as well as the rosary Mama had made for her.

Clare had a whole cabinet full of dolls. She decided to take two of the humblest ones, dolls she'd made herself. Clare had admired

Verily's cornhusk doll, how the husks had been molded like clay to make a head, bodice, arms, and skirts. Her friend explained how to soak the husks in warm water so you could turn and shape them. Verily's mother had learned from an Indian woman in Virginia.

Myra in the spinning house had helped Clare and Verily dye cornhusks with walnut, indigo, cochineal, and tumeric. Since Clare and Verily had to work with the husks while they were still damp, some of the dye seeped into their hands, and it showed on Clare's skin in particular. Her father was aghast, and Aunt Hortense was furious. She made Clare scrub her hands with lye soap till they burned and wear gloves even inside till the stains faded. Aunt Hortense forbade Clare ever to do such a thing again.

She didn't care. Her dolls were beautiful. Her father and Aunt Hortense couldn't understand how Clare could want something so "simple" when she owned a dozen china dolls. But Clare felt pretentious playing with them. She was *proud* of her cornhusk dolls as if they were her own children. And she liked that they didn't have faces. It was difficult to imagine that her china dolls were angry or sad or frightened or joyful during the adventures she invented for them, because they always wore the same placid expression. Her cornhusk dolls could be *anything*.

Clare made an angel, a French duchess in a tall wig, and a doll in a bonnet and crinoline who might have stepped off the streets of Charleston. But her favorite dolls were an Indian maiden with a papoose on her back and an Indian brave to protect her. These were the dolls she took to Barhamville.

Where the other girls laughed at her. "You brought *rag* dolls?"

"They're made of cornhusks, not rags," Clare defended. "I made them myself."

"You have to make your own dolls—out of pig food?!" The speaker was Floride Butler, though the whole floor full of girls seemed to laugh with her.

Most of the students envied Clare such a roommate; they fawned over Floride, whose father was in the state legislature. They wanted to be part of her not-so-secret society. Floride admitted only a select few, who called everyone else "nons" because they were "non-members." Heaven help anyone who failed to pronounce Floride's name the proper French way—Flor-*eed*—in the hearing of any member. Such a girl was barred forever.

Floride and her friends acted as if nons were non-people who existed only for their amusement. They invented mocking names for nons. On one of their first walks, Clare helped a *Terrapene carolina* cross the road, so she became Turtle Girl. It could've been worse.

Then, Floride and Clare's two other roommates spotted her rosary. There was nothing good Protestant girls hated more than a good Catholic. They *all* prayed before breakfast; like daily walks, it was part of the school's routine. Somehow, Clare's method offended the other girls.

When she'd first arrived at Barhamville, Clare had explained to the headmaster and his wife that it was a mortal sin for her to attend a Protestant service. Dr. Marks and Mrs. M were Methodists, but reluctantly they agreed that Clare could remain in her room and pray on her own while the other girls were in chapel.

One Sunday, when Clare knelt for her prayers in her room, she opened her round wooden rosary box to find it empty. She frowned and began searching the rest of the little drawer in her bedside table. Had she forgotten to put her rosary away last night?

This wasn't just any rosary. Mama had made it for her First Communion—not only fastening the crucifix and the beads together with silver wire but *growing* the beads. They were the seeds of Job's Tears plants, dove grey and earthy brown, shaped like fat teardrops and lustrous from the contact of Mama's own hands as she'd worked. The rosary had taken Mama nearly a year to complete. Clare couldn't have lost it!

She looked underneath her bed, then yanked open the drawer of the wardrobe she shared with her roommates. Her rosary wasn't in the pockets of the skirt she'd worn yesterday either!

The other girls were filing out to chapel. "Did you check *under* your bed?" Floride asked behind her.

"Yes!" Clare cried.

"Not *everywhere* under your bed," Floride called back in a sing-song. Clare heard her break into laughter in the hall, joined by their two roommates.

Clare's eyes went wide. No! Floride *couldn't* have…

Clare dropped to her knees beside her bed, stared at the lid of her chamber pot, and swallowed hard. Gingerly, she reached out and lifted the lid. Inside, swimming in Clare's own urine, lay Mama's rosary.

Clare shrieked.

"Do you see a bug, Miss?"

If only! Clare glanced over her shoulder to see one of the school's maids entering with a broom. Clare shook her head and pointed a shaky hand under her bed. "My—rosary…"

The maid, a dark negress, wasn't much older than Clare, maybe fifteen. She knelt beside her to peer into Clare's chamber pot and tsked in sympathy. "Can you get another?"

Clare shook her head more fiercely, tears coursing from her eyes at the sight of those beautiful beads and Christ's crucified body submerged in her waste. Her breaths were so ragged, she almost choked on the words: "Mama made it for me."

"Let's see…" The maid set down her broom and drew a rag from her apron pocket. "Do you have a buttonhook, Miss?"

Clare nodded and tried to steady her breathing. She wiped her nose on her sleeve and fetched her buttonhook from her bedside table.

With the hook end, the maid lifted the dripping rosary from the chamber pot onto her rag, then carried it to the washbasin.

"But we all washed our faces in that!" Clare objected as she stood.

"This is just the first rinse." The maid slid Clare's rosary carefully into the basin, then checked the pitcher. Clare already knew it was empty. "Do you think you can carry the soap dish, Miss?"

"Yes." Clare followed the maid down the narrow servants' staircase to the water pump in the rear yard. There, they set to washing and rinsing Clare's rosary.

Operating the pump for the third time, the maid declared: "Nearly good as new, Miss! Maybe rinse it in some perfume, and—"

Clare didn't let her finish. She threw her arms around the maid. "Thank you!"

The older girl stopped pumping and smiled. "You're welcome, Miss."

"What's your name?"

"Lydia!" shouted Mrs. M as she strode toward them. "We've told you not to speak to the girls, and you've hardly started on the rooms!"

"She was helping me!" Clare protested.

"And you, Miss Stratford!" Mrs. M seemed to tower over her. "We excused you from chapel, not from prayers!"

"I'm sorry, Missus," Lydia murmured, her eyes lowered. Even her shoulders seemed slumped now. "There was an accident..." Lydia scurried away.

"It wasn't an accident!" Clare corrected. "Floride Butler threw my rosary in my chamber pot on purpose!"

NATURALLY FLORIDE CLAIMED she had no idea how Clare's rosary had ended up inside her chamber pot. Dr. Marks and Mrs. M believed her. Floride was, after all, the daughter of one of the wealthiest and most powerful men in the state. Clare's father was a nobody by comparison.

In private, Floride hissed: "A bowl of piss is where Popery belongs. And Papists too!"

Floride and her friends stopped referring to Clare as Turtle Girl and started calling her "the Tattler," as if this were worse than committing sacrilege.

Clare contemplated putting a giant millipede in Floride's bed, but she was certain that would end with the violent death of an innocent millipede.

Instead, Clare wrote to her father and begged him to let her come home. He refused.

Finally, Clare was moved to another room, which she shared with only one other girl: fifteen-year-old Laura Ravenel. She wasn't a Catholic, but she didn't mind that Clare was. Clare could pray and study in peace beside her.

CLARE THOUGHT IT MUST BE MARVELOUS to be a teacher, to hold such knowledge in your head and to make everyone around you more intelligent. She had so enjoyed teaching Verily how to read and write. One day, Clare asked in class how she could become a teacher—and Floride's set found a new reason to mock her. "Nobody *wants* to be a teacher!" they sniggered. Their teacher only hushed them and returned to Caesar and the Rubicon without answering Clare's question.

That evening, Clare asked Laura why she couldn't be a teacher. "Jane Eyre was a teacher!"

"Jane was an orphan," Laura pointed out. "If a girl like you were to become a teacher, it would bring shame on your family— especially your father. It would imply that he was too poor to support you."

Clare wouldn't have minded bringing shame on her father. She wished she were an orphan.

JULY, AUGUST, AND SEPTEMBER were an oasis on Sullivan's Island in the company of Verily and the shorebirds. Her friend told her about the books she'd been borrowing surreptitiously from the plantation's library. "It's like my mind isn't a slave anymore, Miss! I can escape from the Château d'If and find treasure and attend balls!"

Clare and Verily read more books together, careful to stay out of sight and hearing of Clare's father. They helped loggerhead turtle hatchlings reach the sea. David remained in Paris, but he still wrote.

As Clare prepared to return to Barhamville, she decided she didn't mind so much, not with Laura there. But Laura Ravenel was gone. She'd become Laura Wentworth, and she was on a Grand Tour of Europe with her new husband. How Clare envied her.

Clare's new roommate was younger than her. Victoria might have been named after a queen, but she was so shy, she seemed to close up every time Clare spoke to her. If Clare were mean, she would've called Victoria "Turtle Girl." Finally Clare gave up.

She tried to speak to Lydia again while she was scrubbing the corridor, but the maid whispered: "You'll get us both in trouble, Miss."

Clare raised her chin. "Then I'll pray for you. I'll pray the Blessed Virgin will watch over you and that Mrs. M won't be so short with you and that you never have to fish *anything* out of a chamber pot again."

Lydia smiled a little. "Thank you, Miss—but I ain't Catholic."

"That doesn't mean I can't pray for you!"

So Clare threw herself into her studies. She did well on essays, but in the oral examinations she always stumbled. She'd known the answers minutes before, but standing up there with everyone staring at her, she would start stammering as the answers scurried just out of reach. She would always rush back to her seat with tears burning her cheeks.

In the sciences, Clare learned botany and astronomy, which she liked, and a little entomology, which she loved. But the school's study of animals ended there. Clare wanted to know so much more. How did birds and Monarch butterflies manage to fly south in the fall, when they had neither maps nor compasses to guide them? How did frogs and turtles survive hibernating for months, submerged beneath frozen water and mud without food or oxygen? Why weren't there dinosaurs anymore? She knew baby mammals and baby humans grew inside their mothers—but how did they get in there? How did they get out? And where exactly did they grow?

It had something to do with a woman's "special place," she knew. When she was hardly more than a toddler, Clare had reported her amazing discovery to her mother: "There's a hole there!"

"There is indeed, *a chuisle*," Mama confirmed, withdrawing Clare's fingers from their explorations and guiding her to the wash-basin. "That is a very special place. It makes you a girl. When you become a woman, that place can make you a mother. One day, I promise to tell you all about it. But for now, you mustn't worry it with your fingers. You must only wash like I showed you and be patient."

"But…what if water and soap get in there?"

"They'll run right out again when you stand up. The hole isn't deep. Splash yourself with some fresh water if you wish, or pat yourself with a damp cloth. But don't scrub and don't poke, *a chuisle*. You might hurt yourself. You must protect your special place."

Clare had promised to obey. But Mama had died before she could keep her own promise.

Twice since, Clare's fingers had tentatively returned to the place. The hole felt like a tiny circle. The second time, she'd been so bold as to tilt a small mirror toward the place. What she saw was so strange and frightening, she dropped the mirror and would've broken it if she hadn't been on her bed. The area between her legs looked almost like a wound. The pink flesh there was so delicate and tender, she feared she'd already injured herself.

So Clare touched the area only lightly and briefly, in order to clean herself, and she tried not to think about her special place. But she carried it with her always, and she worried constantly: *Is this normal? Am I ugly?* Would Mama have said something, if she was deformed?

With Mama gone, Clare had no one to ask about the place. She wouldn't have asked Aunt Hortense if she were the last woman on Earth. After Mama's death, Aunt Hortense had been horrified to learn that Clare bathed in the nude, even though she did so in a closed room with only Verily to see her nakedness. Verily was nearby to fetch dropped soap, towels, and a clean chemise at the end. Aunt Hortense insisted that Clare bathe *in* a chemise, which made cleaning more complicated.

Whenever she visited (which was often), Aunt Hortense also insisted on sitting with Clare during her baths. Aunt Hortense did nothing useful; she only sat glaring at the curtained window or into the fireplace. Every now and then, she'd glance back at Clare. The first time Clare's hand (which was holding a soapy sponge) had ventured between her legs, Aunt Hortense had pounced like a hyena. She'd yanked Clare's elbow back till it struck the rim of the tub. "You know you aren't ever to touch yourself, *down there*?" she hissed. "It's filthy and wicked and dangerous!"

"Yes, Aunt," Clare had mumbled, rubbing her aching elbow. "Mama told me."

CLARE COULD ASK VERILY, but her friend was a year younger—and might colored girls be different from white girls, "down there"? Why hadn't Clare thought to ask David before he left for Paris? She could write and ask him to send her a drawing of a normal girl's special place. But Clare knew Mrs. M opened students' letters sometimes. She didn't want the headmistress to forbid David to write her or send her drawings ever again.

Since she'd started school, Clare hardly saw Grand-père René and Grand-mère Anne anymore. Clare spent her summers on Sullivan's Island, while they remained in Charleston. Anne was easily embarrassed, but René was a doctor like David. He would know what was normal and when Clare should be worried. If she ever had a moment alone with him, and if she could muster the nerve to ask.

Clare knew boys and men did not have such a place between their legs—or at least, she knew their special places were very different. If male humans were anything like male horses, they had dangly appendages instead: two that hung together inside a bag of flesh and a longer one that retracted into their bodies. She knew that cutting away the parts inside the bag made a stallion a gelding and meant he could not father foals. The retractable organ made less sense to her. She didn't understand why it needed to be so long. Female horses and female humans urinated without such a thing.

Clare had scoured artwork to discover if male humans possessed the same set of organs, but the answer eluded her. The painted or sculpted men were always covered by drapery just there. Once, she'd seen a male statue clothed only in a fig leaf, which bulged outward. That was as close as she came to solving the mystery. It was maddening, to see men every day and yet have so few clues about their true appearance.

David's medical books would have told her everything, she was certain; but on Church Street and on the plantation, Aunt Hortense had purged the libraries of anything she considered inappropriate for a young lady. Clare had hoped to find answers at school, yet her books and her teachers remained silent on the questions she truly wanted answered. How could she be a good wife to a doctor if she understood so little about the human body?

At least Clare overheard two other girls whispering once, so she knew not to worry when the hair between her thighs and in her armpits started growing in darker. Apparently the new hair was part of becoming a woman, like the way her breasts were becoming full instead of flat. From artwork and from seeing her mother in her chemise, Clare had known to expect breasts.

The other girls simpered about their burgeoning womanhood and how it allowed them to attract men. Floride and her friends delighted in collecting as many proposals—as many "victims"—as they could. Clare didn't understand such behavior. She thought you either loved somebody or you didn't. Making a young man believe you cared for him and then mocking him in his absence was simply cruel.

At night in her bed, Clare longed for the sands of Sullivan's Island and the gardens of Stratford-on-Ashley. She longed for Verily's company. Most of all, she wanted David.

She was fourteen years old now. She knew of girls who'd married at fourteen. When David returned from Paris, he would see that she'd changed—or at least, that she was changing, that she was ready to become a wife. His wife.

All she had to do was survive school, and her future with him could begin. David would rescue her from her father and Aunt Hortense, and Clare would make him happy ever afterward. She didn't know yet how wives made their husbands happy. But one way or another, Clare was determined to learn.

CHAPTER 11

I have pitied doctors from my heart. What does the lovely flush in
a beauty's cheek mean to a doctor but a "break" that ripples above
some deadly disease? Are not all her visible charms sown thick
with what are to him the signs and symbols of hidden decay? Does
he ever see her beauty at all, or doesn't he simply view her profes-
sionally, and comment upon her unwholesome condition all to
himself? And doesn't he sometimes wonder whether he has gained
most or lost most by learning his trade?
— Mark Twain, *Life on the Mississippi* (1883)

D avid had promised Clare letters—but he could tell her little
about his work in Paris. What it was like to follow a famous
doctor around the hospital wards with hordes of other students
from all over the world, clamoring for a view of the patient he was
prodding by candlelight. To sit on hard benches with little foot
room, listening to lectures, his pen scratching frantically in his notebook to catch every detail.

These things, at least, David could mention to Clare in passing.
But he could never describe to a ten-year-old girl the stench of
putrefying bodies in the Amphitéâtre d'Anatomie. Many of the

medical students took up smoking to mask the smell. David preferred to anoint himself with bay rum. The corpses of men, women, and children were delivered each morning like loads of firewood. When the medical students were through with the cadavers, the dismembered bits of human were tossed to dogs kept caged in the alley for that very purpose.

David could write to Grandfather about these things. As fellow medical men, *they* could discuss when to employ a Simpson forceps and whether stuffing a wound with charpie allowed for better drainage. Such topics would never do for Clare or Grandmother.

Grandmother's chief concern was whether David attended Mass every Sunday. He assured her he did, and it was mostly the truth. But in their vast empty churches, these Parisian Priests seemed to be mumbling only to themselves, and God felt very far away.

When Uncle Joseph had celebrated Mass, David had sensed God's presence. Now, he felt it most when he touched his Cosmas and Damian medal—the certainty that he was not alone. Medicine was David's true religion now. How could he honor the Creator any better than by studying and healing the human body, His most perfect creation?

David suspected he would have gone from the hospitals, the lecture theatres, and the dissecting rooms straight back to his lodging and his books, if not for Clare. After all, he was in Paris to learn, not to enjoy himself. But he needed pleasant experiences to relate, so he ventured out to the gardens, museums, and theatres.

Every day, David saw French children scamper past him: playing with hoops and balls, pursued by parents or maids. He could imagine Clare here so easily, walking beside him down the avenue des Champs-Élysées and through the Jardin du Luxembourg, marvelling at the architecture, the fountains, the parterres. He wished Clare's father would allow her to visit. Instead, David must be her eyes.

David had explained to Edward that most foreign medical students remained in Paris for only a year or two, as a capstone to their American or Scottish degree. But David wanted to learn all the

Paris doctors and hospitals had to teach him; he wanted to obtain a *Doctorat en Médecine*, which would take at least four years. David had broached the subject with Clare's father in considerable trepidation. Instead of balking at the expense, Edward had actually seemed relieved. David could only conclude that his guardian wanted to be rid of him for as long as possible, whatever the cost. Edward probably hoped David would never return.

David hated owing such a man anything. Edward had agreed to fund his education, and David would ask for nothing more. He lived simply. His fluency in French allowed him to tutor other English-speaking students; and in his second year, one of his professors trusted him to translate his newly published obstetrical text into English. With this money, David bought gifts for Clare and bought himself occasional tickets to plays and operas.

Clare wanted David to describe even his meals, but he assured her they were quite boring. He could not bear to abstain from all alcohol, coffee, and flesh as Sylvester Graham had advised in his *Lecture to Young Men on Chastity*, but David thought the man had been onto something. Fasting and avoiding rich foods had helped Uncle Joseph to decrease "the concupiscent excitability and sensibility of the genital organs." More or less.

Dining well was not only expensive but also required David to dine in company, and his fellow students were always teasing him about not having a *grisette*. These were young working women, seamstresses and shop girls, who supplemented their income by attaching themselves to young men. A *grisette* fell somewhere between a prostitute and a courtesan. Some *grisettes* were even faithful; but when this year's student or artist left Paris forever, the girl would simply find another.

In fact, David had sought out a landlord instead of a landlady because he'd heard Paris landladies delighted in matching students with *grisettes*. David had only to visit the patients at the Hôpital du Midi to come face to face with the dangers of debauchery.

The Hôpital du Midi was not the only Parisian hospital that treated venereal diseases, but it specialized in them. If David did not wish to endure the groans and the effluvia of living patients, he could inspect the wax preparations at the Musée Dupuytren: the temporary lesions and permanent, hideous deformities of gonorrhea and syphilis. There were no cures for these diseases, and the treatments—mercury and silver nitrate—caused their own painful symptoms. David would never understand how his fellow medical students could risk a lifetime of suffering for a few minutes' pleasure. Like Uncle Joseph—even more than Uncle Joseph—David's only mistress would be his vocation.

And perhaps a woman made of wax. The École de Médecine's anatomical museums contained the most fascinating and grotesque exhibits David had ever seen. Wet preparations suspended in alcohol, such as stillborn Siamese twins; dry preparations, such as a mummified monkey head; bones both normal and terribly twisted; and things that had never been alive. These could be horrible, like the syphilis moulages. But one was stunning in its beauty: an Anatomical Venus from the Florence workshop of Clemente Susini.

Inside a glass and rosewood case, she lay supine on a bed of scarlet silk complete with a tasselled pillow. Glass eyes peeked between heavy lids, and real golden hair cascaded over her bare shoulders. Her eyebrows and eyelashes also came from a real woman, her wax lips parted in an expression both languid and ecstatic.

Uncle Joseph had told David about the wax effigies at the tombs of Roman saints, enclosing their bones. Secular Paris preferred to worship this uncanny goddess of art, science, and beauty—in fact, the Anatomical Venus lay in what had once been the refectory of a Franciscan convent. Unlike the saints, this wax woman was entirely naked, apart from her pearl necklace and the band of gold in her hair that resembled nothing so much as a halo. Neck arched, arms slack, nipples erect, she raised one leg as if in modesty, but her pubic hair—also real—remained visible.

Just above her *mons veneris*, up her sides, and across her neck (half-concealed beneath her pearls) ran a seam. Her torso could be opened as easily as her glass case, revealing layer upon layer of meticulously rendered organs and finally, a wax fetus curled in her womb.

Here was a cadaver that would never putrefy. But if instruction was her only purpose, why didn't she lay flat? Why the silk bed and pillow? Why the pearls? Why was her countenance, every curve of her body, poised between pain and pleasure?

This, David knew, this uniquely feminine perfection, was why other men risked syphilis. *He* must look but never touch. Or at least, he must never touch with pleasure.

David was concentrating in obstetrics in order to become an *accoucheur*, a male midwife. One of his classes at the Hôpital de la Maternité was actually called "a course of touching." The *toucher* was a major reason students came to Paris from all over the world. Most women would sooner die—and many did—than allow a man not their husband to see them unclothed, let alone touch them, even if the man was a doctor. Frenchwomen had no such scruples.

During the *toucher*, woman after woman allowed the professor and each student to insert his fingers in her vagina and feel for the mouth of her womb: how the os uteri changed throughout a pregnancy and the *ballottement* of a healthy fetus in response to an examination. Twice, the professors included women who were not pregnant, so the students could feel the difference. Unlike the patients, these women were paid for the invasion of their persons. To David's consternation, the women cooed and sighed at the attention. They were whores (supposedly clean), taking the opportunity to advertise the quality of their parts and their responses.

Just as David's height was a benefit when other students crowded around a patient, his long fingers were well suited to obstetrics. Eventually, his hand stopped trembling and patients' vaginas became no more arousing than their ear canals.

This was as it should be. No woman in his care would suffer postpartum hemorrhage as Tessa had, and no woman would die from puerperal fever as his mother had—not if David could prevent it. In order to be a good *accoucheur*, he must approach his patients with a mind unclouded by lust. Familiarity bred indifference. This was the other reason he had chosen midwifery: to inoculate himself against temptation. Women's genitals were problems to be solved and nothing more.

Breasts were a more stubborn enticement. He saw inflamed and diseased ones at the hospitals, but not often enough to combat the flawless breasts he saw every day. He needn't even enter the Louvre: female statues in every park seemed to thrust their pert nipples toward him. Not to mention the perfect round breasts of the Anatomical Venus. Was any woman of flesh and blood so exquisite?

He resolved never to find out. During the nights of Carnival, he remained shut up in his room, far away from temptation. All around him, Parisians flocked to masked balls, where they drank themselves into stupors and pawed each other in the shadows. Behind his barricade of books, David reread the dreadful consequences of masturbation so many times, he could recite them like an incantation: indigestion, tinnitus, epilepsy, consumption, paralysis, blindness, insanity, death.

Carne-vale—the Italian original meant "farewell to flesh," because Carnival preceded Lent, when the faithful must abstain from meat. But David was bidding farewell forever to another kind of flesh. Men of God and men of science were in complete agreement: giving in to lust was both filthy and dangerous, and self-abuse was the worst depravity of all. What better proof could God have given them of the organ's ignominy than by forcing man to piss and ejaculate through the same canal? Continence marked the difference between a gentleman and a beast. David must become nothing more than a detached medical mind operating trained eyes and skilled fingers that diagnosed but did not dwell.

He purchased a set of colored pencils and took drawing lessons, initially to illustrate his case notes more precisely. But he soon realized that if Clare's father refused to bring her to Paris, David could send pieces of it to her. He sketched Notre-Dame and the Arc de Triomphe; the view from Montmartre; the pigeons roosting outside his garret window; diners at a café; artists copying the Mona Lisa inside the Louvre. David himself was hardly da Vinci, but his anatomical illustrations were accurate, and Clare praised his drawings of Paris.

David indulged her whims whenever he could, to assure Clare that in spite of Floride Butler's cruelty, her father's neglect, and her mother's absence, she was loved—she *mattered*. Facial hair was all the rage in Paris, David told Clare, but he couldn't decide on his own whiskers. Could she help him? He sketched several options for his chin and cheeks, some of them deliberately silly. Clare chose a small Vandyck beard, which he liked too: a neat mustache paired with a strip down his chin.

In one of Clare's letters, she enclosed a smaller, sealed note that she begged him not to open but only to lay on the tomb of Héloïse and Abélard. He entered the gates of Père Lachaise Cemetery and walked the steep hills of that vast city of the dead till he found their Gothic monument. Beneath a canopy of stone, the lovers' statues reclined side by side, dressed as abbess and abbot, their hands clasped in prayer above their chests. David curled Clare's letter and tucked it between Héloïse's fingers, then sketched the scene as proof he'd fulfilled his charge. On one of the other tombs, he spotted an ouroboros and drew that for Clare too.

Most of all, David sketched the Jardin des Plantes. This had begun two centuries before, in the time of *The Three Musketeers*, as the medicinal garden of the king's physician. Now, the Jardin des Plantes was a sprawling research center open to the public: an amphitheatre with free lectures, an extensive library, laboratories, homes for the professors and their families, conservatories, gardens, mineralogy specimens including precious gems, and an enormous natural history museum that attracted visitors and students from all over the globe. The most illustrious men of science had taught here: Buffon, Lamarck, Geoffroy Saint-Hilaire, Cuvier, and all the de Jussieus.

David could imagine Clare racing him to the top of the labyrinth. His legs might be longer, but she could cheat by darting *underneath* the yew hedges as he saw other children doing. He imagined Clare gaping at the giant water lilies, *Victoria amazonica*, whose leaves were so large she could sit on them. But Clare's favorite part of the Jardin des Plantes wouldn't be the plants, David knew—it would be the menagerie.

So he spent hours outside the pens and the magnificent glass and iron cages, drawing the elephants, lions, tigers, zebras, giraffes,

camels, llamas, pythons, chameleons, cassowaries, and ostriches—
even two placid buffalo from the American West. Clare needn't
travel on the overland trail and risk Indian attack to see buffalo; she
could come to Paris.

The grand buildings of the Jardin des Plantes also contained
animal wonders: whole rooms crowded with nothing but insect specimens and a whale skeleton that filled an entire corridor, while
stuffed turtles soared overhead. The interior galleries contained
some two hundred thousand specimens, gathered all over the world
and arranged in accordance with the Great Chain of Being.

This classification system had begun with the ancient Greeks
and had been refined over the centuries. The Great Chain showed
that every creature on Earth existed in a hierarchy, from the simplest
organisms like sponges and worms up through fish, amphibians,
lizards, birds, and mammals till creation reached its highest perfection of beauty and intelligence in man. Or to be more precise: in a
white man.

For a long time, David stood before a case containing a stuffed
orangutan, an ape with black skin and shaggy red hair. Beside it
stood painted plaster casts of a Hottentot, an African, a Red Indian,
an Oriental, and a European, in that order. The races of man had
been ranked like this for at least a century, David's guidebook
reminded him. Each race had its own peculiar attributes. As the
great Carolus Linnaeus had described them in his *Systema Naturae*:

EUROPEAN: White, sanguine, muscular. Gentle, acute, and inven-
tive. Covered with close vestments. Governed by laws.

ASIAN: Sallow, melancholy, stiff. Severe, haughty, and greedy.
Covered with loose garments. Ruled by opinions.

AMERICAN: Red, choleric, erect. Obstinate, merry, and free.
Paints himself with red lines. Regulated by customs.

AFRICAN: Black, phlegmatic, relaxed. Crafty, indolent, and
negligent. Anoints himself with grease. Governed by caprice.

Scientists had confirmed this hierarchy again and again. Dr.
Peter Camper of Amsterdam measured the facial angle of each race

and determined that Africans' skulls closely resembled the apes, whereas Europeans' skulls were the least like apes. Dr. Samuel Morton of Philadelphia measured the capacities of human crania to determine the relative size of their brains. African crania allowed for the smallest brains; European crania, the largest brains.

More and more men of science argued that the differences between the races were so vast and so fixed that the races must be separate species. Mankind had not descended from a single Adam and Eve and spread out across the Earth, degenerating from the Caucasian ideal into Asian, American, and African. Instead, God must have created each race separately on its own continent. This theory of polygenesis had distinguished supporters in France, Britain, and America. They included Swiss-born Harvard University professor Louis Agassiz, who had lectured in Charleston.

For such men, the Hottentots of southern Africa did not even qualify as a human race. Hottentots inhabited a lower link in the Great Chain of Being, closer to this orangutan. The painted plaster cast standing before David had been taken like a whole-body death mask from the most famous Hottentot, Cuvier's Hottentot Venus.

She'd been exhibited in London first, where crowds flocked to ogle her enormous buttocks and to whisper about her primitive genitalia, which she kept hidden between her thighs. She'd been displayed in a cage and named after the goddess of love in order to mock her. When the English tired of this Hottentot Venus, her keepers had brought her to Paris, where the great Georges Cuvier and his colleagues examined her eagerly. She refused to open her legs for the men. But after her death, she was powerless to stop them.

Forty years ago in this very museum, Cuvier had dissected her, paying special attention to her famous "Hottentot apron," her elongated labia minora. He pickled her genitals in alcohol so that other men could come see them too. In a second jar, Cuvier preserved her brain. He discarded the rest of her organs and flesh but reconstructed her skeleton, which hung in another display case.

"She knew at least four languages, Sara Baartman."

David had sensed that other visitors were circling around him, but only then did he realize someone was standing beside him. David turned his head to see a young, well-dressed black man. The stranger's French was fluent, though tinged with irritation and an American accent.

"That was her name: Sara Baartman," the black man continued. "But no one bothered to put that on the label, and I imagine it's not in your guidebook either."

"No," David acknowledged.

"What *does* it say about her?"

Reluctantly, David looked back down to the open page, because he knew what it said. "Only…a phrenological joke: 'We would recommend those endowed with the bump of amativeness not to dwell too long on the charms of the Hottentot lady, which grace the glass-case in the centre.'"

The man scoffed and averted his eyes for a moment. "You are a tourist, *monsieur*?"

"A student."

"Do the French make sense to you yet?" The man motioned to the display in front of them, from orangutan to Hottentot to African up to European. "They consider *this* the pinnacle of science. And yet Frenchmen abolish slavery and admit *me* to the Sorbonne!"

It was true: in the hospital wards and lecture halls, David had seen mulattos and Africans, as well as Turks and Malays, scurrying after the doctors and scribbling notes along with the white students. Even as the professors discussed Nott and Gliddon's *Types of Mankind* and de Gobineau's *Inequality of Races*, David had seen little difference in the way these colored men were received. Only visiting Americans refused to dine at the same restaurant or share the same cadaver with black men.

"In my own country, I am a permanent alien. The nation of my nativity, where my parents and grandparents were born, refuses to issue me a passport, because a colored man cannot be a United States citizen." The man's voice rang with indignation. "But if we learn *their* language and adopt their ways, the French are willing to overlook our dark skin and our tiny brains."

The black man strode away. David remained at the display case.

He wondered what had prompted the man to speak so boldly to a stranger. Had the man detected David's own African blood in the black curls spilling under his top hat and in the fullness of his lips? Had the man simply noticed how long David dwelt "on the charms of the Hottentot lady"? Or had some recent insult provoked this audacity?

David's eyes returned to the Hottentot Venus, Sara Baartman. The plaster cast of her body had been painted to mimic the living woman, complete with her remarkable buttocks—and her dangling labia, if you looked between her thighs. Her plaster eyelids were closed in death, her mouth agape as if in horror at what had been done to her. She was short and she was fat, light-skinned with large, dark areolas and wooly hair. But the longer David stared through the glass, the more Sara's face radiated her humanity and the injustice of her placement here, beside the orangutan.

Frenchmen, science, race—his own place in this Great Chain of Being, as a mulatto practicing medicine—none of it made sense. If South Carolinians knew David's grandfather had been born a slave, they would never have allowed him to study alongside white men, let alone practice medicine. Colored men had their place at the Medical College of the State of South Carolina, it was true. Colored men swept the floors and cleaned the windows.

Most of all, their corpses filled the dissecting tables. No one wanted their loved ones dismembered, and Charleston was no Paris —no metropolis of a million people and a dozen hospitals with an endless supply of paupers. But Charleston did have slaves. And like the Hottentot Venus, slaves had no more rights over their bodies in death than they did in life. To learn how to treat wealthy white patients, Charleston medical students mutilated dead negroes—even live ones, from time to time. Negroes did not feel pain or grief the way white men did, wrote the scientists. You needn't waste your anesthesia on them.

Finally, Sara's shocked expression became too much for David to bear. He closed his guidebook and left Cuvier's museum.

On the way back to his lodgings, David saw the posters for a new museum of wax figures, one intended not only for medical men but also for the public at large: Dr. Spitzner's Grand Musée Anatomique et Ethnologique. "Art, Science, Progress!" declared the advertisements, and "Know Yourself!" David would have dismissed the museum, but the posters listed the exhibit's most popular figures —and two of them were modelled after Emperor Napoléon III and Empress Eugénie. The figures even wore real imperial clothing.

In spite of Clare's entreaties, David had decided not to apply to the American ambassador for an audience at court. If Clare were here with him and she had no other escort, David would not hesitate. But court dress was a significant expense, and David had no personal interest in meeting the Emperor and Empress. Instead, he'd sketched for Clare the Imperial Guards, wearing plumed helmets and steel breastplates over their azure tunics. He'd described the fireworks bursting over the Seine during the Fêtes Impériales.

Now, if David visited Dr. Spitzner's museum, he could view the famously beautiful Empress Eugénie almost in the flesh, in one of her own fashionable gowns, and sketch her for Clare. He resolved to go the next day.

David was unprepared for what greeted him. At the entrance, on a dais beside the ticket booth, the figure of a young woman reclined in a case of metal and glass. He thought at first she was an Anatomical Venus, but she wore a sheer white summer dress. Her posture was even more abandoned, one hand flung over her head and her face half-hidden in her arm. David approached to see her better—and started. The woman was *breathing*.

As if she were a patient in a swoon, his gaze leapt to her face to make a diagnosis. The woman's rosy cheeks seemed to glow with health, and her lips looked almost moist—but he knew a skilled wax modeller could achieve such effects. Her eyes finally gave her away. Each lash was expertly planted, but no eyes flickered beneath her lids. Nor did the rise and fall of her chest affect the platysma muscle in her neck. She was an automaton, nothing more.

But *what* an automaton, uncanny in her semblance of life. The sheer sleeves of her dress revealed the perfection of her arms, and beneath her white bodice, her chest continued to breathe. David wished that he could peer beneath her clothes, that he could see inside her and understand how she worked. Had she been an Anatomical Venus once, and the breathing mechanism was inserted where her organs had been?

"Our Sleeping Venus is based on a figure by Curtius," came the voice of the ticket seller, also a young woman. "Do you know him, *monsieur*?"

David nodded. "Philippe Curtius, the physician and wax modeller who trained Madame Tussaud."

"That's him," smiled the ticket seller. "They say the Sleeping Venus of Dr. Curtius was so beautiful, a banker fell in love with her. The banker begged Dr. Curtius to let him work in the museum, so he could always watch over her."

When the girl said no more, David prompted: "Did Curtius let him?"

The girl laughed. "They say Curtius referred him to the Hôpital de Bicêtre."

David blanched. Bicêtre was an insane asylum. But as David gazed down at the Sleeping Venus, he did not think this banker so very mad.

Arm in arm, a couple approached the ticket booth, but the man glanced uncertainly at David.

"I'd like a ticket," David stammered, fishing out his wallet.

Nothing else in Dr. Spitzner's collection compared to the Sleeping Venus. The museum had its own Anatomical Venus, which Dr. Spitzner himself dissected every half-hour, lifting out each set of wax organs and laying them on a nearby table as he explained their names and functions. A cautionary gallery featured moulages of venereal disease like those at the Musée Dupuytren, but added the disfiguring consequences of masturbation. Wax torsos with compressed organs showed women the dangers of tight-lacing their corsets.

In the Galerie d'Ethnologie, an American Indian wearing only a breechcloth raised his lance as if ready to plunge it into every passing visitor. Nearby stood a family of Niam-Niams, something between monkey and human. Recently discovered in central Africa, the Niam-Niams were a cannibal tribe who had tails. Or so French travellers reported.

David thought the wax Empress Eugénie in her court finery garish compared to the Sleeping Venus in her simple white dress. He found himself returning to Dr. Spitzner's museum again and again to watch the Venus breathe—as if one day she would open her eyes and smile at him.

He tried not to let any of the ticket sellers see him more than once. They were all young women, *grisettes* he supposed. Most attempted to flirt with him. Such women always made him uncomfortable, and he wanted to be alone with his Venus.

He couldn't quite explain his obsession, except that this beautiful woman with honey-brown hair trapped in a case of metal and glass reminded him of Tessa. Clare's mother had even owned a sheer white dress like this, and his last sight of her had been through the glass viewing window in her iron coffin.

Night after night in his dreams, David raced through the streets till he reached the Sleeping Venus, threw aside the lid of her cage, and freed her. She always came alive in his arms with a sigh of delight.

"Do you think she's awaiting her lover?" one of the ticket sellers suggested. "Or that he's just left her?"

David felt his own cheeks flushing. He watched the face of the Sleeping Venus as if he could discern her thoughts, when he knew her head was empty. Yet every time he visited the Sleeping Venus, he felt his breaths fall into unison with hers.

Once, David summoned the courage to ask the ticket seller: "What makes her breathe?"

The girl pretended to be offended. "Dr. Spitzner has sworn me to secrecy, *monsieur!*" Then, the ticket seller crooked a finger at him. David approached cautiously, and the girl whispered: "It's clockwork. Her chest is full of clockwork."

David knew the Sleeping Venus didn't dream of him. He knew she didn't need saving. He knew she would go on breathing after he left Paris—indeed, after he was dead. But that didn't stop him from sketching her from memory, over and over, at the edges of his medical notebooks. Each time, she looked more like Tessa.

Every day, David passed the model makers' shops in the Quartier Latin. He imagined saving and saving till he could commission a wax Venus who would be entirely his own. After all, few medical students left Paris without visiting these shops, without bringing home a wax preparation, a whole skeleton, or a specimen of some sort. Such objects were the badges of a true scientist. They reassured patients of their doctor's extensive education. Nothing could be more natural than to own an Anatomical Venus to amaze his colleagues, instruct his future apprentice, or demonstrate the location of organs to future patients.

But the truth was, David didn't want his own Anatomical Venus, with dissectible innards. He wanted his own Sleeping Venus. A woman to whom he could unburden all his secrets, who would not recoil when he whispered: "For all intents and purposes, I am a negro and a murderer." A woman he could never hurt, because her heart was made of clockwork.

David imagined himself in his future parlor with no companion but the Sleeping Venus laid out on a sofa. He imagined himself reading her the newspaper and talking to her as if she were alive. He imagined a patient spying him through the window and having him carted away to a madhouse.

What he truly wanted was a living woman. But he could not take a wife any more than he could take a *grisette*. If he held out any hope of forgiveness for what he had done to his brother, his life must be a perpetual Penance. For David, it must always be Lent, never Carnival. The pleasures of a wife, of her company, of her body, were indulgences he would never deserve.

He returned home with only a trunk full of books and a case full of surgical instruments.

CHAPTER 12

If we could read the secret history of our enemies, we should find in each man's life sorrow and suffering enough to disarm all hostility.

— Henry Wadsworth Longfellow, *Driftwood* (1857)

When she was sixteen, Easter decided to kill him.

It was the only way she could be free. For a while, she considered going to Matilda for a charm to keep Cromwell away from her. But that would be breaking her vow of silence. If it didn't work, word might get back to him, and he might take it out on Verily as he had threatened to before.

After Miss Clare left for school, Cromwell had given Verily her own little bedroom in the house slaves' quarters, so she wouldn't realize Easter was going to him. Verily was so absorbed in her reading now, she hardly paid attention to Easter anyway.

Awake or asleep, with him or by herself, Easter dreamed of vengeance. She would need cunning or a weapon, or both, to overcome his strength. Easter knew oleander was poisonous—and she worked every day in the kitchen. But poison seemed as uncertain as voodoo. What if she didn't give Cromwell enough? Even if she managed to steal a gun, Easter wouldn't know how to use it.

A knife would be easiest. Yes, slitting Cromwell's throat would be the quickest and surest way—though she dwelt more often on thoughts of gelding him like a horse and slicing off his precious prick. That would kill him too, she was certain, and make him suffer much more; but it might also give Cromwell a chance to react and stab her back before he bled to death. So Easter settled finally on cutting his throat first and unmanning him afterward, so at least everyone would know why he had been killed.

The trouble was *when* to do it. After he fucked her, Cromwell always left before he fell asleep. Easter would have to go to him this time, attack him in his own bed while he slept. If she did it during the summer, when he was alone in the Big House, then maybe she could return to her room before anyone discovered he was dead. It would be difficult to contain her pleasure the next day, when she awoke to the screams of the maid who had found his corpse.

Stealing a knife from the kitchen while Phoebe's back was turned proved easier than Easter had thought, though her pulse was racing as she slipped it from the table into the pocket of her pinafore. Phoebe's stream of gossip did not falter. Easter smirked to herself, thinking, *She'll have much more to gossip about this time tomorrow.*

After midnight, Easter crept up the back stairs without a lantern and prayed Cromwell would be sound asleep. Beyond the white columns, magnolia blossoms rotted sweetly in the sweltering June air. As she snuck around the veranda toward the open windows of Cromwell's bedroom, she feared he'd hear her heart pounding, even above the drone of the night insects.

A faint light bled across the veranda from Cromwell's room. Was he still awake? Easter held her breath and peered inside.

He'd left a small lamp burning on his bedside table. She found Cromwell himself through the mosquito netting draped over his half-tester bed. He lay on his side, and his eyes looked closed. In the heat, he'd kicked off his sheets and wore only a pair of cotton drawers. Sweat shone on his pale skin and pasted together the strands of his dark blond hair.

Easter clenched her jaw in determination and stepped across the threshold of one of the floor-length windows. She kept her eyes on Cromwell, who twitched a little but slept on.

She withdrew the knife from her pocket, and its rough antler handle reassured her. To make it cooler, Cromwell's bed had been pulled away from the wall, but not enough for her to fit. She should attack him from behind at least, so he'd have trouble grabbing her if he woke. She tiptoed around the bed.

Gingerly, careful not to make a sound, she began to draw the mosquito netting away from the head of the bed so she could slip inside it. Then her hand stilled, and she frowned. There was something wrong with Cromwell's back. Easter had never seen it before; he'd never removed his shirt in her presence. Cromwell's shoulders were crisscrossed with *scars*. Not as deep or as numerous as the whip scars she'd seen on the backs of so many slaves, but kin to them—the tracks of a switch, perhaps, laid on without mercy. How would a white man acquire such scars?

The harsh singing of the insects sagged then, and in the brief stillness Easter heard other sounds she realized were coming from Cromwell as he slept. He was curled on his side with his knees drawn up and his fists balled against his face. If he were anyone else, she would have said he was trembling. His murmurs were nothing like the disgusting grunts he emitted while he was with her. She could make out only a few whimpered words, high-pitched and fragile like a child's voice: "Please don't... *Please...*"

Easter wavered for only a moment, shifting back on her heels. But in that moment, her foot slipped on the mosquito netting pooled around the bed. She fought to regain her balance and lost her grip on the knife. It fell from her hand, thumping and clattering against the floorboards.

Cromwell started awake.

Easter cursed in her head and dove for the knife. As she groped across the floorboards and through the pooled netting, her attention kept darting upwards.

Cromwell scrambled till he was sitting upright on the bed, eyes whipping around the room as if to remember where he was, sucking in and out great gasps of bewilderment. He swiped at the tears and the snot coating his face. He'd been *crying*.

Finally her fingers found the knife.

"Easter?"

She froze. What the hell did she do now?

"I didn't tell you to meet me tonight." Snot thickened his voice. Cromwell pulled his knees toward his chest, grimacing and pressing his fingers against his temple. "What are you doing here?"

Should she pretend she *wanted* him? Even the thought revolted her. Easter snatched up the knife and sprang to her feet, thrusting the blade into the space between them.

Cromwell hardly flinched. He considered the knife, then her. Tears still glazed his eyelashes. "You've come to murder me, then?" He sighed, dropped his head into his hand, and muttered: "Well, get on with it or get out of here."

Easter stared at him. He sounded *resigned*. Was Cromwell saying that if she lunged for him right now, he'd let her slit his throat? What the devil had he been dreaming about?

It might be a trick. He'd proven time and again that he was stronger than she was. Wasn't he just as likely to turn the blade on *her*? If Cromwell killed her, he'd only to make up a story to tell Master Edward. Easter's life was worth nothing but her purchase price.

She couldn't risk it. She couldn't leave Verily alone with him. Easter no longer had the advantage. She'd missed her chance—maybe her only chance.

Her arm sagged. She drew the knife against her chest like a shield and turned to leave.

"Come back, Easter."

At first, she tensed. But he sounded almost apologetic. Easter peered over her shoulder.

Head still in one hand, Cromwell motioned vaguely toward his bedside table. "Pour me a brandy."

Her hand tightened on the knife. She turned away. "Pour your own fucking brandy."

. . .

Two DAYS LATER, Cromwell rode back to Charleston without bothering her once. In his absence, Easter convinced herself that it was over now: she had spared his life when she could have taken it. He would honor that, and leave her alone for good.

But he didn't. When he returned to the plantation the following month, Cromwell whispered in Easter's ear that she was to meet him in Miss Clare's bedroom that night, as though nothing had happened. Maybe he thought Easter and the knife had been part of his nightmare.

Maybe he'd apologize. Maybe he'd thank her for letting him live. Maybe he'd say she needn't come to him ever again.

Maybe he'd punish her for refusing to pour his brandy. Or for trying to kill him. Or for failing to do so.

Easter knew remaining in her own bed would only forestall the inevitable. He would simply confront her the next day, as he had in the attic.

When she entered the room, Cromwell was sitting up against the pillows of Miss Clare's bed wearing nothing at all. He'd never done that before, been completely naked with Easter.

It *was* July.

Cromwell was reading a thin little volume balanced on his hairy thighs. He did not bother to glance up. "She's quite the romantic, our mistress."

He was talking about a thirteen-year-old girl.

"Shakespeare's sonnets are well thumbed." Cromwell lifted the book and raised his voice with mock gravity: "'Shall I compare thee to a summer's day?'" He chuckled and snapped the book shut. "In this climate, that is hardly a compliment." He discarded the book on Miss Clare's bedside table. "How are you, Easter?"

"Fine." *Until now.*

"You're still getting your monthlies?"

Easter bristled. Did he think some hysteria of pregnancy was the only reason she'd defy him or want to kill him? "Yes," she hissed.

He raised his eyebrows and motioned towards himself. "Come." His tone was arrogant. He had no doubt she'd obey.

Absolutely nothing had changed. "What if I refuse?"

Cromwell sighed and slumped a little, irritated but not angered by the delay. "Must I repeat myself, Easter?"

"You said you'd tire of me."

He shrugged. "I'd said 'I'll probably tire of you.' But I haven't. You should take that as a compliment. No whore has ever pleased me as long as you have, Easter." He rose from the bed and strode toward her, his prick swelling as his gaze travelled her body. "'Thy black is fairest in my judgment's place.' You *were* pretty. You *are* beautiful."

She thought he was trying to look her in the eyes, but she wouldn't give him the satisfaction. Did he expect her to preen like a peacock at such flattery?

Cromwell brushed her cheek with his fingers. "You are fulfilling your name, Easter: you are always renewing yourself." Finally he dropped his own gaze. "No matter what I do to you."

His fingers went to the hooks at the front of her dress, and she closed her eyes. She felt herself falling, like an animal caught in quicksand.

In truth, only her dress, chemise, and drawers fell in a heap at her feet. This, too, was new: even in summer, even when he undid the neck to reach her breasts, he'd always left on her chemise. He'd never undone her head wrap either. She wished he'd let it alone. Her hair was one part of her she'd been able to keep from him.

She felt Cromwell tracing his fingers down her bare shoulder. "Quite beautiful." He took one of her hands and tugged her toward the bed.

She didn't resist. You could survive quicksand if you didn't struggle. Better her than Verily. Easter wondered if she'd ever escape him. He'd be more cautious now. He'd be sure not to let down his guard. Maybe he'd stripped off her clothing and her head wrap to assure himself she no longer had the knife.

Cromwell started with Easter's breasts, which he usually ignored after a few unpleasant squeezes. Now, he spent an inordinate amount of time stroking and sucking her nipples. He murmured things that might have been compliments. Easter heard her name more than once, but she wasn't listening.

He inserted the pessary with a care that approached gentleness and then, he *stayed*: fondling her inner thighs, kissing and *licking* her cunt. Easter covered her face and gritted her teeth. What the hell was he doing? Why wouldn't he just *finish*?

When he finally pushed his prick into her, he *kept* kissing her breasts and her neck and murmuring her name. He put her hands on him, and she felt the ridges of his scars beneath her fingers. He came very loudly and collapsed on top of her. Even after his breathing slowed, even after she felt his prick go limp and flop out, he still lay there, clinging to her with his face in her neck.

Easter stared at the music box on Miss Clare's dressing table, grateful she couldn't see herself in the mirror, and wished Cromwell would leave. Even if he weren't pinning her down, she couldn't leave first, because she had to take care of the sheets—change the ones they'd soiled for fresh ones. In some ways, she preferred the tomb.

At last Cromwell shifted, raising his head and propping himself on his elbows. Easter kept her face turned away so she wouldn't have to look at him.

He brushed his fingers around the curve of her ear and into the tight curls beyond. "Why didn't you kill me?"

Because I didn't think I'd succeed. She wanted to ask about his nightmare, about the scars on his back. When he'd placed her hands there, was that an invitation? Did he *want* her to ask? She'd spent three years in his grip, and she understood so little about him.

Did she really want to?

"Easter?" he whispered.

She just wanted this to be *over*. Sore from his rutting, lying in a pool of his spew, with his sweaty, hairy skin plastered against hers, all she could think of was sarcasm. "Because I'm falling in love with you."

He sucked in a breath, and his body recoiled till he was braced on his arms. He stared down at her with such intensity, such seething breaths that finally she gave in to curiosity: Easter turned her head to look back at him. But before she could meet his eyes, he struck her hard across the face and shoved himself away from her.

Easter gasped in the shock of it. Never before had he struck her. When she'd talked back to him, it had *amused* him.

For explanation, she got only Cromwell's backside as he stormed out.

HE NEVER STRUCK HER AGAIN. He still asked her to meet him several times a year, but something in him had changed. There was a sadness about him now. He spoke about himself very little but said her name often. He asked her questions that were not rhetorical. She answered as briefly as possible.

He brought her a tin full of coconut oil, which Easter appreciated. He seemed to care when he really hurt her, and he did it less often. But he stayed longer afterwards, watching her, as if he were waiting for something. He never removed his shirt again, and he never explained his scars.

CHAPTER 13

She had
A heart—how shall I say?—too soon made glad
…as if she ranked
My gift of a nine-hundred-years-old name
With anybody's gift.
— Robert Browning, "My Last Duchess" (1842)

Tessa would not have approved, Edward thought as he sat in his office staring down at his new will. Five years ago, the spring before she died, his wife had challenged him on a much smaller matter concerning Lucas Cromwell.

Over breakfast, Edward had informed Tessa that he had offered Lucas rooms in both the plantation mansion and the house on Church Street, for the steward's convenience and Edward's. Lucas had accepted the previous day, and he would be joining them by the end of the week. Edward announced this news over a meal, with Clare present, so that his wife could object only in glares.

Then Edward retreated to his office, where Tessa cornered him. "In our *home*, Edward? With *Clare*?"

"What does Clare have to do with it?" Tessa did nothing *but* invite strangers into their home: that damned priest, his doctor father, *and* his niece and nephew. Edward welcomed *one man*, his friend and his most vital assistant, and suddenly their home was in danger.

"Who *is* this man, Edward? Why do you place such trust in him?"

"Because he has proven himself worthy of that trust! If it weren't for his management—"

"Mr. Cromwell is hiding something. I am certain of it. Every time I try to draw him out, to ask about his past, he deflects my questions."

"He wishes to maintain his privacy! I would think you of all people would be more welcoming to someone who comes from nothing and hopes for transcendence."

His barb missed her entirely. "What sort of 'nothing' does Mr. Cromwell come from? Do you know *anything* about him?"

"Do not think I enter into such an alliance lightly, Tessa!"

"What is he even doing on this side of the Atlantic?" she pressed.

Edward sighed and resigned himself. He strode past her and closed his office door. Still he stood for another moment debating, eyes lowered. "Promise me that what I confide to you will remain in this room."

"Of course."

"Lucas does not even know I am aware of it." Edward lifted his eyes to his wife's, begging her to keep her promise. "He would be mortified if he knew. He has told me only the barest outline." Edward returned unsteadily to his desk. "But people talk...and I have investigated."

"You have?" Tessa's surprise was insulting.

Edward nodded. "I hired someone in the Detective Service, as they call it in England." He sank into his chair and stared at his paperweight. "This man discovered, discretely, that Lucas is the illegitimate son of an earl and a chambermaid."

Finally Tessa was still and attentive.

"The chambermaid died at his birth. Lucas was left without a friend in the world—his father, least of all. You may have heard of the practice of baby farming: unwanted children killed by neglect. Somehow, Lucas survived, so his father deposited him in a school— if one can even call it that." Edward grimaced. "How the teachers there disciplined their charges was not nearly so monstrous as... what the older boys did to the younger ones."

Edward had told the detective he wanted to know everything. He had been mistaken. How a man—how a boy—survived such a violation, Edward could not even imagine. Nothing he could do for Lucas now was too generous, because nothing could make up for such suffering. The earl was the true bastard, a man too blind and selfish to see what a miracle a son was.

Tessa only looked puzzled. "I don't understand. What did the older boys do to the younger ones? Bully them?"

"Yes," Edward agreed readily. Let her think it had ended at that. "Then Mr. Dickens published that Nickleby book; the public became aware of such institutions; a campaign was launched; and many of the schools were closed, including Lucas's. He ended up under the indifferent 'care' of a distant relative here in Charleston. Perhaps his father thought the climate would finally kill him. But in spite of everything, Lucas has thrived." Edward laid a hand on his desk in finality and raised his eyebrows, daring her to argue. "Now you know all." Or enough, at least. "Lucas deserves your compassion, Tessa—not your scorn."

She did not look convinced. "Thank you for telling me, Edward. But I still do not want that man in this house."

"I have made my decision, Tessa."

EDWARD REGRETTED NOTHING. He knew he and the plantations wouldn't have prospered these past five years without Lucas's dedication and ingenuity. Tomorrow, Edward would have his new will notarized; and should anything happen to him, Lucas would become master of the Sea Island plantation. He would also manage Stratford-on-Ashley until Clare married.

It was only just: expanding into cotton had been Lucas's idea.

He was the one who had pulled the Stratford estate out of debt after the death of Edward's father. In truth, Edward wished to will Lucas Stratford-on-Ashley itself. But the rice plantation had been in Edward's family for five generations. Clare was, ostensibly, his daughter: she must become its mistress.

NORMALLY, SUMMER WAS EDWARD'S LEAST FAVORITE time of year. The threat of fever made it too dangerous to ride his fields, the activity he liked best in the world. Many planters fled to Rhode Island or even Europe during the sickly season, but Edward could not bear to go so far. The theatres and museums David wrote about —those did not interest Edward in the slightest. The land was what mattered. The land was what endured. If you learned its moods and treated it right, it would return to you not only sustenance but fortune.

Not that Edward didn't trust Lucas to manage crises with the slaves or the irrigation if he went away for a few months. Lucas would keep everything in order and probably even improve it. But he did not love the land the way Edward did. Just like the rice and the cotton, Edward had roots here. His great-great-great-grandfather was buried in the soil of Stratford-on-Ashley.

The land knew when you loved it, when you belonged to it, and when you saw it only as a tool, Edward was certain. He would not abandon his plantations for Europe or Rhode Island. He would go no farther than Sullivan's Island, so he would always be near his fields, whenever they needed him.

In July, there was little to do but sweat, read agricultural journals, and await the harvest. He was doing all three on the back porch of his Sullivan's Island cottage when Clare and her maid dashed up the path from the beach, chattering like parakeets. On the other side of the porch, they rucked up their skirts and petticoats even further—all the way to their knees—to wash the coating of sand from their feet and ankles.

Till now, Edward had hardly paid more attention to Clare than he did to her maid. Both girls existed only at the edges of his vision, inexplicable creatures he had to tolerate but rarely concern himself with—whenever possible, he left discipline to his sister Hortense. Edward had hardly noticed Clare's absence at school, except that the plantation house and the Church Street house became blissfully quiet.

But sometime this past year while she was at Barhamville, Clare had undergone a transformation. As Edward watched her pouring water from a pitcher down her slender white calves, he realized she was shaped like a woman now, not some slip of a girl. When he wasn't looking, Clare had turned into her mother. She was fifteen, only a few years younger than Tessa when Edward had met her. Edward would never forget his first sight of Tessa.

HE'D BEEN TRAINING AS A LAWYER THEN, under his eldest brother, Miles. Edward had been at their law office, reading Blackstone's *Commentaries* and trying not to nod off, when the bell over the front door chimed. Eager for any distraction, Edward looked up and saw a vision.

Her day dress was only a faded print, but somehow this made her face even more exquisite, like a shepherdess in a fairy story who discovers she's really a princess. Edward could hardly believe she was flesh and blood. She looked like something from a painting. She seemed to light the whole room like a visiting angel.

The sublime young woman flitted to the desk of their Irish copyist, Mr. Conley, and tried to show him the contents of her basket. Intent on his work, Mr. Conley hardly looked up but indicated that she should set her offering beside him.

"Is our Irishman a married man, then?" Edward asked his brother, watching the young woman stroke Mr. Conley's shoulder. How could the man ignore such beauty?

"Hm?" Miles followed Edward's gaze. "No, that's his sister."

Edward released his breath.

"But I forbid *you* to take your luncheon, little brother, until you finish that chapter."

Edward did not obey till the woman flitted away. He knew he had to see her again.

THEIR FAMILY'S CHRISTMAS BALL was approaching, which Edward's father threw for their best business associates. Shouldn't they invite their clerk and copyist as well, Edward proposed to his father? Along with their families? In the spirit of Christmas?

"You just want to get under Miss Conley's skirts," chuckled Miles.

This finally piqued their father's interest. "Is my little Eddy finally ready to make a conquest?"

Edward blushed. He was the youngest in his family, separated from his two older brothers by four older sisters. Their father persisted in calling him "little Eddy," though he'd turned twenty-one months before. Miles too continued to treat him like a child.

Edward might still be a virgin, but that was only because whores and wenches frightened him more than they excited him. Edward wanted a woman all right, but he wanted to be her first and only man. A woman's innocence and purity—those were what truly excited him. Miss Conley was a good Catholic girl; she must be even more virginal than Edward.

He wished his father and brother wouldn't speak of her in such a vulgar manner just because Miss Conley was poor and Irish. Naturally a certain part of Edward wanted under her skirts. But the rest of him wanted to meet her first.

His father agreed to extend the invitations—and glory of glories, both of the Conleys attended their ball.

THAT EVENING, LIKE SO MANY BEFORE, Edward had grown intolerably bored dancing with all the same Charleston coquettes, enduring their conceited giggles and their batting eyelashes. They were all reproductions of one another. They hardly needed names.

Then, he spotted his angel draped in sky blue, seated in a corner beneath a garland of holly. Yet she looked so forlorn. Miss Conley stared at the floor, her cinnamon-colored ringlets dangling forward, past her delicate ears and over her pale cheeks. Her green-ribboned dance card hung limp from her wrist. In spite of the vivid shade, her dress was hardly a ball gown, and she was not wearing a single item of jewelry. Edward saw a cluster of women sneering and whispering about her.

The women he could understand, but could the other men truly not see past the simplicity of Miss Conley's attire? Hers was a natural and effortless beauty, not one that had to be forged, like the other girls'. Unclothed, free of their artifice, they would become drab; but Miss Conley would remain stunning.

Her brother sat down beside her. Edward saw his chance for an introduction and started toward them. But on the way, he passed the resting orchestra. The conductor was just resuming his post. Inspired, Edward leaned over and whispered in the man's ear. Since Edward's father was paying him, the conductor nodded his assent.

Edward strolled toward Miss Conley and her brother. He pretended to notice the Irishman for the first time and to take little notice of his sister. "How are you enjoying the festivities, Mr. Conley?"

"'Tis all quite marvelous," the Irishman smiled, his eyes skimming over the buffet table and the dancing floor, though the latter was currently empty. "On the estate back in Ireland, we'd hear the music from such gatherings, but the only way we'd gain entrance would be if we served the food!"

"Well, that is American democracy for you, Mr. Conley."

"I told you it would be different here, Tessa," the Irishman said to his sister.

Tessa! Edward sang in his head. The angel was named Tessa! She gave her brother a small smile. Her eyes were a bottomless gold.

"Have you met my sister, Mr. Stratford?"

"I have not." Edward bowed. "A pleasure, Miss Conley."

The Irishman continued the introductions. "Tessa, this is Mr. Edward Stratford, the brother of Mr. Miles Stratford. You may have seen him in the office."

Behind them, on cue, the orchestra conductor announced a

Virginia reel.

Edward grasped the lapel of his coat, as this seemed a confident stance. "Would you care to dance, Miss Conley?"

She drew in a breath of surprise, the slender cords of her neck tensing.

"Unless someone else has claimed the next one." Edward glanced at her empty dance card.

"No— Yes. I mean…" Miss Conley dropped her gaze to the floor again, blushing prettily as she tried to compose herself. Then she gave a nervous laugh, like tinkling bells. "I should like to dance, very much. But I'm afraid I don't know the steps. Is a Virginia reel anything like an Irish reel?"

"They are cousins, Miss Conley," Edward promised her. "And if any of the steps are unfamiliar, I shall be happy to guide you." He offered his hand, and the angel took it. Even through his glove and her lace mitt, he thought he could feel her heart racing. Or perhaps that was his heart.

As Edward led her onto the dance floor, he heard a few condescending whispers. Tessa's eyes flitted toward the speakers and she hesitated, but Edward recaptured her attention. "You'll pick it up in no time, Miss Conley," he assured her as they took a place at the end of the set. "Just watch the women above you. Whatever you need to do, they will do first."

Miss Conley nodded nervously, while Edward thought: *No woman could be above you, my angel.*

The conductor directed the orchestra to begin. Edward bowed, and Miss Conley curtseyed back. "Simply follow my lead, Miss Conley." They advanced toward each other. He extended his right hand. She mirrored him, and they turned around each other. The left hand followed, and then both hands together.

The lead couple galloped down the middle of the set, then swung around each member of the opposite sex. Edward watched Miss Conley's shy smile grow bolder, watched her opening like a flower. By the time it was their turn to gallop, she was giggling. Edward saw too that she had won over the men. They were not blind. But Miss Conley was Edward's.

They tried a few other dances, and laughed over their missteps. By the end, she was flushed and panting and Edward was in love. They sat together and sipped wassail and talked and talked. They were both the youngest of seven children. They both felt out of their element here, yet neither of them cared.

Mr. Conley had seemed happy to have Edward keep his sister company during the ball. But when Edward paid his first call at their miserable little room near the wharves, the Irishman's demeanor changed. He became protective and wary. Edward realized that Mr. Conley feared his intentions.

Edward tried to assure the Irishman that they were honorable. He knew Miss Conley was no bauble to be plucked, fondled, and discarded. She was a treasure who must be surrounded with treasures. Edward sought out the things that brought a flush of pleasure to her cheeks: a potted Christmas rose; a night at the theatre; a necklace.

Like her brother, Edward grew protective of his treasure. The thought of Miss Conley laboring day after day over other women's dresses to support herself! The thought of another man abusing her or enjoying her! There was only one way Edward could keep Miss Conley safe.

She did not accept his proposal immediately. He'd taken her for a walk along the Battery. Her eyes widened, but she turned away from him and gripped the railing, looking out to sea. "Have you spoken to my brother, Mr. Stratford?"

Edward admitted he hadn't. "Do I need his permission?"

"I-I think it would be proper, with our father so far away."

Edward frowned. "You don't think your brother will object?"

Still she wouldn't look at him. "I'd like his blessing."

That wasn't really an answer, but Edward already had a solution. "I've been meaning to speak to Miles, about taking your brother on as an apprentice. Then he cannot object to our marriage! It's what your brother has always wanted, isn't it, to become a lawyer? He'll be able to marry that sweetheart of his all the sooner!"

"You are too generous, Mr. Stratford."

"Edward, please." He lifted her hand from the railing and squeezed it. "May I call you Tessa?"

She nodded, but her eyes remained on the sea. Tessa must be thinking about her parents and brothers back in Ireland. It was a pity they wouldn't be able to attend her wedding, but soon he and Tessa would make their own family.

OR SO EDWARD HAD THOUGHT. He mounted her often enough—he was sure a houseful of children would follow. Burying himself inside her was the most astounding thing he'd ever experienced.

In their marriage bed, Tessa was receptive, but nothing more. At first, her reserve had not bothered him. She'd bled, hadn't she? She was his and his alone, his pure angel. He understood that decent women did not feel pleasure as men did. But as the nights passed, Edward started wishing he could inspire something more in her than that polite smile.

Before they had been wed six months, the omen came: her receptive body rejected his first child. She was beyond consolation. She wilted like a bruised flower.

Now the fire Edward had seen in her returned only when she argued with him. They found so many things to argue about. Tessa saw nothing objectionable in singing in public like a harlot. He'd grown up with slaves and knew their tricks, and still she thought she knew better how to manage them. She hated Lucas because his surname was Cromwell and because he was English. She nagged Edward because he no longer attended Mass with her.

How she loved her rituals. Her Works of Mercy. Her priest. Oh, the fire in her returned when he visited. The two of them would make love with their eyes as though Edward were blind. As if this were not trespass enough, when her paramour's sister died, Tessa welcomed his niece and nephew as though she had given birth to them herself. She who had borne only dead things.

Edward couldn't refuse the orphans. That would make him unchristian and cruel; that would make Tessa even more impossible to live with. Edward did not mind the girl so much. But when stranger's fever struck the city, *she* was the one who perished. The image of the priest survived, like a weed that was impossible to kill.

Then, an apparent miracle: Tessa's belly began to swell. The fourth month, the fifth…still this child endured. But the labor nearly killed Tessa; the baby was a daughter; and Dr. Lazare said there would never be a son.

The man might be lying, Edward thought. After all, he was the priest's father and David's grandfather. It could be a family conspiracy.

When Edward tried to share Tessa's bed again, she resisted him. "Please, Edward. You heard what Dr. Lazare said. I can't, anymore. It would be sinful."

Edward was sinful—that was what she meant—for still wanting his wife, when they could no longer "be fruitful." Did she expect *him* to live like a priest, while she lusted after hers? *That* was less sinful than soothing your own husband?

Edward knew what his father had done. His father's body servant resembled him perversely, his father's image in brown, like a counterfeit coin. Living proof of his liaison with a negress. Edward found none of the slaves attractive, not even the mulattos. He wanted Tessa, his angel with the appetite of a demoness.

Edward had suspected for years that she and the priest did more than ogle each other. Still he did not confront Tessa. As long as Edward did not ask, he could hide from the truth. He could tell himself all was well and her betrayal was only imaginary.

Finally, he could bear it no longer, the knowing-but-not-knowing. He decided he could face anything but this limbo of uncertainty. He wanted proof she was betraying him. He charged the house slaves to spy on her. One of them did.

His pure little wife liked to be fucked against garden walls, it seemed. Tessa was no demure flower who found copulation objectionable. She was a whore who found her husband objectionable.

Edward discovered that jealousy excited him too, because Tessa didn't belong to anyone else; she belonged to *him*. Even as he wondered if the priest was her only lover, Edward still wanted Tessa. He never stopped wanting her.

Every time Clare called the priest "Father," Edward would wonder if it were true, if the girl was his bastard. A single, solitary child, after seven years of trying?

The girl had always seemed like a changeling. Sometimes Edward imagined that, after failing the traditional way, Tessa had conceived a child through witchcraft. For all their Catholic mummery, the Irish were pagans at heart.

Edward also recalled a conversation he'd had with David once, about the tiny monsters the boy had been watching through his new microscope. These creatures had no need to couple. They simply had to break off a limb, and from it would grow an exact replica of themselves.

Edward had never believed in immaculate conception, but perhaps there were ways Tessa could create a child on her own: entirely herself yet entirely a separate person, a double alike in every respect save the difference of years.

So seeing Clare growing into a replica of her mother did not really surprise Edward. In fact, it made perfect sense. As did his desire for her.

Edward had never wanted another woman the way he had wanted Tessa. For one thing, he'd never seen another woman as exquisite as Tessa. But that wasn't the only reason he'd remained a widower. What if his second wife couldn't bear him sons either? What if his second wife also took a lover? Wouldn't that prove some fault lay with him? Edward didn't think he could bear the shame.

He felt no shame in this, in desiring the replica of the only woman he had ever loved. Surely something a man had fed and clothed for fifteen years became his property. Even if Clare were his daughter, what could belong to a man more completely than something that had come from his own body?

He'd pulled Tessa out of poverty, given her everything she could ever want, defended her whenever someone tried to make an Irish or a Catholic joke in his presence, looked the other way while she fucked her lover, remained faithful even to her memory—and for what?

After everything Tessa had put him through, all the grief she'd caused, she'd left him this gift. This perfect, undefiled part of herself. Like an apology. Like his reward. It would be wrong *not* to appreciate it.

On Sullivan's Island, in the summer heat, Clare would sometimes sit reading in her room wearing nothing but a chemise. Edward invented questions to ask her. She'd glance up when he entered the room, but she'd never move to cover herself with a wrapper or a shawl. Even as she answered, her eyes would return to her book. She had no idea whatsoever where Edward's eyes were.

But her chemises were so baggy, and her drawers added yet another layer. Even in the heat, with perspiration helping it cling, the linen concealed so much. Breast, hip, and thigh were tantalizing swells and shadows beneath the fabric—but he needed more.

Edward waited for night to fall and listened for water pouring, for Clare's maid filling her bath from the cistern. When she finished, the girl tossed the buckets under the cottage, which stood on stilts to help it weather storms.

Edward found that if he upended one of these buckets and stood on it, his eye line would rise to just the right height. Clare's window was always open for the breeze. Gauzy curtains covered it, but these did not quite meet in the middle. Edward could peer between them.

He'd never been so grateful for the small size of their copper hip bath, which made the tub easy to transport and fill. It also meant that most of the bather remained exposed to the air. After she peeled off her chemise and dropped her drawers, Clare would step in, and the water would reach no higher than her calves.

She would prop one dainty foot on the lip of the tub, sponging herself free of saltwater and sweat, all the while thrusting her luscious little ass toward the window. If she sat, only her hips would be submerged, with her obscenely long legs hanging out of the tub. In either position, her breasts remained visible, round and perfect like a pair of ripening apples.

Edward wondered if she might rub herself. But Clare skimmed the sponge over her nipples and cunt as casually as she soaped her elbows and knees. Humming to herself like a child, she seemed totally ignorant of her womanly parts and their allure. This knowledge excited Edward all the more. Unlike Tessa, her daughter was pure. An utter innocent. She'd probably never seen a cock before.

Edward certainly wouldn't remarry now. A woman would only ferret out his secrets. Perhaps in time, Lucas would come to love the land as much as Edward did. Lucas would not be Edward's heir by blood but by choice. That was something. But what to do with Clare?

Edward knew what he *wanted* to do with Clare. In her innocence, she might even let him. If he told her all fathers did this with their daughters, that it was a father's right, Clare might believe him. He had studied the law, and he knew he had little to fear. Cases had been thrown out because the girl offered no resistance, so how could she say she hadn't consented?

Clare might be more fertile than her mother. What could be more perfect? Edward would have his heir at last. With horses, it was called in-breeding, and fillies mated to their sires often produced excellent foals.

With humans, it was more complicated. Who would they name as the father? Was Lucas that loyal? He'd kept Edward's other secret all these years. But slaves could spy on their masters as well as their mistresses. If Edward indulged himself and the truth became public, what would people think?

Surely most men would secretly envy him. But outwardly, they might shun him. Edward had seen former Governor James Henry Hammond's hopes for a Senate seat derailed when voters (and their wives) learned he'd been fondling his four young nieces. Last year, the decade-old scandal had dimmed enough that Hammond finally got his Senate seat. Still, a decade was a long time to suffer.

Edward had no political aspirations himself, but even a man who owned an island could not operate entirely independently. Achieving the greatest crop yields in the state would mean nothing if no one bought Edward's rice or his cotton.

This truth made him hesitate. Doing more than watching Clare would be a tremendous risk, Edward knew. And watching was so delicious. For now.

CHAPTER 14

That most delightful, that enchanting, though somewhat dangerous, entertainment, a masked ball. … Society finds itself relieved from the superstition of etiquette, and revels in that unchartered freedom.
— William Landor, "The Masquerade: A Tale of the South" (1845)

David had remained in Paris for five and a half years. Completing his thesis on the use of anesthesia in midwifery while tutoring fellow students and ogling wax women had taken longer than he'd anticipated. He might have remained in Paris for the rest of his life, but the city was already crawling with doctors.

Charleston did not exactly lack for medical men, but they were always in demand. The Lowcountry was one of the unhealthiest places on Earth, prone to epidemics of fevers like the one that had taken David's sister Sophie. As a German visitor had written: "Carolina is in the spring a paradise, in the summer a hell, and in the autumn a hospital."

David returned in the spring to reunite with his grandparents. Uncle Joseph was still assigned to the missions north of Beaufort, and they usually had to go to him. Rather than taxing the old couple, these journeys seemed to rejuvenate them. By the end of the year, Grandfather would celebrate his seventieth birthday. He wore glasses now, but otherwise he appeared as hale and hearty as ever. Although Grandfather's hair had gone white, he showed no signs of baldness, which boded well for both Joseph and David.

Henry and May were approaching seventy themselves. They still lived on the property, but they did only light work. Even before the death of Henry's mother Agathe, Grandfather had hired two free black women, sisters named Delia and Violet, to perform the heavy tasks. Delia was an excellent cook, and Violet was especially quick with Grandmother's signs.

David himself was rusty, but the language of signs was coming back to him. He recognized Clare's sign name, with the scurrying mouse paws. His own childhood nickname for the girl: *souris*. Grandfather helped David understand what Grandmother was telling him: Clare had graduated from Barhamville. 'She will be so eager to see you!'

David wanted to see Clare too. "But tomorrow is Shrove Tuesday," he pointed out, signing what he could and waiting for Grandfather to translate the rest. "She and her father will be occupied with the Mardi Gras ball." These United States were a Protestant nation, so Charlestonians did not celebrate Carnival. They had Race Week. But since Edward's brother Laurence had married into a New Orleans family, the Stratfords had hosted a masquerade ball at Stratford-on-Ashley every Mardi Gras.

'What better night to see Clare again!' Grandmother asserted. 'She has a lovely costume. She described it to us last Sunday when we saw her after Mass. It's an animal, of course—but I won't tell you which one. You *must* see her in person.'

"I...couldn't expect to stay overnight at Stratford-on-Ashley on such short notice," David demurred.

'Then you'll stay at an inn,' Grandmother suggested.

"It would be too expensive."

"You are our only grandchild," Grandfather said aloud while

signing the words for Grandmother. "You can borrow Cassique and my gig."

David sighed and admitted: "I'm not sure Edward would even receive me." He could at least see Clare at Mass…

'The man agreed to look after you as if you were his own son,' Grandmother insisted with her hands.

"Edward is hardly in my debt," David argued. "Quite the opposite."

"If he doesn't yet know you've returned, then he won't have told his slaves *not* to receive you." When Grandfather translated this, Grandmother slapped his arm playfully.

David chuckled. "Why do you want me to go so badly?"

"Because Clare needs you, David. You know how lonely she's been these past five years. The girl didn't make a single lasting friend at school. We Lazares are all she has."

'I don't understand it,' Grandmother fretted. 'Clare is the sweetest, most caring…'

"She's too shy; she's too Catholic; she's too fond of toads." Grandfather shrugged. "*We* know her worth, but I don't think Clare does herself. Her aunt is an absolute harpy. She criticizes everything the girl does, including attending Mass. Your grandmother and I get only a few minutes with Clare at church before Hortense drags her away. Your company would mean the world to Clare, David."

He raised his hands in submission, a sign that needed no translation. "All right; all right. I'll try."

'Try?' Grandmother echoed with her hands.

"I don't have a costume!"

Grandmother smiled. 'Leave that to me.'

To David's amusement, Grandmother produced a brown monk's habit. The first year David was in Paris, before Clare left for Barhamville, she had succeeded in obtaining her father's permission for "Grand-père René" and "Grand-mère Anne" to attend the Mardi Gras ball. In the end, a patient's difficult labor had called

Grandfather away that evening, and Grandmother refused to attend without him.

But Grandfather had intended to dress as Friar Tuck, and Grandmother had saved his costume and mask. Even the sandals fit. The Grandmother of David's childhood would never have allowed her husband or grandson to wear a religious habit to a costume ball. She would have been scandalized at the mere suggestion. Grandmother must be mellowing in her old age.

As she admired him in his habit, little did Grandmother realize that David was actually keeping one of the Counsels of Perfection, albeit for his own reasons. In fact, his chastity exceeded Uncle Joseph's.

David packed his costume, a nightshirt, and his shaving things into a portmanteau. Grandfather acquainted him with his gig and with his carriage horse, Cassique. David travelled up the peninsula in trepidation, and not only because of his limited driving experience. He found the inn near Stratford-on-Ashley that Grandfather had suggested and changed into his monk's habit, still wondering if this was a wasted journey.

But when David announced himself at the Stratfords', Edward's butler simply bowed in greeting. "You will find that Master Edward is dressed as Henry the Eighth tonight, Master David."

"Thank you, Pharaoh." David sighed with relief, entrusted Cassique to a groom, and replaced his simple black mask. He thought wearing the hood of his habit a touch too dramatic, so he left it hanging down his back and followed the veranda around the house. Clare might have raced around the plantation barefoot, but he felt very strange treading these familiar boards wearing sandals.

A Mardi Gras masquerade at Stratford-on-Ashley was considerably more dignified than in Paris. No one was permitted to throw flour on the masquers; less flesh was on display; few people drank to the point of collapse—and all of those were men.

As David stepped off the lower veranda, he saw that Edward had constructed the temporary dance floor between the back of the mansion and the gardens. His slaves had done the actual work, of course, laying out the low cypress platform and covering it with two beautiful falsehoods: a painted floor cloth that resembled black and white tiles and wooden columns that mimicked marble.

This roofless temple, the gardens, and the verandas of the mansion teemed with the voices and colors and ruffles of a hundred swirling costumed bodies: queens and pirates, soldiers and Indians. David saw a woman dressed as a nun, but he did not introduce himself. The fluid tones of the hired orchestra drifted from a smaller platform.

David had forgotten how much of a paradise spring in Carolina truly was, with a lushness Paris could not match. Almost absurd in their abundance, the pink and white blossoms of the azalea hedges glowed in the light of the Japanese lanterns strung from the magnolia trees. The weather too was heavenly: few insects yet and just enough of winter's chill tarrying in the evening air to invigorate the dancers.

David soon spotted Henry VIII in his feathered cap, embroidered doublet, white hose, and codpiece. Other guests clustered around him, paying their compliments. David knew he should do the same. Instead, he accepted a coupe of champagne from a passing slave and hid in his mask awhile longer.

Clare's father had chosen Henry VIII—did the man appreciate how fitting that was? Edward was dressed as the king who had destroyed five wives in his quest for a son—though in the end, his legacy was a remarkable daughter.

Tessa was worth at least five queens. Yet she had been dead for more than seven years, and Edward remained a widower. He'd never been handsome, but his looks were inoffensive, and he wasn't yet forty-five. Most importantly, Edward owned two plantations and a fine house in Charleston. He might easily have remarried and achieved the son he lacked. So perhaps he *had* loved Tessa, in his vampiric way.

But as David stood there, staring up at the sweep of stairs where Tessa had died, he still couldn't forgive Edward. The man might not have been anywhere near her, but he had killed his wife just the same. Edward's cruelty and neglect had caused either her despair or her distraction. David supposed none of them would ever know what had really happened that day seven years ago when Tessa had fallen to her death. Not unless they conducted a séance and spoke to her from beyond the grave.

Then, as David watched the portico on the upper veranda where Tessa had taken her last steps, her ghost appeared from the shadows.

David nearly choked on his champagne. It wasn't— It couldn't be— He wasn't *that* drunk!

Was no one else seeing this? No one was screaming, and David was afraid to tear his eyes away in order to judge their reactions. Not afraid of Tessa but afraid she would disappear. *Her* slender neck; *her* full pink lips, parted in anticipation; *her* beautiful face in the shape of a heart; *her* abundance of honey-brown hair, pinned up but untamed... She was standing there just above him, leaning over the balcony...

Slowly, David realized that the woman he'd taken for a ghost was dressed like a swan. Her beaked mask was pushed above her forehead; her gown was covered in white feathers; and pleated wings billowed from her gloved arms. One delicate hand rested on the balustrade, and from her wrist dangled a turquoise bracelet. A snake swallowing its own tail.

Merciful God. The woman was *Clare*.

David had known time was passing those five and a half years he'd been living in Paris. Yet in his mind, Clare had remained the ten-year-old girl he'd left behind, small enough to scurry under yew hedges and sit on lily pads without capsizing. While he'd been drawing the Sleeping Venus, turning her into Tessa, Clare had been here, becoming her mother in the flesh.

Without his conscious decision, his eyes were feasting on that flesh, not only the furrowed brow and straining neck and bare shoulders but lower, just above her corseted bodice, where—

Close your eyes! David shouted in his head. *Look ANYWHERE else! She is your SISTER! You are a monk! Fling up your hood and flee before it's too late!*

Before he could obey his own admonitions, Clare saw him. She frowned. "David?" Then her face transformed into a smile like a moonrise. "David! You're back!"

He finally managed to look away from her. His attention darted to the place Clare's father had been standing. But Edward was gone.

Clare flew down the stairs that had killed her mother. David stood transfixed as she unfurled the pleated white wings attached to her arms and flung them around him. Propelled by the gust of her enthusiasm, her feathered skirts engulfed him like a snowdrift. She wore petticoats but no hoops. Instead of her mother's gardenia, Clare smelled of roses.

She was as warm as fresh piping bathwater, as warm as the unholy movement happening inside his monk's habit. *"Bump of amativeness,"* indeed. So much for inoculating himself against feminine charms. David tried to push Clare away.

"I thought you were Father Joseph at first, but his hair's going grey—and you're wearing the Vandyck!" Clare pulled back just enough to lay one white-gloved hand against his face, her thumb stroking his mustache through the silk. "It's even more dashing than I imagined!"

As her finger caressed his lips, Clare seemed oblivious to the female gasps and male sniggers around them. David heard. Charleston was not Paris.

One woman in particular stalked up to them from the direction of the stairs. Dressed in green, she glared at David and Clare through her peacock mask, her jaw set and her nostrils flaring with disapproval.

"I— She's my sister," David stammered.

"She is *not!*" the peacock woman hissed like a snake. He realized she was Clare's aunt, Mrs. Hortense Fernande. "Release him *at once!* Restore your mask!" she commanded her niece. "And how many times must I tell you: do not leave my sight!"

Mercifully, Clare dropped her hand from David's face and stepped back. But instead of restoring her mask, she took his hand and drew him toward the magnolia trees, away from so many eyes. He managed to deposit his champagne coupe on a table along the way.

When she had him in the lantern light on the other side of the tree line, Clare took both his hands in hers. "Oh David, I love your costume! It's like we planned it!"

David's attention flickered back to Hortense. She'd pursued them behind the magnolia trees, huffing her displeasure. David thought a fire-breathing dragon costume would be more appropriate than a peacock. "Planned what?" he asked Clare.

"Our costumes!" She tapped the beaked swan mask on her head and opened her pleated wings. "You're Saint Francis, and I'm a bird!"

Only Clare would make such a connection. Only Clare. To hear that familiar, inimitable exuberance bubbling from a *woman's* lips... His mouse had become a swan. David had only to do the mathematics: Clare was *sixteen* years old. Sixteen years and two months. Women became wives and mothers at such an age. No wonder her aunt was guarding Clare like a jealous dragon with its treasure.

"Can you see me?" Clare asked David.

He could see nothing else.

"*My* mask makes me feel more like a blinkered horse than a swan!" She pushed David's simple black mask up his forehead.

He did not resist. He tried to forget Hortense, who'd crossed her arms over her chest and paced a few feet away. As Clare reacquainted herself with his appearance, David marvelled at hers. Above guileless amber eyes fringed by long lashes, Clare's delicate brows arched into the gentle slope of her nose and the open petals of her lips, each matchless feature complementing the next, like a masterwork by Botticelli. The kind of beauty that took a man's breath away.

The two brown nevi beneath the corner of her left eye rendered her technically imperfect, but to David, they were touchstones: proof this beautiful woman was Clare. In Paris, his patients had informed him that such *envies*, "longing marks," resulted not from a mother's desire for a child but from her carnal desires.

All David knew for certain was: he wanted to kiss the little moles. He wanted to kiss every part of Clare he could see—and every part he couldn't. His muscles tensed and strained and warred inside him, but he forced himself not to lean closer.

Just to stand in her presence… What was that painting technique he'd learned about in Paris? *Sfumato*. Clare's beauty seemed to diffuse all around her, enriching everything, making the lanterns brighter, the magnolia leaves more vivid, the music sweeter…

"Dance with me, David?"

He glanced back to her glaring aunt. "I-I'm sure your card is full for the entire evening."

Clare fingered the dance card hanging from her wrist. "I saved every other dance for you."

"But you didn't know I was coming."

She caught the edge of her lower lip between her teeth. "A lady can hope."

Her aunt stamped her foot and interrupted: "A *lady* would wait for the *gentleman* to ask!"

Clare did not miss a beat. "Ask me, David?"

Dance with me, souris. Dance with me for the rest of my life. But David couldn't make his mouth express his thoughts, wasn't sure if he wanted to express them.

He didn't even *like* dancing. So as not to embarrass Edward, David had accepted the lessons of a dancing master during college, but he hadn't attended a single ball in Paris.

"Please?" Clare's forehead rippled up in that adorable way she had, the way that made it impossible to refuse her anything. David could only pull his mask back into place and offer her his elbow.

Clare beamed and restored her own mask. She slipped her gloved hand inside the crook of his robed arm and followed him up onto the dance floor. Clare pushed the ends of the swan wings from her wrists to her elbows. The orchestra conductor announced that the Congress of Vienna was next, and the dancers formed themselves into an enormous ellipse.

David hesitated. At the corner of his vision, he saw Hortense watching them from below the platform. "Isn't this a waltz? I'm sure I don't remember—"

"You're wearing sandals," Clare responded bravely. "If you tread on my toes, it will hardly hurt at all."

A waltz was also for couples. You didn't change partners. He shouldn't be doing this. Not with anyone, and especially not with Clare. He could blame his sandals; they were scarcely fit for dancing; he should—

But when Clare moved her body close to his and her feathered white skirt brushed his robe, some primitive instinct gained control of his brain. David found himself sliding his right hand around her corseted waist and holding out his left hand. Clare slipped her slender gloved fingers into his and rested her other hand on his shoulder, revealing her wings again. David trembled at her warmth, at the reminder that she was flesh and blood and not an angel of his imagination.

Somehow, his feet remembered the steps of the waltz well enough not to collide with the other dancers or crush Clare's toes. As the man, he was supposed to be leading, but Clare guided *him*, pressing gently on his shoulder or hand whenever David started to move in the wrong direction. She did not seem to mind this impromptu tutoring. Perhaps it even amused her; Clare's face was alight with joy through every averted misstep and every faultless figure alike.

David wore no coat beneath his monk's habit; his arms were sheathed only in cotton shirt and the thin brown wool of his robe. His hands and wrists were utterly naked; he hadn't expected to dance, and gloves were inappropriate for a mendicant friar. As their positions shifted with each twirling figure, Clare's slender arms grazed his back and his chest. The feathers of her bodice caressed his palms and his fingers.

Even more distressing—even more thrilling—again and again, as their arms twined and untwined, his bare wrists hovered *so close* to the top of her corset. So close he could feel the heat of her rising flesh with each of her breaths. This Venus was wide awake; her head was anything but empty; and her bodice contained wonders far more extraordinary than clockwork.

～

IT WAS HAPPENING ALL OVER AGAIN, like some sort of ghastly echo. The uncle had stolen Tessa from him; and now, the nephew was stealing her daughter. As Edward watched David waltzing with Clare, he nearly hurled his dessert fork between the boy's eyes.

He so like his uncle, she so like her mother. Had the boy dressed as a priest in order to mock him? Never had Tessa looked happier than with her priest. Never had Clare looked happier than in this moment. His hair like a puddle of darkness, hers like a pool of light —he looked like some demigod, she like the newly born goddess of love. Edward had always felt like a mud splatter against such beauty.

Did that give Tessa the right to make him a cuckold? Did that give Clare the right to throw herself at the last man on Earth Edward wanted for a son-in-law? Edward would be damned if she married a Lazare.

David must have sent word somehow. Clare had known he was coming. That was why she'd dressed like a harlot.

WHEN EDWARD'S SISTER HORTENSE had seen the low cut of Clare's swan bodice, she'd been horrified. "You will have it altered at once!" Hortense had demanded.

"There isn't time, Aunt!"

"Then you will wear a fichu and cover yourself!"

"Fichus are for old women!"

His sister looked ready to strike the girl, so Edward stepped between them. "Let me see."

Clare raised her chin in defiance and pointed her breasts at him.

Edward tried not to gape. Her mother might have looked delectable naked, but Tessa had always chosen such conservative dresses. Perfection like that should be brandished, not hidden.

It wasn't as if you could see Clare's nipples: only two luscious mounds every time she inhaled. It wasn't as if anyone would touch them.

"It's Mardi Gras," Edward had reasoned. "The rules are different." He himself would be wearing a codpiece. "Besides, she'll be masked."

"She insists on wearing this *snake*." Hortense yanked on Clare's bracelet. "Someone will recognize her."

"No they won't!" Clare argued. "You wouldn't let me wear it during Race Week, and before that, I was in school! No one else has seen it for years!"

Women did have their whims. Especially Edward's women. "She can wear the dress as it is—and the snake." He tried to soothe his sister: "Nothing will happen. You'll be watching her. So will I."

Hortense huffed and pouted, finally muttering: "At least her mask will cover up those moles."

DAVID MUST HAVE RECOGNIZED THE SNAKE, or Clare had found him, or the gods had simply flung them together for amusement. Edward had hoped David would catch the pox from some French whore and never return. In his letters from Paris, the boy hadn't alluded to a woman even once. Edward had assumed David was being discreet. Had the priest's double been biding his time, waiting for Tessa's daughter to ripen?

Now Edward regretted letting the girl expose herself. But was there any point in trying to restrain her? Nothing Edward had ever done kept her mother from betraying him. Not tenderness, not indifference, not severity. She was Venus pursuing her Adonis, no matter who she hurt and no matter the cost. Edward was only Vulcan, spying on his wife from the shadows.

Tessa's beautiful daughter wanted what she wanted. Sooner or later, Edward would have to surrender her. She would fling herself into that flame regardless of him. All Edward could do was watch her burn.

He reached for another glass of champagne, then went to find something stronger.

CHAPTER 15

Many a young life is battered and forever crippled in the breakers of puberty; if it crosses these unharmed and is not dashed to pieces on the rock of childbirth, it may still ground on the ever-recurring shallows of menstruation…ere protection is found in the unruffled waters of the harbor beyond the reach of sexual storms.
— Dr. George J. Engelmann, "The American Girl of To-day" (1900)

The waltz ended. At least David was able to sit down, on one of the stone benches in the garden beyond the dance floor. He was feeling light-headed. Clare's Aunt Hortense perched on a bench nearby. Clare seemed to dislike the orange swan beak between them as much as David did; she raised her mask again. Every time he looked at Clare, she grew more beautiful and more dear to him. He had not thought it possible.

Clare squeezed one of his hands with her gloved one. She asked him about the Atlantic crossing and his last days in Paris. David tried to concentrate on his answers. Solicitude flowed from her like perfume, as if he were the only person in the world, or the only one who mattered. She was more intoxicating than the champagne. He could live on nothing but the succor of her voice, the comfort of that little crease between her eyebrows, the strength of her hand in his...

Loud male laughter pierced their bubble of happiness. Clare started and released David's hand. A man wearing a devil costume sauntered up, assessed David's monk's habit with a snigger, and then addressed Clare. "When you're through confessing, little angel, what do you say I teach you a few new sins?"

David's hands clenched into fists. At the edge of his vision, he saw Hortense spring to her feet.

Clare did not need either of them. "I am a *swan*, not an angel, sir," she replied with great dignity. "And I shall be confessing to this kind friar for a *very* long time. So please, sir: go to Hell."

David couldn't help but chuckle. The devil snorted and staggered off again. Hortense sat back down.

"Oh David, I was so afraid something would happen to you!"

"Unlike my uncle, I am not actually a cleric, and I *will* hit the next man who speaks to you like that. I may or may not tend to his bloody nose afterward."

"Not just now!" Clare laughed. She might be dressed like a swan, but she laughed like an angel, pure and light. "I meant in Paris." The thought extinguished her joy. "At the hospitals. I was so afraid for you."

"I was never in any danger," David lied. "I have Cosmas and Damian to protect me."

"You're still wearing my medal?"

"Of course."

"May I see it?"

As David reached into the neck of his monk's habit, another male voice interrupted them: "P-Pardon me, miss?"

David looked up to see a young man with auburn hair who was wearing a jester's costume. The man glanced at Clare's sparse dance card in the lantern light. "M-May I have the next d-dance?"

As she restored her mask, Clare's expression was an unconcealed scowl.

The young jester gazed at her so earnestly, so forlornly, David actually pitied the boy. David wished he had some way to converse with Clare privately. He could speak in French, but most well-bred Charlestonians knew it. Then he remembered: Clare had learned his grandmother's language. 'Do you recognize him?' David asked with his hands, motioning to the jester, who gaped at their wordless communication.

'Yes,' Clare answered in signs. 'He's harmless.'

'Then you should dance with him.'

"I don't want to!" Clare cried aloud.

The young jester mumbled an apology and stumbled over his oversized shoes as he tried to withdraw.

The last thing David wanted was to relinquish Clare, but he knew he needed a few minutes alone. Quickly, he stood. "To my immense disappointment," David called after the young jester, "the lady has refused to dance with me a second time."

The young jester returned eagerly, and Clare stabbed David with her eyes.

'Don't be rude, *souris*,' he signed.

Clare sucked in a breath and rose to her feet. She hesitated just long enough to let David change his mind. When he only clasped his hands behind his back in dismissal, Clare allowed the young jester to lead her toward the dance floor. Hortense followed her niece like a shadow. Clare glanced over her shoulder, but she was not looking at her aunt.

David wanted to race after Clare. But he needed to think, and he couldn't think in her presence. He walked away from the dance floor, through the garden of azalea and myrtle hedges sprinkled with a few lingering camellias. Clare had been so delighted to see him; she was always delighted to see him…

Sixteen. She was sixteen years old, and David was twenty-seven. But he had only to consider the guests at this ball to find even greater disparities of age between husbands and wives—or to find married cousins.

No blood bound David and Clare. He was only her father's ward. Yet David had all but witnessed Clare's birth; he had watched her grow up; they were practically brother and sister. He should be recoiling from this desire. The Church would deem it incestuous. Long ago, Clare's uncle Liam had married David's aunt Hélène, and Clare's mother had been Uncle Joseph's lover. Clare called David's own grandparents Grand-père René and Grand-mère Anne.

All this Clare knew, as she thought she knew David. But he couldn't ask her to marry him without telling her what she was marrying. David would have to tell Clare about Ian. This was a girl who grieved when she found a dead cicada. David had abandoned his newborn brother to die in the middle of the wilderness. Once she learned the truth, how could Clare ever trust David with their own children?

David would also have to tell her his other secret. The one about his grandfather: "Grand-père René" had been born to a slave woman on Saint-Domingue. René was a *quarteron*, in English a quadroon—more or less. Grandfather had said his mother was half Yoruba and one quarter Dakota, which muddled things. But the Indian race was closer to the Caucasian in the Great Chain of Being. African blood was the true impediment.

Grandfather René's children were essentially octoons, one-eighth black, which made David one-sixteenth black. The Saint-Domingue planters had a name for this too: *mamelouque*. One-sixteenth, barely six percent, *still mattered*—because a single drop of ink, like a single drop of poison, ruined an entire pitcher of milk.

No one understood how his six percent African blood might affect David's children. He could marry a white woman like Clare and father a black baby. Such a child would make her an outcast. No matter how much David loved Clare or their child, everyone else would point and stare and flay her with their tongues.

If his ancestry became public knowledge, David would become a permanent alien in his own country. In the words of the Chief Justice of the Supreme Court in its decision about Dred Scott, colored men were "altogether unfit to associate with the white race either in social or political relations, and so far inferior that they had no rights which the white man was bound to respect." How could such an impotent being protect his wife and children?

Assuming Clare even survived the childbirths. In the Paris hospitals, David had watched thousands of women suffering horribly to bring forth new life. After all these years of study and of practice, there were so many complications he could do nothing to prevent or to solve. He had been powerless to help as mothers screamed and bled, convulsed and died—and he'd wondered how any man could claim to love a woman and then do *that* to her.

David realized he'd stopped at the edge of the plantation's cemetery. How many hopeful mothers lay beneath these cool white stones? Spanish moss waved from the oak limbs in the moonlight, rippling like shrouds awaiting fresh corpses. Tessa had nearly succumbed to a hemorrhage after Clare's birth, and David had watched his own mother die of childbed fever.

But when he closed his eyes and saw Clare, selfishness still throbbed inside his trousers. If his innocent sixteen-year-old sister knew what he ached to do to her...

David must end this before he dragged Clare into the filth of his lust. He must relinquish her *tonight*, once and for all. Clare might think she wanted him too, but she didn't understand what that meant. She would be happier without him.

In time, Clare's infatuation would fade. Uncle Joseph's mistake had been to give Tessa hope. David must be wiser. He would write to Clare. He would tell her none of this, but somehow he would explain why he was wrong for her.

Before he departed, David knew he should speak to her father. He should thank Edward for his education and offer his services should the man ever need a doctor. Reluctantly, David turned back toward the mansion. He passed through the garden and haunted the edges of the crowd, looking for Henry VIII but not finding him. David gave the dance floor a wide berth. Where might Edward have gone?

David visited the stable and asked a groom to ready Cassique and his gig. Then David decided to try Edward's office. The man did like to drink, and that was where he kept his whiskey. David entered the mansion through the front hall so he could use the interior staircase. He avoided Tessa's staircase.

Compared to the bustle of the party, the inside of the mansion was eerily still—though David could swear he heard footsteps somewhere above him. Perhaps Tessa's ghost inhabited this place after all. David shivered. The chandelier shining down on him did little to dispel his foreboding.

He'd just started up the steps when Clare appeared at the top of the staircase. "David! Thank God!" She was panting, and tears glistened on her cheeks. "I need you, right now!"

David felt his brow furrow beneath his mask. Clare's mask was entirely gone, and she wasn't wearing her gloves anymore. Had that young cad torn them off in order to slobber on her? David would kill him. He raced up the stairs to meet her. Where was her aunt when Clare actually needed her? Didn't Clare know better than to retreat into a bedroom with a man? On this floor, there were nothing but bedrooms and Edward's office. "Did that bastard touch you?"

"What? Who?"

"The jester!"

"Mr. Arrington?" Clare still looked puzzled. "No! We only danced. Then I felt queer and I came to lie down—that's why I have to talk to you!"

David frowned and peered at her in the candlelight. "Are you ill?"

"Yes! I-I think so." She dropped her eyes to the rug. Her face looked so pained. "I'm not sure. Come with me?" Ostensibly, it was a question, but Clare snatched one of his hands and towed him after her.

"I'm afraid I didn't bring my medical bag, *souris*."

"But you still have your head!"

In spite of himself, David chuckled as Clare led him down the dark hallway—toward her bedchamber. David knew which room it was. He'd entered it many times during her childhood. She'd fetch him to see her latest insect or reptile pet. He'd fetch her for dinner. He'd wander inside to pet Mignon, who loved to curl up on her bed.

But Mignon had died years ago, and Clare was no longer a child. David resisted her grasp with just enough force that Clare released his hand as she crossed the room's threshold. She'd lit a lamp on the bedside table already. A blue-and-gold, double-burner Argand lamp that had belonged to her mother, David remembered.

It illuminated David's drawings of Paris, framed and hung on every wall. The buffalo robe lay folded between the rose curtains at the end of Clare's bed. The music box David had given her sat on her dressing table, and tucked into one side of her mirror was the test drawing of his own beard. This room was as full of David as it was of Clare.

She stood next to the bed, one of her fists balled up against her mouth, the other palm against her bodice. Her swan wings hung limp at her back. David wanted to step inside, to comfort her, to ask what was wrong and make it right. Instead, he looked back to see if anyone had followed them. The hallway was empty.

As a child, Clare had run from propriety as if a swarm of yellow jackets were chasing her, always gambolling in the sunlight without a hat and developing freckles, or yanking off her boots and stockings to wade into a pond in pursuit of a bullfrog. But if David stepped inside this bedroom with her now… A tarnished reputation was not something that would fade with time or could ever be washed away. Even if she wasn't his sister, David had a responsibility to protect her.

If they left the door open, David reasoned, maybe it would be all right.

Clare turned back, yanked him over the threshold, and slammed the door. Still she did not speak. She only crossed the floor again, turned, and sank onto the edge of the bed. Her swan mask and her gloves lay discarded on the buffalo robe. Clare's tear-streaked face told him she needed his counsel even more than his protection.

Cautiously, he stepped toward her. Doctor and patient, he reminded himself—nothing more. "What are your symptoms, *souris*? Why do you think you're ill?"

"Maybe I'm not! Maybe I danced too vigorously, and it's some kind of injury… Aunt Hortense says I do *everything* too vigorously."

"Injury?" David stepped closer, his gaze tracing her slender white arms and bare shoulders. "Did you find a bruise?"

She stared up at him with such fear in her eyes. "You'll tell me the truth, won't you, David? No matter how terrible it is?"

Standing before her now, he pushed his mask up to his forehead. "Of course I will."

"If it's bad, if it's some kind of cancer, I want to hear it from *you*."

"*Cancer?*"

"Promise me, David."

"I promise I will tell you the truth, Clare. But first, you have to tell me what you saw and what you're feeling."

Slowly, with a wince that worried David a great deal, with a rustle of petticoats and feathery skirts, Clare drew herself onto the bed. She lay back against the counterpane, perpendicular to the pillows, and stared up at the canopy as if she were trying to divine her fate from invisible stars. One white dancing slipper dangled off the bed, her other leg canted beneath her skirts like an Anatomical Venus. If David didn't know better, he would have thought Clare was seducing him.

Her words were low and anguished: "I'm *bleeding*."

"Where?" Since she seemed to be presenting her foot, David eased off her slipper and inspected her in the lamplight, looking for evidence of a wound. He saw nothing through her stocking but delicate toes and a fine ankle.

"I think— I don't even know the proper name—or any *improper* ones... Aunt Hortense took away all your medical books." Clare drew in a ragged breath. "I saw the blood in my chamber pot. Does that help?"

David's hand stilled on her ankle. *Oh, souris—no one ever told you!* One of his professors had mentioned it in a lecture: fourteen, fifteen, sixteen—these were the usual ages of menarche, the first menstruation. But Clare's mother had died seven years ago, and David suspected that her aunt would sooner swallow poison than utter the word "vagina."

David smiled, though she couldn't see it. "That helps a great deal."

Clare looked back at him hopefully. "You know what this is?"

"Yes," he assured her. "And first of all, Clare, there is nothing wrong. This isn't a cancer, and you aren't injured. Sometimes it's called 'the female disease,' but it's *supposed* to happen."

Clare propped herself on her elbows and frowned at him. "What?"

David realized he was still holding her foot. He released it. "Did none of the girls at school mention when they started bleeding?"

"I-I don't think so." Clare looked away and mumbled as if to herself: "I didn't like school very much. Not the other girls, at least."

"Perhaps they mentioned 'periodical pains'?"

Clare's eyes grew wide and leapt back to his. "The older girls were 'poorly' a lot, and they got to stay in their beds all day. I just thought they didn't want to go to class. I heard one of them mention a curse?"

David nodded. "They meant this blood. It happens to all young women at your age."

Clare flopped back against the bed again. "I'm so stupid."

"No you're not."

Clare emitted a little moan and placed her hand flat against her bodice again.

"Do you need— I have a handkerchief somewhere." David started rucking up the skirt of his robe to access his trouser pockets.

"Would you fetch the towel from my washstand?"

David did so and handed it to her, then turned to face the closed door. Behind him, he heard Clare's petticoats rustling. He watched the space under her door, but the shadows remained untroubled. "Is there *anyone* who can help you? Another woman, I mean? I understand some of them fashion a belt, and attach linen cloths to it, in order to catch the blood…"

"I can ask Verily. She has an older sister. Do colored girls get 'periodical pains' too?"

"They do."

"I'm so stupid," Clare repeated.

"You are not the first girl to be confused or frightened by this, *souris*. But it's perfectly normal. It's simply part of becoming a woman, like, um…" He was thinking about her breasts again. He'd actually started to turn around. David planted his feet.

"Like…?" Clare prompted.

Damn it, now he *had* to give an example. "Like the way you're growing thicker hair in certain places now." *"Certain places?"* He couldn't afford to be prudish about this. Prudery was the reason Clare had remained ignorant for so long.

He was a doctor. He'd had his fingers inside hundreds of vaginas and delivered hundreds of babies, for Heaven's sake. He could use the correct words.

Instead, David concluded lamely: "When these things happen, when she starts bleeding every month, a young woman can become a mother."

"It's safe to turn around," Clare informed him. Then she echoed, incredulously: "Every *month?*"

"I'm afraid so." David turned slowly.

Clare still lay perpendicular on the bed, though now both her knees were raised beneath the imperfect veil of her petticoats and skirts. She'd restored them, more or less, tossing them downward unevenly. Her lovely feet remained visible: one slippered and one only stockinged. She'd tucked a pillow under her head and interlaced her fingers primly over her bodice, as if waiting for an examination.

David rounded the bed so he wasn't staring through her open legs. "Maybe thirty years from now, when you're too old to bear children, your 'monthlies' will stop." When he reached the far side of the bed, he realized he should have carried over a chair. Instead, he sat gingerly on the edge of the buffalo robe, near Clare's face on the transplanted pillow. Her discarded mask and gloves lay between them. "But until then, every four weeks or so, you will bleed for a few days."

"What exactly is bleeding?"

"The blood originates in your uterus." David clasped his hands in the lap of his robe. He had to do something with them, besides reaching for Clare. Lying supine like that, her breasts looked especially voluptuous. "You said you feel queer—you are feeling the muscles of your uterus contracting to expel the blood. The path it takes to exit your body is called a vagina."

"Why?"

"It's Latin for 'sheath,' I understand." God give him strength. Next she was going to ask what was sheathed there.

"No, I meant: why is my uterus bleeding, if it isn't injured?"

David grimaced. He didn't want to admit the truth: that men had spent lifetimes studying the female body, yet so much of it remained a mystery. The reasons women menstruated remained conjectural. Some doctors thought menstruation signalled a woman's most fertile days, like a female animal going into heat. This made little sense to David. Most couples wanted nothing to do with each other while the woman bled each month. What kind of signal was that to perpetuate the species?

Beneath his monk's habit, the restlessness of his own damn loins, while Clare lay here and bled and gazed up at him so trustingly, proved his nature was as much animal as human. "Well, your uterus, it's also called a womb. When you conceive, that's where the child will grow. While it's growing, the child needs...nourishment, and the collection of blood inside a mother's womb seems to serve that purpose. But every month, if you're *not* with child, your body sheds the old blood."

Without looking away from him, Clare played with her ouroboros bracelet. "Like...a snake shedding its skin?"

"More or less. Then new blood collects, and it's shed again, and so forth...until, there is a child."

Against the pillow, Clare nodded solemnly. Then, hesitantly: "David, how does a child...enter my womb?"

He stood up quickly. He realized he was making a sound, like a steam pipe releasing, a sustained: "*Uh...*" He clamped his mouth shut, gulped, and decided: "I think that's all you need to know for the present. Try ginger tea to ease the cramping, and—"

"You promised to tell me the truth, David!" Clare did not move, and somehow this vulnerability made her accusation all the more forceful.

"I have! I have been forthright!" David opened his hands as if asking for a divine blessing—or immediate assumption into Heaven. He needed to escape somehow. "But there are some things—"

Clare managed to catch one of his hands with hers, squeezing it pleadingly. "Will you at least tell me what it's called?"

Intercourse? Connexion? Fucking? There were so many names.

She attempted to clarify: "*Your* vagina?"

David pulled his hand away. "I do not have a vagina!" *That* wasn't a sentence he'd ever expected to utter.

"I meant: what men have instead of a vagina. What is that called?"

"You do realize, Clare, that you should never utter the word vagina in polite conversation?"

"But this isn't polite conversation!" Clare propped herself on one elbow, while David paced at the end of her bed. There wasn't much room. "This is like my final college course—the things no one else would teach me. Teach me, David! What is it called, your not-a-vagina?"

The penis was actually comparable to the clitoris, not the vagina. And he couldn't say *any* of this—not to her. "Clare, I—"

"You either urinate with it, or you plant babies with it," Clare prompted, as if this would help him. "I don't even know which!"

"Both," David admitted between his teeth.

Clare's eyes went wide in horror. "*Both?* How is that…clean?"

"There is a valve, at the end of the urethra, to prevent…" David covered his face with his hand and trailed off.

Clare pressed on. "It's called a urethra? *Your* vagina?"

"No! We both have urethras!"

"Then what—"

David gripped one of the bedposts as if he were anchoring himself in place, because inside his monk's robe, his penis seemed to be urging: *If you don't want to name me, why don't you SHOW me to her? Let her touch me!* "I am not talking about this any longer, Clare."

"Are you saving it for our wedding night?" Only Clare could ask such a question, with her legs spread beneath virginal white skirts on her own bed, and look simultaneously like an innocent and a temptress.

His throat was making that steam pipe sound again.

Clare's head fell back against her pillow, her loosened hair wild and exquisite. "I know; I know—a lady would wait for the *gentleman* to ask." She turned her face to him. "But you needn't be anxious, David! My answer is 'Yes!'"

"You had *better* be proposing, Mr. Lazare!"

David nearly leapt out of his robe. He whirled around to see Clare's aunt striding into the room—with Clare's father bracing an arm on the doorjamb just behind her. Hortense looked ready to castrate David. Edward looked ready to decapitate him. Instead of rendering them ridiculous, their masks only made them more menacing.

"Whether Miss Stratford will accept you is another matter altogether!" Hortense cried.

Edward remained on the threshold, looming with kingly reserve.

Clare sat up too quickly; she moaned and placed a protective hand between her parted thighs.

"My God." Hortense gaped, her eyes ricocheting between Clare and David. "You didn't just— You actually deflowered her! At a costume ball! Dressed as a monk! Of all the heinous, irreligious—"

"You don't understand, Aunt!" Clare interrupted. "I'm bleeding!"

"I should hope you are! I've tried very hard to keep you pure—and for what?"

"I haven't touched her," David broke in. He'd touched Clare's hand and her foot, but that was beside the point. "It is *menstrual* blood, Mrs. Fernande. Clare's menses started tonight. She thought something was wrong with her, so she consulted a doctor—because you were so busy 'keeping her pure,' you neglected to prepare her properly."

"Oh." This deflated the woman's outrage for only a moment. "Well, that is no excuse for being alone with her in a bedchamber. This is not Paris, Mr. Lazare!"

"*I* brought him here, Aunt!"

"Did you even for one moment stop to think how that might look, you little chit? Close your legs, damn it!" Hortense leaned toward her niece and actually shoved Clare's knees flat against the bed. The girl cried out, but her aunt paid no attention. "You couldn't even keep your mask on! Barely a month in society, and now *everyone* has seen you behaving like a harlot!"

David tried to interpose his body between the girl and her brutal aunt. "Clare is not—"

"I wasn't talking to you, Mr. Lazare."

"I don't care!" Clare shouted as if she wanted the whole plantation to hear her. "It doesn't matter what anyone else thinks!" She snatched David's hand and pulled it against her breast. "I want to marry David, and he wants to marry me."

His hand twitched, but he couldn't pull it away. Hortense was finally speechless. With considerable trepidation, David turned his head to Clare's father.

Edward finally spoke, in a growl: "I think the boy and I should discuss that alone."

David swallowed, nodded, and withdrew his hand.

CHAPTER 16

"You know we are not really so much brother and sister as to make it at all improper."

"Brother and sister! no, indeed."

—Jane Austen, *Emma* (1815)

Edward made haste to his office and let the boy trail after him. Edward flung his floppy Tudor hat on the sideboard and poured himself another whiskey. His hands were shaking and half of it ended up on the rug. After seeing Clare on the bed like that, with her legs spread, what Edward really needed was a few minutes alone. But he would take a whiskey. He could not drink it fast enough. Why in God's name hadn't he selected a larger codpiece?

The boy was babbling: "I apologize sincerely and profusely for the way this must look, sir. You have every right to demand that I marry your daughter, but—"

Edward was gripping his glass so hard he feared it might shatter in his hand. "Did you fuck her?"

The boy winced as if Edward had slapped him. Oh, Edward liked making him squirm. "No, sir. I swear to you on her mother's grave: I did not touch your daughter. Not even as a physician. It was a verbal consultation, nothing more."

Was it possible? "Did anyone see you come upstairs together?"

"I don't think so. They couldn't have. We passed no one."

The whiskey was doing its work. Edward felt calmer already. "Then perhaps this little debacle isn't as damaging as my sister thinks." After all, would Clare's becoming unmarriageable really be so terrible? It would mean Edward could have her to himself.

"I love your daughter, sir—but it is because I love Clare and want what is best for her that I must beg you not to insist on our marriage."

Edward lowered his glass. "What?"

"There are things you do not know about me, sir." The boy dropped his eyes to the floor. "Things that are permanent impediments to your daughter's happiness."

Edward narrowed his eyes at the boy. What impediments might he mean? Perhaps he *was* riddled with the French pox. Or he had a mad wife locked in an attic. Yet David had had the same woeful, condemned look about him since he was a child. Often, like right now, his pained expression resembled a clock wound too tightly. Perhaps the boy was impotent?

"Suffice it to say: I cannot in good conscience make Clare my wife."

"Do you intend to make her your mistress?"

"No, sir!"

Edward saw on the boy's stricken face that he felt it too: the way Tessa's betrayal, his uncle's betrayal, lingered in the room between them like the scent of the spilled whiskey.

"I must cut myself from Clare's life like a surgeon excising a cancer."

"Oh." Edward set down his glass on the sideboard. "Well, I agree that is best. We both know what she is like. Were you to attempt to remain friendly with her, Clare would continue to cling to you, pleading and hoping…"

The boy nodded. "'I must be cruel, only to be kind.'"

· · ·

"Don't lay there soiling everything." Aunt Hortense peeled off Clare's remaining slipper. "We must get you out of these clothes. Why are there never slaves around when you need them?" She reached up Clare's legs to rip off her garters.

Clare flinched at her aunt's roughness but did not move from her sitting position. She'd vowed never to ask Aunt Hortense about these things, yet the words haunted her: *"You actually deflowered her…"* "What did you mean, when you said you *hoped* I was bleeding, and you didn't mean m-menstrual blood?"

With Clare's left stocking hanging limp from her gloved hands, Aunt Hortense paused to glare at her. "A pure girl bleeds on her wedding night, and it has nothing to do with menstrual blood. If she doesn't bleed, her husband knows she's been wicked."

"H-How?"

"Because the first time you lie with a man, or if you ever violate yourself, it tears you open. There is blood and there is pain." Aunt Hortense yanked off her other stocking.

Clare swallowed. She didn't want to know any more; and yet— "V-Violate myself?"

"This is precisely what I was trying to prevent." Shaking her head, Aunt Hortense crossed around the bed to Clare's back. "Knowledge is the root of all sin. Pure girls are ignorant girls."

Clare tried to look over her shoulder. "But—"

Aunt Hortense forcibly turned Clare's head forward, her gloved, bony fingers digging into Clare's jaws and the sides of her neck. "The place where you are bleeding—the place *above* where you are bleeding—keep your fingers away from them."

The place ABOVE where she was bleeding?

"Do you hear me, Clare?" With one hand, Aunt Hortense kept Clare from turning her head. With the other, she jammed a loose hairpin back into place.

Clare winced. "Yes."

"If you ever try to touch yourself, you will injure yourself." Aunt Hortense tore each swan's wing from Clare's back. "You will soil yourself. You will start shaking, and you will go mad." Now Aunt

Hortense grabbed Clare's chin and forced her to turn her head. "Don't ever say I didn't prepare you, niece."

For a moment, Clare heard only her own terrified breaths. Then, in the hallway, David's low voice: "Thank you, sir."

She didn't care about the pain or the blood or her bare feet. Clare wrested away from her aunt, scrambled from her bed, and flew into the hall. David had said "Thank you" to her father! That meant he'd agreed to their marriage! "David!"

He'd already walked past her bedchamber. He was nearly to the staircase. He paused but did not turn around.

Clare bounded to him. "When are you coming back?"

Still David did not turn. "I'm not coming back, *souris*."

Why wouldn't he look at her? "You mean…we'll meet you in Charleston?"

His head turned just enough that he could look over his shoulder. He'd put his mask back on. "I mean: I cannot marry you, *souris*."

Clare sucked in a breath, whirled around, and glared at her father. He watched from the hallway behind her, next to her aunt. "You cannot prevent this, Father!"

"He didn't, Clare." Finally, David turned around. "Your father and I are in agreement."

"*What?*"

"I'm sorry, *souris*." Behind that mask, his face was unreadable.

Her voice wavered. "You…*don't* want to marry me?"

"I cannot marry you."

"D-Did you meet someone in Paris?"

"No."

"Is it because I'm so ignorant?"

"Of course not."

"Is it because I'm too bold?"

"No, Clare."

"Then *why?*"

"Because I love you, Clare."

Her hands balled into fists at her sides. "You're not making sense, David!"

"I know. But I won't hurt you, Clare."

Her eyes darted back to her aunt, then to the floor. Her voice dropped to a whisper. "It's painful the first time; I know that now. I'm prepared."

Clare looked up to see David grimace behind his mask. So it was true, what Aunt Hortense had said: it would *hurt*. "That's not what I meant, *souris*."

"Then explain it to me!" Clare clutched the front of David's robe with both hands. He did not react, not even when tears spilled from her eyes. She hated that her father and her aunt were witnessing her humiliation. "Tell me the truth!" Clare begged David. "How can you refuse to marry me and then tell me you love me?"

"Surely you understand that there are different kinds of love, Clare." With agonizing affection, he brushed the loose hair from her eyes. The touch of his fingertips felt like fire against her skin, branding her with his tenderness and his betrayal. "All your life, you have been my sister. A brother loves his sister, but he cannot marry her. It would be wrong."

"But you—" *You've been staring at my breasts!* Clare shouted in her head. *I know you have!*

For a moment, David's fingertips rested at the side of her face. "You must believe me, Clare: I am walking away because I love you." He turned, pulling away from Clare's grasp.

Her legs wobbled. She nearly fell. "No." Clare tried to stagger after him, but Aunt Hortense caught her shoulders. "No!" Clare screamed, thrashing against her aunt till her father came to restrain her too.

As David vanished down the stairs, her aunt and her father dragged Clare into her bedroom in tandem, as if she were the inmate of a madhouse and they were her keepers. Before Aunt Hortense slammed the bedroom door, she instructed Clare's father: "I think you'd better station yourself in the hall till she's calm." Her father grumbled a reply.

Clare crumpled onto the floor, tears pouring out of her. For five and a half years, she had imagined this day in her head. David would return and see she was no longer his little mouse but a woman. He would take her in his arms and declare his love and she would swoon with happiness.

Instead, she was sobbing so hard she might swoon. And no one was here to catch her.

"Why don't we let in some air?" Aunt Hortense said almost soothingly. She struggled with one of the triple-hung windows facing the veranda. "Where *is* that black wench when you need her?" she scolded a second time, when it was Aunt Hortense who'd told Verily to help Easter and Phoebe in the kitchen.

Numbly, Clare watched her aunt shove up the lower two window sashes, then attempt unsuccessfully to pull down the bottom one, muttering all the while. Right now, the window was a door. Clare had used the triple-hung windows that way all the time when she was a girl.

She could escape through the window *right now*. Clutching the bedpost, Clare pulled herself to her bare feet. She shoved past her aunt and raced across the upper veranda. She gripped the railing to halt her momentum, nearly toppling into the darkness beyond. Desperately, she peered over the edge.

Below her, on the drive, David strode toward Grand-père René's waiting gig.

"David!" she shouted.

He stopped, hesitated, and finally looked back. Framed by his black mask, his eyes seemed to sparkle like sapphires hidden in a cave. Were they glistening with tears, or only with lantern light? Beneath his mustache, his lips parted. But he did not speak.

"Don't leave me here!" she cried.

David only brought his fists to his heart to sign: *I am sorry, souris.* The little mouse feet of her sign name had never looked so forlorn.

Behind her, Aunt Hortense hissed: "Clare! Come inside this instant!"

Below her, David lowered his eyes and turned away. Without so much as another glance, he climbed into the gig and took the reins.

Clare collapsed in a puddle of skirts and feathers, still sobbing his name.

Aunt Hortense yanked on her arms, but Clare clutched the balustrade as if it were a raft and she were drowning at sea. She choked on her tears, only dimly aware that David was pulling around the drive and disappearing through the gates.

It had all been so perfect! David returning *tonight*, more handsome than ever, with those curls like ebony shavings, still wearing the Vandyck beard she had chosen for him and the Cosmas and Damian medal she had given him! He'd waltzed with her and caressed her with his eyes—and then her horrid leaky vagina had ruined everything!

"Clare!" Aunt Hortense admonished. "What will people think?"

Had Clare done something else to make David discard her? Surely he didn't think she took *other* men into her bedroom and asked them about private parts? She was his; she had always been his… Had he never wanted to marry her? But he'd given her the ouroboros bracelet! A snake, like Prince Albert's engagement ring to Queen Victoria! A symbol that meant "Our love will go on forever"!

This couldn't be how the story ended—how any of the acts ended! The hero didn't abandon the heroine!

By this point, Aunt Hortense had sunk her fingers into the hair on the top of Clare's head. Before she could pull, a male voice interrupted her, not Father but Mr. Cromwell:

"May I be of assistance, Mrs. Fernande?" He was dressed as a knight and certainly playing the part.

Aunt Hortense released Clare's head and stepped back, muttering.

Mr. Cromwell crouched beside Clare. "I understand you aren't feeling well, Miss Stratford. Hadn't we better get you inside, out of this chill?"

Clare did feel cold. The fight had drained out of her with the blood. When Mr. Cromwell gently rubbed his chainmail gauntlet over her bare wrist, as if he were steadying a spooked horse, Clare let her arms go limp. She let Mr. Cromwell unwrap her fingers from the posts of the balustrade and take her up in his arms. Aunt Hortense accompanied them back to Clare's bedchamber. Clare pressed her face against Mr. Cromwell's breastplate and imagined he was David.

Mercifully, Aunt Hortense left her alone that night. Clare lay against her buffalo robe and stroked the hair as if it were David's curls. She imagined his scent lingered here: sharp and earthy like Caribbean spices.

He'd admitted he loved her. She couldn't believe he saw her only as a sister. She couldn't believe he didn't yearn for her like she yearned for him. Did he not think her strong enough to be a wife, a mother? She could bear pain, for his sake. She was bearing it now.

Wherever Clare's father was—probably drunk—he did not object when she re-lit her lamp in the small hours. She caressed each of David's drawings as if one of them held a clue, as if some hidden detail could answer her question: *Why? Why do the people who love me not love me enough to STAY?*

CHAPTER 17

I have wept and wondered whether every manly aspiration of soul had been crushed in the colored man, or does he pander to the notion that he belongs to an inferior race?
— Reverend John Day, a man of color, "Sentiments on Colonization in Liberia," *Philadelphia Colonization Herald* (May 1854)

David had to share a bed at the inn. As he stared into the darkness, listening to his bedmate's snores, he battled the temptation to sneak back to Stratford-on-Ashley in the middle of the night and beg Clare to elope with him.

He needn't even beg. But David must be wiser than the romantic dreams of a sixteen-year-old girl. *She will be happier without you,* he told himself again and again.

David rose at the first hint of dawn and declined breakfast. Fortunately, Cassique had slept better; he trotted back to Charleston with little guidance. David's head remained a muddle.

He returned to find his grandparents still at their breakfast table. They greeted him eagerly and invited him to join them.

Grandfather set down his newspaper. "Did you have a memorable night?"

'Hasn't Clare grown into a beauty?' Grandmother prompted in sign. 'So much like her sweet mother!'

Then, in unison: "Tell us everything!"

David narrowed his bleary eyes at his grandparents, realizing why they'd been so insistent that he attend the ball. "You were matchmaking."

Grandmother admitted the truth with a shy smile into her teacup.

Grandfather continued to sign for her benefit, while declaring aloud: "Why shouldn't we want the two young people we love most to make each other happy? You already adore each other."

David sliced a muffin in half and said nothing.

Grandfather frowned. "I take it there were complications."

David stirred butter into cold grits. He looked to his grandmother, who was usually so concerned with Church law. "Have you forgotten that Clare and I are related by affinity, that my aunt married her uncle?"

The smile fell from Grandmother's face, and she averted her eyes for a moment.

"Of course we haven't forgotten, David," Grandfather answered testily. "Your grandmother and I think about your aunt Hélène *every day*. But this situation is why the Church invented dispensations. I will happily pay the tax for you!"

"I am no longer welcome beneath Edward's roof."

"Then elope! I will help you!"

"Clare is a child."

"As you saw for yourself, that is no longer true, David. She came out last month, during Race Week. Other men are courting her."

David glanced apologetically at Grandmother. "Clare's menarche happened *last night*. She thought she had a cancer."

Grandmother made a small sound of sympathy and rose from the table, leaving David and his grandfather alone.

"I should have made certain Clare knew what to expect," Grandfather sighed. "Since she started at Barhamville, I've hardly had a moment alone with her. I tried to broach the subject once, but Clare's aunt interrupted us. She practically chewed my ear off. She reacted as if I were a dirty old man and said such things were her prerogative, so I assumed… I shouldn't have assumed."

"I'm sure Clare would have sent for you if I hadn't been there." Without much appetite, David swallowed another bite of grits. "Why is this so important to you, Clare and myself?"

"Because that young woman is dear to me, just as her mother was. She is dear to all of us—your grandmother and uncle too." Grandfather stared into his empty teacup. "We couldn't save Tessa. But we can save Clare."

"Save her from what, exactly?"

"From her harpy of an aunt and her inebriate of a father, first of all." Grandfather pulled off his glasses and tapped his newspaper. Even upside-down, David could see the column was about slave sales. "From this beautiful city's damned peculiar institution and how ugly it makes *everything*. From marriage to a slave-owner—a man who cares only about acquiring her father's plantations and what a beautiful ornament she'll make on his arm. A man who will smother Clare's curiosity and intelligence. A man who 'came of age' by raping a slave woman, who will force Clare to watch while his bastard children grow up around her."

"I am hardly the only man in South Carolina with a conscience," David argued.

"You are the only one she loves."

"She is sixteen years old. She is bound to fall in love again."

"You speak as if Clare were *any* sixteen-year-old."

Of course she wasn't. Inside the body of a goddess, she possessed the heart of a saint, the soul of a poet, and the mind of a scientist.

"Are you truly willing to leave her happiness in the hands of a stranger?"

My hands are bloody, and they always will be. If Grandfather knew the truth about baby Ian… He loved Clare as if she were his grand-daughter. He'd never let her marry the man who'd killed his grandson.

Grandfather cleaned his glasses, tucked them back behind his ears, and sat waiting for David to continue the conversation.

Finally David set down his spoon and pushed back his chair. "I won't be giving you great-grandchildren. I'm sorry."

Grandfather stood too. "Why not, David?"

"I'd be a terrible father."

"The men who think that are the very ones who care enough to get it right."

David strode toward the staircase, eager for the refuge of his room.

Grandfather followed him into the hall. "Is this about my mother? About our African blood?"

His hand on the newel post, David hesitated for only a moment before he started up the stairs.

"You are just like your uncle!" Grandfather called after him. It was not a compliment.

"That is not the only reason." David kept climbing.

"What are the others?"

David paused at the threshold. "What I do with my semen is my own business." He closed the door decisively behind him.

In the hall, Grandfather laughed heartily. But when he was through, he shouted: "This isn't over, David!"

DAVID TRIED TO UNPACK more of his things and organize his books, but his eyes and his head ached from lack of sleep. He kept seeing Clare's stricken face when he'd told her he couldn't marry her. Her final cry haunted him too: *"Don't leave me here!"*

David knew Grandfather was right: this slave society bred violence like a poisonous weed fouling the water. At South Carolina College, David had witnessed the brutal tempers of his fellow students. Less than three years ago, South Carolina Representative Preston Brooks had caned Massachusetts Senator Charles Sumner nearly to death on the floor of the Senate. What might such men do in private?

This culture of violence infected even the slave-owners' wives and daughters, like Clare's vicious aunt. But mostly, women were its victims, white as well as black. Clare might marry a brute. Someone who beat her, who forced himself on her, who kept her with child year after year after year. Someone whose roving prick would curse her with syphilis.

Clare might just as well marry a gem, or someone harmless like Mr. Arrington, David told himself. *You are not her only hope. You are no spotless knight in shining armor.*

She had looked at him as if he were exactly that. David pulled out his notebook and began sketching Clare leaning over the balcony, beaming at the sight of him like a princess in a tower. If she knew the truth…

Clare deserved so much more than he could give her. She deserved a younger man unburdened by secrets, not a husband whose millstones would crush her spirit and drown her dreams. If David told her what he'd done to an innocent child—if he told her what the cross in his blood might do to *their* innocent child—Clare's bright eyes would turn away in fear. David could not bear to watch her suffering for love of him.

His vision blurred. He pressed so hard, he tore the paper. David tossed the pencil aside and closed his notebook. His fingers twitched in protest, caressing the cover as if it were Clare's skin.

He decided to rest for a few minutes. He collapsed on top of his bed.

He dreamt of Clare. Her joyous smile; her slender feet; her shapely breasts. Her words replayed in his head, amorous even when she hadn't meant them to be:

"Teach me, David!"

"Aunt Hortense says I do EVERYTHING too vigorously."

As a young man, David had overheard Tessa's passionate cries when Uncle Joseph visited her in secret. The old French wives' tale claimed Clare's mother had stamped her daughter with that insatiable desire; the proof was right there, in the *envies* at the corner of Clare's eye…

How would David's little sister react if he whispered hot in her ear "I want to take your nipples in my mouth"? If he pulled her atop him and urged "I want you to ride me like a whore"? Would Clare cry out in longing and satisfaction as her mother had?

Uncle Joseph had said once that if you were asleep, it didn't count as a sin, because you couldn't give your consent. But what if, when you woke, your hand wouldn't stop?

Even if Joseph were in Charleston, David wouldn't have confessed to him. Not this sin. But David knew he couldn't resist this vice on his own, and medicine's methods for preventing self-pollution included caustics and castration. He decided to consult a Physician of the Soul first.

So that afternoon, David walked to the beautiful new brownstone cathedral and knelt inside a confessional to vomit up his ugliness. "Bless me, Father, for I have sinned."

On the other side of the grille, the unfamiliar Priest made the Sign of the Cross over him. David saw a bald head rimmed with white hair, and the man seemed to be suffering from shortness of breath. David suspected pulmonary emphysema—then reminded himself that the Priest was supposed to diagnose *him*, not the other way around.

David crossed himself. "I confess to Almighty God, to Blessed Mary ever Virgin, to all the Saints, and to you, my spiritual Father, that I have sinned. It has been…months since my last Confession." He'd stopped confessing regularly in Paris. His sins were always the same.

In spite of his labored breathing, the elderly Priest sounded cheerful. "And what brings you back today, my son?"

Lust. Such a small, simple word, for such a cataclysm. The marks on Clare's cheek were *moles*—not proof of latent carnality. She was sixteen years old and practically his sister. "I have…impure thoughts."

"Are you married, my son?"

"No."

"Have you given in to these lusts?"

"Never…with anyone else." David grimaced and closed his eyes. "When I was younger, before I understood the moral and medical gravity of…the solitary sin, I often— But I thought I had conquered this."

"What do you think has changed, that your sin returns to you?"

Even behind his eyelids, David could see her. "My desires have a focus now. So bright she blinds me."

"You speak of a young lady?"

"Yes."

"Is *she* unmarried, and a Catholic?" The Priest's tone was definitely cheerful now.

"Yes…" David answered slowly, because he could follow the man's implication.

"Such temptation is unique, my son, in that the Lord has given us a means to sanctify it. Your Penance is enviable: you may satisfy your desires without sin—indeed, through a Sacrament."

David gritted his teeth. "What is my Penance, Father?"

"I have given it to you: Matrimony." Why was everyone so keen to marry him off?

"I cannot perform your Penance, Father."

"Why not, my son?"

"Because I cannot marry! I cannot bind an innocent girl to me, when…" Where did David even begin?

"You have another sin to confess?" the Priest prompted.

"Seventeen years ago, Father, I committed the oldest sin of all."

At last the Priest was silent, waiting for him to continue.

"Cain and I will share a circle in Hell."

Still the Priest did not speak.

David actually peered through the grille, to make certain the man had not suffered a heart attack. The eyes of the old Priest were closed, but his hurried breathing persisted. David had laid a great weight on this frail man: the knowledge that he shared his confessional with a murderer. But David's own burden felt no lighter.

What the Priest finally said was not what David had expected: "You are mistaken, my son. The first sin was not Cain's or even Adam's. It was Lucifer's. It was pride."

David scoffed. This was theological quibbling.

"Have you confessed this sin before?"

"Yes."

"The Priest granted you Absolution, and you did your Penance?"

"I am doing it." David's whole life must be a Work of Mercy, a perpetual Penance. Marrying the girl he loved was out of the question.

"Your voice sounds young yet," the Priest continued. "If you committed this sin seventeen years ago, you must have been——"

"Ten. I was ten years old. Well past the age of reason."

"Even for a grown man who sins with full knowledge and deliberate consent, even for 'a sin that cries to Heaven for vengeance,' *God forgives*. Think of King David. He is called 'beloved of God'—a man who committed adultery, and then murdered the woman's husband in order to have her for himself."

David had not asked for a sermon—particularly not one about his shameless namesake.

"To deny Our Lord's forgiveness is to deny His mercy. But even denial can be forgiven, if it is repented. Think of Saint Peter. Upon him, Christ built our Church." The halting way the Priest spoke as he struggled for breath imbued each word with more power: "Or do you imagine that *you*, of all men in all ages, have managed to commit a sin so grievous that God Himself cannot forgive it? If that is true, my son, then you *have* repeated Lucifer's error."

Lust, self-abuse, and fratricide were not enough for this man? He had to accuse David of following the Devil? This Priest understood nothing. David stood and banged open the door of the confessional in his haste.

The Priest did not pursue David but called after him, loud enough for half the cathedral to hear: "My son! You cannot be forgiven until you confess your true sin!"

PART IV
WHERE HE IS WANTED

1859-1860

C‍HARLESTON, S‍OUTH C‍AROLINA
AND S‍T. J‍OSEPH, M‍ISSOURI

Far off thou art, but ever nigh...

— Alfred, Lord Tennyson,
In Memoriam (1850)

CHAPTER 18

No place in the United States offers so great opportunities for the acquisition of Anatomical knowledge, subjects being obtained from among the coloured population in sufficient number for every purpose, and proper dissection carried on without offending any individual in the community.
— Dr. Thomas G. Prioleau, Dean of the Medical College of South Carolina, to the state legislature (1824)

David had returned to Charleston on the 7th of March and attended the delightful, disastrous Mardi Gras ball on the 8th of March. Before the month was out, he'd secured an appointment as one of the two House Physicians at Roper Hospital on Queen Street. His grandparents claimed they were proud, but they exhibited more dismay. The House Physicians were required to not only reside at the hospital but also take their meals there.

'Your home is one block away!' Grandmother argued. 'Surely they could make an exception for you.'

'If a stabbing victim arrives in the middle of the night, you would let him bleed to death before a messenger can fetch me?'

Grandmother frowned, then amended: 'You could dine here, at least. We just got you back!'

'I'm sorry, Grandmother. It's not possible.'

In truth, David was grateful for the restrictions. No longer living and dining with his grandparents meant he could escape their nagging about his celibacy. Confining himself to the hospital grounds also meant he could pretend he did not reside in the same city as Clare. Better that David live like a cloistered monk, safe from temptation.

Unlike the foreboding District Jail on the other side of the block, Roper Hospital seemed a pleasant prison. Opened only three years before, the hospital looked like the offspring of a Venetian palace and a Tuscan villa. Adorned with bracketed cornices and topped with finials, six square towers marked the structure's four corners and entrance. Elegantly arched and columned, three-story loggias fronted the two wings of wards stretching between the towers. If the patients were ambulatory, they were allowed to convalesce on these loggias until evening.

High ceilings and a constant perforation of windows allowed for ventilation of the interior spaces as well. At the building's heart lay a library, a pathological museum, an amphitheatre for lectures, and the physicians' offices and quarters. Ornamental, kitchen, and medicinal gardens surrounded the grand Italian structure. So did an iron fence with a locked gate.

David was no idle emperor in this palace, and the hospital's guests were no sybarites. Wealthy patients, and patients aspiring to wealth, convalesced in their homes and had their physicians attend them there. Only the poorest and most desperate invalids resorted to a hospital.

Unlike the Consulting Physicians and Attending Physicians, who visited like gods descending from Olympus, the House Physicians seemed to be doctors in name only. David's duties were a wearying, demeaning combination of clerking and nursing.

He ensured that each new patient was bathed prior to admittance. He kept a Case Book, which was examined by a committee for accuracy and thoroughness at random intervals. David also maintained the hospital's "Black Book," in which he recorded the names of the disorderly patients and their offenses. He superintended the nurses and the dispensing of medicines. He ensured that the orders of the Attending Physicians were carried out. He organized the instruments in the surgical ward. He conducted the postmortem examinations and deposited any interesting specimens in the pathological museum. He was not permitted to discharge patients.

All the better, David thought, to combat his supposed pride. Examining lice-ridden scalps; lancing boils; wrestling lunatics into straight-jackets; and doing interminable paperwork—all for a paltry hundred dollars a year—certainly kept a man humble.

THE WARDS WERE ORGANIZED by malady, by sex, and by race. Nearly half of the patients, including the lunatics, were black. Some of these men and women were free, but most were slaves.

David remembered reading an argument by William Gilmore Simms, Charleston's great man of letters. He found it again in the hospital library:

> The absence of all care for the morrow, for the future, for their own support in age, and the support of their children…and the generally inferior activity of their minds, cause their freedom from this dreadful malady. Certain it is, that we have few or no madmen among the negroes.

David knew the state lunatic asylum in Columbia also had negro inmates. Apparently Mr. Simms had visited neither.

David wondered how his fellow House Physician, Dr. Pickens, explained the slaves in their maniac cells. He decided to read Mr. Simms's argument aloud at dinner.

Dr. Pickens paused with a piece of mutton halfway to his mouth and frowned at David. "Simms is many fine things, but he is not a doctor. The 'inferior activity' of a negro's mind doesn't *prevent* madness—it *predisposes* him. If his master doesn't manage him properly, a negro's brain easily succumbs to drapetomania or dysthesia aethioptica."

"Drapeto...?"

"They're mental diseases peculiar to negroes," Dr. Pickens explained around his mutton. "Dr. Cartwright named them years ago."

Dr. Pickens returned Simms's "The Morals of Slavery" to the hospital library and found the relevant issue of *The New Orleans Medical and Surgical Journal*.

"DISEASES AND PECULIARITIES OF THE NEGRO RACE, BY DR. CARTWRIGHT OF NEW-ORLEANS," David read. "DRAPETOMANIA, OR THE DISEASE CAUSING NEGROES TO RUN AWAY." The subtitle unsettled him, so David retreated to his quarters to read the rest.

> The cause, in the most of cases, that induces the negro to run away from service, is as much a disease of the mind as any other species of mental alienation, and much more curable, as a general rule. With the advantages of proper medical advice, strictly followed, this troublesome practice that many negroes have of running away, can be almost entirely prevented...

The Old Testament name for the negro race, Dr. Cartwright claimed, "declares the Creator's will": negroes were Canaanites, descended from Noah's cursed son, Ham, and Ham's son Canaan. Canaanite meant "submissive knee-bender." Even in

> the anatomical conformation of his knees, we see 'submissive knee-bender' written in the negro's physical structure. ... If the white man attempts to oppose the Deity's will, by trying to make the negro anything else than 'the submissive knee-bender'...the negro will run away.

A negro would run away only if his master attempted to treat him like a man? Surely Dr. Cartwright couldn't be serious. David had dissected hundreds of cadavers, and he'd never noticed anything different in the conformation of a black man's knees.

At least Dr. Cartwright advocated keeping negroes well fed and clothed and giving each family their own cabin. But

> if any one or more of them, at any time, are inclined to raise their heads to a level with their master or overseer, humanity and their own good require that they should be punished until they fall into that submissive state which it was intended for them to occupy... They have only to be kept in that state and treated like children, with care, kindness, attention and humanity, to prevent and cure them from running away.

Dr. Cartwright did not stop there:

> DYSAETHESIA AETHIOPICA, OR HEBETUDE OF MIND AND OBTUSE SENSIBILITY OF BODY—A DISEASE PECULIAR TO NEGROES—CALLED BY OVERSEERS, 'RASCALITY.' ... They wander about at night, and keep in a half nodding sleep during the day. They slight their work... They raise disturbances with their overseers without cause or motive... It makes man like an automaton or senseless machine...

Wasn't that what a master wanted, an automaton to do his bidding? And if slaves left their cabins at night, they did not wander aimlessly; they were visiting relatives on other plantations or attending secret meetings.

"Slavery improves the negro in body, mind, and morals," Dr. Cartwright concluded.

> There is a radical, internal or physical difference between the two races, so great in kind, as to make what is wholesome and benefi-cial to the white man, as liberty, free institutions, etc., not only

unsuitable to the negro race, but actually poisonous to its happiness.

If the races were so different, why did the Attending Physicians lecture about how to treat white patients while demonstrating on negro cadavers?

A FEW DAYS LATER, after obtaining permission from his Attending Physician, David dined with his grandparents. They insisted that he leave his cloister occasionally. David braced himself for news of Clare. His grandparents still saw her at Mass from time to time.

She'd asked about him. She was not yet betrothed. Someday, when Clare was safely wed, David hoped they might be friends again. But while she remained free, he must live on these scraps.

Uncle Joseph was visiting too, from his new parish of St. Patrick's on the Charleston Neck. Grandmother and Delia made sure the table was laden with delicacies David couldn't get at the hospital and Joseph couldn't get at his presbytery: venison pastry, potatoes à la Lyonnaise, Spanish cream... In the seven years since Tessa's death, Joseph had slowly relaxed his asceticism, and he complimented the cooks. But Clare's ghost and Dr. Cartwright's theories continued to haunt David. He couldn't muster much of an appetite.

After dinner, Grandmother's new friend came to fetch her for Vespers: Mrs. Doherty, who had lost her hearing with age and was eagerly learning Grandmother's signs.

David, his uncle, and his grandfather retired to the piazza to drink port and watch the lamplighters illuminating the city. A Priest flanked by two doctors. Much as his grandfather and uncle perplexed and irritated him sometimes, David knew they were good men trying to do their best for the world. They did it more selflessly than David accomplished his own Works of Mercy. Even now, Grandfather and Joseph were discussing their charges: naming no names, laughing without a trace of cruelty, only genuine affection for patients, parishioners, and each other.

At times like this, David regretted that the Lazares were a dying breed, that there would be no more Priests or doctors or anyone else to follow after them. For a few minutes, David could forget they descended from slaves, that they would always carry that burden.

He waited for a lull to ask: "Have either of you heard of Dr. Samuel Cartwright, of Louisiana?"

"Dr. Drapetomania?" Joseph scoffed.

"Yes," Grandfather answered through gritted teeth, leaning forward in his chair to stare at David. "Tell me you haven't swallowed that man's balderdash. He has as many critics as converts, thank God. A few decades ago, it was Benjamin Rush claiming 'Negritude' was a form of leprosy. Now anyone who resists slavery must have a disease."

In the fading light, David stared into his port. At the time of his death, Dr. Benjamin Rush had been the nation's preeminent physician. He'd trained in Edinburgh and London. He'd signed the Declaration of Independence and taught at the University of Pennsylvania. He'd also been an abolitionist. If a man like that thought negroes had leprosy...

"Tell me, David," Grandfather pressed, "who is madder: the 'master' who claims another man is his property, or the 'slave' who seizes his 'unalienable Right' to 'Life, Liberty, and the pursuit of Happiness'?"

Dr. Cartwright had claimed the equality in the Declaration of Independence applied only to white men. David did not have an answer to Grandfather's question, so he evaded it. "Not all of our colored lunatics are slaves. Some are free."

"In this city," Joseph asserted, "no man or woman of color is truly free."

Grandfather agreed. "No matter his age, no matter how many generations his family has been free, *every* free colored person is required by law to attach himself to a white guardian. Every free colored person is also forced to pay an annual capitation tax. They cannot vote, and they have a curfew. Imagine what that kind of humiliation does to a person: to be treated like a perpetual child, like a prisoner always on parole but never pardoned. If one or two of them run screaming through the streets, I can hardly blame them. Slavery and submission are *no one*'s natural state. Man walks on two legs, not four."

This reminded David of Dr. Cartwright's Biblical allusions. He asked his uncle: "Does Canaanite even mean 'knee-bender'?"

Joseph shrugged. "The meaning of 'Canaan' is obscure. But it's irrelevant. There is no Biblical or classical basis whatsoever for connecting the 'curse of Ham' with blackness. Noah cursed Ham's son Canaan. Dark-skinned Africans are the descendants of Ham's son *Cush*, who wasn't cursed at all. In the Middle Ages, European lords claimed their white *serfs* descended from Ham and Canaan, in order to justify *their* subjection. It wasn't until the seventeenth century and the rise of the African slave trade that 'scholars' decided Ham was black and African slavery was God's will. The so-called 'curse of Ham' is all self-serving misinterpretation and outright falsehood."

Grandfather was grinning at Joseph. "You can see why Bishop Lynch banished him to the Beaufort missions, can't you?"

"And then recalled me when I had the audacity to offer reading lessons at my Sunday Schools." Joseph sighed.

David frowned, trying to understand why the Bishop should object to catechumens learning to read. Then David remembered: one of his uncle's Colleton County missions consisted of negro parishioners—slaves who worshipped at a remote church called St. James the Greater. "Do you mean: even at the St. James mission?"

Now Joseph grinned. "Especially at the St. James mission."

David glanced toward Archdale Street, only a few steps from the piazza. "You were breaking the law."

"Do you really think Bishop Lynch is going to have one of his own Priests arrested?" Grandfather chuckled.

Joseph sat back in his chair. "As a wise man once said, 'There is only one sin our Church cannot bear: the sin of scandal.' Besides, many of the St. James parishioners could already read. All I did was provide books and a safe place where they could continue to learn."

"Someone else might have discovered you," David pointed out. "Like their masters."

"How do you think Bishop Lynch found out? It was a risk I was happy to take—a risk I *am* happy to take."

Slowly, David realized that at St. Patrick's, Joseph still had slave parishioners. David's eyes widened.

"You don't approve, David?" Grandfather asked, his tone indicating that he already knew David's opinion—and he did not care.

"I think you're being foolhardy," David answered regardless. "How can it be worth the risk? A slave with the ability to read only learns about things he can never have."

"Slaves are men and women and children first, David," his uncle insisted. "Slavery is a condition, and it is temporary. You know what happened at Harper's Ferry, what happened in Haiti—what nearly happened here in Charleston. Slavery is an abomination, and God will not allow it to continue. Country after country has seen that and abolished it already: Spain, Britain, France, Denmark… It's only a matter of time before our government abolishes slavery too."

"Do you really think South Carolina and all the other slave states will stand by and let that happen?"

"I didn't say it would be easy. But whatever the cost, I plan to do everything in my power to prepare for that day. Maybe I won't live to see it, but I think you will."

David could certainly see why Bishop Lynch wanted Joseph close enough to keep an eye on him. David glanced back to Archdale Street. The gaslights were glowing now. David felt more exposed than ever.

"We're shocking you, aren't we, David?" Grandfather observed. "Treason, madness—they're a matter of perspective. But right and wrong—those never change."

THE FOLLOWING MONTH, David admitted a young slave woman named Dido to the hospital. She seemed to exhibit the symptoms of drapetomania and dysthesia aethioptica. Her new master was at his wit's end with her. In the middle of the night, someone had raised the gates on his rice fields, drowning the fragile new shoots. Someone had also opened the chicken coop, the hog pen, and the cow pasture, letting the animals run wild. Her master, his overseer, and his driver sat up at night to discover it was Dido. She seemed to be in a state of somnambulism, unaware of her actions. So her master chained her in the barn at night.

Her strange activities only shifted to daytime. Instead of hoeing weeds, she chopped up the young corn plants. Dido claimed she'd gone into a trance and didn't know what she was doing. In this state, she would wander through her master's house, singing to herself in some African language, frightening her mistress and the children. When flogging produced no results, Dido's master sent her to Roper Hospital.

Apart from her scars, Dido's only visible symptom was poor nutrition—but this was true of most slaves. While David examined her, the negress sang in her incomprehensible language, even as she watched him make notes in his Case Book. Then, Dido broke off singing and simply watched David in a way that unnerved him.

So far, the negress had exhibited no violence toward persons, David reminded himself. The nurse had checked her for concealed weapons, and besides, Dido was entirely naked now. The nurse was a colored woman too. The white nurses refused to attend colored patients.

Since she was no longer singing, David asked: "Can you answer a few questions for me, Dido?"

"You first." He wondered that anyone could look so confident naked.

"I told you my name: Dr. Lazare. That is all you need to know about me."

"I got one question, that's all. Surely you got time for one question."

David sighed. "Very well."

"You got a touch of the tar-brush yourself, don't you, Doctor?"

David tried not to react. He failed. His eyes leapt to the nurse, who was filling the hip bath. He hoped the running water had obscured Dido's question. "What is that supposed to mean?"

"You know what it means," the negress smirked.

"I know nothing of the kind." He motioned to the tub. "Your bath is ready. Clean yourself up."

Dido stepped in and plucked up a sponge. She waited for the nurse to carry her clothing away, while David returned to his Case Book. Then Dido resumed: "Don't worry, Doctor: your secret is safe with me. Just as long as you don't declare me cured anytime soon."

David had heard of slaves shamming physical ailments to escape work, but feigning lunacy was new to him. He gaped at Dido.

"You keep staring at me like that, I'll claw your eyes out. Then *nobody* will doubt I'm mad."

David did not turn his back—it was against the rules to leave a patient unattended—but he did avert his eyes. "You *want* to be locked in a cell?"

At the edge of his vision, Dido shrugged. "I hear we get to walk in the garden."

"Once a day."

"I hear the food ain't half bad, and the beds ain't even on the floor." She turned on the tap again. "I ain't never had a real bath with running water neither."

"It's not really running water. It comes from a tank on the roof. We have a cow who walks on a treadmill to pump it..."

Dido shut off the water. "Least it ain't me on that treadmill."

David swallowed. Charleston's Work House stood on the other side of this block, next to the District Jail. David had never been inside the Work House, but he'd heard the stories—and the screams. Only last week, a slave who'd been caught in a Work House treadmill had been carried to the hospital. David and Dr. Horlbeck had had no choice but to amputate the man's leg. Even then, they hadn't been able to save him. His dismembered cadaver still lay in the dead house.

Dido's voice brought David back to the present: "Every day I'm here, my master has to pay for it, don't he?"

"He does."

Dido settled back into the tub. "Yessir, I'm feeling like a queen right 'bout now." She looked out toward the loggia. "It's a damned sight better than being trapped in them rice fields: dragging my feet through muck from can see to can't, sun burning my eyes and my skin, never knowing when a snake or a gator gonna decide I done offended him, getting bit by every gnat and fly and skeeter in the Lowcountry—all for nothing 'cept to make Master richer." Her voice dropped. "Never knowing when he gonna come after me, neither."

For a long minute, David stared at the oiled cloth beneath Dido's tub. "I'm only a House Physician. The Attending Physicians make the final decisions. But I can make recommendations. I'll recommend that you receive the House Fare, same as the staff receive—that's full meals with meat every day but Friday. I'll also recommend that you remain here a fortnight."

"Can't you make it any longer?"

"You're as sane as I am, Dido."

"Don't you mean: 'You is the most dire case I ever seen, and the only cure is Northern climes'?"

David actually chuckled, that this place—which white patients saw as a last resort, which he'd chosen as a prison—was a refuge to a slave. "I'll push for a month if I can."

So often, as David walked the wards, those endless rows of beds with mosquito netting draped over each one, he'd think of coffins and shrouds. He'd wonder what the point of it all was: he and the other doctors were only fending off Death for a little while. Even successful births felt like hollow victories—he knew many of those children wouldn't survive to their first birthdays.

Then he'd remember Dido sighing in her bath, sitting in the garden, savoring beefsteak and pudding. David had only been able to give her a month's reprieve, but he'd seen what that month had meant to her.

There was always a chance. A chance that, sustained by her holiday, Dido would live to see freedom, whatever that might mean. A chance that one of the babies David delivered would live to accomplish great things.

His brother would never have such a chance, because of David. So he locked himself in this prison, a block away from his family, who would never have to bear the burden of what he'd done. And at night, David shut himself in his cramped little cell and only dreamt that Clare lay beside him.

CHAPTER 19

Why does the slave ever love? Why allow the tendrils of the heart
to twine around objects which may at any moment be wrenched
away by the hand of violence?

— Harriet Jacobs, *Incidents in the Life of a Slave Girl, Written by
Herself* (1861)

Everyone loved a wedding. Everyone but Easter.
Slaves' weddings pleased Master Edward so much, he
contributed most of the feast and gave even the house slaves an
extra half-day off work. For the master, a wedding meant family ties
that would discourage the couple from running away. It meant children, which meant more slaves—more profit.

Still the slaves celebrated this little island of happiness. Not all
masters allowed their negroes to choose their own spouses. On one
of their neighboring plantations back in Virginia, the master had
paired off his strongest "wenches" with his strongest "bucks" so they
would "breed the best stock." He didn't care if the man and woman
loathed each other.

Master Edward wasn't like that. He knew slaves naturally sought
solace in each other to survive the terror and drudgery of their lives.

He let Chloe and Cato and all the other couples find each other. Once, he'd purchased a woman from another plantation, when his valet fell in love with a neighbor's maid.

But Easter knew love was impossible for her. Even if Cromwell permitted her to marry—which she doubted—what man would ever want a woman as soiled as she was? Even if a man could overlook what Cromwell had done to her, how could Easter let another man touch her without recoiling? Even if Cromwell dropped dead tomorrow, she would be his forever.

For her, other people's weddings meant nothing but pain. *She* would never be the woman standing there in a pretty dress, gazing at the man who loved her and anticipating how he would show his love once they were alone.

Yet here Easter sat beside her sister, watching the festivities by the light of a bonfire. On Easter's lap sat a plate she'd barely touched. Grief always stole her appetite. The other wedding guests had had no such problems. Often, the only meat the field hands got were the animals they raised, hooked, or trapped on their own. They did not let Master's generosity go to waste. Picked to the bones, the carcasses of two roast pigs still hung over barbecue pits. Large kettles held the remains of hoppin' john and collard greens. On the long tables behind Easter and Verily, skillets lay gutted of crackling bread.

To their right was the dancing. Even those not on their feet were smiling and clapping out the tune to the music of a banjo and a fiddle. Cuffee and Quash accompanied them, playing tin buckets and pans as if they were drums. South Carolina masters did not permit real drums, the kind whose sound carried for miles, because a long time ago African-born slaves had used them to communicate between plantations and plan a rebellion.

The dancers started the juba, making their bodies into instruments too. Slapping their hands against their thighs, together, and against their chests with dizzying rapidity, like leaves in a hurricane, they sang:

"We sift the meal, they give us the husk
We bake the bread, they give us the crust.
We fry the meat, they give us the skin
And that's the way they takes us in…"

"Easter!" Verily elbowed her. "Do you think he's looking at you, or at me?"

Her sister was sixteen now, and she chattered endlessly about the young men on the plantation and in Charleston. It was exactly what Easter wanted for Verily—a normal life where men promised happiness instead of dread—yet Easter could not help but envy her sister as she envied the bride and groom. "Who?" Easter asked dully.

"Shadrach!"

Easter's heartbeats sped up, and she followed Verily's eyes. The new blacksmith sat against the thick trunk of a sycamore, the light of the bonfire playing over his long limbs, smiling face, and short, full hair. Fortunately, Shadrach was watching the dancers now, so Easter could stare at him without fear of discovery. She couldn't help staring. Shadrach was the handsomest man she'd ever seen. His light-colored, lightweight summer clothing contrasted strikingly with his dark skin—almost as black as the iron he forged—and showed off the contours of muscle across his arms and chest.

She'd snuck glances since his arrival last month, watching Shadrach as he worked and chatted with the other women. He'd tried to speak to Easter too, but she'd always found an excuse to hurry away, like she had with every other man who'd shown interest. She knew such conversations would lead only to disappointment for both of them.

Shadrach cheered and applauded the juba dancers, then looked back to Easter and Verily. Easter dropped her eyes quickly.

"He's coming over!" her sister squealed.

Easter hoped Shadrach sought Verily. To ensure he had only one choice, Easter rushed from her seat toward the safety of her quarters. Behind her, the juba callers began a new song:

"Old black bull come down the hollow,
He shake his tail, you hear him bellow.
When he bellow he jar the river,
He paw the earth, he make it quiver…"

Easter herself jumped at the sensation of a strong, callused hand catching hers. She sucked in a breath and glanced back to see Shadrach. She tried to pull away, but he didn't let go. "Won't you dance with me, Easter?"

"I-I…" His eyes were as dark and inviting as drinking chocolate —but she knew better than anyone how easily a man's fine appearance could deceive. She stared down at Shadrach's broad hand smothering hers, at the strength of that extended arm. This man bent iron to his will. What might he do to a woman who displeased him?

Shadrach frowned. "Easter? You ain't afraid of me, is you?"

She didn't answer, only pulled her hand from his.

He let her go. "That the *last* thing I want. I upset iron, not women."

Now Easter frowned in confusion, glancing up to see one side of his beautiful lips curved in a smile. "Upsetting iron is when you…" He started to make the hand motions, like he was gripping a hammer and tongs, then brushed the idea aside. "Come by the smithy sometime, and I'll show you. I seen you, lingering at the window."

Easter was grateful he couldn't see her blush.

"*Come in.* Ask Verily—she'll tell you I don't bite."

Ridiculous jealousy stabbed Easter in the heart. The way her sister spoke about Shadrach, like he was a magnificent, untouchable god, Easter knew already that nothing had happened between them.

"But your sister, she still a girl." Shadrach took Easter's hand again, so gently this time, brushing her knuckles with his thumb. "A man, he wants a woman, like you."

Easter swallowed. Being a woman wasn't always a good thing.

Shadrach glanced back to the wedding party. "Don't you like to dance?"

Easter looked away and murmured: "I ain't done it in a long time, and..."

"You ain't in the mood for dancing?"

She shook her head, squeezed his hand in apology, and drew hers away again.

"How about I just walk with you, then?"

"A-All right." It *was* a bit of a walk back to her quarters behind the Big House. She wondered if Cromwell was lurking somewhere in the darkness, and the thought quickened her steps.

Shadrach looked up to the full moon and smiled. "It ain't right, a beautiful woman like you being alone on such a night."

Easter loved the sound of Shadrach's voice, deep and rich but bright with confidence. She wished she could listen to those notes all night. But it was cruel to encourage him when there was no hope. The words hurt her chest, but she forced them out: "You don't want me, Shadrach."

He only chuckled. "Ain't that for *me* to decide?"

Easter clenched her fists in pain and didn't answer, knowing Cromwell had decided for them five years before.

"Why wouldn't I want you, Easter?"

"Because...you look at me, and you think you see beauty—but you don't know me at all."

"I know you save the best bits from Master's table for the chillun. I know you got a different head wrap for every day of the week. I know you talk to Master's hens when you collect their eggs. And I know you watch me when you think I ain't paying attention. *All* of that makes you beautiful."

Easter shook her head. "But you can't see..."

"Can't see what, Easter?"

"How—" She stopped walking and stared at the dirt beneath her feet. "How soiled I am, inside."

"You mean you been with a man before?"

Easter nodded sharply.

"Was it your choice?"

Easter's throat clamped nearly shut. "No."

"Then it don't count, Easter."

She covered her mouth with her hand and stifled a sob.

"You want to tell me about it?"

"No."

Shadrach hesitated. Easter was sure he'd give up on her, but instead he asked: "How about I tell you about me, then?"

She wiped away the tears clinging to her cheeks and nodded. "I-I'd like that."

The massive branch of a live oak spread out along the ground nearby. Shadrach sat down on it, and Easter sat beside him. For several moments, he was quiet. The chorus of frogs and katydids nearly drowned out the distant music of the wedding celebration. Easter breathed in the sweet olive somewhere ahead of them and watched clouds chase each other across the moon.

Shadrach began, his voice low and mournful. "I only really been with one woman, and she was my wife. Her name Thisbe. We loved each other something powerful. But our master, if'n one of his women didn't have a baby after a year with a man, he'd sell her. Just like that."

Easter drew in a sharp breath and turned to look at him, but Shadrach's eyes remained on the moon. This was why the preacher who'd joined Chloe and Cato tonight had asked them to vow "till death or distance do you part." No slave had the power to promise forever.

"After he sold my Thisbe, Master Dickson 'married' me to a widow who'd already had chillun. Cretia liked me well enough, but she didn't *want* me—and she didn't want any more chillun. Cretia didn't care if Master sold her, since he'd already sold her chillun. But Master Dickson heard Cretia and me was living like sister and brother. One night, I came back to our cabin to find Cretia cowering on the bed and Master Dickson smokin' in the corner. Said he'd sit there and watch till I'd 'covered' my woman. 'I ain't your stud horse,' I said. 'That's exactly what you is, boy!' he shouted back.

"Didn't matter how much Master Dickson beat me—I wouldn't obey him. I even struck him back a few times. We was like two gamecocks circling each other. I could see on his face he wanted to kill me, but I was too valuable and he was too greedy. I kept running off till he sold me. I guess maybe I thought I could find Thisbe, if'n the traders took me far enough and I asked enough people. But it's been near seven years, and I ain't even heard word of her."

"But...you always seem happy. You're always joking and flirting."

Shadrach met her eyes in the moonlight. "There's this Gullah proverb my mother taught me: 'If'n you hold onto your mad, it will kill all your glad.' Took me years to realize she was right. If we let our lives stop because of what they done to us, they *win*, Easter. We can't let them win." Shadrach brushed his fingers over the back of Easter's hand where it lay on her lap. "Now, won't you tell me your story?"

Easter turned her face to the ground. "I-I can't." She stood, but she didn't step away. "Verily don't even know it."

Shadrach paused before he spoke. "It was a white man, wasn't it?"

Is, Easter thought—but better to let Shadrach think the white man was in the past. She nodded.

Shadrach stood beside her. "How old were you?"

The tears returned. She couldn't stop them. "Thirteen."

"Oh, Easter." Shadrach touched her cheek. Though his fingers were thick with calluses, his touch was remarkably tender. "He's damned lucky he ain't here right now, that white man. I'd kill him."

Easter stared into his beautiful face, hating the darkness for hiding so much of him. "They'd kill *you*."

"I'd let 'em do it, if it would change what he done to you." Shadrach shook his head. "I know that ain't possible. But I ain't him, Easter. I'll be good to you, if you let me." He squeezed her arm gently just below her shoulder. "Will you think about it?"

Easter nodded but said nothing. She wiped her tears on her sleeve and started back toward her quarters.

Shadrach walked beside her in silence till they passed his black-smith shop. He tilted his head in its direction. "Come inside some-time and I'll show you how I upset iron." He grinned, his teeth flashing white in the moonlight. "I mean it. I'll teach you the parts of an anvil and everything."

Easter couldn't help but smile in return. "Anvils got more than one part?"

"Yes, ma'am! Anvils got faces, shoulders, waists, and feet—just like women. But women is a little bit softer."

In spite of herself, Easter sniggered.

Shadrach stroked his chin thoughtfully. "Leastways, that's how I remember it."

Easter narrowed her eyes. "You talking like you ain't touched a woman in years. You touched me not ten minutes ago."

"That don't count."

"I don't count?"

"'Course you count. But I only touched your face and maybe your shoulder. I ain't touched your waist or your feet at all. I'll let you know about those, soon as you make up your mind."

Now, Easter laughed. He was full of contradictions, this slave who let no man master him. Shadrach was so confident that Easter would say yes—yet when a woman said no, he'd endured beatings instead of forcing her. Shadrach could joke even with pain sunk deep in his bones, and in the space of a few minutes, he could take Easter from despair to joy.

She smiled to herself all the way up the steps of the kitchen house and into her bedroom. From her window, she watched Shadrach saunter back to his cabin.

Easter didn't think of Cromwell again till she started unhooking her dress. Then, she sank onto the edge of the bed and closed her eyes in dread.

CHAPTER 20

St. Joseph, Missouri

Were there a possibility of success, how soon would the pipe of peace be thrown aside, and the yell and whoop of war be heard instead? And who would blame them?

— Mary Eastman, *Dahcotah; or, Life and Legends of the Sioux* (1849)

É sh felt something jab his side and started.

"Wake up, boy," barked Lieutenant Gates. "We're here."

Ésh leaned toward the window to see, but the stagecoach sloshed through a mud hole, jostling his view. "Here?"

The bluecoat replaced his hat. "The ferry landing across from St. Joseph."

Ésh must still be dreaming; he must be having a terrible vision; he could not be seeing what he thought he was seeing out the window. He could only echo: "St. Joseph?"

"It was founded by Papists."

"Papists?"

"What are you, a mockingbird?"

Ésh wished he were a bird—he wished he had wings to carry him far away from here, to carry him back home. Instead, he clutched his parfleche of clothes against his chest and stumbled from the stagecoach, his body sore from so much sitting. But outside the contraption, the view was no different. It was *worse*, because he could see more at once.

Ésh gaped across the curve of muddy river like a discarded fingernail, past the piss-yellow bluffs to the thousands of buildings on the other side. There *must* be thousands, of all shapes and sizes, choking the hills and plains. Most of the buildings looked sturdy and permanent, not sloppy like the stations along the stagecoach trail and nearly all the dwellings at Fort Laramie.

Moving amongst the buildings were hundreds and hundreds of *veho*: walking, riding horses, and driving wagons. Beyond the buildings stretched field after field, most brown and empty now but scraped into ordered rows. In others, cows and horses grazed. The buildings and fields seemed to go on forever.

"This is…" Ésh stammered. "This is always here? It is not a special gathering?"

"This is *nothing*." Gates laughed. "St. Joseph is a *town*. Nine thousand people, last I heard."

There were three times as many *veho* in this one settlement as there were men, women, and children in the entire Zizistas nation.

"This is tiny compared to a city—and sleepy compared to what this place looks and sounds like in the spring, when emigrants are heading out West. Charleston, where you're headed, that's at least four times the size of St. Joseph. There are twenty-five, thirty *million* of us on this continent, boy—and more arriving in the ports every day."

Ésh did not know what "million" meant, but the way Gates said the word, Ésh knew it must be a number even larger than a thousand. He hardly saw the "ferry" that carried them across the river. He was too busy staring at the tall white buildings in the middle of the river, which belched black smoke and *moved*. Gates called them "riverboats." These too were filled with people, but not all of them were *veho*.

When Ésh reached the other side of the water, he saw that one of the riverboats was also disgorging people. After the *veho* stepped off, a group of people with dark skin followed. They were all connected together with chains like the ones Ésh had worn around his ankles at Fort Laramie.

He had heard of black white men. There were women and children too. Most of them kept their eyes on the ground, and *veho* with guns stayed close to them. It was winter now and the air was cold— Ésh had been wearing his buffalo coat for days. But these dark-skinned people were dressed in thin, ragged clothing.

Gates saw Ésh looking at the people. "You've never seen negroes before, have you? You'd better get used to them, boy; you'll be seeing a lot more of them where we're going."

Farther down the riverbank, a group of negro men without chains were loading great bundles onto a second riverboat. Ésh knew the *veho* kept negroes as slaves, but he didn't really understand what that meant. "They are your captives?"

"More or less. Our grandfathers captured their grandfathers and brought them here to serve us."

And generations later, the *veho* still forced these people to serve them? No Zizistas treated captives so cruelly. Instead, they would become part of the tribe, honored like any other Zizistas.

Gates saw Ésh was displeased and chuckled. "If this family of yours still exists, they may own negroes themselves."

Ésh hoped not. "Why do the negroes not run away?"

"Because they can't take care of themselves. Negroes may resemble men, but they're only simple-minded brutes—only beasts of burden."

Zizistas treated beasts better than the *veho* treated these negroes. Beasts were their brothers, fellow creations of Maheo, and they had many things to teach humans. Animals had things to give humans as well, their hides and flesh and bones—but animals *chose* to give themselves to hunters, and hunters never accepted these things without thanking the animals for their sacrifice.

Ésh had heard that the *veho* made slaves of Indians too, even allies of the Zizistas like the Dakota. If his white family had slaves,

Ésh would know at once that they were the worst kind of *veho*: selfish and lazy. He would cease to wonder if he would have been happy with them. He could turn around and never think of them again.

"They completed the rail line from Hannibal last February," Gates declared as if this were important. He seemed to be pointing (with his finger, in the rude way of *veho*) toward puffs of black smoke several buildings away. "Priest-ridden or not, that makes St. Joseph the westernmost outpost of civilization. We'll need to change trains several times and cross a few more rivers by boat, but essentially we can follow those rails all the way across the continent to Charleston."

Gates led Ésh through the paths between buildings, which were filthy with mud, manure, and piss. For once, Ésh was glad he wore thick *veho* shoes instead of his moccasins. He clutched the parfleche full of his proper clothes, the ones his mother had made, tighter against his chest. Finally, they stepped up onto a wooden floor over-flowing with people. Beside it waited a line of small buildings—or maybe long stagecoaches? The tallest of these objects was black and belched black smoke.

At the window in a nearby building, Gates traded coins for colored pieces of paper. Then the bluecoat led Ésh toward the line of stagecoaches. Gates climbed into one of them, but Ésh hesitated. "This is the train," Gates grumbled. "This is how you get to Charleston."

How did it move? As odd as they were, Ésh could understand the stagecoach and the riverboat; one was carried by horses and the other by water. This train had neither, though there seemed to be a metal path underneath it.

The large object at one end of the train, the one that was smok-ing, suddenly let out a shriek. Ésh jumped and nearly dropped his parfleche.

"Fine. I'll leave you here. Makes no difference to me. In fact, it gets me home sooner." Gates disappeared into the train.

Ésh had to find his white family. He sucked in a breath and followed Gates. They crossed through and stepped between the parts of the train, which was already filled with *veho*. Beneath their feet, the wood floor was often stained with a sticky brown liquid. "Tobacco juice," the bluecoat muttered. "You'd better get used to that, too."

Tobacco was for smoking and for offering to the Sacred Powers. These *veho* did nothing right.

Gates found them a place to sit, and Ésh settled uneasily beside the window. Unlike the openings in the sides of the stagecoach, these were covered by glass. Outside, the wind was ruffling skirts and snatching hats. Inside this train, he felt nothing but a slight shudder. It was unnatural.

He was looking for a way to open the window when part of the train shrieked a second time. Then the space around him jerked backward, taking Ésh with it. Here he was again, facing West as they travelled relentlessly East. He hoped his stomach wouldn't react as it had on the stagecoach.

The two *veho* across from him treated the train's churning start with unconcern. They only spit streams of the dark liquid toward a tall metal bowl at their feet. Not all of the tobacco juice made it into the bowl. Ésh drew his feet tighter beneath him and returned his attention to the window.

The glass held his reflection almost like a mirror. Ésh might be wearing a buffalo coat made by his Zizistas mother, and his ears might be pierced six times. But his tanned skin was growing pale in the weak winter sunlight. His eyes were green, and his hair was yellow and short. It was the face of a *veho* staring back at him.

Ésh remembered the badger's prophecy. The part that had already come true: his hair had been cut, by the doctor at Fort Laramie. The part that had yet to happen: he would die before his hair grew long again.

He must be brave. He must tolerate the sights and sounds and smells of his enemies. He must learn about these *veho* contraptions. He must learn where he had come from.

DAY BY DAY, train by train, city by city, Ésh learned what millions of *veho* meant. He saw no buffalo or antelope or elk. The only horses were saddled or tied to wagons or trapped inside fences. In the *veho* lands, so much of the Earth looked bare and rutted like the wide path of the overland trail. Through the train windows, Ésh watched more buildings and people slip past him than he could count in a lifetime.

Long ago, the prophet Sweet Medicine had warned the Zizistas about these *veho*. He had described their strange clothing and the hair on their faces. Sweet Medicine said they would bring wonderful things, like mirrors and sugar. But the Zizistas should not take these gifts, because the *veho* would bring terrible things too, like drunkenness and sickness. Sweet Medicine had seen what would happen if the Zizistas did not heed his warnings: the *veho* would keep coming. They would never stop, and the People would die.

Ésh had heard the Sweet Medicine stories all his life, and still he had not believed that the *veho* were different from any other enemy. Not until their power swallowed him. Not until he saw their numbers with his own eyes.

In many places, there were more negroes than *veho*. But they were always serving the *veho* or going where the *veho* wanted them to go. The negroes walked along paths chained together. They rode on the same trains as Ésh and Gates, but at the end with the baggage. The negroes built new paths. They moved the dirt around in fields. They pulled out tree stumps. They built fences.

The *veho* loved fences, and they loved to yell at the negroes while they watched them work. In one field, a *veho* was beating a negro man tied to a post till blood flowed from his back. Two negro women watched, clutching one another and sobbing. The man's mother and wife? Ésh could not hear their cries, but he felt their agony just the same. He wanted to leap from the train and strike down the *veho*. He wanted to shout to the negro man and the women: *Run!*

But where could they run that no *veho* would find them? Numbers did not make you right, but they did make you strong. One day, would the *veho* force the Zizistas to serve them, to cower before them like this?

Millions of *veho* meant the Zizistas could not win. There would always, always be more *veho* to fight. Somehow, the Zizistas must learn how to live beside the *veho* without losing their lives, without losing everything that mattered.

Ésh must help the People, but he knew he could accomplish nothing alone. Too much about these *veho* remained a mystery to him. He could not even read their signs or their books. He needed *veho* allies, if such a thing was possible. Gates was not an ally, Ésh knew. But maybe Ésh's *veho* family could be, or the girl he had seen in his dreams. He wanted her more than ever. He wanted her to make him forget, if only for a little while. He hoped she had not given up on him, that she was waiting for him even now.

CHAPTER 21

STRATFORD-ON-ASHLEY PLANTATION
CHARLESTON, SOUTH CAROLINA

All married women, all children, and girls who live on in their
father's houses are slaves.
— Mary Boykin Chesnut, Diary (February 25, 1865)

Seated in front of her dressing table, Clare gazed down at the
small ceramic jar of lip coloring in her hand. She was contem-
plating smearing it all over her face and going down to greet Mr.
Percival Arrington like that as if nothing were amiss. The thought
alone made a smile tug at her lips for the first time that morning.
Would mussing her coiffure enhance or undermine the effect?

Clare would love to see the look on Mr. Arrington's face at such
a display, but most of all she wanted to witness Aunt Hortense's
reaction. Her aunt had been so sure Clare's "shameful behavior" at
the Mardi Gras ball would scare away all her suitors—but that was
precisely what Clare wanted.

It was true that Clare had had fewer callers since Mardi Gras,
but a handful remained persistent. Her father's plantations were too

great a temptation. Clare knew *those* were what the young men really wanted, not her. She wanted none of them. And the thought of having any of those men do to her the thing that hurt, the thing that made children possible...

Most of her suitors made her skin crawl. When they bent to kiss her glove, she could hear it in the sugary tones of their voices, see it behind their simpering expressions: they were thinking about doing *the thing*. Even with Aunt Hortense there as chaperone, they held Clare's hand too long and sat too close. And the casual way they spoke about disciplining slaves...

Other suitors, like Mr. Arrington, were not horrible. They might make some girl happy. But that girl was not Clare. The longer she was forced to converse with them, the more they bored and irritated her. They had only a handful of mildly interesting things to say, and by their second visit, they would be repeating themselves, while Clare gritted her teeth and pretended to be entertained.

If Clare married one of these men—a man she did not love, a man like her father—she would end up as miserable as her mother. Clare could become mistress of Stratford-on-Ashley and strive to ease the lives of the slaves—but what power would she really have? She was only a woman. Her husband would make every decision. She would be his property, too.

David didn't want her father's plantations. He could be a doctor anywhere. She didn't want to be a Charleston lady, planning teas and balls. She wanted to roam the woods. She wanted to keep caterpillars and reptiles. David wouldn't mind her pets. He encouraged her love of crawling, scampering things. He understood who she really was and loved her for herself.

David would come to his senses eventually. For nine excruciating months, Clare had dragged herself through the motions of propriety and politeness, only pretending to consider other men. The pretending stopped *now*.

"Verily, help me out of this dress."

Her friend looked up from the newspaper she was reading. "But I thought Mr. Arrington was—"

"I shan't be accepting Mr. Arrington's suit or anyone else's!"

Clare untied one of her embroidered undersleeves and tossed it on her dressing table.

"Are you certain, Miss?" Verily asked, moving behind her.

"Absolutely! Perhaps I'll go North and live with Uncle Liam and become an abolitionist like those scandalous Grimké sisters! You could come with me!"

Verily's fingers paused on the hooks at the back of Clare's bodice. "What about my sister?"

Clare frowned. She'd forgotten about Easter. Father might give her *one* servant... She discarded her lace collar and shrugged. "It was only a fancy."

Uncle Liam and Mama's other brothers in New York City already had a score of children and their aging mother to support, Clare knew. Would she be a help to them, or only a burden? Clare couldn't imagine having to live in some cramped tenement. The only animals she'd see would be cockroaches and rats.

Perhaps Clare could join the Sisters of Our Lady of Mercy right here in Charleston. As a postulant, she could teach and nurse. Clare could prove to David that she'd make a good doctor's wife, and it would be months and months before the Sisters would expect her to take final vows. By then, David would realize how much he needed her.

Verily had finished unhooking Clare's bodice. Clare pulled it off and stood up from her chair so her friend could undo her pink skirt. As soon as it was over Clare's head, Aunt Hortense rapped on the door.

"Clare! Mr. Arrington is waiting!"

"I'm not coming."

"Pardon?"

"I'm not coming," Clare repeated with more emphasis while she unbuttoned her corset cover. "Tell him I am indisposed; tell him whatever you like." Verily was helping Clare shed her petticoats. "I shall write him a letter and make my apologies, but I am not doing this anymore!"

Aunt Hortense flung open the door to find Clare standing in her corset and crinoline. "What in Heaven's—" she spluttered. "What do you mean, you are 'not doing this anymore'?"

"Courting. I will not sit in that parlor and pretend to be interested in those men any longer." With Verily's assistance, the cage crinoline collapsed at Clare's feet. "From now on, I will accept callers only if their last name is Lazare." Clare stepped out of her crinoline.

Aunt Hortense threw the door closed behind her and stormed across Clare's bedchamber. "How many times must I tell you, girl: David Lazare made his choice." Clare drew in a breath to argue, but Aunt Hortense plowed on: "It's been *nine months* since the Mardi Gras ball. Has Mr. Lazare contacted you even once?"

"No, but—"

"He has forgotten you, Clare. You must forget him, or you will die an old maid."

"Then I'll die an old maid!" Clare plucked out hairpins and tossed them on her dressing table, letting her hair tumble across her shoulders and down her back. "Or I'll become a nun!"

That vein in her aunt's temple was throbbing. "You cannot do this to your father! You are all he has! You know how much this plantation means to him!"

"Then I'm *not* all he has, am I?" At the edge of her vision, Clare saw Verily attempting to conceal a smile.

"You are his one and only heir!" Aunt Hortense shot back.

"He has Mr. Cromwell."

"Mr. Cromwell is not your father's flesh and blood. *You* are the only one who can give your father grandchildren. Would you send him comfortless to his grave?"

Without waiting for Verily to loosen the laces, Clare unhooked the front of her corset. "I will not marry a man I do not love!"

"Cease this romantic poppycock, Clare! You are no longer a child! You were born to wealth and privilege. With that comes the responsibility to—"

"I don't want it!" Clare let Verily take her corset. "I don't want any of it!" Clare flung open her wardrobe.

"You don't want your pretty clothes?" Aunt Hortense motioned toward all the linen and silk. "You don't want a fine meal three times every day?"

Clare snatched up her blue and gold wrapper—Mama's blue-and-gold wrapper—and pushed her arms into the sleeves. "They didn't make my mother happy, did they?"

"Your mother was an ungrateful harlot who got what she deserved."

Clare sucked in a breath, and her hands clenched so tightly, her fingernails shot pain into her palms. She wanted to strike her aunt.

"You will dress and come down to the parlor and converse with Mr. Arrington like a proper young lady, or you will not eat."

Clare tied the sash of the wrapper with finality. "Then I shall starve."

FORTUNATELY, HER FATHER DISAGREED about allowing Clare to eat. "She's sixteen," he soothed his sister over their turtle soup. "Why rush?"

Aunt Hortense only glared at both of them.

After dinner, Clare retreated to the library, hoping to find a romantic novel to cheer her and to spite her aunt. Perhaps she would revisit *Pride and Prejudice*, which proved a man could be a blockhead and yet realize the error of his ways.

As Clare stepped over the threshold, she smiled at the familiar gilded leather spines lined up so neatly in the polished mahogany bookcases—each a world waiting to be discovered, each rendered luminous by the late afternoon sunlight streaming through the windows. Then she realized that someone else had come to peruse the library's treasures. "Good afternoon, Mr. Cromwell."

"Good afternoon, Miss Stratford." His voice was amiable, but he did not look up from his book. Her father's steward sat in one of the red wing chairs, where David had sat so often. This wasn't the first time Clare had happened upon Mr. Cromwell in the library. She peered surreptitiously at the spine of his book. *The Prince*, it said. Had he come in search of a romantic novel as well?

Clare strolled to Miss Austen's shelf. But as she reached for the first volume of *Pride and Prejudice*, Mr. Cromwell spoke again:

"Did you know Verily can read?"

Clare's hand froze, and she nearly forgot to breathe. She dared not look around at him, or Mr. Cromwell would read the guilt on her face. The hairs at the nape of her neck tingled with fear. "P-Pardon?"

For teaching a slave to read, not only could Clare be fined a hundred dollars, she would go to prison. From the Lazares' upper piazza, you could see the District Jail. It was a looming, terrifying place, the tops of its walls like gaping teeth. The Jail was something out of a Gothic novel—but it was *real*. And for sending her there, Mr. Cromwell could collect fifty dollars. Did her father pay him that much in an entire month?

"I spied her teaching the new blacksmith how to spell his name with soot," Mr. Cromwell continued calmly. "And while you were away at Barhamville, books kept disappearing from the library and then reappearing."

Verily would face worse than prison. She would be whipped. Could she even survive fifty lashes? What else might Clare's father do to her? He'd said once that a literate slave was a ruined slave. A literate slave would start to get *ideas*. She could write her own passes and leave the plantation whenever she wished. Clare's father might *sell* Verily. She would never see her sister again. Clare gripped one of the bookshelves and closed her eyes as the gravity of what she had done seeped like lead into her bones.

"I do hope Verily's teacher will instruct her to be more careful in future."

Clare released the terror from her lungs and slumped forward, bracing her forehead against the back of her hand. "Th—" She almost said *"Thank you,"* but caution told her this was too close to confession. "That is wise advice," she amended.

Clare wanted to snatch up *Pride and Prejudice* and race from the room; but this too would announce her guilt. Mr. Cromwell had spoken as if he already knew Clare was to blame, but she must *admit* nothing. She swallowed and forced herself to browse the shelves a few minutes before claiming the three volumes of her novel.

When she turned back toward Mr. Cromwell, she saw his eyes remained on his book. But as she passed beside him, he said: "I hear you might take the veil." His tone remained nonchalant, as if their previous exchange had never happened.

Clare raised her chin and attempted to match his serenity. "I might."

He glanced up, but it was only a glance. "That would truly be a loss to mankind. But I do not blame you in the slightest for rejecting those insipid suitors. A woman like you must find a man worthy of her."

Clare's body felt weak again. The three volumes of *Pride and Prejudice* nearly tumbled from her arms. "A w-woman like me?"

"A kind heart, a quick mind, a beautiful face—you possess it all, Miss Stratford." Mr. Cromwell closed his book, stood, and met her gaze with his intense grey-blue eyes. His demeanor radiated sincerity without a trace of fawning. "Don't suffer any man who sees you only as a means to an end, who won't cherish everything you are and everything you can become." He strode away without another word.

Her heart racing, Clare collapsed onto the wing chair he had vacated, her books spilling onto her skirt. Her cage crinoline and corset separated her from the chair seat; but when she placed her hand against the arm, she could feel the warmth of Mr. Cromwell's body lingering in the red brocade.

Mr. Cromwell had been in her father's employ since she was seven years old. But that was all he'd ever been to Clare: her father's secretary, then his steward. She'd never thought of Mr. Cromwell as a *man*. Not until now.

When she tried to read *Pride and Prejudice*, each time Mr. Darcy spoke, she heard Mr. Cromwell's voice.

THAT EVENING, MR. CROMWELL JOINED THEM for supper, as he often did. Clare tried very hard not to stare at him, but she failed miserably. He felt her staring, because amusement quirked his lips. More than once, Mr. Cromwell caught her gaze, and his smile became conspiratorial. His eyes, like a troubled sea, more grey than blue, sparked with invitation and mischief.

Neither her father nor her aunt noticed these exchanges. But Clare's cheeks flamed with nervous delight.

Why had she never noticed how handsome Mr. Cromwell was? He might have been a sculptor's model for Apollo. Refined yet thoroughly masculine. His dark blond hair was the color of cool wet sand, always tidy yet always carefree. Mr. Cromwell's elegant side whiskers also fit him perfectly. They framed his face to the corner of his jaw, then grew thinner and pointed toward those playful lips.

Though it made Clare feel disloyal to her Irish mother, Mr. Cromwell's English accent thrilled her—so crisp and confident. He was a fine dancer and an even better equestrian. Mr. Cromwell seemed to *belong* on a dance floor and in a saddle. He even rode a white horse like the knights in tales of chivalry.

Mr. Cromwell was at least as intelligent as David, maybe more so. When she'd discussed literature at the dining table, Mr. Cromwell had proven discerning and perceptive. He was a reader like Clare. His vocabulary was astounding; he understood the power and the magic in words.

Mr. Cromwell had always been kind to Clare and to Verily, but keeping the secret of Verily's lessons went beyond kindness. It was rebellion. He knew slaves had minds as hungry as his own and did not condemn them for it.

Unlike Clare's other suitors, Mr. Cromwell was not a Carolinian. He was not tied to this land. He could take her to see Paris or Rome —perhaps they could even live abroad. If David truly didn't want her, perhaps the answer to all her problems had been *here* all along.

IN BED THAT NIGHT, Clare tossed and turned. The day after tomorrow was the eighth anniversary of her mother's death. Mama had disliked Mr. Cromwell, Clare remembered. Had her mother only been prejudiced against him because of his accent and his name?

At dawn, Clare pulled on Mama's blue-and-gold wrapper again. She was careful not to wake Verily, who slumbered on her trundle-bed. Clare hurried down the back stairs that had taken her mother's life.

The moment she stepped onto the grass, her slippers began to collect dew. Mist transformed the back garden into a labyrinth, concealing what lay around the next bend in the hedges. But Clare had learned the way to her mother's tomb long ago.

The fragrance of unseen sweet olives lured her on. Roses lingered and camellias burst into bloom. Beauty berries, daylilies, and snapdragons greeted her too. Hanging, it seemed, from every bush, draping every flower, were spider webs and strands of their silk, bejewelled with dew that threatened to break their delicate weave. Spanish moss swayed like ghostly fingers gesturing toward the cemetery gates.

Someone had left the entrance ajar. Even here, a spider had been at work: a web dangled in the gap between the two gates. Clare might admire their artistry, but spiders were one of the few creatures she preferred to avoid. She saw no evidence of the web-spinner, so she pushed the gates wider, snapping the dewy strands. They fluttered in the air for a moment, then floated down, limp and useless, against the loops and curls of iron.

A pale gibbous moon sunk over her mother's white tomb, which was slowly turning grey. Clare had always liked the Egyptian embellishments, from the cavetto cornices to the columns that resembled bundles of papyrus stems, palm leaves, and lotus blos-soms. The Egyptian elements might be exotic and pagan, but they set Mama apart, a permanent declaration that she did not belong here.

The gates of her tomb were always locked. Clare had made the mistake of asking her father for the key while Aunt Hortense was present, and her aunt had dissuaded him. But Mr. Cromwell had been present too. "I'll make you a copy," he'd whispered to Clare, and he'd been as good as his word. Clare wondered if this kindness would have softened her mother's opinion of him.

Clare unlocked the gates and started down the steep staircase. The sun had yet to reach here; she realized she should have brought a lantern. Instead, she proceeded slowly, bracing one hand against the cool marble wall. Little by little, her eyes adjusted to the faint light.

Ahead in the gloom, the white angel took shape, mourning over her mother's sarcophagus. In the far wall, the Blessed Virgin stood in her niche, flanked by inverted torches that promised eternal life but offered no light. Clare padded around the sarcophagus and groped for the box of lucifer matches behind the little statue. She found the sandpaper and struck a match once, twice, thrice before the end ignited. She touched it to a votive candle and let the match die.

As if her mother lay inside and not beneath the floor, Clare placed a hand on the cool sarcophagus. Her fingertips traced the inscription, the letters of her mother's name. "I don't know what to do, Mama. I was so certain David was my future, but... Is it Mr. Cromwell? Will *he* take me away from here? I don't want to leave you, Mama, but— I don't *belong* here. I don't know how much longer I can bear all this pretending. Should I join the Sisters of Our Lady of Mercy? Should I wait for David?"

In the silence, one word seemed to echo back to her: *Wait...*

"How much longer, Mama? What—who—am I waiting for?"

The tomb only tossed the word back again: *Wait...* Clare's ears must be playing tricks on her.

"Will I ever be happy, Mama?" she wept. "Will I ever escape this place?"

This time, there was no answer.

Desolate, Clare returned to her bedchamber.

Verily was awake. "I suppose you'd better return this to the library for me, Miss," she sighed, holding out a book. Last night, Clare had told her friend about Mr. Cromwell's revelation and reminded her of the need for secrecy—for both their sakes.

Clare saw that Verily had been reading Alfred Tennyson's *Maud, and Other Poems*. "Did you enjoy it?"

"Very much!" her friend whispered back. "I can see why you like him."

Clare smiled. "Which verses were your favorites?"

Verily found the page and showed her. "This part here. The rhythms mesmerize me, and the words are so romantic!"

While her friend did up her hair, Clare reread the part of *Maud* that Verily had chosen. The desperation in the words, the Language of Flowers—the more Clare read, the more the words seemed a message from her mother. The poem's narrator was a man, but by the penultimate stanza, Clare had flipped the gender; not "She is coming" but "*He* is coming." It sounded like a promise:

He is coming, my life, my fate;
The red rose cries, "He is near, he is near;"
And the white rose weeps, "He is late;"
The larkspur listens, "I hear, I hear;"
And the lily whispers, "I wait."

Clare closed her eyes and echoed: "I hear, I hear... I wait."

CHAPTER 22

I believe that the white race are special favorites with our Heavenly Father; that he made the negro for their benefit, just as much as I believe that he made for our use the horse, the cow, or the sheep... Freedom, amongst negroes, is just as useless as razors amongst children.

— Mary Herndon, *Louise Elton* (1853)

Easter decided Shadrach was worth the risk. Cromwell had never actually forbidden her to take up with another man. As long as she obeyed when Cromwell wanted her, what did he care who she spent time with? For almost six years, her body had been his alone. Cromwell owed her this. He owed her a great deal more, but she would take this.

She began visiting Shadrach as often as she could. With him frequently hired out to other plantations and her endless duties in the kitchen, this wasn't often at all. But it was often enough to live on. When Phoebe figured out where Easter was going, she teased her but also released her from the kitchen as soon as possible each evening.

At first, Easter wanted to keep her fondness for Shadrach, and his for her, a secret. She knew in her gut that the news would make Cromwell angry. But she soon realized that secrecy was impossible. It made no sense to Shadrach, who wanted to shout her name from the roof of the Big House. He didn't understand that the white man who'd abused her was still abusing her, that the man passed his smithy nearly every day. Easter had told Shadrach about her family, about the journey from Virginia—about everything but Cromwell. Shadrach asked if it was a slave trader who'd raped her, and she let him believe it.

She and Shadrach were rarely alone. He lived in a cabin with three other unmarried men, who often came and went in the evenings when Easter was free to see Shadrach. Meeting him in her own room made Easter nervous, with the bed gaping at her like a promise she wasn't sure she could keep. So she usually came to his smithy, where young Cudjo helped tidy the place and served as Shadrach's striker. Easter thought of Cudjo as young, though he was her own age. But she felt older than nineteen, closer to Shadrach's twenty-seven.

Shadrach usually had visitors. After they'd finished their tasks for the day, the men often gathered at the smithy to discuss the latest news, like Mr. Brown's raid on Harper's Ferry in Virginia. The plantation's youngest boys, the ones who had few duties yet, hurried to watch Shadrach work whenever they could.

The plantation's girls also came to admire the blacksmith. Even after Shadrach made it clear that he'd chosen Easter, they lingered and giggled and sighed, tossing her envious glances. Verily too had pouted for a full week, but finally she began to treat Shadrach like the brother they'd lost.

Something about the shower of sparks and the alchemy of smithing mesmerized them all. Shadrach took iron, one of the hardest things on Earth, turned it as soft as clay, molded it however he wished, and then rendered it strong again. He might be a slave, but he was also a god. A negro wielding such power was a sight to behold. One could almost believe Shadrach did the work for his own pleasure.

It had been years since Master Edward had had his own blacksmith. He'd been ordering parts from Charleston, sending out his repairs, or hiring smiths from neighbors. Ironically, it was Cromwell who'd convinced him to purchase a blacksmith again, arguing that Shadrach would earn back his price in a few years' time, since they could hire *him* out to neighbors.

After Shadrach labored from dawn to dusk forging iron for another white man, he would have to surrender his wages to Cromwell, who always knew the promised amount. To show his generosity, Master Edward would always have Cromwell return a few coins to Shadrach. The myth of Shadrach's power would shatter, until he picked up his hammer again the next morning.

As he worked, Shadrach told Easter about his grandmother, who'd lived in Africa till she was Easter's age and survived the terrible passage. Shadrach told Easter what it was like when he'd run away from his old master for a few days. He explained his leather apron, his bellows, his forge, his slack tub, and all the parts of his anvil.

She saw in his face how much he longed to explore *her* parts. But every time Shadrach drew her close, she still tensed while memories assaulted her, memories of terror and pain that would not let her go.

"It's all right, baby," Shadrach would whisper. "You take your time finding your way to me. I ain't going to pretend slow is easy, but nothing good ever is. Waiting ain't going to kill me."

Easter could not bear to ask: *"What if I'm NEVER ready?"*

Even in the kitchen, wherever she was on the plantation, Easter would hear the voice of Shadrach's hammer ringing out strong and true. It seemed like an echo of his own steady heartbeat, like he was calling out to her: *I love you. I'll wait for you.*

ON SUNDAYS, she and Shadrach snuck into the carriage house so they could be alone. Finis, the old coachman, always saw them enter, but he was their ally. Finis treated the coaches as if they were animals in his care, and Shadrach's skill at repairing their undercarriages met with his approval. Finis asked only that Easter and

Shadrach's clothes be free of grease and soot before they climbed inside any of Master Edward's fancy carriages. Finis did not want the Master asking about mysterious new stains on the upholstery.

One day, just before Easter and Shadrach darted into the carriage house, the honking of geese drew their eyes upward to a great arrow of birds in the sky.

"Looks like they going North," Shadrach murmured. "They don't have to ask anyone; they just pick up and go. They is free."

In the safety of the Master's blue brougham, Shadrach said: "You know, there's free colored people in Charleston ride around in carriages as fancy as this one. Even more in the North and in Canada. You ever think about it? Being free?"

Easter stared out the front window of the brougham at the empty driver's seat. Her eyes took in the call bell and all the fittings of the plush cream interior. The little mirror that folded open. The holders for a cane, a parasol, a fan, and calling cards. She could not imagine *belonging* inside such a carriage. But ever since she'd met Shadrach, and ever since she'd heard about John Brown... "I think about it almost every day."

"What would you do, if you was free? Would you want to be a cook?"

"I enjoy cooking for people I love." Sometimes she brought sweet potatoes to Shadrach's smithy and baked them in the coals of his forge. Nothing had ever tasted as good as those potatoes. "But I wouldn't want to cook in another person's house or in some kind of hotel for the rest of my life. Sewing—that's different. That lasts." She ran her fingers over the brougham's gold-and-blue embroidered window pull. "If I were free, I'd want to be a—what they call it—a *modiste*. Make *fine* clothing for free colored ladies. Find the fabrics and the styles that make each woman really see herself for the first time. Make her proud of herself. That's what I'd do, if I were free." She looked back to Shadrach. "If you could choose, would you still be a blacksmith?"

He nodded. "The men in my family have worked iron for hundreds of years—long before we was slaves."

"There are blacksmiths in Africa?"

"'Course there are. They important men there. My father wanted me to be one too—that why he named me Shadrach. He was going to name my brothers Meshach and Abednego—but turned out, I was his only son. I'd still be a blacksmith, all right, but I'd do more than this repairing of plows and hoes." He motioned dismissively in the direction of his smithy. "A man can't find much satisfaction in that kind of work, not if that's all he does. You ever take a real good look at the gates of this plantation?"

Easter thought of the gates on Miss Teresa's tomb, and she tried not to shudder. But those were cast iron, made in a factory.

"Ain't they something?" Shadrach continued. "And they're simple compared to some of the fences and gates in Charleston! *That's* what I want to do. Something that makes people stop and stare, it's so beautiful. Something that didn't exist till I dreamed it and drew it out of the iron." He spoke with his hands, gesturing with such passion that the brougham trembled in place. "I want to create something so fine and so strong, people will still be using it a hundred years from now. And I want to train every boy that comes to me how to work iron, so he can make whatever *he* want to make."

Easter's smile mirrored his till she realized: "You want a son."

Shadrach's arms sagged, and his face fell. "I do. But there ain't no hurry, Easter."

She drew in a breath and forced her lips back into a smile. "Let's get one thing straight right now: I ain't fond of the names Meshach *or* Abednego."

Shadrach chuckled. "Fair enough!"

ONE SATURDAY, she helped Shadrach shoe a horse by handing him tools while Titus, one of the grooms, held its lead rope. Their horse nickered in greeting, and another animal snorted in response. Easter looked up to see Cromwell seated on his white gelding at the edge of the smithy yard, his jaw clenched and his eyes narrowed in a scowl. He *knew*.

Shadrach remained intent on his work and did not raise his eyes till Cromwell had disappeared into the trees.

As soon as Easter left Shadrach, Cromwell intercepted her and demanded she meet him in the tomb that evening. He was rougher with her than he'd been in years, in such haste he forgot the pessary —and he still didn't seem satisfied.

But Cromwell said nothing about Shadrach, and he did not threaten Verily. He spoke only six words to Easter: "Shut up!" when she tried to remind him about the pessary, and "Don't forget the syringe" as he was leaving.

As she injected the vinegar, Easter worried that Cromwell would press Master Edward to sell Shadrach. She worried that Shadrach would learn the truth about Cromwell; that Shadrach would kill him; and that Master Edward would hang Shadrach.

Instead, the next time Master Edward hired Shadrach out, Cromwell took his wages and gave him nothing back. Easter wondered if Cromwell had convinced Master Edward to keep all of Shadrach's wages, or if Cromwell was pocketing the difference himself.

Shadrach fumed about it to Easter. "It's like they're striking me 'cross the face, handing me dimes like I'm a child, when I'se the one done all the work. But that's the only money I got, to save up or to buy something nice for you..."

"I don't need anything but you," Easter assured him.

So Shadrach *made* her a Christmas gift. With his most delicate tools, he forged a pendant that to Easter looked like an elaborate heart made of scroll-work.

"The buckra will think it's only a heart, if they see you wearing it," Shadrach winked. He called the pendant a *sankofa*. He said it was a symbol from his grandmother's people, the Akan. It meant: *Learn from the past so you can change the future.*

"What are we learning?" Easter asked him.

"Right now, it means: we've all lost someone." Shadrach knew Christmas was difficult for Easter; it reminded her of the jail yard in Charleston and the last time she'd seen Pompey and Mama. "We got to remember them—but in order to make us stronger, not to break us. It means we got to hold on tight to what we got."

Easter wore the *sankofa* proudly, though she was careful not to let Cromwell see it.

"I can make you a ring too," Shadrach suggested. "Wouldn't be gold, but…"

Easter swallowed. "You mean, a wedding ring?"

"I do." Shadrach grinned. "Whenever you're ready, *I do*."

She wanted to marry him. Of course she did. But… "Not yet." Easter closed her eyes so she wouldn't see the disappointment on his face. "Not until I know I can be a true wife to you."

Shadrach only repeated: "Whenever you're ready, Easter."

ANOTHER DAY in the privacy of the brougham, he let her see the hideous mass of scars on his back. His repeated punishments for running away, for refusing to be the master's stud—and for refusing to make shackles. He'd rather be whipped himself than forge something that would keep another man a slave.

"Master Dickson wasn't the last to beat me," Shadrach muttered. "One of the overseers liked to say: 'Ain't no feeling in a nigger's hide.' If I screamed, he'd say I was faking it. After he whipped me, he'd grind red pepper in the wounds, just to make sure they'd hurt."

Easter shuddered. Yet she wished she could have been there with him, to soothe Shadrach's lacerated back and distract his mind. She touched the ugly ridges on his beautiful flesh, then kissed the perfection of his shoulder.

His chest was flawless too, hard as his iron and yet fluid, shifting with each little movement. Dark as midnight and more vital to her than her next breath. She loved this man. More importantly, she *wanted* him. She wanted to give him a hundred hours of pleasure for every hour of pain he'd endured. She still didn't know how long it would take to conquer the terror lodged deep inside her, but the more time she spent with Shadrach, the more certain Easter became: together, they would defeat it. She kissed his shoulder a second time like a promise she intended to keep.

He sat there watching her admire him, grinning his lopsided grin. "What you thinking?"

Easter blushed. "That it don't matter what they done to you: you are the most beautiful man I've ever seen."

"*I'm* thinking: I wish she'd kiss my mouth instead of my shoulder."

Easter sat back a little. She avoided his eyes and admitted: "I-I don't know how. I've never…"

Shadrach sounded surprised, but not disappointed. "You *never* been kissed?"

Easter shook her head. It wasn't something Cromwell had ever wanted.

Shadrach stroked her hand. "Would you let me teach you?"

Easter caught the inside of her lip between her teeth, then looked back at him. "Just kissing?" She might *want* more; she might be nearly ready; but she did not want their first time to be inside a carriage, no matter how fancy.

"Today, just kissing," Shadrach agreed.

Easter nodded her permission. He held her gaze and placed his gentle, callused hand against the side of her face. He brought his mouth to hers and closed his eyes. She closed hers too. She felt his warm breath, then the brush of his lips, startling and soothing all at once. She wasn't sure what to do, so she remained still. Caressing her cheek with his thumb, Shadrach kissed her lightly once, twice, three times—then pulled back.

"How you feeling?" he whispered.

"F-Fine," Easter stammered, her eyes fluttering open. Was that it?

"You don't sound sure."

She watched his lips, so close and yet so far. "I feel pretty good."

"Only 'pretty good'? You a tough woman to please."

"I ain't! But…"

Shadrach grinned. He must have noticed how she was staring at his lips. "Don't worry. I ain't finished yet." He brought his warm mouth against hers again. This time, Easter opened her lips. As their kiss deepened, fear fled and happiness overtook her. How could this one point of contact send sensation flooding all the way to her toes?

Yet it wasn't enough. She pulled him closer, one hand gripping his shoulder and the other sliding downward to feel his heart racing beneath her palm. Shadrach groaned but didn't stop kissing her.

Then they both jumped at a sharp knocking on the window behind Shadrach. They gasped and broke apart to see Finis standing just outside the brougham, though he was looking toward the carriage house entrance. "Master's coming!" He glanced inside and glowered. Easter realized that from the coachman's angle, it must look doubtful that Shadrach was wearing anything at all. "You best not be getting no *substances* on my seats," Finis scolded them, striding back to the front of the carriage house.

Shadrach pulled his shirt on, and he and Easter scrambled from the brougham, smothering their laughter as they fled. They climbed through the back window of the carriage house, where she embraced him tightly—and realized Shadrach's body was eager to do more than kissing.

She tensed instinctively. He started to speak, probably to apologize, but she wouldn't let him. Easter touched his face and promised: "Soon."

CHAPTER 23

We drove past a white man, who (as is common in Charleston) was correcting his negro in the street. The poor fellow was writhing under the cruel infliction of a flagellation... My companion, fearing lest the sight might provoke in me some exclamation, nudged me violently with his elbow, saying at the same time, hurriedly, "Don't heed, don't heed."
— John Benwell, *An Englishman's Travels in America* (1853)

É sh began to think he would spend the rest of his life on a train. He and Gates even ate and slept on the "cars"—or at least, Gates ate and slept. Ésh only attempted to do so. There was a place to relieve yourself on a train, but nowhere to bathe. Ésh couldn't be certain, but he thought the other "passengers" stank even worse than he did.

He tried to sit by windows and keep them open, but this allowed smoke to blow in. Gates and the other passengers also complained about the cold. It was mild compared to winters on the prairie. They must be in the Big Freezing Moon now, and there wasn't even any snow here.

At last, Gates announced that they had reached Charleston. Ésh staggered from the train. He saw very little; his eyes and his head ached. Gates found them a "cab" which took them to a "boarding house."

There, Ésh collapsed, even though it wasn't dark yet. Since he disliked *veho* beds, he dragged a blanket onto the floor. Exhausted as he was, throughout the evening and night, the strange sounds of this place kept waking him.

IN THE MORNING, Ésh remained weary, but the thought of washing roused him. The *veho* idea of a bath involved very little water, however. They spread a slick cloth on the floor under a large bowl, and they wet themselves from two smaller bowls in a "washstand." No wonder the *veho* smelled. Ésh did the best he could. At least he was able to shave.

Much as he hated it, he continued to wear *veho* clothing. At Fort Laramie, Dr. Johns had given him two sets. While Ésh was resting, Gates had had their spare clothes cleaned. That was something.

Ésh wore his medicine pouch under his shirt. He tucked the rabbit skin with his *veho* family's names into a pocket. He left his buffalo coat at the boarding house. The weather was cool but not cold, and he had noticed that the farther East he travelled, the more people stared at him in the coat. Ésh preferred to watch these *veho* without their watching him.

When he ventured outside with Gates, Ésh saw that there were as many negroes in Charleston as there were *veho*—maybe more. Some of the negroes were dressed in plain clothing, and some wore fine coats. But even these did not make the *veho* respect them.

Across the street, through a line of sad little trees, Ésh saw a young negro boy in a fine coat, hardly older than his brother Tahpeno. The boy was hunched up, cowering and whimpering while a *veho* beat him with a stick and yelled at him. Ésh stopped and stared. Other *veho* passed the man and boy, most only glancing at them and hurrying by. Some acted irritated—but at the *boy*. A pair of *veho* actually laughed as they walked by.

Ésh didn't care how tired he was or how many horses were

crossing in front of him; he could not stand by and do nothing like these *veho*. He stepped down into the street, but Gates grabbed his arm. Ésh glared over his shoulder and tried to pull away. That he could not do so proved how weary he still was.

Gates held him firm and growled: "You won't last long in Charleston if you try to interfere with a man disciplining his own property, boy."

Ésh looked back across the street. Finally the *veho*'s rage seemed to be spent. He lowered his stick and strode away from the young negro. Slowly, the boy straightened himself. Blood ran down the side of his head. He pulled a small white cloth from his pocket and held it to the wound. He trembled. The *veho* looked back and barked at him to hurry up. The boy followed the *veho* until Ésh lost sight of them.

Reluctantly, Ésh returned to his own path alongside the street and followed Gates to their destination. He called it "the post office," but he also called it "the Exchange." It was a large and important-looking building, with tall windows. Around these and the three doors, it was white, but most of the walls were the color of deerskin. They climbed steps to a platform at the center and entered one of the white doors.

Inside, Ésh found a place to sit down. He hadn't slept through the night since they'd left Fort Laramie. He hadn't slept well since he'd left the Zizistas.

Gates scowled at him but approached a young *veho* behind a barrier of wood. Gates introduced himself, then said: "That young man is Mr. McAllister. He is seeking his family. They've been separated for a long time. Has a David or a Sophie McAllister ever picked up mail here?"

"Not to my knowledge," answered the young *veho*. "But let me see if Mr. Huger is available. He's been postmaster here since before I was born." He asked another young *veho* to "watch the desk" and disappeared into another part of the building.

While he and Gates waited, Ésh pushed himself to his feet and walked to the tall windows at the back of the building. He'd seen something outside that he'd taken for a forest of bare trees, yet the forest was shifting. Now, he could see that these "trees" sprouted from enormous boats, which floated on a wide expanse of water.

"That's the Cooper River joining the Atlantic Ocean," Gates informed him.

Ésh watched the great boats passing each other, some of them coming to settle at paths of wood on the water. Many of the boats belched black smoke like the trains. "Those are not riverboats."

"Those are *ships*, boy—ocean-going vessels. Every white person on this continent, they or their grandparents came here on a ship. Every negro did too."

Ésh wished no *veho* had ever thought of these ships. Then the *veho* would have stayed where they belonged—far away from the Zizistas—and the negroes would not be their slaves.

Huger appeared, a man who had seen perhaps seventy winters. He said that a John McAllister sometimes received mail here, but no David or Sophie. Huger remembered that there had been another McAllister in Charleston perhaps twenty years ago. "I can't recall his Christian name, but it was something unusual—it wasn't David."

Gates frowned. "So this John McAllister wasn't here twenty years ago?"

Huger shook his head. "I believe he's a recent immigrant."

Gates sighed but asked: "May we leave a message for him?"

"Of course."

Gates wrote a few lines on a piece of paper, folded it, and handed it back to Huger with a coin. Ésh knew these coins were how the *veho* asked each other to do things or give them things. Sometimes they used colored pieces of paper with drawings on them instead. The *veho* did not believe in trade. Where this "money" came from, Ésh did not know.

"You might place a notice in the newspapers," suggested Huger.

"I thought of that," answered Gates. "Where is the nearest office?"

Huger motioned back the way they'd come. "The *Mercury* is just past the Bank of South Carolina on Broad Street. It will be on your right."

Gates thanked the man, and then he took Ésh to this *Mercury*. It consisted of several young men writing at desks. A white stone carving of a man's head and shoulders watched over them. Gates spoke to one of the living men, who gave him a tall piece of paper full of tiny marks and symbols in exchange for a coin. Soon, Gates was writing on his own smaller piece of paper. He asked Ésh for the rabbit skin again, and he seemed to be copying the information as Mé'hahts had copied it from the cave on Independence Rock. When Gates was finished, he showed the paper to Ésh. "What do you think?"

Ésh stared at all the little black marks, then reminded Gates: "I cannot read."

"Ah. Yes. It says:

NOTICE: Seeking information on a David and Sophie McAllister who passed Independence Rock on the Overland Trail in July 1841. Reply to Mr. McAllister at Mrs. Kerrison's Boarding House on Church Street."

Gates explained that if Ésh had any family still living in Charleston, or if there were any people in Charleston who'd known his family, one of them might read this notice and come to find Ésh.

Then Gates took him back to the boarding house. In a room below the one where they slept, they ate slices of fatty pink meat and something similar to a prairie turnip. A young negro girl served them, and Ésh had seen a negro man working in the "garden."

Ésh ate slowly, not only because he kept thinking about the boy being beaten on the street and because he disliked the food but because his weariness would not leave him. He wondered if all he needed was a good rest, or if he would never sleep well again.

Gates, meanwhile, ate quickly and spoke with his mouth full of food. "Well, boy, I've done what I can for you. If you need help, ask Mrs. Kerrison. She seems kind enough."

Kind people did not own slaves.

"When we get back to the room, I'll give you the remainder of what Major Day and Dr. Johns provided for you. If you're careful, it should keep you for a month. You'll need to find some kind of employment before then."

Ésh lowered his fork and frowned. What was this "employment"?

"The notice in the newspaper will run for a week. If you want to repeat it, you'll have to pay again. You'll also have to pay Mrs. Kerrison again in a week."

Why couldn't Gates do these things? With every unfamiliar word, more and more weariness clouded Ésh's head. "W-What is a week?"

Gates glared at him. "Seven days. You remember where the post office is?"

"I-I think so."

"You'll have to return there in person to find out if John McAllister replied to my message."

Ésh did not comprehend what was happening till Gates replaced his hat and stood. "You... You are leaving?"

"I was your escort, boy. I am not your father. You are a mostly grown man; it's time you learned to look after yourself. You understand the language well enough."

Ésh did not think he understood the language at all.

"There's a ship leaving for Savannah in an hour." Gates held up the newspaper he'd bought. "I'll be damned if I miss Christmas with *my* family just because you lost yours twenty years ago."

Ésh choked down a few more bites of food, then followed Gates up to the room. The bluecoat was stuffing the last of his belongings into his bag.

Ésh glanced at the water pitcher and bowl. "Can I have your razor?"

Gates sighed. "Fine." He found his razor and slapped it on the thing he'd called a dresser, beside several pieces of colored paper and a few coins. The bluecoat picked up his bag, but at the door, he looked back. "Good luck, boy."

When Gates was gone, Ésh opened the window and leaned heavily against it. But the smells here were all wrong. Everything smelled rotten. He could not even look up to the Sky or down to the

Earth, because part of the building, a part without walls, stretched outside the window. Nor could Ésh see very far in any direction; more buildings blocked each way.

Ésh closed the window and peeled off every one of his *veho* clothes. He dressed himself again in his breechcloth, leggings, moccasins, and fringed shirt. He felt better, but he was still weary. He pulled the padding from the bed onto the floor. He curled up on his side and buried his face in his buffalo coat. Even that didn't smell right anymore, but the texture of the thick hair comforted him.

CHAPTER 24

The frequent drumming which is heard...the citadel, the guard-house, with its martial ceremonies, the frequent parades of militia...might lead one to imagine that the town was in a state of siege or revolution.

— Frederick Law Olmsted, *A Journey in the Seaboard Slave States* (1856)

His sleep was fitful, but Ésh woke feeling a little more clear-headed. He remembered what his grandfather had taught him: every morning, you should honor the Sun and the Earth and the Four Directions. In spite of all the strangeness around him, the Sacred Powers were here too.

Ésh could not pray within walls, but he was not eager to meet any *veho* on his own. He opened the window again, and he recalled that when he and Gates had arrived, Mrs. Kerrison had said they could sit on the "piazza." Perhaps from the edge of it, he could see the Sun and the Earth.

Ésh climbed through the window, but scarcely had he stood up when a female voice shrieked on the other end of the piazza. He looked over to see the negro girl of perhaps fourteen winters who had served him food before. Now, she was seated in a chair with a needle in her hand. In her lap was a dress, in addition to the one she was wearing. Her eyes were wide, her mouth open.

"I am not going to hurt you," Ésh told her.

The voice of Mrs. Kerrison called from inside the house: "Betsy? What's the matter, child?"

"Th-There's a savage on the piazza, Missus!"

"A *what?*" Mrs. Kerrison opened the door onto the piazza, the one between the rooms. She too started when she saw Ésh. The small grey-haired woman sucked in a breath and brought a hand to her throat as if she feared he might cut it. Then Mrs. Kerrison leaned forward and narrowed her eyes at him. "Mr. McAllister?"

Since that wasn't really his name, Ésh only repeated: "I am not going to hurt you." He was glad to see that Betsy looked more intrigued than frightened now.

"Wherever did you get that costume?" Mrs. Kerrison asked.

Ésh did not want to trust this woman. She owned slaves. But what other choice did he have? He would never find his *veho* family or return home without help. When Betsy had screamed, Mrs. Kerrison had sounded concerned, not angry. Perhaps there was some kindness in her. While Ésh decided how to answer, he looked down at his buckskin shirt. He admired the green dye and caressed the fringe beneath his sleeve. "My mother made this."

Mrs. Kerrison looked more confused than ever. "Your mother...?"

"She is a—you would say she is a Cheyenne Indian. I am Cheyenne too." He'd lowered his eyes again on purpose, so he would not see Mrs. Kerrison or Betsy's incredulous expressions. He hurried to explain: "I have been with the Cheyenne since I was born. *Almost* since I was born. I must have had a white mother, too. I came here to understand what happened to my white family."

"But why come to Charleston?"

From his room, Ésh retrieved the rabbit skin with his family's names on it. Mrs. Kerrison had Betsy bring breakfast out to the piazza and let her remain sewing nearby while Ésh told Mrs.

Kerrison what he knew and what he and Gates had done in Charleston so far.

"I cannot believe Lieutenant Gates left you here alone!" Mrs. Kerrison exclaimed. "You might have ended up starving on the streets!"

"I am not going to starve. I am a good hunter. I can make a bow, and—"

"Oh *no*, child! You cannot go about hunting other people's livestock. Every animal here *belongs* to someone."

Ésh frowned. "But outside the city, there are woods. We passed them on the train."

"Even there, the land and the animals on it—wild animals like deer and turkeys—belong to someone, Mr. McAllister. The rules are very different here."

Ésh stared down at his plate, at the strange *veho* foods. "I need money." He knew he would need it to return West as well, for the trains and riverboats and stagecoach.

"Yes, child. Until you can find your family, you will have to find employment."

"What is employment?"

"Oh dear. You do work, and your employer pays you money."

Ésh wondered if the negroes were paid for the work they did. He glanced at Betsy, who sat sewing at the other end of the piazza. The girl smiled back shyly now.

"What an Indian can do here, I'm not certain…" Mrs. Kerrison said as she sipped her tea. "We must think of other ways to contact your family. We could try the Presbyterian Church at Meeting and Tradd. It's full of Scottish families, and McAllister is a Scottish name." She set down her cup. "But you understand, child—if it has been twenty years since you had a McAllister relative in Charleston, you may *never* find them, or any word of them."

"Yes. I understand."

As much as his family, Ésh wished he could find the girl from his visions, but he had no idea where to begin looking. He hadn't even seen her face. He knew nothing about the girl except the dark honey color of her hair and the sound of her voice. Now that he had heard *vehoá* speaking here in Charleston, he'd realized that the girl's voice sounded similar to theirs—he was in the right place. If only the black wolf would return to guide him.

AFTER BREAKFAST, Ésh dressed again in his *veho* clothes. He did not need anyone screaming at the sight of him as Betsy had. If he could not find his family, he could at least learn about the place where they had lived. It amazed him that even in the Big Freezing Moon, many plants here were still green. There were even a few flowers.

Along one little street ran a red-brown wall, and two kinds of roses climbed over it. They must be related to the rosebushes that liked to grow along streams back home: the centers of the flowers were the same, the leaves were similar, and the stems were prickly. But these roses had an enormous number of petals, and the pink ones smelled almost like plums. In this wall with the roses was a door with a round window at the top, and inside the wall he could see even more green. Every garden in Charleston was like this: the plants were trapped behind walls and fences. Just like the people.

At dinner in the middle of the day, Mrs. Kerrison told him about a place called White Point, where the city met the ocean. "It's a public garden, filled with trees. You might like it."

She was right. There were still fences, but they were low, and there were many gaps. In this garden at the end of the city, there was a great stretch of grass and tree after tree. Birds nested in some of them. Beyond the trees, water lapped at the Earth, and the Sun danced on every wave.

Ships passed over the water, growing larger as they approached and smaller as they drifted away. This must be the ocean. In the distance, he saw more land and trees. He wondered if that was Scotland, where his *veho* family had come from.

At White Point, he was surrounded by beauty and sometimes even quiet, like sitting in the middle of prairie grasses or on the side of a mountain. This was not a real forest, but the air was cleaner; and when Ésh sat on the Earth beneath one of the trees, he felt happier.

He closed his eyes and prayed silently to the Sacred Powers. He thanked them that he had made it this far and asked for their guidance. How could he find his *veho* family? How could he find the girl from his visions? How could he help the Zizistas remain free as long as possible? He stayed till the Sun set, watching and listening for a sign.

All that happened was: one of the nesting birds pooped on his shoulder. He wasn't sure how to interpret that. Ésh thought the Sacred Powers had not heard him.

But when he rose to return to Mrs. Kerrison's, he saw two horses tied to one of the fences. Between his imprisonment at Fort Laramie and the journey here, it had been nearly two moons since he'd ridden a horse. Far too long.

He wished he could steal one of these horses. He could do it so easily; their owners were not even nearby. But Ésh knew that *veho* did not consider horse stealing brave; he would only make the animal's owner angry. So he settled for conversing with the horses in Zizistas and their own silent language.

As the animals returned his greeting with their breath, Ésh realized: *horses* were how he could make money. In this city brimming with strangeness, these beautiful animals were something he understood. He could blend into their herd far more easily than into the *veho*.

Ésh told Mrs. Kerrison about his idea.

"Of course!" she cried. "You'll have to watch the Wanted advertisements in the newspapers for anyone needing a groom." She saw Ésh didn't know the word. "That's what we call a man who works with horses: a groom."

Ésh admitted to Mrs. Kerrison that he couldn't read.

"Oh dear. I wish I had the leisure to teach you, child, but I do not. I will, however, peruse the papers on your behalf."

No one responded to the notice Gates had placed in the paper. John McAllister did leave a reply at the post office, but it was only to say that he'd been in Charleston less than a year and had no knowledge of a David or Sophie McAllister. Nor did anyone at the Presbyterian Church know of Ésh's family.

Mrs. Kerrison read the Wanted advertisements in the newspapers every day. The only mentions of grooms were notices about negro grooms for sale.

Mrs. Kerrison was distressed that Ésh did not find his family in time for Christmas, though the celebration meant nothing to him. It seemed to involve eating a lot of food and singing to the *veho* god.

Ésh said his own prayers. In a low voice, he sang the prayer of a Zizistas scout in enemy territory:

> "Wolf I am.
> In darkness
> in light
> wherever I search
> wherever I run
> wherever I stand
> everything
> will be good
> because Maheo
> protects us."

Ésh begged the Creator to guide him. "Why am I here?" he asked again and again. But how could Maheo answer when there were so few animals in this city to carry a sign to him? Ésh wished his grandfather were here. He was a medicine man; he could recognize signs even in a place like this. Ésh's money kept decreasing, and he was no closer to accomplishing anything.

He wondered if he should offer his flesh. Then he remembered how the bluecoats at Fort Laramie had thought him crazy for cutting himself. The *veho* did not understand that such sacrifices pleased Maheo. The doctor at Fort Laramie had talked about a terrible place called an asylum. If he was locked up, Ésh could not help the People.

He also remembered what the girl in his vision had said: *"Your flesh is more than acceptable. But I prefer it on your body."* Ésh wished she would visit his dreams again. He thought of the black-and-orange butterfly she had shown him. *"This is how you'll know you've found us,"* she'd said. But it was too cold now for butterflies. Even the flowers were sleeping.

He found himself returning to the wall with the roses that had smelled like plums, though the petals had all fallen. Once on the little street, he heard the beautiful voice of a young woman singing. The language wasn't English, and each note glided over him like honey—like the girl's voice in his vision. But this song ended too quickly; Ésh could not even determine which house it had come from. He peered in the gates and fences all along the street, searching for her, but he got nasty looks from the negroes and *veho* inside. Some of them yelled at him. He did not hear her voice again, and Ésh decided she could not have been *his* girl.

He still wasn't sleeping through the night, but he grew more accustomed to the city's rhythms, its sights and sounds and smells. He needed to learn as much as he could about these *veho*. Yet he found himself spending most of the day watching negroes. They made more sense to him and frightened him less. He was not a very good scout.

In the mornings, he would watch negroes bring wagons full of strange things to the market buildings. The negroes sold things they'd made: baskets and chairs and clothing. But mostly, the negroes sold things to eat. Birds Ésh recognized, though the colors and sizes might be different: ducks and geese and turkeys. The negroes sold the fat animal he'd eaten at Mrs. Kerrison's, which was called a pig. They sold fish larger than Ésh had ever seen and other strange, smelly creatures who came from the ocean.

Throughout the day, negroes would walk the streets pushing carts or balancing trays on their heads. "Shrimp! Get your fresh shrimp here!" they cried, or "Chestnuts! Fresh roasted chestnuts!"

Ésh passed streets where negroes themselves were sold, and he was careful not to pass that way again. He discovered that for a few coins, some negro women and some *vehoá* would let you use them for a few minutes. Ésh wanted to use them. But the women did not look very clean, and he had so little money.

Every evening, church bells would ring, and drums would rattle and rattle till the bells rang again. *Veho* dressed like bluecoats marched through the streets, carrying muskets with knives on the end. These men drummed not with their fingers or with sticks wrapped in hide, like the Zizistas did, but with bare sticks. The sound from their drums was very different from Zizistas drums. This drumming was sharper and harsher. Ésh disliked the sound from the start, but he grew to hate it. While the *veho* soldiers marched through the streets, striking their drums, Ésh would see negroes hurrying through the city. After the bells rang the second time, he would see no more negroes.

He asked Betsy why this was. "That be the curfew," she explained while she hung his spare clothes up to dry in the yard. "The City Guard arrest any negro they catch in the streets after nine o'clock—even free negroes. Unless they can pay the fine or their master agree to pay it, they get whipped." She shuddered.

"There are free negroes? How?"

"Some of 'em work and work till they able to buy their freedom. Some got freed by their masters—mostly in their wills, when their masters didn't need 'em no more."

"Why can't negroes be out at night?"

Betsy glanced through the hanging clothes and then back over her shoulder to make sure no one else was nearby. "'Cause buckra—white men—they is afraid of us. Afraid we gonna meet in secret and plan things."

Ésh dropped his voice too. "Like an attack?"

Betsy nodded.

"Why *don't* you attack?"

"'Cause we've tried it before, and we didn't succeed," Betsy muttered. She saw Ésh's wide eyes and explained: "Not me. Other negroes tried to rise up, years ago. But even if we got free for a little while, where we gonna go? Charleston ain't anywhere near Canada. There's too many buckra out there waiting—buckra with dogs and guns."

"But you would escape, if you knew you could get away?"

"Ain't no use thinking about it, Mr. McAllister. I know I is one of the lucky ones, with my Mama and Papa right here." She looked back to the kitchen, where her mother was the cook. "Mrs. Kerrison gets into tempers sometimes, but she ain't a bad Missus. Mostly, I'se worried about what will happen when she's gone."

Ésh began avoiding the City Guard, and their massive Guard House on Meeting Street, as if they might arrest *him*. He also noticed that no negroes ever visited White Point Garden. Betsy said negroes weren't allowed there. Ésh supposed this was how White Point had gotten its name. If it weren't for his yellow hair and his *veho* clothes, he probably wouldn't be allowed either.

Ésh liked White Point Garden less knowing this, but he enjoyed breaking the *veho*'s selfish rules. He felt less trapped there, sitting under a tree or staring out at the water. He wished he could swim in the water. He was sure it would be cold, but he hadn't had a proper bath in moons.

Ésh WALKED TO EACH of the "livery stables" in the city and asked if they needed another groom. The stable owners wanted to know who else had employed him. When Ésh tried to explain, they heard only the halting way he spoke. The stable owners dismissed him without giving him a chance to prove himself.

At one of the stables, a young negro groom noticed Ésh's strange speech and his piercings, six holes cut in the rim of each ear. Though Ésh wore no ornaments, the groom was intrigued. Thirteen-year-old Zeke wanted to see Ésh's Zizistas clothing and hear his story. In exchange, whenever the white man who owned him was gone, Zeke taught Ésh about *veho* horses.

Ésh learned the shapes, textures, and parts of *veho* saddles. These were something in-between the small pad saddles Zizistas men used—hide stuffed with grass or hair—and the sturdy saddles of Zizistas women, which had high cantles and pommels made of wood. A few Zizistas men owned bridles with metal bits, though Ésh himself preferred a simple buffalo rope looped through his horse's mouth. He already knew that the *veho* attached metal shoes to their horses' hoofs.

He'd also noticed that *veho* horses used their voices more often than wild horses or Zizistas horses, who understood that loud noises attracted predators and enemies. While most *veho* were shorter than most Zizistas, their horses grew larger. Perhaps this was because the *veho* horses ate different food—even in winter, when Zizistas horses often had to eat cottonwood bark, the *veho* had plenty of dried grasses and grains to give their horses.

But this rich and varied food came at a terrible price. No Indian would force a horse to go faster by digging little spikes into his sides. Many *veho* horses never walked or ran free; they left their stables only when someone was mounted on them or when they pulled a wagon or carriage behind them. At all other times, the horses lived within walls and fences.

Some even died of this imprisonment, Zeke explained, if a horse tried to roll in his stall and became "cast" against a wall. Powerless to regain his feet in this position, the horse could panic and injure himself past curing, or he could suffocate on his own blood as it pooled in his lungs.

Trapped inside a small room each night and pinched inside *veho* clothing each day, Ésh thought he understood. The cramped way these *veho* lived was unnatural.

Most *veho* treated their horses the same way they treated negroes, as if horses and negroes existed only to serve them. Any beast or man who defied them or even annoyed them must be punished. The *veho* did not understand that horses were brothers and allies, who would choose to help you if you asked them properly and proved yourself a trustworthy leader.

The *veho* loved to race their horses, but they did not care for the animals, train them, or even ride them. Their negroes did all these things. The *veho* wanted "jockeys" who were as small as possible, so they found cruel ways to make their negroes stop growing. Zeke's brother Abe was a jockey. His master not only starved him but also forced Abe to sit inside a mound of steaming horseshit every other day, sweating and sweating till he weighed less than his little brother.

Zeke and Abe had different masters, and they were lucky to see each other once a moon. Zeke wished he and his brother could live

free out West with the Zizistas. Ésh wished that too. He wished he
had more to give this young man than stories. As he sat under the
trees at White Point, Ésh would imagine that he and Zeke and Abe
were stealing hundreds of *veho* horses and galloping free all the way
to Zizistas country.

CHAPTER 25

I think I could turn and live with animals, they are so placid
    and self-contain'd,
I stand and look at them long and long.
— Walt Whitman, "Song of Myself" (1881)

In the Hoop-and-Stick Game Moon, what the *veho* called January, Ésh was walking to White Point Garden when he saw a black horse tied to a fence, waiting for its owner. He remembered the black horse he'd tried to steal in the mountains, the one belonging to a *veho* officer, the horse that had gotten him captured and sent to Fort Laramie. If it weren't for that horse, Ésh would still be with his Zizistas family. If he stole this horse right now, could she carry him back to them?

He stopped and greeted the mare by offering his knuckles. She sniffed his hand and accepted his company. Ésh had lived with horses all his life; he'd been learning their silent language for nearly nineteen years. Perhaps the little beaded horse charm in the medicine pouch around his neck helped him too.

She was bored, the mare said by lashing her tail and stamping her foot. He scratched her shoulder where she could not reach and loosened her lead rope just a little, pretending it would be easy to escape with her. The mare nuzzled him hopefully, tickling him with her whiskers. Perhaps he could simply walk her around a little?

Then, he heard a girl screaming. The screams came from the direction of White Point, but they grew louder and closer. A small girl clinging to a small horse dashed right past Ésh. Behind them, a man was yelling too: "Louisa! *Hold on!* Someone, please—stop that pony!"

Suddenly, Ésh had a reason to *ride*. He pulled the black mare's lead rope free from the fence, and she pricked her ears toward him in excitement. "I need your help," he told the mare in Zizistas. As he leapt into her saddle, Ésh heard a man shouting protests from the piazza above them. "I need your horse!" Ésh called in English as he squeezed the mare's sides with his calves. "I will bring her back!"

Ésh urged the black mare after the girl and her pony. With the warmth and power of a horse beneath him, he felt like a Zizistas again—like a man instead of a ghost. United with another being, he felt more like himself. The mare was eager to run, and the confidence in his posture told her not to be frightened when people cried out in alarm.

Yet this city was no open plain. Every few strides, some new barrier loomed: a carriage or a cluster of City Guards. Ésh would have ridden over the guards happily, but he didn't want the survivors to chase him down, and he didn't want the mare to be hurt. She met each challenge, swerving right and then left and then right again in response to his guidance. More and more of the cramped, smelly city disappeared behind them. There was nothing so thrilling as seeing the world pass between the ears of a horse.

Finally Ésh spotted the girl Louisa ahead, still clinging to her running pony and still screaming. Ésh brought the black mare alongside them and told her with his posture to match the pony's gait. *Keep pace, keep pace*, he told the mare without words.

Ésh knew if he grabbed for the pony's reins first, it might whip its head and throw off the girl. He must rescue her first. The pony was shorter than the mare, but far away on the prairie, while riding a running horse, Ésh had snatched a bow and a shield off the ground; he knew he could do this too. He held on with his legs and leaned sideways, stretching farther and farther till he'd caught the girl under her arms.

She was too frightened to release her grip on the pony's mane.

"I have you!" Ésh cried.

At last, the girl let go. As soon as Ésh pulled her onto the black mare, Louisa twisted and clung to him instead.

He kept the black mare at a run till he'd grabbed the pony's reins. With gentle insistence, he commanded the small horse to heed him. He slowed both animals to a walk, then a stop. They'd nearly run out of city.

"You O.K.?" Ésh asked Louisa. Zeke had taught him this alternative to "all right."

Louisa was still clutching him tight, her blonde hair loose across her face. She looked about eight years old. "There was a dog!" the girl panted. "It snapped at Sunshine and scared him! He's a good pony, really he is! Is he hurt?" Louisa stretched to look at her pale yellow mount.

"I don't think so." Ésh peered down at the pony, who was winded but calming. "Do you want to ride him on the way back?"

Louisa hesitated and gazed up at Ésh, her arms still encircling his neck. "Could I stay with you a little while longer?"

Ésh chuckled. "O.K." He turned both horses back toward White Point, at a walk this time.

"I've never seen a man with pierced ears before. Are you a pirate?"

"What is that?" Ésh spotted a water trough and directed both horses toward it.

"Pirates are bad men who sail ships and steal things. They were hanged on White Point. Papa was telling me. He said they wore gold earrings."

"You think I am a bad man?"

"No," Louisa smiled. "You are a good man. You saved me."

Ésh had borrowed the black mare because he'd wanted to feel hoofs pounding under him again—saving this girl had only been an excuse. One less *vehoá* hardly mattered to him. But glancing down at Louisa's little face smiling up at him, he was glad he'd saved her.

Her father was happiest of all. When Ésh lowered Louisa into the man's arms, he cried: "Oh, thank you, sir! Thank you!" The girl babbled about how Ésh had plucked her from the galloping pony.

The owner of the black mare was waiting too. Reluctantly, Ésh dismounted. He tied Sunshine to a fence and returned the mare to her owner. "I told you I would bring her back."

"That was some quick thinking, son," said the man. "And some impressive riding."

"How can I ever repay you?" asked Louisa's father.

Ésh thought about how little money he had left at Mrs. Kerrison's. He patted the pony's neck. "Do you need a groom?"

Louisa's father frowned. "No, I-I'm afraid I don't."

"Neither do I." Yet the owner of the black mare smiled. "But I might know someone who does. How do you feel about working for a colored man?"

Ésh had learned that if a negro was free, he was called a colored man instead. "If he has horses, I do not care about anything else."

THE OWNER OF THE BLACK MARE took Ésh to a farm outside the city. He had purchased the mare from the farm's owner, a man named Mr. Alexander. He was a "mulatto," which meant some of his ancestors were white and some were black. Mr. Alexander bred and trained horses, and he had many foals coming this year. He could use another groom, he said.

Mr. Alexander's current grooms and trainers were all negroes. It seemed most white men wouldn't work for a mulatto. This colored man owned slaves himself—that was what surprised and displeased Ésh.

But he needed the money this employment could bring, and Mr. Alexander seemed an improvement on a *veho*. His slaves respected him rather than feared him, and Mr. Alexander trusted them to run the farm in his absence. Ésh was also relieved to see that the man let his horses run free in pastures most of the day. When he spotted a black-and-white paint, Ésh knew it was a sign.

Mr. Alexander asked if Ésh could work on Sundays, because two of his negroes, Jesse and York, had "abroad marriages." This meant nearby planters owned their wives, and the couples spent most of the week apart. The women did not have to work on Sundays, when Jesse and York wanted to spend the day with them. But Mr. Alexander's horses needed care every day. Ésh said he would be happy to work Sundays.

Mr. Alexander was impressed by Ésh's rescue of Louisa and the story of how he'd come to Charleston. Mr. Alexander was even more impressed by Ésh's skill with his horses. He had Ésh retrieve a stallion from a paddock, and Ésh proved himself able to command the animal without either words or blows. Ésh's methods differed from his, but they interested Mr. Alexander.

Leaning against a fence, staring out at his fine mares, Mr. Alexander observed: "I hear Indians are fond of stealing horses."

Ésh decided the man's expression was amusement rather than suspicion. With a smile, he asked: "Do you wish me to steal someone's horses for you?"

Mr. Alexander laughed.

He agreed to hire Ésh for a month, maybe more. So Ésh said good-bye to Betsy and Mrs. Kerrison, who promised to forward any messages from his family.

The black-and-white paint soon became Ésh's favorite charge. She was a sweet-tempered mare, but Mr. Alexander had been unable to sell her, because *veho* did not value "piebalds." Her former owner had named her Medusa after a monster. Ésh thought Mr. Alexander didn't mind so much that no one else wanted the paint mare, because he was fond of her as well.

Mr. Alexander gave Ésh permission to wear his Zizistas clothing and to hunt on his land, as long as he gave his kills to Hephzibah, their cook. Mr. Alexander also agreed that when the weather was warmer, Ésh could make himself a hut of branches and blankets and sleep outside.

There was even a stream where Ésh could bathe, and he was

delighted to discover that soapweed grew here too. Mr. Alexander called it yucca. Ésh preferred the lather its roots made to the harsh soap of the *veho*. The stream was cold, but he didn't care. He might spend every morning shovelling manure, but Ésh felt clean and free for the first time in moons.

He was sleeping through the night again. Out here amongst the pastures and woods, Ésh could no longer hear the drums of the City Guard. The sounds and sights and smells felt right again, more like home. Ésh was surrounded by grazing horses, grassy Earth, and open Sky, not walls the *veho* had made. There were trees no *veho* had planted, whose shape and scent he recognized, sharp and strong. He could place his hand on the rough bark, close his eyes, inhale pine, and imagine he was back in the mountains.

Maybe he would never find his *veho* family. But here, he'd found peace, and he could make enough money to return home. Maheo had not forgotten him.

Mr. Alexander was away often; he spent whole days in Charleston or in the "upcountry," considering new horses to purchase or new stallions to cover his mares. Because he was a colored man, Mr. Alexander could not leave the state during these journeys, or South Carolina would not let him return.

Even within the state, he had to travel with a white partner, since many *veho* mistook Mr. Alexander for a slave. One evening, Ésh came upon these two men when they were not expecting him. The way Mr. Alexander's hand was touching his partner's face, the way they started apart at his approach—Ésh knew these men did more than work together, that they were like the halfmen-halfwomen of the Zizistas.

Ésh had learned that the *veho* shunned such people. With only a smile, he tried to tell Mr. Alexander and his friend that *he* knew they were holy. Halfmen-halfwomen had powerful love medicine. Ésh hoped it was a sign that the girl from his visions might still find him.

ÉSH'S APPEARANCE AND WAYS amused his fellow grooms. At first, the men spoke *about* Ésh frequently but *to* him as little as possible. He could not blame them: Mr. Alexander was paying him to do the same kind of work they had to do for nothing.

Then the negroes tried giving Ésh orders as if he worked for them. He obeyed without complaint. He wanted to show the men that he was not arrogant and lazy like so many *veho*. By his second week, the other grooms began to accept him and even teach him things. There was always more for Ésh to learn.

One evening, they all sat inside the main stable, cleaning the saddles and bridles while rain poured down outside.

Ésh was pondering what to do about his name. Whenever someone said "Mr. McAllister," it still sounded strange to him. The name felt like a saddle made for someone else. He could tolerate it now and then, but he longed for a better one. The negroes had simple names: Jesse and York and Ben.

"You don't have a Christian name?" asked Ben.

Mr. Alexander had asked the same question, so Ésh knew what Ben meant. "If I do, I do not know it. The name the Cheyenne call me, it is Mo'ohtáwo'neh."

York tried to say it back, but gave up halfway through with a chuckle. "What now?"

"It means: Black Wolf," Ésh explained.

At this, they all laughed. Jesse, whose skin and hair were almost as dark as a crow's feathers, motioned to Ésh's yellow hair. "If you'se black," he grinned, "what does that make us?"

Ésh remembered his boyhood name. Unlike Mr. McAllister, it fit him. Unlike Mo'ohtáwo'neh, it was short and simple. "When my mother found me, she named me Ésh."

The other men paused in their work and considered this, each of them murmuring the word like the first notes of a song.

"I like it," York decided as he returned to polishing a bit. "Ain't pretentious. A man who wears a diaper shouldn't have no pretentious name."

Ésh scowled. He glanced down at the wide strip of elk hide that passed through the cord around his waist and between his legs. "It is a breechcloth—not a diaper!"

York tilted his head, as if to see the garment from a different angle. "Looks like a diaper to me."

"A *looong* diaper," Jesse agreed. "A little *too* long, if you know what I'm saying. You ain't fooling nobody with that thing, Ésh."

His face grew hot. "The ends only reach my knees! At dances, many warriors in fancy dress, their breechcloths drag on the ground!"

At this, the other men laughed loudest of all. "Can you imagine," York grinned, "me going to meet Lizzie for a dance with such a thing strapped 'tween my legs?"

Lizzie was York's woman. Ben had Hephzibah, who cooked for them and washed their clothes, and Jesse had Affy.

Ben saw Ésh wasn't smiling. When he'd recovered his breath, Ben assured him: "We is just playing with you, Ésh. Don't get many chances to laugh at a white man. Leastways, not to his face."

I'm NOT white, Ésh wanted to say. But he knew it wasn't entirely true. He also understood that these men didn't mean to be cruel. As they sat there, laughing about the size of Ésh's *véto'ots* and how he was dressed like a child, Jesse and York and Ben didn't know how much Ésh envied them their women—how much he hated being a virgin.

He had only the girl who visited his dreams, whose voice and hair were like honey. Last night, she'd returned to him. Still he did not see her face, but she whispered: *"I am near, my love. I am coming."*

PART V
COMMUNION

1860

CHARLESTON

I find thee; I am safe, and strong, and glad.

— Elizabeth Barrett Browning,
Sonnets from the Portuguese, XXVII (1850)

CHAPTER 26

I have been told that the white man, who is almost a god, and yet a great fool, does not believe that the horse has a soul. This cannot be true. I have many times seen my horse's soul in his eyes.

— *American: The Life Story of a Great Indian, Plenty-Coups, Chief of the Crows* (1930)

Clare survived the next Mardi Gras ball only by escaping it. Her upset stomach wasn't entirely feigned. She couldn't stop thinking of the last ball. Surely David was missing her too. When would he regret his decision and come back to her?

She would give him till Easter Sunday, Clare decided. What better time for a new beginning? If David hadn't reached out to her by Easter, she would allow Mr. Cromwell to court her. She knew he was still interested. She could tell by the way he looked at her. Perhaps only jealousy would spur David to action.

Meanwhile, Aunt Hortense remained determined to mold Clare into a model wife. This meant learning how to run a household. Clare liked learning how to make things in the kitchen. She found the scents and textures both exciting and comforting, and she felt accomplished when her cake or pastry turned out just right. Verily's sister Easter never said much of anything. But Phoebe was good company; she always had gossip.

Baking, sewing, and arranging flowers (but *not* gardening) seemed to be the only activities a lady was allowed to do with her own hands. Clare knew her mother had helped in the plantation's sick house, but Aunt Hortense forbade Clare to enter this cabin until *after* she was married. Clare supposed there was a chance she might see a naked man there, and she was more disappointed than ever.

"Running a household" meant ordering the slaves around, and Aunt Hortense berated Clare that she was not "firm" enough. "Give them an inch," her aunt declared ad nauseam, "and they'll take an ell!"

Clare didn't understand all the fuss. The slaves had been working here for years already. Why did they need her telling them what to do? If the spices *had* to be locked up, why couldn't Phoebe keep the key? Aunt Hortense acted as though the cook would bathe in rosewater and stuff her mattress with saffron if no one was watching.

To escape her aunt, Clare renewed her interest in sketching and painting. She found it soothing. Most of all, creating art was an excuse to take her phaeton out to some far meadow on the plantation and remain there for hours. Aunt Hortense railed about the dangers of alligators and negroes.

Fortunately, her father had been strangely indulgent since Clare returned from Barhamville. She didn't know why, but she wasn't going to look a gift horse in the mouth. Her father allowed her artistic excursions as long as Clare followed his rules. She must take Verily, who had to prove herself capable of handling the carriage horse. They must return before dusk. They must remain on the plantation but stay away from the rice fields. And they mustn't approach any creatures.

Clare kissed her father's cheek in delight and promised to obey. Even if she didn't *quite* follow the rule about creatures. She never brought any back with her, but she loved sketching them. Her paintings were mostly landscapes, since trees and barns held still.

Her first subject was her grandfather's old stallion barn. It held only hay now. Before her birth, Clare's grandfather had attempted to breed racehorses, but he hadn't been very good at it. He'd invested far more than he ever made back in stud fees or winnings at the Washington Race Course outside Charleston. Her father and Mr. Cromwell had sold off the stallions years ago.

The grey brick stallion barn remained, looking like a picturesque country church with its steeply pitched roof and its pointed arches over each window and door. It was not the most elaborate Gothic Revival outbuilding around Charleston, but it was theirs and Clare was fond of it.

Every passing day brought her closer to Easter with no word from David. In an effort to distract herself, Clare ventured past the stallion barn. She saw the horses grazing in their neighbor's paddock and fell in love. They weren't just any horses: one was a black-and-white paint.

Clare stopped the phaeton. She hadn't seen a piebald or skewbald horse in years, and that was on a visit to Aunt Amelia in Greenville. Charlestonians considered such animals ugly. But Clare knew Indians valued paints, and she adored them.

Great splashes of black and white adorned the mare's coat. Even her mane and tail were parti-colored. The horse reminded Clare of her dearly departed piebald cat, Mignon. His paw pads had been an adorable motley, spotted with both black and pink. Clare's favorite flowers were variegated too, like the Jaune Desprez roses climbing over their garden gate in Charleston. Why settle for one color when you could have two or three?

Dimly, Clare knew that her placid carriage horse, a chestnut gelding named Arthur, had taken her inattention as an opportunity to crop grass on this side of the fence. At the corner of Clare's vision, Verily looked up from her book.

Clare didn't take her eyes from the mare, as if afraid she might vanish. "Isn't she beautiful?" Clare sighed.

"Which one?"

"The paint!"

"She's...whimsical," her friend acknowledged. Verily's reading was certainly expanding her vocabulary.

Clare passed her the reins, climbed down from the phaeton, and approached the serpentine fence. "Would it be all right if I painted you, beautiful girl?"

The black-and-white mare actually raised her head and regarded Clare. Clare gasped. One of the paint's eyes was pale blue. She was both breathtaking and unearthly. Yet Clare wasn't frightened. If such a creature were hers, what might Clare call her? Whimsy? Caprice? Shadow?

Mirage, Clare decided as she sketched the paint mare. She'd always liked the word, the way it rolled off her tongue.

The next afternoon, Clare returned to the eastern fence with Verily. The paint and her paddock mates were cantering around the enclosure, kicking and nipping playfully. Even with her own kind, Mirage displayed none of the viciousness Clare had seen in some mares.

As she watched, Mirage flopped down on her back, rolling in the dirt to rub off her winter coat. Clare laughed. The mare righted herself and fixed Clare with those beautiful, eerie eyes, one brown and one blue. Clare held her breath. Mirage walked straight toward her.

"Verily, look!" Clare cried. "I think she recognizes me!"

Her friend hardly glanced up from her book. "Don't let her bite you, Miss."

Clare turned back to the approaching Mirage and tried to dismiss the suggestion. She knew as well as anyone how terrifying a horse could be. But in the mare's pricked ears and calm gait, she read only curiosity. Mirage came to one of the places where the fence zigzagged outward. Clare drew in a breath, pulled off her driving gloves, and held out her knuckles. Mirage's great pink nostrils flared with interest but without aggression. Her whiskers tickled Clare's skin.

"Good afternoon, beautiful girl." Clare stroked Mirage's forehead, between those mesmerizing brown and blue eyes. A horse's great, dark, round eyes always looked wise and bottomless to Clare. But Mirage's blue eye was something else entirely. It resembled nothing so much as a fortuneteller's crystal ball, as if Clare's fate might lie hidden inside.

Clare felt unworthy to stand in the presence of such a creature, yet she yearned for Mirage to stay near her. "I wish I had a carrot or an apple to give you." Despite the mare's ethereal appearance, Clare suspected Mirage would respond to earthly pleasures like any horse. Then she remembered: "I do have mint candies!" Horses loved mint!

Clare ran back to the phaeton and found her reticule. She withdrew two Bêtises de Cambrai.

Verily eyed her. "Aren't those from France?"

"Yes," Clare answered defensively.

Her friend sighed and returned to her book.

Mirage's nostrils were fluttering again. Clare placed one of the candies on her palm and held it out. The mare's extended lips slurped it up, and she seemed to roll the candy around on her tongue before she swallowed it. She stretched out her neck to ask for another. Clare grinned and granted it. This time, Mirage licked the candy from her palm, and kept on licking in order to gather the last traces of flavor. She exhaled minty breath and reached out for more.

"I think that's enough for today, greedy girl." Clare caressed the mare's velvet muzzle, then forced herself to step back from the fence.

For a long minute, they stared into each other's eyes across the barrier. *I know you,* said Mirage's mystical blue eye. *I like you, because we are the same. Come again, won't you?* Slowly, Mirage pulled her head over the fence and returned to her paddock mates. Clare could hardly bear to let her go.

She thought back to her childhood pony and all the joyful mornings they'd shared, cantering through the gardens and woods and fields. Sometimes David had accompanied them on his uncle's horse or one borrowed from her father. Clare wished girls were allowed to ride astride, but she'd found her balance on a sidesaddle eventually.

After Clare grew too big for ponies, she'd tried to ride a horse. Her second day so far off the ground, her new horse had spooked and bolted when a screaming flock of Carolina parakeets exploded from the trees. Clare had broken both bones in her lower arm in the fall.

The carriage ride into Charleston had taken almost two hours, even with Finis pushing the horses. Every second, every jiggle of the carriage was excruciating. Clare had been certain she'd faint from the pain; she'd *wanted* to faint; but she never had. She remembered every second.

The skin hadn't been broken, and Grand-père René had set the bones with his usual skill. Clare had healed. But the memory of that pain remained with her. When she'd tried again with other horses, the animals had sensed her fear and become skittish themselves. Clare's nervousness screamed *"Threat!"* The horses hadn't understood that the threat was *them*, and their anxiety only increased Clare's.

Then she'd gone away to school. By the time she returned, Clare had decided she could love a horse just as well from the ground or from the seat of a carriage.

But standing here watching Mirage, Clare longed to communicate with her in the way you could only do from the saddle, to know her and join with her. Clare might love turtles and butterflies, but she was lucky if they tolerated her. A cat was only an amusing companion. But a horse could be your friend—a friend who would lend you her strength and her speed and transform you into someone new, someone better. All you had to do was love her.

Clare decided she'd been a coward long enough. If only she could have a calm, intelligent, beautiful animal like Mirage for a partner, she knew she'd be able to ride again. She'd be able to *soar*.

Clare turned to Verily. Her friend had had to give up riding too, when Clare stopped. "Verily, isn't that Mr. Alexander's land?"

"Yes, Miss."

"He sells horses, doesn't he?"

"Yes, Miss."

"Maybe he'll sell me Mirage!"

.   .   .

AT SUPPER THAT EVENING, Clare announced: "I want to start riding again. And I found the *perfect* horse. She belongs to our neighbor, Mr. Alexander. I've met her across the fence, and—"

"You're walking up to strange horses?" Aunt Hortense interrupted.

Clare ignored her. "She's as gentle as a lamb, Father! Couldn't you purchase her?"

"It will have to wait, Clare. Lucas and I are leaving for the cotton plantation tomorrow morning."

"What makes this horse special?" Mr. Cromwell asked. "What drew you to her?"

"She—" Clare hedged, lowering her eyes to her quail. She suspected her aunt would disapprove of a paint. "She came right up to the fence to greet me. I didn't even call her. The other horses paid no attention to me whatsoever, but Mirage…the way she looked at me, it's like *she* chose *me*."

"Mirage?" Aunt Hortense bristled. "How do you know its name? Did that colored man speak to you?"

"No, Aunt," Clare sighed. "I don't know her real name. But Mirage fits her."

"What does she look like, this Mirage?" asked her father.

"She's…black and white."

"Black with white markings?" Mr. Cromwell prompted. "Does she have stockings?"

Clare knew he was only trying to make friendly conversation. But his probing made Clare grimace. She supposed there was no point in withholding the truth. "She's a paint."

Mr. Cromwell smiled. "A piebald?"

Clare nodded. She glanced at Aunt Hortense, and she knew she'd been right to dread her reaction.

"I haven't seen one of those in—"

"Out of the question!" Aunt Hortense proclaimed. "Ladies do not ride piebalds!"

"Why not?"

"It's undignified!"

"How extensive is the discoloration?" Clare's father interjected. He was frowning too. "Would your saddle blanket hide it?"

"Mirage isn't discolored! She's beautiful!"

Clare's aunt glared at her. "Is it wall-eyed?"

"One of her eyes is blue," Clare admitted.

"You cannot trust a wall-eyed horse!"

"Glass eyes are unsettling," Clare's father agreed.

"A horse can see perfectly well with a blue eye," Mr. Cromwell informed them.

"It should be doing tricks in a circus!" Aunt Hortense declared, motioning with her knife. "Or pulling a plow!"

"Just because you cannot see her worth doesn't mean she's worthless!" Clare cried. "The Godolphin Arabian was used as a *carthorse*. The Godolphin Arabian, who sired the world's best racehorses!"

"Clare!" her aunt admonished. "A lady does not speak of such things!"

"What?" Clare drew her arms out of the way so Austin, the footman, could take her plate. "Covering?"

Her aunt spluttered.

In truth, Clare had only a vague idea what occurred when a stallion covered a mare. But the look of horror on her aunt's face was well worth the fib. Mr. Cromwell tried vainly to suppress a chuckle.

"I won't let you turn this family into a laughingstock!" Aunt Hortense slapped Austin's wrist with her napkin when he attempted to take her plate. "Your father has indulged your whims long enough!"

He cleared his throat. "I'm sure we can find a suitable mount for you."

"But I don't want another horse! I want Mirage!"

"You shouldn't be riding at all," Aunt Hortense persisted. "You could be thrown again! How many times must I remind you, Clare: you are your father's only child. You have a responsibility to this family."

"To serve as a broodmare, you mean?"

"I think it's time Lucas and I retired," Clare's father suggested loudly. "We've an early start tomorrow."

Clare couldn't give up now. "What if I never take Mirage off the plantation? She could be a secret!"

Her father set his napkin on the table and stood. "We will discuss this when I return, Clare."

As he and Mr. Cromwell disappeared into the hall, Aunt Hortense bustled after them. "Edward, you cannot be considering—"

Clare was the only person left at the table. Austin offered her rice pudding. She accepted quickly and strained to hear her father's reply.

"I'll be gone for a week, Hortense. I'm sure this will work out on its own. Clare may lose herself in a new obsession. Or someone else may purchase this horse in the interim."

As their footsteps receded, her aunt muttered: "I will make sure of it."

Normally, rice pudding with rosewater and cinnamon was Clare's favorite dessert. Tonight, she hardly tasted it. How dare Aunt Hortense insult Mirage. How dare her father think her so fickle. Clare wouldn't rest till Mirage was hers.

CHAPTER 27

The majesty of men themselves is best discovered in the graceful
handling of such animals.
— Xenophon, *The Art of Horsemanship* (circa 350 B.C.)

All night, the words haunted Clare: "I will make sure of it."
What had her aunt meant? Would she send one of her vile
sons to purchase Mirage and send her far away?

Aunt Hortense wasn't at breakfast, so Clare couldn't ask her.
She'd sent her maid with a message:

> Your willfulness has given me a headache. We will continue our
> lessons tomorrow. Stay away from the piebald!

Clare wolfed down her breakfast and asked Phoebe to prepare a
picnic, so she could spend all day disobeying. At the very least, she
would paint Mirage, capture her forever on canvas.

Clare had Finis harness Arthur to the phaeton, and she directed
the gelding to the east fence at once. But Mirage and her paddock
mates were nowhere to be seen. Carefully, Clare stood up in the
carriage and peered over the serpentine fence.

What if Aunt Hortense had already sent word to someone, who was examining Mirage right now? Her new owner wouldn't see how special she was! He might hitch her to a plow and whip her!

Clare wasn't going to let that happen. She sat down again and urged Arthur toward the gate near the old stallion barn. Since the barn held only hay now, hardly anyone used the gate anymore, but it was still there, leading onto the back road. She could be at Mr. Alexander's stables in a quarter of an hour. She'd beg him not to sell Mirage. She'd learn Mirage's real name.

"Hold these." Clare handed Verily the reins and climbed down from the phaeton.

"What are you doing?" her friend asked as Clare unlatched the gate.

"I am protecting my horse!"

"We can't leave the plantation, Miss!"

"We'll be back before anyone knows we're gone."

Verily narrowed her eyes.

Clare nodded at the book in her friend's lap. "Don't you want to *have* an adventure instead of only reading about them?"

"Trespassing on the neighbor's property is an adventure?"

"We won't be trespassing! The first thing I'll do is find Mr. Alexander."

"And the first thing he'll do is send you home."

"I have to try, Verily! Didn't you see the way Mirage looked at me? She knows we belong together!"

"I think she was looking for another fancy French mint."

"It was more than that! We have a connection!"

"I think that horse bewitched you."

"Please, Verily?"

At last, her friend laughed a little. Then Verily tucked her book away. She clicked her tongue, and Arthur walked through the gate.

Clare closed it quickly, climbed back into the phaeton, and took the reins. A few minutes later, she'd found the gate onto Mr. Alexander's property. It was open. Clare directed Arthur down the lane. She looked around for Mirage but didn't see her. She wondered where to begin asking. The house, she supposed.

First, she needed to find a water trough for Arthur. She heard water splashing and followed the sounds to the other side of a barn. Where she saw a young Indian, washing his arms at a pump. Not a single scrap of clothing covered him above his waist. Clare's mouth dropped open, and her hand must have tightened on the reins— Arthur stopped obediently.

What the man did wear was tanned and decorated animal hide: quilled moccasins, fringed leggings, and striped breechcloth, just like in books. But his hair was short and blond. His skin was white, or at least it wasn't red. Yet that skin still marked him as Indian: the man's back was to Clare, and she could see clearly the deliberate scars at his shoulder blades, the remnants of some Indian rite.

Mirage must be *his*. Clare wondered if he'd ridden the mare all the way here, and how far they'd come. She felt her anxiety about the beautiful horse melting away. This man was kind to Mirage, Clare was certain. He understood how special she was. Clare could turn the phaeton around and leave right now, before anyone knew she'd come. She should.

But she couldn't.

Verily spoke for her: "You don't see that every day."

The young man at the pump turned around, shaking the water from his arms. Clare had never seen a man with such arms—or such a chest. For that matter, she'd never seen a man's arms or chest before, outside of paintings and statues. Even swimming on Sullivan's Island, David had never taken off his shirt.

This man was as magnificent as a statue, yet he put marble to shame. His was a breathing, rippling body. Droplets of water clung to his skin, shifting and joining. Not only his pattern of scars transfixed her: there were gorgeous undulations to his shoulders, his stomach, and his—well, *breasts*. His nipples were the color of hazelnut shells.

Clare forced her gaze past the decorated pouch around his neck, past his collarbones, up the strong column of his neck, and her fascination only increased. Something in the man's face—the slant of his nose? the shape of his lips?—seemed so familiar…

"Good morning," those lips said with a grin. That grin! Those eyes—the color of Spanish moss touched with starlight. His eyes darted between Clare and Verily till they settled on Clare. She thought the man was well aware she'd been staring at him—was still staring at him—and that he didn't mind at all. Like a young racing stallion, he luxuriated in his beauty and his power.

Now that she had his permission to admire him, Clare struggled to keep her attention from sliding downward again. "I-I came about a horse."

"We have many horses here." The man glanced toward the barn beside them. "One more, now."

Clare drew in a breath, glad both of the news itself and the distraction. "A new foal?"

The man nodded. "She gave us some trouble." His accent was different from any Clare had ever heard, pleasant and precise with its own unique cadence.

"But she and her dam are all right?"

"Yes."

"M-Might I see them? I'll be quiet, I promise!"

The man smiled again. "Come with me."

Clare forced her eyes to her friend and offered her the reins. "Verily, would you mind...?"

"I'll look after Arthur, Miss." Verily looked wary. She accepted the reins, but she whispered: "You look after yourself."

"I don't know what you mean." Clare readjusted her shawl and climbed down from the phaeton. As she followed the young man into the barn, Clare realized he was even more naked than she'd thought. His leggings and breechcloth were two separate garments: as he walked, she saw crescents of bare flesh appear in-between. Glimpses of thigh. Of *buttock*.

So she threw etiquette aside and introduced herself. "My name is Clare Stratford. I'm your neighbor to the west."

"My name is Ésh." He was closer to her own height than either David or Mr. Cromwell. Clare liked that. It was easier to look into his eyes. He wasn't so intimidating.

Ésh turned his attention down the wide aisle of the barn, where a negro was exiting a box stall. "Has she stood up yet, Ben?"

The black man, who was thirty perhaps, saw Clare and dropped his gaze. Ben's brow furrowed in confusion and concern. She knew he was wondering why a young white woman was visiting without a visible chaperone. "Not yet, but I think she's nearly there. Good morning, Miss."

"Good morning." Clare held her head high as if nothing were out of the ordinary.

Ben seemed to hesitate, then left them slowly.

With Ésh, Clare peered through the bars over the door of the stall to see a grey mare with her muzzle in a bucket. A pace behind her, a dark brown foal was testing her new legs. The filly got her front hoofs planted, but the back ones flailed beside her till she flopped over in the straw.

"Oh!" Clare cried in sympathy.

The grey mare jerked up her head, eyeing Clare with suspicion.

She almost raised her hand to her bonnet—should she take it off? did it make her look large and threatening?—but she knew a sudden movement would only make things worse.

Beside her, Ésh blew out an exaggerated sigh through his nose. This seemed to calm the mare, who returned to her bran mash.

Her stubby little tail flicking in the straw as if she were winding herself up, the brown foal tried again—and collapsed again when her spindly legs wobbled out from under her. Clare longed to help, but she knew this was something the filly must learn to do on her own.

As much as Clare wanted to watch the foal take her first steps, she remained acutely aware that a half-naked man stood beside her. She felt very warm. She kept stealing glances at him. Ésh must be nineteen or twenty, she decided. She had so many questions: Which tribe had he lived with, and for how long? Why had he come to South Carolina? What was in the pouch around his neck? How had he obtained the long scar just below his shoulder? Did he usually wear earrings?

He was wearing a breechcloth, leggings, and moccasins. She was wearing boots, stockings, garters, drawers, a chemise, a corset, a corset cover, a cage crinoline, a petticoat, a skirt, a bodice, under-sleeves, a collar, a shawl, gloves, and a bonnet.

The wide rim of her bonnet made it difficult to study Ésh surreptitiously; she had to turn her whole head. She watched his head tilt toward her just a little, and she watched a broad grin spread over his face. Once again, Ésh knew she was staring at him.

Clare felt her cheeks going hot and returned her attention to the foal. The newborn drew her front legs beneath her, heaved herself upward, and planted her back legs. Clare gasped with delight. She'd done it!

But the filly's front hoofs began sliding forward and outward. Her back hoofs went wide too, till the poor little horse was flat against the straw again, her legs splayed out in four directions. Clare covered her mouth and giggled. So close!

The mare finished her breakfast and turned to lick her daughter's neck. Encouraged, the filly struggled anew and slowly righted herself. She swayed, she tottered, but she remained on her feet. Clare wanted to cheer.

"Does she have a name?" Clare whispered to Ésh.

"Not yet." He stepped back from the stall.

"What about…" She followed him toward the harness room, which smelled wonderfully of leather. A fringed buckskin shirt hung from one of the hooks. At first, Clare was only disappointed Ésh intended to cover himself. But it *was* March. She was wearing a wool dress and a shawl.

Then, as Ésh pushed his arms inside and pulled the garment over his head, Clare really looked at his shirt, and horror stole her breath. Unlike his leggings, his shirt wasn't decorated only with buckskin fringe. It was decorated with *hair*: strand after strand of black and red and white hung from each arm and each side of his chest like trophies.

How many people had he killed? How many white people—old people—children? If he'd been wearing that shirt when she first saw him, Clare would have turned around and fled. Now, she was alone in a barn with a murderer, and her legs wouldn't move.

His hand smoothing down his ghastly trophies, Ésh turned back to her. "What about...?"

"Are—" Clare choked out. "Are those scalps?"

Ésh laughed. He held out his arm toward her to give her a better look.

Clare winced.

"This isn't human hair. It's from the horses I've captured."

"Oh." Slowly, Clare returned his smile and let down her guard again. It helped that Verily was standing just outside the harness room now, though her friend's arms were crossed in impatience. Clare pretended to ignore her. "The horse I came about, I think she must be yours. The black-and-white paint?"

Ésh grinned even wider. Clare could see he was fond of Mirage. "I take care of her, but she is not mine."

"Then she is for sale?"

"Yes."

"I met her over our fence, you see, and I've fallen in love. Could I meet her properly?"

"She is in the east paddock today. It is not far." Ésh pointed with his chin toward the other end of the barn and started toward it.

Clare followed, and Verily shadowed her. "What's her name?"

"Medusa."

"That's a terrible name!" Clare scowled. "Pegasus, perhaps... although he was a boy..."

Outside, Ésh led Clare and Verily down a gentle slope, toward a giant live oak. "I know Medusa was a monster. Who was Pegasus?"

"Medusa's son—a winged horse."

"All horses have wings."

"I suppose they do," Clare agreed, longing to ride more than ever. "I've been calling her Mirage. Don't you think that fits her better?"

"What does Mirage mean?"

"A mirage is...a vision."

"Yes. I like that better. Jesse says it is bad luck to change a horse's name, but my people think it is *good* luck." Clare was growing more accustomed to Ésh's pronunciations. His *that* sounded like *dat* and his *think* like *tink*, which reminded Clare not only of the way many negroes spoke but also of her mother's Irish accent.

Before Clare could ask who his people were, Ésh stopped at a gate just beyond the giant oak. On the other side of the fence, Clare spotted Mirage next to one of her paddock mates. They stood with their heads pointing in opposite directions, busily grooming each other's backs with their teeth and tongues. As Ésh opened the gate, Mirage's ears pricked toward them, and she raised her head. She gave her grooming mate a few final nibbles, then trotted over.

Verily decided to stay outside the fence. One of the low branches of the live oak made a bench for her.

Mirage nickered in greeting, and Clare hoped she was coming for her. Instead, the mare went straight for Ésh, nuzzling his hair and lipping his ear. He chuckled and murmured something in a language Clare didn't understand.

When Mirage did turn her head, her nostrils quivered. She thrust her muzzle toward Clare's face and opened her jaws.

Clare sucked in a frightened breath and stepped back. "She doesn't bite, does she?"

Smiling, Ésh looped an arm around Mirage's neck to restrain her. "No, but she does love to eat flowers." Ésh motioned toward the silk roses decorating the inner brim of Clare's bonnet.

"Oh!" She undid the ribbon and hurried back to Verily. Over the fence, she handed her bonnet to her friend. When Clare turned around, she found Ésh staring at her, though he was trying not to. She touched her head. "What? Is my hair all mussed?"

"Your hair…is like honey," Ésh breathed.

Clare dropped her eyes. "S-Some kinds of honey, I suppose." It was more brown than gold.

Had Ésh just complimented her? Was he still staring at her? She'd been so thunderstruck admiring *his* beauty, she'd never dreamed Ésh might find something to admire in her. Compared to him, she was ordinary, and she hadn't made any sort of effort this morning. Why on Earth had she chosen this old green-and-brown plaid? Clare's gloved fingers tightened self-consciously on her ugly skirt.

She only made Ésh pay more attention to it. "Can you ride in that?"

"No." It was a hoop skirt, not a riding habit.

"Then I will show you how wise and gentle she is myself." Facing her tail, he patted Mirage's right shoulder. "My people, we mount from what you call 'the off side.' Many of the horses here, they do not like this. They will not allow it. Medusa—Mirage—she let me the first time." With his right hand, Ésh gripped Mirage's mane just above her withers. Then in one faultless, fluid motion, he leapt up, turning his body in the air, and vaulted onto her back.

Clare gasped. She'd never seen anything so beautiful in her life. He was as graceful as a ballet dancer. One moment Ésh was standing on the ground, and the next he was mounted on Mirage, only the swaying fringes of his leggings and shirt testifying to his flight. Clare wanted him to slide off and do it again. She could watch this man leap onto this horse over and over for the rest of her life and never tire of it.

"You see?" Ésh smiled. "She did not move. She learns quickly. Unless she sees a flower she wants to eat, she always obeys. And every gait is smooth. She is a joy." Without a word or a kick, seemingly without a signal of any kind, Ésh asked Mirage to walk, then to trot. They began circling the paddock around Clare, cantering now, Ésh holding his seat with nothing but supple balance and a handful of mane.

As they flew, man blended into horse, horse into man, his agile legs melding into her powerful sides, her mane flowing into his horsehair-and-buckskin shirt. Clare understood why the Greeks had believed in centaurs. She did not so much want this horse now as envy her.

When Ésh and Mirage eased back to a walk, Clare called: "Where did you learn to ride like that?"

"From my brother Háhkota. He is Cheyenne. I am too."

"Cheyenne? You've come from the Great Plains?"

"Yes." Again without any signal Clare could see, Ésh stopped Mirage.

"What brought you all the way to Charleston?"

"Everything I remember is Cheyenne. My mother and grandfather found me when I was a baby. But as you see, I must have had another family first." Ésh flicked a finger through his golden hair, long enough to be scandalous. "I hoped I would find them here, my first family. But I have not."

"Why did you think they were here?"

"They wrote it on the side of the cave where they left me: *David McAllister, Sophie McAllister. Charleston, S. C. July 1841.*"

Clare gaped. She couldn't breathe. It wasn't possible. David had told them all that his baby brother had *died*—in July 1841, nearly nineteen years ago. But if that baby had lived… "The cave—was it on Independence Rock?"

"How did you…?" Ésh caught her astonishment.

She could see it now. Clare finally understood why Ésh's face was so familiar, why she'd trusted him at once and why she couldn't stop staring. Those were Father Joseph's lips. And that was David's nose. "Ésh, I know David McAllister. I know your family."

CHAPTER 28

[Animals] do not lie awake in the dark and weep for their
    sins,
They do not make me sick discussing their duty to God…
Not one is respectable or unhappy over the whole earth.
— Walt Whitman, "Song of Myself" (1881)

He'd liked her from the start. Apart from Ben's wife Hephzibah, Ésh hadn't seen a woman up close for more than two moons, so he would have been interested in any female visitor. Clare was young and pretty, at least for a white girl. She loved a paint horse, so he knew she was smart.

And the way she looked at him, like she'd never seen a man before, like every part of him was delicious and fascinating… A girl hadn't looked at him like that since— He wasn't sure a girl had ever looked at him like that.

Ésh thought the black girl must be Clare's slave. This fact was not in Clare's favor. But here in South Carolina, so many white people owned slaves. Even people who were partly white owned other people. Mr. Alexander and Mrs. Kerrison had taught him that not all slave owners were cruel. Ésh would wait to make up his mind about that part of Clare till he knew more.

Then she took off her hat, and Ésh had understood. *Clare* was the girl who'd visited his dreams, the one whose hair was like honey. When she'd stood beside him in the barn, he'd thought he'd smelled roses!

Now, she was telling him she knew his white family, after he'd given up hope of ever finding them. He shouldn't have doubted the Sacred Powers. They had sent her to him. They had marked her: Clare's cheek carried two small spots like finger-taps of brown paint.

Ésh swung his left leg over Mirage's neck and slid from her back. He wanted to be closer to Clare; he wanted to hear her every word. "My family is here?"

"Yes! In Charleston!" Clare looked as excited as he was. "Your uncle Joseph is at St. Patrick's; your grandfather and grandmother, René and Anne, are on Archdale Street; and your brother David is at Roper Hospital."

"David McAllister is my brother?"

"Yes, but he doesn't use the name McAllister anymore. That was his father's name—*your* father's name." Clare's eyes were wide with wonder. Like her hair, they were the color of dark honey. Ésh was very glad she'd removed her hat. "He uses your mother's name, Lazare."

"My mother is in Charleston too?"

"No." Clare's excitement faded. "I'm afraid your mother and father both died on the way West."

"And Sophie McAllister?"

"She was your sister. She died a few months before I was born. Her tomb is in Charleston, at St. Patrick's. Your name is carved in the mausoleum above hers, because David told us you died too."

His *brother* had left him in the cave?

"Not the name Ésh, of course—your mother named you Ian."

Ian. Ésh liked it. Short, simple, and easy to pronounce.

"But why would David lie?" Clare's hand was at her forehead as if her head ached, and she was swaying on her feet. "I-I need to sit down."

Ésh opened the gate so Clare could sit on the lowest branch of the giant oak. Her slave looked worried. She handed Clare back her hat, but Clare only held it hanging limply in front of her.

"I've known David since I was a child. He— How could he..."

Ésh saw Clare wanted to think, but he had waited all his life for these answers, and only his brother had them. "My brother David is your friend? Do you think he will visit you again soon?"

Clare's slave scoffed.

"I doubt it," Clare murmured. "It's...complicated." Her face was tight with pain. "David and I—we quarrelled. It's been more than a year since I saw him last."

Ésh couldn't give up now. "Where is this St. Patrick's, and Archdale Street, and..."

Clare's honey-brown eyes fixed on his. She drew in a breath. "I could take you."

"When?"

"Now."

"Miss Clare!" her slave cried.

Clare raised her chin. She looked more determined than ever.

Ésh would take her at her word. "I must speak to Ben, to ask if it is O.K. that I go. Mr. Alexander, he is not here today."

"Yes, of course."

Ésh meant to go directly to Ben. But before he'd even rounded the enormous trunk of the oak, Clare's slave began arguing with her: "We cannot go all the way to Charleston with a stranger, Miss!"

Ésh wanted to know how Clare would respond, how she treated her slave when she thought they were alone. What better way to understand if Clare was cruel or kind? The green leaves and giant bulk of the oak hid him well. All he had to do was pause and listen.

Clare didn't shout at her slave or strike her. Instead, Clare tried to convince the other girl. "We're only going to St. Patrick's. It's on the Neck. And Ésh isn't a stranger—he's a Lazare. He's practically family."

"He was raised by savages! Literally!"

"Indians aren't savages!"

On the other side of the oak, Ésh smiled. He was liking Clare more and more.

"Even *if* he's a Lazare," the black girl argued, "how does that mean you can trust him? His uncle broke your mother's heart, and his brother broke yours."

Ésh's eyes widened. He stared at the rough bark of the oak between them and wished he could see Clare's face. She had been in love with David? Was she still? Was that why she wanted to go into Charleston?

Clare did not contradict her slave; she only insisted: "There is nothing wrong with Grand-père René."

"It's more than ten miles to Charleston! We could be stranded!"

"Arthur is perfectly hardy. It hasn't rained for days, and there isn't a cloud in the sky, so there won't be any mud. We'll be back before dusk."

"Someone will see us!"

"In these bonnets, with the hood of the phaeton up, no one will be able to see our faces unless we're looking straight at them."

"Someone will see us," the black girl repeated more forcefully. "Your aunt or your father will find out, and they will blame me for letting you ruin yourself."

"I'll tell them you objected vehemently. I'll protect you!"

For a moment, Clare's slave went quiet. "I know you'll *try*, Miss. But I don't belong to *you*."

"I have to do this, Verily. It's my last chance."

"Last chance for what?"

"To make my own choice! Father and Aunt Hortense will marry me off, and I'll be trapped, same as Mama was. I know you aren't free, but neither am I. I'd rather be ruined than chained to a man I don't love for the rest of my life."

Verily lowered her voice. "Maybe you got your own chains, Miss, but they're nothing like ours."

"What can I do, Verily? You said it yourself: you don't belong to me. I can't buy you, and I can't free you."

"But you understand, Miss: this choice of yours, I'm going to feel the hurt, same as you. Except it isn't *my* choice. It isn't *my* day."

"Tell me how I can make amends, and I will do it."

Quiet settled. Ésh almost left them. He'd learned what he needed to know: Clare treated her slave like a person, not property. He'd also learned a great deal more.

As he was stepping away, Verily said: "You've brought me particular books before, when I've asked you."

Ésh stopped. He knew it was against *veho* law for a slave to read. Clare only answered: "Yes."

"I've heard there are books written by men who were slaves, after they got free. One of them named Frederick Douglass, another named William Brown. That's the kind of book I really want to read."

"Those are the kinds of books people burn, Verily."

"Will you find one for me?"

On the other side of the oak, Clare hesitated before she made her decision. "I will. I promise."

Ésh heard their dresses rustling in movement. He hurried away.

He found Ben carrying a rope, about to retrieve the red stallion. It was time to lead him along the mares' paddocks. Ben would watch their reactions and see if any of the mares was ready to be mounted. The stallion came to the gate willingly. Head up, lip curled, his nostrils flared as he inhaled the female scents on the breeze.

"You been here more than two months, and you haven't rested a single day," Ben said. "I have no problem with you going to meet your family, or with you borrowing Medusa. If Mr. Alexander were here, I know he'd give his permission too. But you going with a white girl is another matter."

Ésh frowned. "Why?"

Ben looked back toward the foaling barn, where Clare was talking to her brown gelding. "That there is Edward Stratford's daughter. I seen her across the fence. I don't know what she thinks she's doing here, but you got to be smarter, Ésh. White men, planters especially, don't take kindly to young stallions compromising their daughters."

"'Compromising'?"

"Ruining, soiling…"

Ésh thought he understood, and he scowled. "I am not planning to—" Not today, at least.

"If you are alone with Miss Stratford for even a few minutes, that's exactly what her father and everyone else will *think* you've been doing."

Did white men have so little control of themselves and so little respect for their women?

"If you were someone respectable, Mr. Stratford would expect you to marry her. But you are something else, Ésh. I don't know how her father would react. Might arrange it so you can't compromise a woman ever again."

"What do you mean?"

"Ain't it the same with the Cheyenne? You told us the young women wear a protective rope. If a man interferes with it, what does her father do?"

Ésh swallowed. "He kills the man." For a moment, he watched Clare across the distance, while the stallion behind him pawed the ground and whinnied his complaints. "Do white women wear such a rope?"

"I don't rightly know, Ésh. *I* ain't never seen under their skirts. *I* ain't a fool."

But Ésh had dreamed about Clare. Were the Sacred Powers only showing him how he would die? The badger had told Ésh he would not live to be old, and that his death would follow the cutting of his hair. The doctor at Fort Laramie had taken Ésh's hair more than four moons ago. It had already grown long enough to cover his ears.

Surely the Sacred Powers would not let him die before he returned to the Zizistas and shared what he'd learned. Would they?

Across the distance, Clare spotted him and smiled. She left Verily with their gelding and started toward Ésh. He thought again of how Clare had stared at him, and how she'd touched him in his dreams, like a promise.

"Clare and I will not be alone," Ésh explained to Ben. "We will have her maid with us."

"Last I knew, a maid didn't count as a chaperone." Ben eyed the stallion, who was growing more and more impatient. Then he looked back at Ésh and sighed. "I ain't your father, Ésh. I ain't even your employer. I can't tell you what to do. But if you have any sense, you'll find another way to meet your family. Going anywhere with that white girl is dangerous, for you and for her." Ben turned his back and opened the gate.

Ésh watched Clare grow nearer. She'd put her hat back on. Ésh wanted to see her hair again. He wanted to see it loose, cascading to her knees like in his first vision. He wanted to see all of Clare. He feared that if he said no to her now, that would never happen.

Her skin was flushed, from exertion or excitement or both. She glanced toward Ben, who was leading the prancing stallion away. "What did he say?"

"That I am free to go."

Clare grinned. "Truly?"

"Ben also said that going into Charleston with you is dangerous."

Clare opened her lips, but nothing came out. She had beautiful lips. Ésh imagined touching them—kissing them. Clare exhaled and recovered herself. "He's right. It could be dangerous. Are you afraid?"

"No. Are you?"

"No."

"Then let us go."

CHAPTER 29

I once was lost, but now am found.
— John Newton, "Amazing Grace" (1772)

Quite to Clare's disappointment, Ésh changed into a plain brown suit. Even his waistcoat and his bowler hat were brown. He remained handsome—he could be nothing else —but in a subdued way. This effect was on purpose. "I go into Charleston dressed as a Cheyenne, and everyone will stare at us. I do not think you want them staring."

Yet he rode Mirage, a horse whose coat shouted *"Come look at me!"*

This seemed to work to their advantage. When other riders, drivers, and passengers remarked their little group on the road, they noticed only Mirage. The people paid no heed to the nondescript chestnut pulling the nondescript phaeton or to the nondescript women inside. Clare was grateful now for her dull brown day dress with its faded green stripes.

A piebald horse with a blue eye was unusual, but not as outlandish as an Indian riding bareback would have been—Ésh used a saddle and bridle now. After a moment of surprise, admira-

tion, amusement, or disdain, passers-by returned their attention to
the road, the countryside, or each other. Many did not notice their
little group at all.

"I suppose in the West, no one would notice Mirage," Clare
observed, "because there are so many horses like her."

"Yes and no." Ésh kept Mirage at the perfect angle, where Clare
could see him beyond the rim of her bonnet and the hood of her
phaeton and still keep an eye on Arthur and the road. "There are
many paints in the West, but no two of them are the same."

Ésh explained that this was one of the reasons the Cheyenne
favored paints: their patterns were all unique, making it easier for a
hunter or warrior to pick his own animals out of the village's herd
when he needed them. Yet the paints' coats allowed them to blend
into the landscape better than solid-colored horses. In daylight, from
a distance, the horses looked like a pattern of shadows against the
earth. In winter, you could disguise their dark parts with white clay
and blend into the snow. At night, you could darken their white
parts with black mud.

Ésh had snuck close to many enemy villages this way, spied on
them, and then returned with other warriors to capture their
enemies' horses. He was proud of his horse thefts. Hearing him talk
of his daring, Clare couldn't help but admire him.

Beside her, Verily was anything but entranced. Her friend looked
bored, annoyed, and worried by turns. Verily said nothing aloud,
and after a few attempts to engage her, Ésh learned to let her be.
Clare thought all three of them would have preferred to leave her
friend reading under the giant oak. But even Clare wasn't reckless
enough to make such a journey *alone* with a man.

She told Ésh everything she could about his family. "Your father
was a carpenter—he worked with wood. His name was Peregrine
McAllister."

Ésh repeated the name carefully.

"Peregrine means 'foreigner' or 'traveller,'" Clare explained.
"But it's also a kind of falcon—a bird. Some Cheyenne men are
named after birds, aren't they?"

"Yes." Ésh looked pleased.

"Your father came from the Scottish Highlands. Do you know where Scotland is?"

"Across the ocean."

Clare nodded. "In many ways, your Highland ancestors were like Indians: their clan, or tribe, meant everything to them. They were led by chieftains. Long ago, when they went to war with invaders, the tribesmen painted themselves for battle. And they had a reputation for savagery." Clare wanted to ask Ésh if he'd killed anyone in battle, if he did have a collection of scalps somewhere. But the possibility frightened her.

Ésh looked so delighted by this information about his father's people that Clare decided not to tell him about the Highland Clearances—how the Highlanders had been forced off their lands, how they'd been scattered and lost their traditional ways of life.

The news that his grandmother was deaf intrigued Ésh too. "When they wish to trade, tribes who do not know each other's language also communicate with signs. I wonder if her signs are the same."

Clare tried to show him a few, but she had only one hand free. It was too difficult to drive Arthur and sign at the same time. So Clare told Ésh about Grand-père René, Father Joseph, and David.

"My grandfather and brother are both medicine men, and my uncle is a holy man?" Mirage tried to detour toward wildflowers growing alongside the road, and Ésh pulled her away. "Are they good people, my family?"

"The best I have ever known."

Ésh glanced at Verily and frowned. "Do they have slaves?"

"Two. A husband and wife, Henry and May. They are your grandparents' age, and they work very little now. You have to understand, Ésh, the law doesn't allow your grandfather to free them."

"And it is your father who owns Verily?" Again, he looked at her, but Verily was staring at her hands.

"Yes," Clare answered. Her voice had grown weak. She turned to her friend, cleared her throat, and forced strength into her words. "If you were mine, I would free you. I swear it, Verily."

"But you said the law will not allow this," Ésh reminded her.

Verily spoke at last, though she did not meet their eyes. "I could go to Canada, where that law can't reach. But I won't go without my sister."

"The Cheyenne do not have slaves?" Clare asked.

"No."

"But they take captives in battle?"

"It is not the same. Captives become part of our tribe. They work no more than the rest of us. They marry Cheyennes, and their children do not suffer because one of their parents was a captive once."

Ésh spoke of the Cheyenne as if he were still one of them, as if they were his future as well as his past. Clare longed to ask if *he* would marry a Cheyenne woman. Might he *already* be married? She must find a way to the truth. "Will you return to the Cheyenne, do you think?"

"Yes. It is good to know where I came from, but the Cheyenne are my true people. And my family needs me." For a moment, Ésh averted his eyes, lost in some private worry.

She pressed him with other questions about his life in the West. She'd been fascinated by Indians all her life, and she'd read every book she could find about them. But Ésh was better than any book.

She asked about buffalo and antelope and prairie dogs, then circled back to people. None of her questions prompted Ésh to mention a wife or fiancée. Clare supposed this was only just: when she'd told Ésh about David, she'd been careful not to betray her love for him—or the fact that she was making this reckless journey partly in the hope of seeing David again.

Perhaps if Clare revealed herself a bit more, Ésh would too. "I envy you, Ésh: you know where you belong. I thought I knew that, once. Now, I know only where I do *not* belong, that I couldn't bear to stay *here* for the rest of my life."

"Why not?"

"Because, as my aunt is always reminding me, I am my father's only child—his only heir. My aunt and my father expect me to marry a planter's son. A man who has grown up ordering other people around and beating them when they displease him. A man who would be marrying me so he can become master to even more slaves. Most South Carolinians, slavery is all they know, and they accept it as their right. But my mother lived a different life before she married my father. She knew slavery was wrong. She tried to be a good mistress, a good planter's wife. For years she tried. And it killed her. It took her spirit and it killed her."

Ésh was listening so intently, sympathy furrowing his brow; but this was more than Clare had meant to tell him. *"My mother was so unhappy, she took her own life"* was no way to attract a man. Clare concluded: "So I do what I can to escape. I read. I wander the gardens and forests on our plantation. I study animals. I sketch and I paint."

Ésh offered her a small smile. "You take a strange man into Charleston."

Clare laughed weakly. "It is more that, with my mother gone, my own family feel like strangers. Your family, the Lazares, do not think I am odd or unwomanly for collecting caterpillars or chasing lizards. They understand me and encourage me."

"That is what a family should do."

Should, yes. If Clare felt out of place here, in a family who looked like her, among neighbors who looked like her, how lonely Ésh must have felt, growing up with people who looked nothing like him. His Cheyenne family must be wonderful indeed. "Is your Cheyenne mother still living?"

"Yes. She made the clothing you saw."

"What kind of hides were those?"

"Deer and mountain sheep."

"And that was quillwork, on your shirt?"

Ésh smiled. "How do you know about quillwork?"

"We have a little in a museum here."

"What is a museum?"

"A place where we collect beautiful and interesting objects. But your mother's work is finer than the pieces in the museum. She is a true artist."

"That is not even her best work. But I will tell her you liked it. You will make her very happy." Ésh also told Clare about his grandfather the medicine man and his annoying but endearing little brother.

"Oh, I wish I could meet them!" Then Clare blushed to realize the implication. How could she go West and meet his Cheyenne family unless Ésh took her?

He was smiling. "I think my family would like you. You are curious and brave like a Cheyenne."

Clare blushed even hotter. That might be the nicest thing anyone had ever said to her. "Do they speak English too?"

"My mother speaks some English, and my grandfather knows many of your words." He sighed. "My little brother speaks English better than me."

"I think your English is very good."

"You are kind, I think. I know I am still learning."

"Would you teach me some Cheyenne words?"

"First, you must know we do not call ourselves 'Cheyenne.' That is what the Lakota call us. It means 'we do not understand their language.' We call ourselves Zizistas. It means 'the People.'"

"Say it again?" He did, and Clare echoed him as best she could: "Zi-zis-tas."

Ésh taught her the Zizistas word for horse: *mo'é-no'ha*. He taught her black and white and red: *É-mo'ktavo*, *É-vo'kom*, *É-má*. All the while, the horses' hoofs carried them closer and closer to Charleston.

Ésh asked her to sing something for him in Irish. Nervously, Clare obliged. She chose "Trasna na dTonnta," because it was a cheerful song about homecoming, even if it did mention a grave-yard. "Farewell to loneliness," Clare sang in her mother's tongue. "My heart leaps with joy..." Best of all, her performance seemed to please Ésh.

Far too soon, they passed the turn for the Washington Race Course, and it was time to slow Arthur and Mirage to a walk, to cool them down before they reached St. Patrick's. At least this last mile would be a slow one; but it could not be slow enough. Clare had spent the whole morning with Ésh, and she wanted more time.

She interested him beyond her connection to his family, Clare was certain; but did she *captivate* Ésh as he did her? What could she talk about, in these last few minutes (virtually) alone, to communicate that she wanted—needed—to see him again?

"I have a confession to make," Clare blurted.

"What is a confession?"

"It means there is something shameful that I have not told you, because I'm afraid you'll think less of me." Clare drew in a deep breath. "I love horses, truly I do; but I have not ridden one in six years."

Ésh scowled. "Why not?"

"Because I fell. I broke my arm. It was so painful… I've tried to ride many times since then, but I've been so frightened that I will fall again."

"You *will* fall again."

"Pardon?" Her plan wasn't working. He thought her an idiot.

Yet Ésh's smile was warm. "I have fallen from horses many times, and I know I will fall again."

"But you ride with such *confidence*—like you're not on Mirage but part of her."

"First, I learned how to fall. This is important. Second, were you riding with both of your legs on the same side of the horse?"

Clare blushed. They weren't in downtown Charleston, but there were buildings and carriages and *people* all around them now. Anyone could have heard Ésh asking about her legs. "Yes."

"I have seen other white women do this. I do not understand it. You cannot talk to a horse like that. Horses talk with their bodies. If they can feel so little of your body, and you can feel so little of theirs, you cannot calm them or encourage them. It does not work."

"Well, a woman riding sidesaddle carries a whip that serves as her right…limb…" A couple was passing in an open victoria, and Clare felt the woman glaring at her. Verily was too. "I take it Cheyenne women ride astride."

"Yes."

"I *want* to ride that way, but I wouldn't know how."

"I could teach you," Ésh offered, just as she'd hoped. "I can teach you how to fall too."

"I would love that."

"Miss Clare…" Verily interjected in admonition.

Clare had the perfect excuse to ignore her. "We're nearly there! This is Radcliffe Street up ahead." She turned Arthur, and Ésh turned Mirage. "That's St. Patrick's!"

"That is where my uncle the Priest lives?"

"It is." The wooden building looked more like a barn than a church.

Verily stayed with the horses while Clare led Ésh to the presbytery. A negress answered their knock—the Priests' housekeeper, Clare assumed. "Good day," Clare said. "Is Father Lazare at home?"

"Not at the moment. But he said he'd stop back for dinner."

"Will you tell him Clare Stratford is waiting for him in the cemetery? At his family's mausoleum?"

"You're welcome to wait in the parlor."

"No thank you." As they turned to the cemetery, Clare smiled at Ésh. "Let me show you your tomb."

She led him to the mausoleum with LAZARE carved over the entrance. Despite the tomb's purpose, its rosy sandstone exterior always struck her as warm and cheery. The little structure resembled a church more than St. Patrick's did, ornamented as it was by a few Gothic flourishes: gingerbread trim beneath a sharply peaked roof and an open quatrefoil window in each gable. The mausoleum managed to look welcoming without looking ominous, even after a rain, for it was then the resurrection ferns above the entrance seemed to greet you like bowing palm fronds.

The doors were locked, so Clare took Ésh around the back. Here, decorative ironwork supported a climbing Lamarque rose and protected a stained glass window of the Blessed Virgin. Instead of an Immaculate Heart, a golden-orange butterfly with black veins and white spots hovered over her chest.

Ésh gaped at it. He touched the stained glass through the ironwork. "This animal…"

"It's a Monarch butterfly. Do you have them in Cheyenne country?"

"Yes. A butterfly like this, it led my mother and grandfather to me in the cave."

"Truly?" Clare grinned. "I raised Monarch butterflies when I was a girl, before my father forbade it. I think that's why Grand-père René chose a Monarch: I talked about them so often. The man who made this window, your grandfather saved his life. Butterflies symbolize resurrection, you see: a caterpillar seems to die, then emerges from its chrysalis more beautiful than before. René also wanted to honor his great-granduncle Thierry, who was a lepidopterist—someone who studies butterflies. It's a play on your family name, too: Lazare is the French form of Lazarus, a man who rose from the dead." Now, Ésh had fulfilled the promise of his mother's name.

This window held a secret wholly apart from its symbolism. Hidden behind the climbing rose and the decorative ironwork was a little hook for a key. René had shown her years ago. His granddaughter Sophie, David and Ésh's sister, had almost been Clare's sister. Clare had wanted to pay her respects.

She retrieved the key and unlocked the mausoleum's bronze doors. Their green patina was not unlike Ésh's eyes. A blue glow from the window suffused the white limestone interior, sunlight tinted by the Blessed Virgin's robes and glass sky. The vestibule of the mausoleum was a tiny chapel, complete with an altar and a prie-Dieu. The side walls each held three stacked crypts.

Clare touched the highest panel on the right wall. "You see?"

Ésh looked, but he did not see. "I have a confession to make." A shy smile played over his lips. "I cannot read."

"Oh! I could teach you. I taught Verily."

Ésh glanced toward the doors of the mausoleum as if someone living might overhear them. "I thought it was against the law for slaves to read."

Clare raised her chin. "It is."

Ésh's smile returned. "What do the words say?"

"It's your name: Ian McAllister."

They reached toward the carved letters at the same time. For a moment, their fingers interlaced. Clare drew her hand back and blushed. She was wearing gloves, but she felt the warmth of Ésh's fingers nonetheless. It was the closest she'd come to touching him.

"Your parents' names are here too, as a memorial, though they were buried out West." She pointed to the names just above his on the panel: "Catherine Lazare McAllister and Peregrine McAllister."

"These are also names?" Ésh touched the inscription on the crypt below his, then looked across to the center crypt in the left wall.

Clare nodded. "Your sister Sophie and your aunt Hélène. Their bodies do rest here. Hélène died when I was a baby. But you can ask your uncle, Father Joseph, about her. She was his sister. Hélène married my mother's brother, Liam. So you see, you and I are almost family."

Ésh was grinning now. "Almost."

"Clare?" called Father Joseph. He dashed up the mausoleum's steps. "Are you all right?"

"I am marvelous, Father. In fact, 'I bring you good tidings of great joy.'" Somehow Father Joseph's presence made her feel Biblical. How many people ever delivered such news? "I have found your lost lamb, so to speak."

"Pardon?" Still catching his breath, Father Joseph braced a hand against the open door.

"Your nephew, Ian—he is risen from the grave!"

CHAPTER 30

Thy brother shall rise again.
   —John 11:23

"Pardon?" The man called Joseph said again. His eyes rested on Ésh now, his brow a wrinkle of disbelief beneath the wide edge of his low black hat.

Ésh stared at Joseph in return, searching for a resemblance. But his hat and the blue light of this stone tomb hid so much. All Ésh knew for certain was: Joseph was as tall as a Zizistas—certainly taller than Ésh.

Clare was happy to speak for him, so Ésh let her. "The baby your sister Catherine bore at Independence Rock—he didn't die, Father. He grew up among the Cheyenne and became *this man*. His name is Ésh now."

Joseph gaped at him. "W-Would you take off your hat?"

Ésh smiled. "I will if you will."

"Oh! Of course."

Hats in their hands, they gazed at each other in uncertain silence. Joseph's curly hair had been black once, Ésh could see, but much of it was grey now. He was nearly fifty years old, Clare had said. His eyes were the blue of an evening sky. Ésh had trouble finding a likeness between them.

Then the man let out a great sigh, as if he'd been holding his breath for years. "You look like your father. Your blond hair, your green eyes, even your height—they are his."

Ésh realized he'd been holding his breath too. Part of him had doubted: what if Clare was mistaken? But his uncle's words were a balm soothing Ésh's fears. This man recognized him. And there was the black-and-orange butterfly on this tomb. *This is how you'll know you've found us,"* Clare had promised in his vision.

"Ésh has your mouth, doesn't he?" Clare suggested. "And David's nose?"

"Yes." His uncle stepped closer and grasped Ésh's shoulder for a moment, as if to confirm he was real. "Praise God. These are indeed 'tidings of great joy.' I am delighted to meet you, Ésh. However did you find Clare?"

Ésh smiled at her. "She found me."

"He's working for our neighbor!" Clare explained. "Ésh helps care for Mr. Alexander's horses. I saw one of them across the fence and fell in love. She's the black-and-white paint. Did you see her at the presbytery?"

"Wait." Joseph scowled. "You're talking about the plantation."

Clare looked away for a moment. "Yes."

"You came all the way from Stratford-on-Ashley, today, alone?" Joseph's voice boomed like thunder in the hollow space of the tomb.

"I wasn't alone. Ésh was with me. Verily too."

"Clare! What were you thinking?"

"I was thinking: 'Ésh has waited almost two decades to meet you; you and your parents don't even know he's alive; and we—'"

"*Your* family doesn't know you're here, do they?"

"No…" Clare pouted.

"We have to get you home, Clare!"

She crossed her arms over her chest. "The horses need to rest."

Joseph sighed and tapped his hat against his knee. "Very well. We will all go to my parents' house for dinner and let the horses rest." He pointed at Clare. "You will go home immediately afterward."

"Yes, *Father*." Though Clare sounded irritated, she was smiling.

AFTER SOME DEBATE, they decided that Verily would remain at the presbytery to eat Father Joseph's dinner and await their return. He took her place in the phaeton. With Ésh and Mirage following them, Arthur pulled Clare and Father Joseph toward Archdale Street.

Clare asked in a low voice: "Do you think you could obtain a book for me, Father?"

"What book might that be?"

She glanced at the carriage passing on the other side of the street and the people on the sidewalks. "I'll tell you later. Not here."

Father Joseph raised an eyebrow. "All right. As long as *you* promise not to use the mausoleum key again without my permission."

Clare frowned. "Why not?"

"That is a question I cannot answer on the street either. But promise me, Clare."

"I promise, Father."

Perhaps she'd sounded defensive and insufficiently grave. He peered at her doubtfully.

Clare whispered: "I kept your secret with Mama, didn't I?"

The ghost of a smile tugged at Father Joseph's lips, and he nodded.

They drove up the lane at Grand-père René's, and Clare stopped Arthur at the stable.

"I think I'd better go in first and prepare my parents." Father Joseph climbed out of the phaeton. "Would you please give Delia my apologies, Clare, and tell her there will be at least five of us for dinner?"

"At least?" Clare echoed as he helped her down.

"We'll send Violet with a message, but I don't know how soon David will be able to get away from the hospital."

Clare's heart sped up. "I-I'll tell Delia. I can contribute a hamper of biscuits and ham, if that helps."

"I'm sure she'll appreciate it."

Father Joseph disappeared into the house. Henry came to help Ésh with the horses. Arthur; Mirage; Grand-père René's carriage horse, Cassique; and Father Joseph's old grey, Prince, greeted each other with a series of sniffs and snorts.

Clare delivered the bad news to Delia in the kitchen.

"Has the good Father mistaken me for the Lord Jesus?" Delia inquired, one floury fist propped on her hip. "Does he think I can conjure loaves and fishes whenever I please?"

"Maybe this will help." Clare held out her hamper.

Delia accepted it but shook her head. "This meal won't be nothing fancy."

"It doesn't need to be," Clare assured her.

Clare returned to the yard to see Grand-père René and Grand-mère Anne stepping from the piazza in a sort of daze. Ésh smiled and doffed his hat. He strode to meet them in the garden, between the columbines and the azaleas.

Her white hair drawn into a neat chignon beneath her cap, Anne reached out to touch her grandson's face with a trembling hand. She feasted her eyes for a long time before she turned and signed to her husband.

"She says you will not believe her," René translated, "but her hair was yellow like yours once."

"I believe her," Ésh smiled. "Will you tell her she is beautiful, whatever color her hair is?"

His grandfather chuckled. "I have told her that myself many times."

"Tell her this also, then: Cheyennes do not lie."

René obeyed. Anne covered her mouth with her hand, her eyes glistening with tears. Ésh's grandfather embraced him, pulling his grandmother in with them. Clare couldn't help but envy Ésh such a family.

"Joseph tells us you've been travelling all day. Come inside, please." René let his grandson and wife precede him across the piazza and into the house. Then he blocked the door, denying Clare entrance.

Her heart skipped a beat.

His hand on the doorjamb, René glared at her over his shoulder. Despite his spectacles, he might have been some wrathful god, with his flashing blue eyes and his white beard. "You have been reckless, Clare."

She dropped her eyes to the boards of the piazza between them. "I-I know, but——"

"Thank you."

Clare looked up again and saw a smile quirking his lips. She smiled back and followed him inside.

They sat down to the dinner Delia had cobbled together. Clare for one hardly tasted it. She was too busy devouring every word, whether signed with hands or spoken aloud.

Ésh was eager to learn some of his grandmother's signs. He asked about his parents. He told them all about the black wolf who had lent him his formal name. He explained the medicine pouch he wore around his neck. Inside was not only the fur of the wolf but the wings of a Monarch butterfly. He'd also brought a rabbit skin with a copy of the words David had carved into Independence Rock.

"Your Cheyenne mother was very brave, to raise a child who looked like her enemy," René said. "It must have been difficult for you too, being different."

"It would have been easier if I had black hair," Ésh admitted. "My aunt said I was ugly. Sometimes the other boys would tease me and call me Toad Belly."

Clare gasped. She could see from his pained expression that a part of Ésh believed himself ugly.

"My father only—how do you say—tolerated me. And sometimes I thought there must be something wrong with me. It was not only the way I look. I made stupid choices. Selfish choices. I would wonder: 'Is it because I am white?' But my mother and grandfather and brothers, they loved me no matter what I did. They believed I could be better. They made me *want* to be better."

René smiled. "That is what family is for."

'You must come to live with us now,' Anne urged.

Clare held her breath. At Mr. Alexander's, Ésh was her neighbor. If he lived here with his grandparents, when would she ever see him?

Fortunately, the idea troubled Ésh too. "I like working with Mr. Alexander's horses," he explained, "and Ben and the others need my help—there is much to do. But finding you is why I came East, and I will be here only until the summer. Maybe Mr. Alexander will let me stay with you some days and work with his horses other days."

"You mean, you will return to the Cheyenne?" Father Joseph asked.

"Yes. I am happy to know all of you. But I do not belong in Charleston."

Anne whimpered and covered her mouth with her hand.

René forced a smile. "Is there a Cheyenne girl waiting for you?"

Clare dropped her biscuit. No one noticed.

"There was someone I thought I would marry," Ésh admitted with a frown. "Her name is Méanév. I have known her since we were children. She made me better too. But she married my brother instead."

How strange, to think that Ésh had *other* brothers, one older and one younger. Clare kept glancing toward the doorway. David might arrive at any moment. She longed to see him again, but she could think of no way he might explain himself. When she couldn't hold her tongue a moment longer, Clare blurted: "Why did David tell us his brother died?"

Silence fell over the table. Only René's hands moved, translating Clare's question for Anne. They and their son were eerily calm, as if they already knew the answer—or at least, they knew more than Clare and Ésh. Father Joseph had had a few minutes alone with his parents, Clare remembered.

Finally he spoke. "You understand, Clare, that the Seal of Confession forbids me to reveal anything—"

"David told *you* the truth?"

Father Joseph hesitated, his face pained. "He did."

Ésh set down his fork. "You knew I was alive?"

"No. I knew only that you were still alive when— I thought you died in that cave on Independence Rock."

Clare couldn't believe it. "David *abandoned* his baby brother?"

"David was barely ten years old when he made that choice." Father Joseph addressed Ésh. "Your brother had just lost his parents, and then the man who was to take him to safety. There was no wet nurse. David thought there was no way to save you, Ésh, and he couldn't bear to watch you die. I hope you can find the strength to forgive him."

"What is 'forgive'?"

"It means: you know someone has done something terrible, something selfish that hurt you, but you do not condemn him. You love him anyway. The choice David made nearly nineteen years ago, to leave you behind, it has haunted him every day since. A Priest in Missouri gave him Absolution; *I* gave him Absolution; but I don't think David will forgive himself until *you* forgive him. Do you think you can do that, Ésh?"

Ésh closed his eyes. His lips moved without sound. Clare thought he was praying.

Silence crept over the table again. This time, it was broken by the front door opening and closing. Then David's voice called: "Uncle Joseph?"

"We're in the dining room," he called back. No one else moved or spoke, but everyone drew in a breath and held it. Rugs and floorboards sighed under David's feet as he strode through the parlor to reach them.

"What's happened?" Medical bag in hand, David appeared in the doorway.

He sucked in a breath and stopped with a jolt, as if he'd been electrified. But he wasn't reacting to Ésh. David's sapphire eyes were wide with shock because he'd seen Clare. He was still wearing the Vandyck beard!

Yet he did not greet her. Some unspeakable torment distressed his handsome features and he dropped his gaze, then glanced to his uncle and grandparents for an explanation.

Clare forced her eyes shut to stop the tears. David didn't want her. He didn't love her. She would never be his wife.

Beside her, Father Joseph stood. Clare willed herself to concentrate on the true reason she'd brought Ésh to Charleston. Father Joseph placed his hand on the shoulder of his youngest nephew. "David, this is your brother, Ian. He's called Ésh now. That is a Cheyenne name. His Cheyenne mother and grandfather found him in the cave on Independence Rock."

David's blue eyes went even wider and fixed on Ésh.

"Good afternoon, brother," Ésh said without a trace of resentment.

David began shuffling backward toward the parlor, shaking his head. "I— I'm dreaming…" David dropped his medical bag on the floor and staggered sideways.

All of them leapt to their feet. Through the open door to the parlor, they watched David collide with an easy chair and collapse into it. As if the seat bristled with spikes, David doubled up in pain: twisting away from them, hunching his lithe body into an unnatural contortion. His breaths rushed in and out with audible gusts. He sank one hand into his hair and didn't let go. He clutched the other fist against his chest as if he had been paralyzed in the Act of Contrition.

Clare longed to run to him and wrap her arms around him. But what comfort could she be? The way David had reacted—he couldn't even look at her…

Father Joseph saw her hesitating. "Would you come into the garden with me, Clare?" With his hands, he suggested they should leave David and Ésh alone.

Anne accepted. Reluctantly, Clare followed them.

"You're all right, David." Their grandfather placed a gentle hand on his brother's back. "Just keep your head low till you catch your breath again."

The problem with this position was that it kept David staring at the floor. Ésh wanted to see his face. He decided to sit at his brother's feet, crossing his legs like a Zizistas in a council lodge. When David's breaths had calmed, Grandfather René picked up the bag he'd dropped and retreated.

David's body was still doubled up on the edge of his chair, his hand still clenched in his black curls. Black like their grandfather, their uncle, their mother's hair. Ésh envied him that. Finally, David's blue eyes slid to Ésh's face. His lashes were damp. "You look like him," his brother said like a sigh. "Father. Our father."

Ésh smiled. "That is what our uncle said."

His brother closed his eyes. The tears escaped anyway. "I left you." His breaths were speeding up again. "I just *left* you like a piece of refuse…"

"I am not angry, brother. I am grateful."

"'Grateful'?"

"If you had tried to bring me with you, I might have died. If I had lived, I would have grown up here, yes?"

"Y-Yes."

"Our grandparents and our uncle, they are good people." Ésh knew René was listening, though he meant what he said. "They would have done their best to make me a good person too. But if I grew up here in Charleston, I would have been a different person, I think. I would never have known my Cheyenne family or my friend Méanév. They taught me how to be a man, how to think about other people before I think about myself. It took me a long time to learn these things. I am still learning. I am stubborn, and sometimes I am selfish. I am not sure I ever would have learned how to be a man, in a city where there is always a slave to do things for you. So you see, brother, in making me Cheyenne, you made me better. You saved me. How could I be angry at you?"

"I was angry at you!" His brother was weeping. Ésh could see the grieving little boy he had been. "At a baby! For killing our mother. So I tried to kill you."

Ésh shrugged. "You did not succeed. White men are clumsy."

His brother let out a sound that might have been laughter, but it was very snotty.

Their grandfather returned to offer David a handkerchief. "There is something we haven't told you about our family, Ésh. There is a reason so many Lazares have black hair—two reasons, in fact." René peered toward the hall and narrowed his eyes. "I have a pocket globe in my office. Just a moment."

While his brother blew his nose, Ésh raised himself to the long seat called a sofa.

René returned with a wooden case that filled his palm. Inside was a pale blue ball decorated with shapes and words. "Have you ever seen a globe before?"

"No," Ésh admitted. "Also…I cannot read."

"We'll teach you," René promised.

Ésh wondered if David was part of that "we." His brother was still perched uncomfortably on his chair, staring at him in wonder.

René sat beside Ésh on the sofa and lifted the ball from its case. "This is a map, a representation of the Earth."

But…the Earth had four corners.

René turned the globe, then cupped it in one hand. "Fort Laramie is about here." With the other hand, he pointed to the middle of a large reddish shape now on the ball's upper left. "In Charleston, we're about here, on the edge of the Atlantic Ocean." René tapped the southeastern border of the large reddish shape. "Most of our ancestors were born on the other side of this ocean." His fingertip travelled northeast across the pale blue area and stopped at a small yellow shape. "Your father Peregrine was born here, in Scotland." René's finger moved southward a little to a larger yellow shape. "Your Grandmother Anne's parents were born here, in France. So were my father's parents, Marguerite and Matthieu."

Ésh realized that he couldn't have seen across the ocean from White Point Garden. The ocean, and the Earth, were larger than he'd ever dreamed. Was that whole yellow area filled with white people? Was the Earth really round like this?

René tapped an enormous green shape south of France. "But my mother's mother, Àbéní, she was born in Africa."

Ésh's eyes widened. This was why negroes fascinated him, why he felt comfortable with them! "Your grandmother was a negro—a negress?"

René smiled and nodded. "She called herself a Yoruba. That was her tribe." Then anger clenched his jaw. He drew in a steadying breath and released it. "My grandmother Àbéní, your great-great-grandmother, was kidnapped by slave traders—stolen away from her family and forced onto a ship. That ship carried her to Saint-Domingue, on the island of Hispaniola, where my mother Ìfé and I were born." René's finger crossed the ocean again and landed south of Charleston, on a tiny red shape surrounded by blue. "But my mother's father, Tokala, he was born in Canada." His finger leapt past Charleston, up the large red shape. "And *his* mother, my great-grandmother, was pure Santee Sioux."

Ésh could only gape. "We are Dakota?"

His grandfather smiled. "Just a little."

"They are the cousins of the Lakota! The allies of the Cheyenne!"

This was why Maheo had led Ésh's Zizistas mother and grandfather to that cave. Ésh *did* belong with them. He always had. Whether the bands called themselves Lakota or Dakota, the Zizistas called them Inviters and counted them as kin.

"But why did your Dakota grandfather travel to…" Ésh frowned at the globe. "Saint…?"

"Tokala was sent there as punishment. His Dakota mother was a slave, so he was a slave, even though his father was her French master. As I understand it, Tokala was a rebel." René smiled again. "After his mother's death, he burned down his father's house and ran away. The French caught Tokala and shipped him to Saint-Domingue. They thought he would die quickly in the sugarcane fields. Instead, he met a beautiful Yoruba woman."

"But you said Tokala was born in Canada. I thought there were no slaves in Canada."

"There aren't anymore. But there were, for about two hundred years."

"The law changed?"

"Yes."

"Then maybe someday, the law will change here, too."

"I hope so. I dearly hope so."

David finally spoke up, though his voice sounded defeated. "You understand, Ésh, that you cannot go about the streets of Charleston saying slavery should be outlawed? And you cannot tell *anyone* we have African ancestors?"

Not even Clare? Ésh frowned. "Why not?"

Their grandfather sighed. "Because it is dangerous—for you and for everyone in our family."

"Our grandmother doesn't even know," David murmured.

Ésh stared at his grandfather.

René dropped his gaze to the floor. "I should have told her a long time ago. But she is a Charlestonian. She was raised to believe there are two kinds of people: those born to be slaves and those born to be masters. Our own ancestors are proof that most of the world thinks that way."

Ésh scowled. "Only white people think that way."

"Sadly, that is not the case. White people practice cruelty on a larger scale, but it was Indians from another tribe who sold my Dakota great-grandmother into slavery. Some African tribes sell their enemies into slavery too. Humans of any color can be cruel and cowardly—or brave and brilliant and beautiful. If you learn nothing else on your journey, Ésh, I hope you learn that. Being mostly white doesn't make you superior to Indians or Africans. Nor does it make you ugly or selfish. Only your own choices can do that."

CHAPTER 31

To err is Human; to Forgive, Divine.
— Alexander Pope, *An Essay on Criticism* (1711)

Grand-mère Anne hurried to her Mary Garden, knelt before her statue of the Blessed Virgin, and bowed her head.

Clare paced among the azaleas. "Father, do you think David was afraid I'd discover what he did to his brother? Do you think that's why he pushed me away?"

"I think that was one of the reasons." Father Joseph stood still with his hands clasped in front of him. "If it's any consolation, Clare, David has pushed all of us away."

It was no consolation whatsoever. They *had* him; David would always be Father Joseph's nephew and René and Anne's grandson. But David was slipping away from Clare. "If I told him I understand, do you think…?"

The lines around Father Joseph's eyes tightened. "*Do* you understand, Clare?"

"I… I don't know. It's so hard to believe, that anyone could abandon a child like that—least of all David. He's always been the soul of kindness…" Until the Mardi Gras ball.

Father Joseph lowered his gaze to his feet and let out a long breath. "You are so young, Clare. Every year that passes, the Devil gives us more opportunities to make terrible mistakes, to make choices we'll regret for the rest of our lives."

Clare stopped pacing. She remembered how Father Joseph had begged Ésh to forgive his brother, because David couldn't forgive himself. Father Joseph had spoken with such passion, as if the remorse were his own.

Clare glanced at Grand-mère Anne. She was still praying, and she was deaf, but Clare stepped closer to Father Joseph and lowered her voice nonetheless. "You regret not running with Mama and me."

He hesitated, then answered: "Yes."

"Why didn't you?"

"I thought I was doing what was best for all of us. I was certain your father would pursue us and take you from your mother. I thought God would never forgive us, if I abandoned my Priesthood and your mother abandoned her Marriage." His voice wavered, and his weary indigo eyes shone with threatening tears. "But if I had known what the true outcome would be…"

"Do you still believe that? That God would not have forgiven you?"

"I think…cowardice is also a sin. I think I wronged both of you more by refusing." Father Joseph closed his eyes. "A few years ago, our Holy Father said: 'Far be it from us to dare to set bounds to the boundless mercy of God.' It reminded me of the Revelations of Juliana of Norwich: 'His love excuseth us, and of His great courtesy He doth away all our blame, and beholdeth us with compassion and pity…' I think they mean intentions count, and God forgives us when we falter. But sin still has consequences." A tear descended his cheek. Father Joseph brushed it away, but a second soon took its place. He looked at her with stricken eyes. "She is still gone. You still lost your mother, and it is still my fault."

Clare slipped her arms around him and laid her head against his shoulder. "I forgive you, Father."

He let out a shuddering sigh and returned her embrace.

Footfalls crunched an oyster shell path. Clare opened her eyes to see David with his medical bag. She let go of Father Joseph.

David hesitated but didn't even meet her eyes. "I need to return to the hospital." Without another word, he hurried through the gate.

Clare sucked in a breath that was halfway to a sob and turned back to Father Joseph. He clasped her hand in both of his in an attempt at comfort.

In David's wake, Ésh and his grandfather emerged from the house.

Anne had finished her prayers. She was frowning. 'Did you and David argue?' Father Joseph translated for them.

"No. I told him I am not angry," Ésh explained. "I told him I am happy to have two families."

If Ésh could forgive his brother for leaving him to die, Clare knew she should forgive David for breaking her heart, again. But unlike his uncle, he'd shown no contrition whatsoever.

"You'd better not linger," Father Joseph advised. "There are only a few hours of daylight left. And this time, I should accompany you."

"Don't be silly," Clare told him. "You cannot return in the dark. You'd have to spend a whole night away from your parishioners."

"Then I will go," René offered.

"You have your patients," Clare argued. "Ésh and I will be fine."

René frowned and eyed his grandson. "You must take care of our Clare, Ésh."

"I will," he smiled.

'You understand that here, a woman's reputation, her good name, mean everything?' Anne asked.

"It is the same with the Cheyenne," Ésh assured them.

Clare lifted her chin. "The only people whose opinions I care about are standing in this garden." David no longer merited a place on her list. As for South Carolina's other bachelors, Clare *wanted* them to dismiss her as unmarriageable.

Anne still looked uneasy. 'I will fetch your bonnet from the hall —but give me a few minutes.'

René confirmed what her hands had said, then shrugged to indicate that he didn't understand the delay either. "We should get the horses ready."

At the stable, Arthur was dozing on his feet. "I wish we could stay here too, boy," Clare told him.

René admired Mirage, proving his good sense. When they had her saddled and Arthur harnessed to the phaeton, Anne returned. She'd added a veil to Clare's bonnet.

Clare put it on and hugged her. 'Thank you,' she signed, raising her veil to touch her fingertips to her mouth, then gesture toward Anne.

'Thank *you*, for bringing us our grandson.'

Anne embraced Ésh too, then went to her husband and son. Clare didn't recognize all the signs at a distance, but Anne seemed to be confirming that they'd checked the horses' legs and all their equipment for soundness.

Ésh frowned at Clare's altered bonnet. Was he *pouting?* "I cannot see you."

Clare was thankful for the veil, because she was blushing. He *wanted* to see her! She attempted to draw on her driving gloves nonchalantly. "That is the point. Now, I am a woman of mystery."

"But you can see me?"

She couldn't resist the chance to tease him. "I don't need to see you. I only need to see Arthur."

Standing impatiently between the shafts of the phaeton, the gelding joined their conversation by lifting his tail and depositing several globs of manure onto the stable yard.

Ésh burst out laughing. "You choose a horse's ass over me?"

Clare giggled. He'd picked up the most amusing assortment of words.

René approached, raising one eyebrow. "Try not to say 'ass' in polite company, grandson."

"Are we polite company, Grand-père?" Clare jested.

Ésh was grinning too. Clare thought he knew it was a rude word. "What should I say instead?"

"Hindquarters, posterior, rump…"

"There's always the French," Clare suggested.

"Derrière," René agreed, rolling his r's as only a Frenchman could.

"I have not even learned English yet, and now you want me to learn French?"

"You are doing *beautifully*," Clare assured Ésh.

"Fair enough, grandson. We should reciprocate. How would you say that in Cheyenne?"

With feigned innocence, Ésh inquired: "Ass?"

"No!" His grandfather guffawed. "'Beautifully.' 'Beautiful.'"

"In Cheyenne, you must join it with something, so I could say: *Mo'on-mo*." He was looking directly at Clare. "That means: 'You are beautiful.'"

Again, she was thankful for the veil.

René narrowed his eyes behind his spectacles. "Are you certain you don't wish me to come with you, Clare?"

"Of course not. Ésh has been a perfect gentleman."

"Gentlemen do not say 'ass.'" Still smiling, René embraced Clare and whispered: "Take care, dear girl."

"I will, Grand-père."

ALL THESE YEARS, his brother had been alive—Cheyenne but whole and happy and kind in spite of David's sin. The block between his grandparents' house—*their* grandparents' house—and Roper Hospital had never stretched so wide. With every step, the tears threatened to return. Tears of relief and thanksgiving and joy. His brother was *alive*.

David had wanted to touch Ésh's face, to embrace him. His brother might even have allowed it. But David had blubbered enough—he wasn't fit to be in anyone's presence yet.

He hurried through the gates of Roper Hospital and did not stop at his quarters. His cramped little room was like a prison cell; anyone could find him there. His duties could wait a few minutes longer. He climbed the staircase inside one of the towers. The roof was the only place at the hospital he could truly be alone.

Inside the top of the tower, he passed the bats. A few chirped their displeasure at being disturbed. In the dim light through the slatted windows, he saw the furry little creatures flash their leathery wings as they resettled.

The bats made David think of Clare. He'd started to write to her so many times, and the bats had always seemed a safe opening. Most women—and many men—were horrified by these creatures. But Clare would be delighted and curious. She'd want to see the pups. That was Clare, and he loved her for it. He couldn't stop.

David stashed his medical bag and his hat. He emerged onto the hospital's roof, braced his hands against his thighs, and took in great lungfuls of air. He struggled to calm a racing heartbeat that had nothing to do with the stairs.

When he'd first seen Clare sitting at his grandparents' table, an irrational part of David had seized it as a sign. He'd wanted to run to her—to fall on his knees and declare himself in front of everyone: *"You're here! Do you know how many times I have thought of you this past year? I love you, Clare Stratford! Will you have me?"*

Fortunately, this romantic fantasy had expired in an instant, and reason had prevailed—even before his brother's resurrection changed everything.

Later, when David had seen Clare in his uncle's arms, jealousy had twisted inside him—even though David knew it wasn't *that* sort of embrace. Tears wet Joseph's cheeks and Clare's eyelashes. They must have been imagining David's baby brother alone in that cave.

But what had his brother's resurrection really changed about David's future? Ésh's survival didn't erase David's sin but displayed it like a banner for all to see.

Clare must understand now why he couldn't marry her—part of why, at least. She didn't know about the secret he carried in his blood, the other reason he couldn't promise her everything she deserved. She needed a husband who could protect her, who would always make her feel safe. A colored man couldn't give her that assurance any more than an attempted infanticide.

If David loved her, he must let her go. He must leave her to a better man, a man her own age who hadn't blackened his soul.

David strode across the hospital roof till he reached the edge, till the wind tugged at his coattails. He stared past the church steeples to the masts and smokestacks, to the sparkling water beyond. He watched the ships steaming out of the harbor and imagined he stood on one of their decks, bound for Paris—away from the frightening future where every one of the people he loved knew his darkest sin.

But that was cowardice. Even if David's future didn't include Clare, it would include his brother—the brother who had forgiven him.

CHAPTER 32

Who ever loved that loved not at first sight?
— Christopher Marlowe, *Hero and Leander* (1598)

Father Joseph accompanied Clare and Ésh back to his presbytery. She asked Ésh to hold the horses while she went inside with Father Joseph. He'd shown Verily the extra bedchamber and told her she was welcome to use it. Clare suspected her friend had been reading rather than resting, but she'd hid her book in her pocket before they entered.

Clare closed the door and tucked up her new veil. "Verily, tell Father Joseph about the books you want."

She looked uncertain, glancing to Father Joseph and away again.

"You can trust him," Clare assured her friend.

"You…ever heard of Frederick Douglass or William Brown, Father?"

"I have."

"I'd like to read one of their books, or a book by someone who used to be a slave but got free."

Father Joseph considered for a moment. "Are you hoping they will tell you how *you* might get free?"

Verily looked more uncomfortable than ever. Now she glanced nervously at Clare. "Maybe."

"I'm afraid that's unlikely," Father Joseph told her. "These men have to be careful. Anyone can read their books—even slave catchers. If Mr. Douglass or Mr. Brown were to explain how they escaped, it would prevent anyone else from escaping the same way."

"I'd still like to read them," Verily mumbled.

"I will be happy to find you their books, though it may take some time."

"Now you know our secret, Father," Clare prompted. "So why can't I use the mausoleum key?"

Father Joseph hesitated, then smiled. "Our secrets are related. You cannot use the mausoleum key whenever you wish because my sister and niece aren't the only people who sleep there."

Clare frowned. He wasn't making sense.

Father Joseph drew in a breath. "That is to say: my family's mausoleum is also a station on the Underground Railroad. Do you know what that means?"

"Yes!" Clare cried. "Oh Father, you are so brave!"

"Not as brave as the people who've slept inside it—but a tomb was the safest hiding place we could think of."

"'We'?"

"My father was a conductor first."

Of course! Clare should have guessed it.

Verily too was staring at Father Joseph in awe.

He smiled at her. "So if you do decide to escape, Verily, I hope you will let us help you."

THE SUN WAS SINKING. Father Joseph helped Clare and Verily into the phaeton, then held Mirage so Ésh could mount. He promised to pray for a safe journey, and he bid them "*À bientôt!* That is French for 'We will see each other soon!'" Father Joseph explained to his nephew. "Because if you do not visit again in a few days, Ésh, your grandparents and I will come looking for you."

Ésh chuckled. "I understand."

As they followed King Street out of Charleston, Clare and Ésh were finally alone again. More or less. Verily sighed and settled back against the seat of the phaeton.

Clare knew she must make use of these last precious hours with Ésh. Everything she learned about him only intrigued her more, only prompted more questions. A lady did not ask such questions, but then no lady spent all day with a handsome young man who was not her relation. A lady certainly didn't contemplate how she might spend *more* time with such a man. But first, she must test him to see if he trusted her. Only then could she truly trust him. "Ésh…"

"Yes?"

The veil lent her courage. "At your grandparents', you said you'd made selfish choices. What did you mean?"

Ésh averted his eyes. He drew in a breath and released it. "I will tell you the worst things. When I was thirteen years old, I was supposed to be scouting—finding the Pawnee camp so my war party could capture their horses. Instead of returning with news of the enemy's numbers, I stayed to count a coup. The Pawnee saw me, and I ruined the raid. Later, on another raid, I promised a spotted horse to my little brother, but I decided to keep the horse for myself. And after the Battle of Turkey Creek, when we were running from the bluecoats, I passed a Kit Fox Soldier whose horse was trapped in sand. He called out for my help. I could have saved him. But I did not stop. I saved myself."

Even through her veil, Clare could see how much these choices troubled Ésh. Yet she'd feared deeds far more terrible, like the scalping of white women.

"I know now that I was wrong to do those things. I have tried to make them right again. I gave my brother my spotted horse before I left. I cannot give the Kit Fox Soldier his life again, but when I return, I will give his family all my horses."

"It's not as though you killed him."

"It is almost the same."

Ésh had mentioned bluecoats. She knew he meant white soldiers. "*Did* you kill anyone in that battle?"

"Not at Turkey Creek."

Clare's heart raced. "You killed someone during another battle?"

"Crows tried to steal our horses. One of them wanted my horse, and I fought with him. He cut my side, but I got his knife and killed him instead."

Ésh had only been defending himself and his property, Clare told herself. That was more brave than bloodthirsty. Unless... "Did you take his scalp?"

Ésh peered over at her with the corner of his mouth threatening a smile. His expression said *"Of course"* and *"White women ask such strange questions."*

Clare swallowed. "You didn't...bring it with you to Charleston?"

"No," Ésh chuckled. "My Zizistas family has it on display in their tipi."

As if the thing were a work of art! Clare shuddered. She was relieved the scalp was far away, and she was glad it hadn't belonged to a woman.

FOR THE HUNDREDTH TIME since she'd put on that veil, Ésh wished he could see Clare's face. Not only because she was beautiful to look at, but because her face was so changeable, so expressive. He wondered what she really thought about his taking a scalp. He wondered if Clare had gone pink beneath that veil.

At first, the flushing of her cheeks simply seemed strange— Zizistas women didn't go pink like that. But he was learning to read those flushes the way white people read the black marks in books. The color meant she was excited, but Clare could be excited in so many ways: eager, delighted, embarrassed, defiant...

Sometimes, even Clare's neck went pink—the color stopped only at the white collar of her dress. He wondered how far the pink really went. He wondered what color she'd turn if he touched her cheek. If he kissed her lips.

Which he couldn't see at all anymore, through that aggravating veil.

"Your turn," he said.

"Pardon?"

"I told you about my stupid choices. Now *you* must make another confession."

"But I don't have anything to..."

"Not even about my brother?"

She hesitated. "I...don't know what you mean."

"I think you took me to Charleston today because you wanted to see *him*."

"That wasn't the only reason!"

"I think he is more than a friend to you."

"He might have been," Clare admitted in a mutter. "But not anymore. He made it very clear today that he is no longer my friend...or anything else."

"I am sorry," Ésh said, even though he was not sorry. He didn't understand his brother yet or why he would walk away from this brave and beautiful woman; but Ésh liked having her all to himself.

Clare had gone silent. Her hat pointed only toward Arthur's ass. She was so rarely silent, Ésh knew she was hurting. He must take her mind from David.

Yet as Ésh searched for something to say, his mind returned to his brother. David had warned Ésh to say nothing of their African ancestors...but his brother and grandfather had not forbidden him to speak of their Dakota ancestors. Clare seemed fascinated by all things Indian, yet she'd responded so strangely when Ésh told her he'd taken a scalp—an act that filled Zizistas mothers and wives with pride. He needed to know how Clare would respond to the news that he really was part Indian.

They were surrounded by trees and fences now. Ésh made sure no one was approaching in either direction, then declared: "It is my turn again. I have...it is more a secret than a confession. Do you want to hear it?"

"Of course." Even if he couldn't see it on her face, he heard the excitement returning to Clare's voice.

"My secret is: maybe I am not Zizistas by blood, but I *am* Dakota. At least a bit. My grandfather told me his great-grandmother was a Dakota."

"Truly?"

Ésh smiled. He was sure Clare was flushed again. "Yes."

"Your family is full of secrets! Does David know?"

Ésh stopped smiling. "Yes."

"But he read me Mrs. Eastman's book about the Dakota when I was a girl! Why didn't he tell me?"

"I think...my brother is ashamed to be part Indian," Ésh answered carefully. "Our Dakota ancestor, she was a slave in Canada. Her son, René's grandfather, he was a slave in Saint-Domingue."

"*That's* why Grand-père René has a dark complexion—why David and Father Joseph have black hair! They aren't part Spanish at all, are they?"

"I do not think so. My grandfather did not mention 'Spanish.'"

"I thought Grand-père René trusted me!" Though there were no other riders or passengers nearby, Clare seemed to realize how loudly she was speaking. "Thank you for trusting me, Ésh."

He knew he could. "Now, it is your turn to tell another secret."

"Oh! I...well... I lied a little, about buying Mirage."

"What?"

"I *want* to buy her, but I already talked to my father and my aunt. They think piebalds are ugly and unladylike. I don't think I'll be able to change their minds."

"Just because she is not yours does not mean you cannot ride her."

"You meant it, about teaching me to ride again?"

"Did you mean it, about teaching me to read?" Maybe his grandfather would teach him too, but Clare didn't need to know that.

"Of course I did! But will Mr. Alexander let you borrow Mirage again?"

"It is my job to exercise her. We will exercise her together."

Clare giggled. "I might not be able to meet you *tomorrow*. But I'll get away if I can."

"I can wait."

"We'll need somewhere to meet, somewhere we won't be seen." Clare thought for a few moments. "We could use the old stallion barn, the one that looks like a church."

"'Like a church'?" Ésh wasn't sure what that meant.

"It's in the Gothic style, like your family's mausoleum. It's grey brick with pointed white doors and windows and a steep roof. You can see it from the paddock where Mirage was yesterday."

Ésh smiled. "I know it."

"There's a lovely pasture next to it. You can teach me how to fall there."

BY THE TIME THEY REACHED Mr. Alexander's gate, Clare knew she was already falling. Falling into ruin, her aunt would say: Clare had made plans for a tryst with a gorgeous young man—a "savage" by both upbringing and blood. Yet Clare couldn't wait to see him again, no matter the cost, because she was falling in love.

And Ésh must feel the same. When they parted, he said: "I will wait for you tomorrow, and the day after that, and the day after that, if you do one thing for me."

Clare's breaths grew faster. "What?"

"May I see your face again?"

She blushed, tossed up her veil, and held it there while he grinned back at her.

"*Mo'on-mo*," he declared before he disappeared on Mirage. "*You are beautiful.*"

Clare had known David all her life. Ésh had grown up in a different world, and he was still learning her language. Yet after a single day together, Ésh trusted and valued her more than his brother did. Ésh was not secretive or cruel. He was bold and generous. He said what he meant. He told her she was beautiful.

THE MORNING SHADRACH HAD GIVEN HER the *sankofa*, the afternoon they'd first kissed inside the brougham—in her happiest moments with him, Easter had literally been carrying a lie beneath her heart. A lie fathered by Cromwell.

Forgetting the pessary had mattered, terribly. She'd hurried back to her quarters, but she must have injected the vinegar too late to kill his foul seed before it took root.

Life, begun in a tomb.

Occupied with endless kitchen duties and distracted by thoughts of Shadrach, Easter had lost track of the weeks passing. After all, her monthlies had rarely been monthly. She'd missed them without *missing* them, without realizing anything was wrong. She hadn't vomited once. She didn't understand how she could've had a monster growing inside her all this time and not known it.

But she couldn't ignore the signs any longer. She'd never missed three monthlies in a row before. Her head ached, and she was exhausted even on Sundays. She found herself pinching sugar when Phoebe wasn't looking, and she'd eaten half a jar of red peppers in one sitting. Her breasts and her belly were starting to swell.

Easter was furious. Just when Shadrach had shown her a firm path leading up to the sunlight, Cromwell yanked her back into the mire. She wanted nothing more than to kill the trespasser inside her. Easter had heard whispers, about what women in the quarters did when they couldn't stand to bear one more slave: tansy and pennyroyal...

Cromwell had his own ways to end a pregnancy, learned from his whores. He'd told Easter to come to him so word of the child would not spread. But Cromwell had gone to the cotton plantation, and Shadrach had been hired out all the way to Georgetown District. They'd left Easter alone with her thoughts and with the tiny new life inside her.

A life that was helpless and innocent.

Easter's mother and father had both been sired by white men. Those men had not made Mama and Papa ugly or cruel, and their mothers had loved them in spite of their conceptions. This child was Easter's far more than it was Cromwell's. This boy or this girl was descended from those strong, loving, beautiful mothers, from East-er's strong, loving, handsome father.

Easter realized she *wanted* this baby. She simply had to convince Cromwell to let her keep it. Sooner or later, he would notice her belly.

She could tell him it was Shadrach's.

Easter didn't know which she dreaded more: Cromwell's reac-tion to her child or Shadrach's. Shadrach would know she'd been unfaithful, that she'd been lying to him all these months. She could make up new lies, pretend the child's father was another slave, that she'd wanted him. Wasn't that better than letting Shadrach go after Cromwell and be hanged for raising his hand against a white man?

Easter would lose Shadrach either way. She should choose the way that would keep him alive, even if it meant breaking both their hearts.

Unless she surrendered the child. Unless she killed it before Shadrach knew it existed... But how could *that* be right?

From the moment she admitted her child's existence, Easter hardly slept. She lay in her bed, her mind racing, the solution always, always eluding her. She'd tell herself she would puzzle it out tomorrow, but her mind would circle back again and again, desper-ately seeking a new path and finding only brambles.

CHAPTER 33

Fools rush in where Angels fear to tread.
— Alexander Pope, *An Essay on Criticism* (1711)

"Where the devil have you been?" Aunt Hortense demanded from the upper veranda, looming over Clare like an angel of judgment.

A few steps away from the back staircase, Clare paused. Verily stopped beside her, her head bowed in contrition.

The growing dusk seemed to seep from Aunt Hortense's black gown. "I sent Mr. Tilling to look for you hours ago! He said you'd vanished!"

Simple lies are easiest, Clare had decided. Her aunt would never guess she'd gone all the way to Charleston with a strange man. All Aunt Hortense knew for certain was that the overseer had missed her. "Well, I saw Mr. Tilling. I was hiding."

"'Hiding'?" her aunt echoed doubtfully, gripping the veranda railing.

"I *wanted* you to worry. I was angry about Mirage." Both of those statements were true.

Aunt Hortense looked confused. "Angry about *what?*" Her aunt couldn't even remember the name of the beautiful mare.

"Mirage! The piebald!" Clare inhaled a deep breath and forced herself to remain calm. She'd never see Ésh again if she couldn't sweet-talk her aunt into complacency. "But I've had a day to reflect." Clare glanced at her friend. "Verily has been my good angel, pleading with me to reconsider my behavior."

Aunt Hortense squinted at Verily. "She has?"

"I am willing to concede that I may have been headstrong." Clare couldn't be too effusive, or her aunt would realize this remorse was an act. "I may have been ungrateful toward you and my father."

"Is that so?"

"I am willing to set aside the idea of owning the piebald—for now—and consider whatever horses you and my father think more appropriate for me."

Her aunt peered down at her uncertainly.

"I will not even leave the house tomorrow, if you do not wish it."

If anyone had recognized her on the road, Clare reasoned, it would be days before word reached her aunt or her father—perhaps even weeks. She might be living under a Sword of Damocles, but until it fell, she was free. All she had to do was deceive Aunt Hortense and persuade Verily.

When they were alone in her bedchamber that night, Clare watched her friend's face in the mirror. Verily was brushing rose oil into Clare's freshly washed hair. Her friend's features remained placid, revealing nothing.

Clare breathed in the soothing scent of the oil and dropped her gaze to her gold silk dressing gown. If Clare was honest with herself, she was hurt by Verily's wanting to run away. When she'd thought of freeing her maid, Clare had expected that little would change, that Verily would remain and serve her as a free woman. For the first time, Clare wondered if Verily saw her only as a mistress—if they weren't really friends at all.

Clare had no one else. "Do you truly wish to escape, Verily?"

Her maid stopped brushing. In the mirror, Clare watched something flicker across Verily's countenance. Her neck tensed. Her lips parted. Her eyes didn't know where to settle. Was she afraid? Of *Clare*? "I don't want it for me, Miss," Verily answered at last. "I want it for my sister. She's so unhappy, she won't even talk to me anymore."

"Is there something I can do, to make Easter happier here?"

"I don't think so, Miss."

"I don't want you to go, Verily; I will miss you. But if *you* want to go, I will help you and Easter escape—as long as you help me meet Ésh without anyone finding out."

Finally, Verily met her eyes in the mirror. "I think you're foolish to trust him, Miss. I think this will come to a bad end."

"Let me worry about that, Verily." Clare had spent an entire day with Ésh, and he hadn't touched her once—no matter how much she'd wanted him to. "Do we have a bargain?"

Verily's voice grew hard. "You'll find a way to meet him even without my help, won't you?"

"I will." What had Father Joseph said? *"Cowardice is also a sin."*

Verily sighed. "All right, Miss. If you help my sister and me, I'll help you."

THE NEXT MORNING, Clare listened more or less attentively while Aunt Hortense explained the etiquette of hosting a dinner party in excruciating detail. Clare did not conceal her boredom completely —a drastic change in her behavior would only ignite her aunt's suspicions. Clare genuinely tried to parrot back all the rules, but she made many mistakes.

After they'd eaten their own dinner that afternoon, Clare asked: "Shall we continue with my lessons, Aunt?"

"No; no. We'll pick up tomorrow." Aunt Hortense waved her hand in dismissal. "You seem to retain less and less as the day goes on."

"I do think small doses are best," Clare suggested meekly.

"Very well. Go and paint your trees." Aunt Hortense jabbed a finger toward her. "But stay away from the fence line, and if Mr. Tilling should pass you, *greet him.*"

"Of course, Aunt. Thank you, Aunt!" Clare sprang up from the table. She nearly kissed the top of her aunt's head, but she decided that would be excessive.

CLARE HAD VERILY SEND FOR MYRA at once. She was the plantation's best seamstress. Two days ago, the day she'd resolved to ride again, Clare had asked Myra to alter one of her dresses into a serviceable riding habit. The seamstress would leave the blue cashmere skirt full in the back but shorten the front and sides, which no longer needed to stretch over a cage crinoline. Myra would use this reclaimed fabric to form matching trousers.

Clare was delighted to learn that the habit was nearly finished. Myra let her try it on. The seamstress had strengthened the inner thighs of the trousers with leather. Clare hadn't worn trousers since her riding accident. Her skirts concealed them completely, and she was *more* encased than in a cage crinoline, yet she felt very daring.

While Myra made a few last alterations, Clare assessed herself in the mirror. She'd grown up awestruck by her mother's portrait in the library, feeling small and plain beneath such immortal beauty. She'd hated the moles like petrified teardrops beneath her left eye.

Yet Clare's suitors had been quick to flatter her. Such unsolicited, unwanted panegyrics had made her uncomfortable. She'd discounted their praise and worried what the men would expect in return for their flattery. Ésh had said *"You are beautiful"* as if he'd discovered a treasure—with no presumption that he would soon possess it, only joy that such a treasure existed. When he'd complimented her, she'd believed him.

Clare might not be extraordinary like Ésh or her mother, but for the first time she could remember, she saw no faults in her reflection. She looked particularly fine in deep blue, she thought—much better than in yesterday's faded green plaid. Her skin seemed to glow like alabaster, and the blue brought out the gold in her brown hair.

Once, she would have compared the color of this habit to David's eyes and its black piping to his curls. No longer. The habit was sapphire, indigo, Parisian blue—it was hers, and she wore it only for Ésh.

CLARE COULD NOT SET OUT in the phaeton wearing a riding habit without giving away her plans. She had to hide it in a basket and venture forth wearing a hoop skirt. She wore her shortest, most forgiving corset. She made sure her small hat had no flowers on it to tempt Mirage, only ribbons and feathers.

When Clare arrived at the stallion barn, she saw no sign of Ésh. But it was not yet late afternoon—he'd said that was when he could get away, when there was not so much to do with Mr. Alexander's horses. With Verily's assistance, Clare used one of the box stalls to change into her new riding habit.

In the hayloft, Clare found a place to hide the books, slate, chalk, paper, and pencil she'd brought so Ésh could begin learning his letters. For the better part of an hour, Clare sketched, talked to Verily, talked to Arthur, and paced beside the barn. Mr. Tilling rode by, and Clare waved to him dutifully.

Finally, Arthur pricked his ears toward Mr. Alexander's property and lifted his head. Ésh was approaching on Mirage! He rode her bareback and wore his Cheyenne clothing again.

Clare was delighted to see him in his natural state. She left Verily reading and ran to meet Ésh and Mirage. "You came! You brought her!"

"I did." Ésh slid down from Mirage's bare back. She wasn't wearing a bridle either. Ésh untied a rope from his waist, then made a halter and lead out of it.

When he was finished, Clare re-introduced herself to Mirage, letting the mare sniff her and stroking her strong warm neck. "What does Mr. Alexander think you're doing?"

"I asked him if I could ride Mirage when I am not working. It is only—how do you say—a white lie." Ésh grinned. "Are you ready?" He assessed Clare's riding habit, which might be narrower than a hoop skirt but still contained a great deal of fabric. "You can ride in that?"

"Yes. But Mirage doesn't have a saddle. Was I supposed to bring one?"

"No. I will bring one next time."

How those words thrilled her, the promise of a *next time*.

"This time, I want to teach you to listen and speak without anything in the way."

"What do you mean?"

"To listen and speak not with your ears and your voice but with your thighs."

Clare felt heat rushing to her face—and perhaps a few other places.

Ésh didn't see, thank goodness. He was reassuring Mirage by rubbing her forehead. "With your whole body. That is how horses listen and speak."

"You— You want me to ride bareback?"

"I do."

Clare bit her lip and stared at Mirage's back, which was about even with her eye line. The mare was fifteen hands at most—not much taller than a pony, but still a long way to fall. While Clare hesitated, a fly buzzed between them and landed on Mirage's knee. The mare's skin twitched, and one of those terrifying hoofs stomped the ground to expel the intruder. Clare felt the reverberation through her boots. Yet Ésh stood fearless beside the horse, wearing nothing but moccasins on his feet! Clare shuddered.

Her eyes slid forward to Mirage's head. Her blue eye unsettled Clare now, and the mare wore no bit. "There aren't even any reins."

"You don't need any. I will guide her."

In more ways than one, Clare must trust Ésh not to hurt her. She swallowed in determination. "We need a mounting block, a step of some sort..." Clare looked back toward the barn. Verily was watching them with her arms crossed over her bodice.

"You don't need a step either."

Clare returned her attention to Ésh. "But I cannot do what you do—leap up from the ground."

"Maybe someday. Today, I am your step."

"All right…"

Ésh led Mirage to a nearby dogwood tree and tied her lead rope around one of the branches. Fortunately, it was not yet in bloom. "Do you want to mount from the right or the left?"

"The right, like you do." Clare's heartbeat quickened at her own daring. She would learn to not only ride astride like a man but also mount like an Indian.

"Then take hold of Mirage's mane with your right hand and put your left hand on her back."

Clare screwed up her courage and obeyed, trying not to think about the nearness of Mirage's hoofs.

Ésh stood behind Clare and slightly to her right. She glanced over her shoulder to see him peering down at her pleated blue skirt. "You have two legs under there, yes?"

Clare blushed anew. "Yes."

"Bend your right knee and give me your foot."

Her boot lifted as if of its own accord. Ésh caught her ankle with his left hand. Beneath her skirts, his right hand slid up her boot and her shin till it cupped her right knee. Clare couldn't help trembling, but it was not from fear of the horse in front of her. The hands of a man, *this* man, were underneath her skirt, cradling her leg. Silk stocking, cashmere trouser, and leather boot separated their skin, but she could feel the strength of his hands nonetheless.

"Now jump up straight. I will help you."

In a motion both powerful and controlled, Ésh lifted her from the ground. For a moment, she felt weightless, and the sensation of flight was more thrilling than frightening. Then Clare remembered what they were doing. She remembered to lean forward.

She managed to drape herself over Mirage's back, the front of her corset across the mare's spine. Clare heard Mirage snort, and her own body went rigid, certain the animal would bolt. Clare had to remind herself that Mirage was tied and Ésh was still supporting her right leg.

"Good!" he cried. "Now turn forward while you bend your left leg and pull it over her back."

Tentatively and with difficulty because of her skirt, Clare dragged her left knee over, then her boot. Finally she had one leg on each side of Mirage. How strange it felt to have such warmth and bulk so close to her most delicate places. Clare had never dared to sit like this in her life.

Except she wasn't sitting—she was crouching, clinging to Mirage's neck.

"Now sit up," Ésh urged. He'd let go of her. Clare made the mistake of glancing down. The ground looked leagues away. Clare squeezed her eyes shut for a moment. She remained leaning over Mirage's neck and busied herself rearranging her skirt.

Ésh's mouth quirked. "You must sit up sometime."

Clare drew in a deep breath, braced her hands on Mirage's withers, and hesitated. She felt more secure hunched up like this.

"If you fall, I promise to catch you."

"What if I fall off the other side?"

"I can run very fast," Ésh grinned.

Clare laughed. Little by little, she pushed herself upright, till she was beaming down at Ésh in victory. She felt powerful, to have such strength between her legs. She felt united with Mirage instead of simply perched atop her.

Ésh did not look pleased. In fact, he was scowling, glancing to the mare's head, then Clare's skirt. "I think your legs are too tight. Mirage is confused."

The mare's ears were flicking, Clare had to concede.

"She is tied, but she thinks you want to go forward." Ésh tapped Clare's knee through her skirt.

She tensed even more, squeezing Mirage's sides, and the mare did walk forward a step.

Ésh caught her lead rope and directed Mirage to back up again, or else Clare would soon be unseated by the branches of the dogwood. "How do you say…" He demonstrated by loosely shaking his arms.

"Be more loose?" Clare suggested. She tried to obey.

Ésh wasn't satisfied. "Do with your legs what I did with my arms."

Feeling silly, Clare wobbled her legs on either side of Mirage.

"Good! Now to dismount, grip her mane with both hands, and—"

"You want me to dismount already?" Was he giving up on her?

"Then you will mount again. It is good to practice a few times."

Ésh demonstrated how she should build up momentum for her dismount by standing on his right leg and swinging the left one repeatedly. At first, Clare was simply mesmerized by the confident motions of that moccasined foot, the strength inside those fringed leggings. She wished he wasn't wearing his long shirt. She thought of the delicious gaps between his breechcloth and his leggings.

With considerable effort, Clare forced herself to concentrate on her task. She attempted to mimic his motion and got only halfway; she couldn't quite swing her leg back over Mirage's rump. Perhaps there were too many skirt folds in the way. Firmly but gently, Ésh grasped Clare's ankle and pulled her leg all the way over. Then he held onto her waist so she wouldn't topple backward as she slid down from Mirage's back.

Three more times, Clare practiced mounting. Each time, Ésh helped her. Each time, his hand slid up her shin to cup her knee. But his fingers never strayed any higher. As Clare dismounted, she surrendered to the weakness of her unskilled muscles. She liked having Ésh take hold of her ankle and direct her leg. She wished she could turn in his arms and see his face when he did these things. He seemed detached, as if he were only doing a job, and yet his hands lingered on her a moment longer than they needed to.

The fourth time, Ésh allowed her to remain mounted. "Now, you must learn...balance, that is the word. Are you sitting on Mirage's back with both..." He stumbled and tried again. "Is your..." He sighed. "What do you want me to call your ass?"

Clare burst into laughter and hid her face in her hand. "Seat!" she gasped. "My seat!"

"Is your weight the same on both sides of your *seat*? Is one side higher or more forward?"

Clare did her best to recover and assess the position of her ass.

At last, Ésh led Mirage at a walk. Clare grew accustomed to the rhythm of the mare's muscles and bones moving beneath her. Ésh taught Clare how to communicate *stop, go, turn left, turn right* with only her balance, with the subtle position of her seat and her thighs.

Still Clare's hands ached for reins that weren't there. "I feel so helpless," she admitted.

"You must learn that the rider is never in control."

Clare sucked in a frightened breath and clutched Mirage's mane even tighter.

"It is the horse who decides what to do," Ésh explained. "Bits and whips and spurs, they are for riders who are lazy and cruel. Often they do not work, because the horse is bigger and stronger than you. If *she* is frightened, you cannot force her to do something, or you will both be hurt. You must learn her language so you can say: 'I wish you to do this, and you do not need to be frightened, because I will look after you.'"

ALL TOO SOON, the lesson was over: Ésh told her he must return to Mr. Alexander's. When she dismounted, Clare's legs ached, but she wanted to hug Ésh. Instead, she wrapped her arms around Mirage's neck and praised her patience.

"Do you know when you'll visit your family again?" Clare asked Ésh as he unknotted the mare's halter.

"Not tomorrow, but the day after, for two days." He tied the rope around his waist.

"But you'll meet me again tomorrow?"

"Yes." Ésh gripped Mirage's mane and leapt onto her back in the way that stole Clare's breath. "There are many things I must teach you still."

"But I'm not hopeless?"

"No," Ésh smiled down at her. "You are *hopeful*. Is that right?"

"That's right." Clare didn't have the heart to correct him. And he wasn't wrong.

PART VI
HOW TO FALL

1860

CHARLESTON

When I bestride him, I soar, I am a hawk…

— William Shakespeare, *Henry V* (1599)

CHAPTER 34

I'd sleep another hundred years,
O love, for such another kiss…
O love, thy kiss would wake the dead!
— Alfred, Lord Tennyson, "The Day-Dream" (1842)

It rained all night and into the morning. The clouds had blown away by the time Finis hitched Arthur to the phaeton. But between the carriage house and the old stallion barn, the wheels nearly became mired twice. Arthur stared at Clare pitifully, as if beseeching her to turn back.

She persisted, though her own muscles ached from yesterday's lesson. She wasn't accustomed to using her thighs in such a way. At the stallion barn, Clare frowned at the pasture where she'd ridden Mirage. Great bogs of mud occupied it now. She decided it was Ésh's turn; today, she should give him a reading lesson.

She'd envisioned this happening outside as well, but they couldn't sit under a tree in such muck. Besides, they should let the stallion barn conceal them from Mr. Tilling's eyes whenever possible. Yet there was nowhere to sit on the ground floor.

Verily helped Clare change into her riding habit, since it was easier to climb the ladder to the hayloft without a hoop skirt. Clare decided to shed her hat. Her maid sighed and gave her a look, then wandered off with her novel.

Should Clare toss down some hay to sit on? It would absorb moisture from the ground and be ruined. There was a reason hay was stored in a loft.

While she was standing at the top of the ladder pondering this, she heard Ésh's voice calling from below: "Are you up there, *mo'ona?*"

"I am here." Clare peered over the edge of the loft and caught her lower lip between her teeth. "Did you call me beautiful again?"

"Yes." Ésh grinned up at her. "You are learning Zizistas."

Clare felt her cheeks growing warm at his compliment. "I thought *I* would give *you* a lesson today—teach you our alphabet?"

"I will come up." Ésh climbed the ladder. He was wearing a different Cheyenne shirt today, one dyed green. The fringes of buckskin on his arms and legs swayed in the way that made her want to stroke them.

Clare hurried to retrieve her reading materials. "I brought a book I know you'll want to read later on. It's called *Dahcotah: Life and Legends of the Sioux*—about your ancestors! The stories were written down by a woman named Mary Eastman, the wife of the commander at Fort Snelling in Minnesota. Her husband did the drawings." Clare flipped through the pages. "Here's one."

As Ésh accepted the book, his bare fingers brushed Clare's gloved ones. Neither of them shied as they had in the mausoleum. She pointed to the caption. "This says 'Lover's Leap or Maiden's Rock.' One of the stories is about a Dakota woman whose family didn't approve of her beloved. So she threw herself from this cliff."

Below the outcropping of rock, several Indians paddled canoes or stood serenely on the riverbank. Atop the cliff, not one but two figures stood with their arms out as if they were about to jump.

"But we should begin with McGuffey." Clare picked up *The Eclectic Primer* and sat down on the hay. Ésh closed *Dahcotah* and sat beside her. "There are twenty-six letters in the English alphabet. They look a bit different depending on whether they're upper case or lower case." She showed him the two facing pages of letters, and Ésh leaned closer.

She loved the smell of him: clean and wild and animal. Stronger even than the sweet scent of the hay. He smelled of mint—did he apply it on purpose?

"What is this?" Ésh asked, tracing his fingertips over her turquoise ouroboros bracelet. "I like it."

"It was a gift from my mother." And from David. But she must not think of David. "It's a symbol of rebirth and eternal love in the shape of a snake. See how he's swallowing his own tail?" Clare decided *ouroboros* was too complex for a new reader, but she took up her slate and spelled *snake*.

"The s looks like a snake, doesn't it? Now these letters are all lower case. Upper case letters are used for the beginning of sentences and proper names. My name, for example, is spelled C-l-a-r-e." She wrote it in chalk below *snake*. "Only the first letter, C, is upper case."

Ésh looked from the slate to the primer. "The tiny c is almost the same as the big C."

"It is. But that's not true for all the letters. Your name is a good example. I *think* Ésh would be spelled E-s-h. See how the first letter, E, is four straight lines? But there's a curve in the little e."

For a while, Ésh seemed to follow her. But after a few minutes, he stopped saying the letters after she did. Clare realized he was staring at her instead of the primer. "Ésh," she scolded. "You're not paying attention."

"Yes I am," he grinned without taking his eyes from her face.

"Not to the book."

"What book?"

Flattered as she was, Clare lowered the primer and narrowed her eyes at him. "Don't you want to learn?"

"I do not think my head will hold any more today." Ésh sighed and flopped back flat against the hay, setting his fringes to dancing again. "I was awake half the night. Two of Mr. Alexander's mares foaled."

Clare turned so she could look at him without straining. She loved looking at him—and with his eyes closed, she could stare without feeling rude. "Are they all right?"

"One colt, one filly, two dams—all fine."

"I'm so glad."

His hands rested against his stomach. Only one thumb twitched. "I am sorry I am stupid today."

She was simply grateful that he'd come at all. "I could read something to you—one of the Dakota stories from Mrs. Eastman's book."

Ésh laced his fingers and tucked them under his head. "I would rather hear *your* ancestors' stories."

"My ancestors?" Clare considered. "I could tell you one of my mother's stories: the Salmon of Knowledge or the Pursuit of Diarmuid and Gráinne. But Irish stories always end tragically. At the least, they are bittersweet. I prefer stories with happy endings."

"Tell me one of those stories, then. I want to hear what you like, *mo'ona*."

Watching him resting there, more ideal than a Greek statue, did bring a title to mind. "Well…I've always been fond of Sleeping Beauty, or 'La Belle au bois dormant' in the original French. Tennyson wrote a lovely version of it." Ésh looked so innocent, Clare grew bold: she lay down beside him and stared up at the rafters. The thousand little pokes of hay did not bother her, because she knew he was feeling them too. "The Grimm brothers named the princess Briar Rose. Don't tell Father Joseph, but I chose Rose for my Confirmation name because I wanted to be like Sleeping Beauty, not Saint Rose of Lima."

She thought Ésh's eyes were open and his head was turned toward her now, but she dared not look. She clasped her hands over her waist, as if they might go wandering on their own.

"Why do you like this Sleeping Beauty?"

Clare gazed up resolutely at the rafters. "She's like Snow White —she's like a promise that even when everything seems lost, there's still hope. That meant a great deal to me after my mother died. But Snow White's prince, he doesn't do anything to raise her from the dead but move her coffin—and his servants pick it up for him!

Sleeping Beauty's prince is *brave*. He's a warrior. He's willing to risk everything—ghosts, ogres, brambles that have killed other men—in order to save her." Clare sighed. "And now I've told you the story without telling you the story."

Ésh propped his head on one elbow and peered down at her. "Then tell me the ending."

Her heart galloping in her chest, Clare forced her eyes to remain on the rafters. "Sleeping Beauty was cursed to sleep for a hundred years. When her prince finds her at last, he breaks the curse with his kiss, and they live happily ever afterward."

"That is a good ending. Your ancestors were wise."

Unable to resist temptation any longer, Clare glanced toward him. At least she'd *meant* for it to be a glance. But Ésh's thickly lashed grey-green eyes held her captive.

He was watching her with such rapture—and he was leaning closer. "The kiss of a warrior, it has great medicine. But I think you have been the brave one, *mo'ona*—to ride a horse again when you were afraid. To trust me."

Her attention slid to his lips. He had such beautiful lips, the lower one so full and the upper one sculpted like a bow... "I..." Clare stammered. "I want to know you."

"And I want to know you, *mo'ona*."

Did he understand that when she said it, she meant both *"I want you"* and *"I love you"*? Did he mean those things too?

Ésh said nothing more. He waited, his face inches from hers, only his eyes and his breaths caressing her: wordlessly he was asking her permission. His smile was melting all her defenses.

Clare knew she should not permit him such a liberty, not so soon... He'd made her no promises. Her hand flickered between them as if readying to push him away, but the motion faded against her chest. Did she really want her first kiss to happen in a *barn*?

She wanted her first kiss—her every kiss—to happen with Ésh. He was all that mattered, and she would do whatever kept him near her. Clare closed her eyes and surrendered.

The space between them vanished, and his beautiful lips nestled against hers, rough and soft at once. He was so *warm*... What an idiotic thought; of course he was warm. Then all of a sudden the warmth was gone, and she missed it immediately.

Clare opened her lips to protest, rising just slightly from the bed of hay, hand reaching out and knees drawing up as though she might pursue him. But before she could speak a word or even open her eyes, Ésh's hand slipped beneath her head and his mouth found hers again. His press was firmer now, surer, but no less gentle.

She realized her own lips were pursing, returning the kiss. If she was hesitant, it was only from inexperience. Would he think her unwilling? Even through her kid glove, she felt the fringe of his shirt brushing her hand. She gripped the buckskin, holding him to her, afraid he'd pull away again. His warmth was a comfort, an assurance that he was not some fairy tale prince but very, very real...

His mouth shifted ever so slightly, ever so slowly, savoring her as if he had never discovered anything so precious and no amount of lingering would ever be enough. Her mind swam with poetry: *"Our spirits rush'd together at the touching of the lips..."*

When Ésh relinquished her for the second time, Clare sighed with satisfaction and yearning into his mouth. She didn't let go of his shirt, and his hand still cradled her head. Why had he stopped? Had she disappointed him? Had she been too demure? Too eager?

Clare slitted her eyes open to see Ésh turning his head, looking back toward the ladder. Her eyes widened and she followed his gaze.

"I knew it," Verily muttered, rolling her eyes.

Ésh hardly moved. He only grinned. "Have you never been in love, Verily?"

"Love"! He'd said the word "love"!

Clare hardly heard Verily's response. She said something like "It never stuck," then addressed Clare: "Mr. Tilling just passed by. I told him you were resting."

Clare sucked in a breath, let go of Ésh's shirt, and sat up. "Did you bring Mirage inside?"

"Yes, Miss. He didn't see her."

Clare released her breath. "Thank you."

"I suppose I'll take Mirage back outside now." Verily glared at Ésh. "Unless you need me up here, Miss."

Clare knew she was scarlet. "See to Mirage, please."

Verily sighed and disappeared down the ladder.

Sitting beside her, Ésh reached toward Clare and extracted a piece of hay from her head. Sheepishly, she reached up to her mussed hair. One long strand had come loose from its pins. "What must you think of me?"

He fondled the wayward lock, twining it around his finger. "I told you already: I think you are beautiful and brave…"

Clare longed to ask: *"What you said to Verily—did you mean you're in love with me, or only that I'm in love with you?"* Instead, Clare said: "You must think…" She swallowed, turned her back to him, and stood. Her hair slipped from his hand. "I am not in the habit of allowing men such liberties with my person."

Ésh followed her to the edge of the hayloft. "I am happy to hear that, *mo'ona*. I do not like the thought of other men touching you." He brushed the loose strand behind her back. As he did so, his fingers grazed her shoulder.

She shivered, keenly aware of the muscles in that arm, of the force pent up inside him. She'd felt it yesterday, when he lifted her onto Mirage's back. Clare watched Verily leading the mare from the barn and wondered if she should have accepted her maid's offer. "Do you understand, Ésh? You are the first. The power you have over me—it frightens me." Or at least, she should be frightened. "You are stronger in knowledge and in body—you could take from me something I was not ready to give…" With trepidation she watched his reaction, desperate to read the emotions flickering over his face. Sadness? Determination?

"I will *take* nothing from you, *mo'ona*. I promise it on the honor of both my grandfathers. But I will *give* you anything you want…"

Tell me you love me, Clare pleaded in her head.

"…if you do one thing for me now."

Clare held her breath.

"Let down your hair?"

Clare breathed again. Slowly, she reached up and pulled out the pins, collecting them one by one in her palm. Lock by lock, her hair tumbled over her shoulders and down her back to her knees. Ésh watched her as if she were opening the gates of Paradise. He caught a few strands between his fingertips and caressed them. He drew them closer to his face and closed his eyes. "Your scent is like roses…"

"Verily brushes my hair with rose oil, to make it shine."

Ésh seemed to waver on his feet. He released her hair, took her hand, and stepped back toward the hay.

Clare hesitated, pulling away.

Her refusal didn't make him angry. He only smiled and held out his hand again. "I made you a promise, *mo'ona*: you do not need to be frightened, because I will look after you. And I really am tired."

She laughed a little. "I am too—from all that riding yesterday."

"Then we should rest, as Verily said."

Clare began to pin up her hair again.

"Keep it down, please…"

"But I'll be picking hay out of it for hours!"

"I will help you. If we lay on something, it will not be so bad…" To Clare's shock and delight, Ésh pulled his long shirt over his head. Now, he wore only his medicine pouch, breechcloth, leggings, and moccasins—like the first day she'd met him. He draped his shirt over the hay.

"But…the hay will poke you now…" she murmured, trying not to stare at all his bare skin and failing miserably.

"It is for both of us." He tugged her after him as he lay down on one side of the fringed buckskin shirt. There wasn't much room left for Clare, unless… "Come." As she lowered herself, he wrapped his arm around her, drawing her against his body. She had no choice but to lay her head on his shoulder.

She had *every* choice. There was no force in his embrace, only suggestion. Only welcome. Only recumbent strength, warmth, and beauty beneath her. Breaths quickened with awe, Clare rested her cheek against his bare skin, at the edge of one of his scars. Her gloved hand settled just below his right nipple.

Was she dreaming? For three days now, she'd imagined tracing the ridges and valleys of his arms and chest and abdomen with her fingers. Instead of exploring, her hand only trembled; but even through her sleeve, she could feel the tautness of his belly beneath her arm. And the firm warmth of his shoulder and chest beneath her head... Even in her fantasies, she'd not been so bold.

Ésh brushed her kid glove with his own bare fingers. "Do you always wear these?"

"Almost always."

"Why?"

"Because they are...proper..." Her voice faded as her eyes studied his dark nipple.

Ésh lifted her hand with both of his. He undid the button at her wrist and tugged off the glove. "You should not hide these, *mo'ona*," he whispered into her palm before he kissed it. Her other hand, still gloved and tucked between them, felt bereft.

Casual yet possessive, Ésh stroked her loose hair. Then his fingers grazed the moles beneath the corner of her left eye. Clare tensed self-consciously.

"When a warrior paints himself with spots like this, do you know what they mean?"

"No..."

"They are hailstones. They make him fierce."

Clare giggled. "Can women be fierce?"

"The best ones are."

Clare relaxed as she had on Mirage—even more than she had on Mirage. She trusted Ésh completely. She realized she could feel his steady heartbeat against her ear. She never wanted this moment to end. Yet so many mysteries lay hidden within this man. "What does this design mean?" Her fingertip traced the air over the quilled circle on the front of his medicine pouch, quartered into four colors: black, white, yellow, and red.

"It is a medicine wheel. Each color is for one of the Sacred Powers at the four directions. Also the four seasons and the four parts of a man's life. It is a circle with no end. It means we do not die, only change. This gives us courage."

A symbol of resurrection like Clare's ouroboros bracelet or the Monarch butterfly on the Lazare mausoleum. Careful to arch her hand around Ésh's nipple, she brushed her fingers over the jagged scar above it. Beneath her cheek, she could just feel the roughness of a matching scar on the other side of his chest. "Are these from the Sun Dance?"

"Some people call it that, yes. Most Zizistas call it the New Life Lodge."

"There were skewers through your chest, and you danced till you tore them free?"

"Yes."

Clare shivered. She fulfilled her fantasy: she trailed her hand across his broad shoulder and down again, over the undulations of hard muscle sheathed in soft flesh. "And the scars on your arms?"

"I cut away the skin as a sacrifice, so that the Sacred Powers would pity me and guide me."

Clare shuddered. She supposed it was little different from a Catholic flagellating himself, but she could not imagine slicing off her own skin. No wonder Indian warriors were called braves. She grieved that Ésh had marred his perfect body, and yet somehow the scars became him. "Did they answer, your Sacred Powers?"

"Yes. The answer was you."

"Pardon?" Clare raised her head.

"For four days I fasted and prayed, and the Sacred Powers were quiet. Then, they gave me a vision of a woman with hair like yours." His fingers played with her locks again. "With a voice like yours. She told me to follow the wolf who guided me to Fort Laramie. To Charleston. To you. She gave me a black-and-orange butterfly as a sign."

Clare's eyes widened. That was why Ésh was fascinated by her hair and by the Monarch on his family's mausoleum. This *was* a fairy tale: they were meant for each other, just like Briar Rose and her prince.

"You guided me to my first family." Ésh slipped his hand upward till his thumb rested on her cheek. "But I hope that is not everything the Sacred Powers want for us." He caressed the edge of her lips. "It is not everything I want."

Clare wanted him close to her always, gazing at her just like this… She drew in a breath that would determine the rest of her life. "Ésh, would you take me back with you, when you return to your Cheyenne family?"

"Are you sure that is what you want, *mo'ona?*" His eyes were grave, more grey than green in the shadows of the stable. "It is not an easy life. It becomes harder and harder each year, because there are more whites and fewer buffalo."

"But you are going back."

"I do not belong here, or anywhere among white men. None of the Zizistas do. I must fight for them as long as I can."

Clare looked down at his scars from the New Life Lodge, at his medicine pouch. "I know the West is changing, but that is why I must go. I want to see the buffalo, the antelope, and the prairie dogs..." She thought of the beautiful, playful Carolina parakeets, who had filled the trees once, who grew rarer with each passing year. "I want to see Independence Rock, the mountains, and the tipis. I want to draw the Cheyenne like Mr. Eastman and write down their stories like Mrs. Eastman." She met Ésh's eyes again—so warm and vital. "I can help them, Ésh: I can teach the Cheyenne English and teach them to read, so they understand the treaties they are signing. If I remain here, I am nothing—another silent wife. Another powerless plantation mistress. I don't belong here any more than you do."

Still his thumb caressed her cheek. "Will you come as my wife, *mo'ona?*"

Clare gasped. It still wasn't *"I love you,"* but...

"I will be a poor husband at first. I must give my horses to the family of the Kit Fox Soldier. But I will catch more. I will make you proud."

Clare cradled his face in both her hands, one gloved and one bare. "Yes," she cried. "Yes!"

Ésh grinned. "You give me courage, *nazheem!*"

Was he saying he loved her?

Ésh lifted his head till his nose was brushing hers, and she welcomed his renewed kisses. But this time, Clare felt a change. He did not so much invite as pursue her, with a hunger both exhilarating and daunting. His thumb stroked the edge of her lips, pulling gently, as if coaxing her mouth to open. Then something deft and seeking flicked over her lower lip.

Clare realized it was the tip of his tongue. Her breath caught. She wasn't sure how to respond.

Ésh didn't press her. He let his mouth linger against hers for a moment longer; he kissed her one last time with only his lips; and then he lay back against the hay.

Clare tucked her head beneath his chin and returned her gaze to his chest. Brazenly she slid her bare hand down his abdomen to rest beside his navel. Just above the cord of his breechcloth. He was hers now. Almost hers. "When will we go?"

"Your month of May, I think."

Five weeks away at least. A long time to wait—and a long time to keep their secret.

"Do you want to live with my family till then?"

Clare drew in a sharp breath. "No—don't tell your family yet."

"Why not?" She could hear the frown in his voice.

Clare remembered Grand-mère Anne's distress when she'd learned Ésh planned to return to the Cheyenne. How might she react to the news that *Clare* wanted to live as a heathen? Proper white women would sooner kill themselves than become squaws. In James Fenimore Cooper novels, characters called such a fate "degradation" and "worse than a thousand deaths." Certainly Father Joseph would disapprove: how could she attend Mass in the middle of the wilderness? Anne or Father Joseph might send word to Clare's family to prevent her elopement. "I think they will try and talk me out of it."

"Why?"

"Because it's...a little mad: a Charleston girl marrying an Indian." Clare was losing herself in the rise and fall of Ésh's chest. "But it's what I want."

"I want you too," Ésh whispered into her hair.

"I love you." The words sat on her tongue. It meant nothing, Clare told herself, that Ésh hadn't said them. He nearly had.

CHAPTER 35

O Love, O fire! once he drew
With one long kiss my whole soul thro'
My lips, as sunlight drinketh dew.
— Alfred, Lord Tennyson, "Fatima" (1833)

That evening as Clare sat down to supper, Aunt Hortense glared at her and demanded: "Why are you so happy?"

"I'm not, Aunt."

"You were humming in the hall."

Clare picked up her wine glass and hid her smile in it. "The sun came out after the rain, that's all."

"That was hours ago."

"It was a beautiful sunset, didn't you think?"

She must temper her joy, Clare knew. All she had to do was think of the two lonely days ahead, when Ésh would be in Charleston. She almost wished she hadn't introduced him to his family yet.

When he returned to the stallion barn, Ésh greeted her with a grin. "Good afternoon, *nazheem*."

She was wearing a new riding habit, this time of violet silk. "Am I not beautiful anymore?" Clare pretended to pout, even as she colored. He was making her vain.

"More than ever, now that you are *nazheem*." Ésh drew her into his arms. "It means 'my woman'—and also 'my wife.'"

"Which way did you mean it?"

"Both," he smiled.

"But we haven't... Don't Cheyenne brides and grooms exchange vows when they wed?"

Ésh frowned. "'Vows'?"

"When a Cheyenne couple marries, isn't there a ceremony? A ritual?"

Ésh looked uncomfortable. He didn't let her go, but he avoided her eyes. "If you were Zizistas, I would send to your father many horses and other gifts. But even if I had my own horses here, I do not think your father would accept them."

"He would not." Clare forced herself to smile. "I suppose I would be worth very few horses, anyway—I cannot even tan a hide yet."

Ésh met her eyes again. "The horses do not equal the bride's worth. They prove to her father that her suitor is brave and that he can provide for her. When her father accepts, he sends to her suitor other horses and other gifts—they are of equal value or greater. Horses are very valuable, but even a hundred of them cannot equal one woman." Ésh was staring at her lips now.

Clare wasn't finished. She didn't feel like a wife yet. "Does the husband give his new wife a ring?"

"Not when they wed, but when they are courting, yes—he might give her his ring and she might give him her bracelet." Ésh's fingers traced the ouroboros circling her wrist.

With only a twinge of loss, Clare unhooked the turquoise snake's tail from its mouth and offered the bracelet to Ésh.

He smiled and accepted it, though he peered at the clasp. "How do I...?"

Clare wrapped the turquoise snake around his wrist. It was larger than hers; she tucked only the very tip of the snake's tail into its mouth before locking it in place. "Don't let your family see this. They'll know it's from me."

"I will keep it safe." Between her glove and her cuff, Ésh caressed her bare wrist. "I wish I had a ring or earrings to offer you in return. But they are all with my Zizistas family."

Clare smiled at the idea of borrowing earrings from her husband. She'd noticed the empty holes along the rims of his ears.

"It will be difficult to buy something in Charleston without my grandfather or grandmother knowing it—but I will find a way."

"You need to save your money for our journey, don't you?"

"Yes." Ésh scowled.

"Then you needn't buy me anything."

"But it is what husbands here do? Give their wives a ring?"

Movement caught Clare's attention: Mirage grazing in the pasture, swishing her beautiful parti-colored tail to ward off flies. "You could make me a ring! Braid together a few strands of Mirage's hair—then I will have something to remember her by."

"You think like a Zizistas, *nazheem*," Ésh smiled. "It is thanks to Mirage that we found each other. I have her hair in my bag already." He laid his hand against his chest, where his medicine pouch rested beneath his shirt. "When I make you a ring, you will have her medicine too."

"Medicine… I think I know what that means to a Cheyenne. Power and blessing, but also mystery?"

Ésh narrowed his eyes at her. "Are you sure you are not Zizistas?"

Clare raised her chin. "I am now—for my husband is Zizistas."

Ésh did not deny the appellation.

Could it really be this easy, to claim him as her husband? "How do I say it in my new language, 'my husband'?"

"*Na-eham*." Ésh was staring at her lips again and leaning nearer.

Much as Clare longed for him to kiss her, she knew the wife of a Cheyenne warrior must know how to ride. "Teach me, *na-eham*!" Clare broke away from him and darted to Mirage's right side. "I still don't know how to fall!"

Ésh came to stand behind her. "First, you must be able to dismount on your own. Did you practice as I showed you?"

"Of course, *na-eham.*" In the privacy of her bedchamber, she'd straddled a chest and practiced swinging her left leg. Her muscles ached, but they were growing stronger.

Clare mounted with Ésh's help. This time, he made no secret about caressing her leg, but his hand climbed no higher than her knee. Then, with great effort and a little grunting, she showed him she could dismount without his assistance. Ésh was pleased.

There was more than one good way to fall, Clare learned. It depended on what her horse was doing. First, Ésh explained how Clare could push her body away from Mirage's and land on her feet. Then Ésh taught Clare how to roll to safety instead.

Either way, she must relax her muscles—something she still found difficult. Clare remembered the dream she'd had shortly before her mother died, how she'd fallen from a great cliff. Even after Clare started awake in her bed, the terror and the nothingness clung to her. Now, she was less nervous when Ésh kept close by, when she knew there was someone to catch her—or at least help her up again.

On her sixth or seventh try, Clare rolled into Ésh and toppled him like a ninepin. They ended up tangled in the grass, laughing. She relished the chance to feel his warm body against her, his strong arms protecting her. For a moment, their heads were so close that she saw only his golden hair and felt his breaths tickling her neck.

"Am I doing better, or worse?" she panted.

"Better!" Ésh declared. "I am proud of you, *nazheem.*" He said the words against her skin, nipping Clare's chin and the corners of her lips with admiring little kisses. If he only did this, Clare would go boneless—she would fall forever and feel nothing but pleasure. When he brought his mouth fully against hers, she closed her eyes and parted her lips.

Ésh lost no time. She felt his tongue teasing her lower lip again, and she remained unsure what to make of it. When Clare was little, she'd stuck out the tip of her tongue in concentration and been completely unaware of it, till Aunt Hortense had scolded her out of the habit.

Yet the quick movements of Ésh's tongue seemed purposeful. He was exploring just inside her lips now, lapping at her, tasting more and more of her. She realized her own tongue was rising to meet his, eager—or at least willing—to accept what he offered, to taste more of him herself.

He moaned and dove deeper. It was the strangest sensation, to have a part of his glorious body thrust inside hers. It was astonishing and intoxicating, for someone as ordinary as she was to be connected, literally connected, to someone as singular and dazzling as he was.

Yet he thought her beautiful. He'd asked her to be his wife. And Ésh was clearly enjoying their kiss. One of his arms held her tight to his chest, and his other hand was kneading her shoulder like the paw of a contented cat. Ésh's tongue was like velvet as it circled, retreated, and pursued.

Cautiously, then with more confidence, Clare learned to respond, to challenge and tease him. Her hands explored the contours of his back, his arms, his shoulders. She wished he wasn't wearing his shirt. Her fingers sank into his hair.

Only when they were both breathless did Ésh pause with his forehead against hers. "I am *very* proud of you, *nazheem*," he gasped. "You learn fast."

"I have an excellent teacher," she giggled. But the words made her realize: Ésh kissed and flattered her with such skill because *someone else* had taught him. Clare sat up and turned away from him.

Ésh kissed the nape of her neck. "Is something wrong, *mo'ona?*"

Had he called other women beautiful? "You're very good at this."

"Thank you."

She heard the grin in his voice. Clare glowered at him over her shoulder. "That wasn't a compliment."

He frowned. "What do you mean?"

"I mean: You must have had a great deal of practice." The words came out sharp as quills. "And I don't like the thought of other women touching you any more than you like the thought of other men touching me."

"I have kissed other women," Ésh admitted. The crease between his eyebrows irritated her. It said: *What did you expect? Isn't it obvious all women adore me?*

If she was to give herself to him, soul and body, she must face this and try to put it behind her. "Have you…done more than kissing? Have you…" She didn't know how to finish.

His face softened. "No, *nazheem.*"

Clare sucked in a breath. "Truly? You understand what I'm asking?"

"I think so."

"You've never…joined with a woman?"

"No."

Clare turned back and threw her arms around his neck, pulling his gorgeous virgin body against hers. "I cannot tell you how happy that makes me, *na-eham*—to know you are mine, truly mine, and no one else's. I will be a good wife to you, I swear it."

"I think you will be a *very* good wife," Ésh said in a voice that was almost a purr, staring at her in a way that sent shivers of anticipation through Clare's body.

But before his mouth could reach hers, Verily interrupted them. "Mr. Ésh!" Clare's maid called as she raced up to them. "You must get yourself and your horse inside the barn! Mr. Tilling is coming!"

Ésh seemed to be running before he'd even regained his feet. He snatched up Mirage's lead rope and towed the reluctant mare inside.

Clare tidied her hair as best she could, and Verily thrust her book into her hands. Clare plopped down in the grass again, hoping a sitting position would disguise the fact that she wasn't wearing a cage crinoline. If the overseer noticed anything amiss with the volume of her skirt, it did not inspire commentary. He merely tipped his hat and rode on.

As soon as Mr. Tilling was gone, Clare flew into the barn and into Ésh's arms. She nearly swooned with relief and delight, but Ésh didn't let her fall.

The next day, they barely accomplished anything in the way of riding, and no reading whatsoever. Each kiss she thought might be the last became another, as if a new decision to cease was resolved and overturned between each. Why should they hurry? What did riding or reading matter when they had *this*? Suddenly nothing in the world felt more natural than sharing his mouth.

CHAPTER 36

Love creates a likeness between that which loves and that which is loved.

— Saint John of the Cross, *The Ascent of Mount Carmel* (1619)

If he'd misled Clare, it was only a white lie, Ésh reasoned. He might have "done more than kissing" with Nataane; he might have intended to "join" with her—but in the end, he *hadn't*.

How was Ésh to explain that he'd shot too soon and ruined it, when he was still learning Clare's language? When she might not know how a man's *véto'ots* behaved? If she did know, Clare might doubt his ability to be a good husband, when he couldn't control himself.

He would learn, Ésh vowed. He would make certain that didn't happen again. He would leave Clare sated, not disappointed.

He wanted to please her—a white woman!—as he had wanted to please no one else. Always before his first concern had been pleasing himself. He was older now, not as stupid or selfish as he'd been even a few moons ago. He understood that you could not enjoy a woman's body without becoming responsible for the woman to whom it belonged.

What did it matter if Clare's skin was not tawny and her hair was not black? She was beautiful in her own way. She was as pure as a Zizistas woman yet as passionate as a Cloud woman.

When he first saw her, he'd assumed she was like other white women: a fragile doe, easily startled. But as she grew more comfortable and confident with him, in her kisses another kind of creature emerged: his equal, cautious yet bold, beauty and strength intertwined. A mountain cat, perhaps.

In order to keep her, he'd have to satisfy her. Ésh tried to recall everything his Zizistas grandfather had taught him about women and about his own body. Everything he'd learned from listening to and peeking at his father and second mother when they came together under or over their buffalo robes. Everything other Zizistas had told him. Everything Nataane had shown him. Everything he'd overheard Jesse and York and Ben saying about their women.

Altogether, Ésh knew a great deal, but his knowledge remained incomplete. In order to please Clare their first time together, he would need to ask specific questions. Like how to stop himself from finishing too soon. The way the grooms spoke about women's breasts also intrigued Ésh. To the Zizistas, breasts were only for nursing babies.

From the expression on Ben's face when Ésh mounted Mirage in the afternoons, Ésh knew the man had guessed where he was going —and that Ben disapproved. So he was unlikely to help. Jesse or York would probably answer Ésh's questions, but he feared they might give him bad advice on purpose for their own amusement.

Who did that leave?

ON HIS NEXT VISIT to Archdale Street, Ésh found Grandfather René reading on his "piazza." His left foot was shoeless, propped up and wrapped in white. "What happened, Grandfather?"

René peered at Ésh over his spectacles. "Unfortunately, I do not have your way with horses, Ésh. Or perhaps my reactions are not as quick as they used to be. My foot ended up underneath Cassique's hoof. I feel like a fool and it hurts like the dickens, but I'll mend. I hope *you* are well?"

"I am, Grandfather."

René returned his attention to his book. "And how is Clare?"

"She is good." Ésh smiled. "She is learning to—" He broke off when he realized that he'd already revealed too much.

René narrowed his eyes as if he were trying to read Ésh's expression instead of his book. "You've seen her since the day she introduced us, haven't you?"

Zizistas did not lie. So Ésh looked toward the garden and said: "Maybe."

"How many times?"

"A few." Ésh met René's blue eyes. "I am teaching her to ride."

"In secret, I imagine?"

"I cannot meet her openly."

René closed his book. "Horseback riding isn't all you're doing, is it?" René did not wait for Ésh's answer; he knew it already, and he was scowling. "I saw how you two looked at each other. You are playing with fire, Ésh, and you are destroying that young woman's reputation. I shudder to think how her father will react. When you return to the Cheyenne, you will be abandoning Clare to face the consequences of your actions alone. That is the behavior of a coward and a scoundrel."

Ésh did not recognize the last word, but the way René spat it, Ésh knew it was an insult. And he wouldn't let even his grandfather call him a coward. Ésh must tell him the whole truth. "When I go, she is coming with me, as my wife."

For a moment, René gaped at him, as if this were somehow worse than deserting Clare. "You met her a week ago—you hardly know her."

"I know everything I need to know. You and my grandmother and my uncle have known her all her life, and you like her."

"If you think so highly of our opinions, then sit down and *listen*." Nervously, Ésh obeyed.

"Answer me honestly, Ésh. Have you explained to Clare what living as a Cheyenne would mean?"

"She knows."

"Do you intend to take additional wives?"

Again Ésh avoided his grandfather's gaze. Those blue eyes seemed to understand everything before Ésh had arrived at a decision himself. "Maybe." Why should he deny himself a true Zizistas wife, who could teach Clare everything she needed to know? She'd be like a sister to Clare.

"If that is your intention, Ésh, end this *now*. That young woman has known enough heartbreak already. Clare needs a husband who will consider her feelings first, last, and always—who will remain faithful to her and her alone. I don't care if polygamy is customary among the Cheyenne—to a romantic young woman like Clare, it would mean degradation. You would humiliate her. She would never forgive you. If Clare goes West with you, she will be sacrificing *everything* for your sake. The least you can do is give up other women. Do you hear me, Ésh?"

"Yes," he answered without opening his clenched teeth. The thought that he would never, ever join with another woman, or with a Zizistas woman—Ésh did not like it at all.

"Have you lain with Clare? Do you understand what I mean by that?"

"Yes. And we have done nothing but kiss."

"That had better be all you do, until you are both absolutely certain that this is what you want—most especially, that this is what *she* wants."

"She is not happy here, Grandfather."

"You believe you can make her happy, in a strange land among strange people?"

"They will not be strange to her for long."

"Would *you* give up everything for *her*?"

"She does not ask me to."

"She may, Ésh. A year from now, two years—if she is miserable, you must promise me that you will bring her back to us. Ideally you would remain with her. But if you cannot find a way to live in her world, at the least you will free her. If the two of you cannot find happiness together, you will allow her to find it without you. Promise me, Ésh."

"I promise."

"Before you touch her again, you will also give her my letter. You will watch her read it, and you will bring her answer back to me."

"What letter?"

"The letter I am about to write."

"My grandmother and my uncle and my brother—will you tell them about me and Clare?"

"Not until I read her answer."

In order to give his grandfather time to think and write to Clare, Ésh spent the rest of the day with his uncle. Before dinner, they accepted David's invitation to visit him at his hospital.

His brother guided them through the "wards" and explained the work of a *veho* medicine man. In the way he spoke to his "patients" and the way they greeted him, Ésh could see that David was a good doctor. He was especially tender with the women and babies.

His brother also asked Ésh many questions about his life, but David still appeared uneasy and sad. Ésh stood before his brother, happy and grown, yet he thought David remained haunted by the crying baby he had been. It was as if his brother dragged invisible buffalo skulls behind him from skewers that never tore away. Suffering might please Maheo, but the Creator did not want anyone to suffer forever.

Ésh wondered how David would respond when he learned Clare intended to go West with him.

Ésh was particularly intrigued to learn about his uncle's work, how white men spoke to their Creator. So many of the things Joseph did that afternoon reminded Ésh of his Zizistas grandfather's medicine. Joseph also sang to the Creator and made offerings to him. He burned incense and myrrh as the Zizistas burned sage and sweet grass.

With his uncle and with the family's permission, Ésh visited the house of a man who was near death. Instead of shaking a buffalo-skin rattle to drive away evil, Joseph shook a silver ball on a handle. The ball held holy water, and his uncle sprinkled it in each corner of the sick man's room, as a Zizistas medicine man would expel spirits from each part of a patient's lodge.

Joseph and other Catholics often fasted for days so that the Creator would pity them. Though his uncle no longer followed the practice himself, Joseph told Ésh that many Catholics also made themselves bleed as a sacrifice, just as the Zizistas did.

In some ways, the *veho* and the Zizistas were not so different. They both believed that the Creator had come to Earth and lived among them. But Maheo had only taught his people how to make arrows and fire, how to hunt and how to live. The white men's Creator had come to Earth so he could suffer and die for them. When Catholics whipped themselves or wore garments that left their skin raw, it was to imitate their Creator. A representation of his sacrifice was called a crucifix, which white men often carried with them. A crucifix also adorned their places of worship.

Ésh was more comfortable within the walls of Joseph's church than he was within other walls. It was like a permanent New Life Lodge. Ésh could see how much his uncle loved his Creator. Joseph said his "God" had died for all humans, Zizistas as well as white men.

Outside in the graveyard, Ésh asked: "Is your Creator the same as our Maheo, then?"

"There is only one God, Ésh. He must be the same." Joseph was tidying the bushes in the graveyard, collecting the wrinkled flowers in a sack. He said it would encourage the bushes to bloom again.

Overhead, a flock of birds chattered to each other in a tree, then burst into the sky. "But Zizistas also believe there are spirits living beneath the Earth and at the four directions—the Sacred Powers. We believe each animal has great medicine, too. I do not think white men believe this."

"We do not. Or at least, Catholics do not. Throughout history, there have been many kinds of 'white men.' Some have worshipped animals and trees."

"Then not all white men believe in Hell?"

Joseph paused in his work, his hand full of dead flowers. "You know about Hell?"

"A Black Robe spoke to my friend Méanév when we were children. She tried to explain Hell to me." Ésh's eyes settled on the tomb that held the bones of his sister Sophie and his aunt Hélène. "We decided it was so terrible, it could not be true—to suffer even after you are dead."

"What do the Cheyenne believe?"

"That after we die, we go to be with the Creator. That in the Land of the Departed, there is always plenty of game, and everyone is happy. The Dakota believe the same." Ésh glanced behind him and saw no one. "Do you know what the Yoruba believe?"

"I see my father told you about his African grandmother," Joseph smiled. "Among other things, the Yoruba believe the souls of the departed can return in new bodies."

"You and I are part Dakota, part Yoruba, and part French. Where will we go when we die?"

"I am a Priest, Ésh. I believe in Hell. But I hope it is very sparsely populated." Joseph continued to gather the dead flowers in his sack. "The longer I live, the more I am convinced that God is truly merciful. We all must suffer. But in the scope of eternity, our suffering will be brief and our joy will be boundless."

Ésh asked Joseph to repeat this in simpler words.

His uncle chuckled, apologized, and did so. "You're not even nineteen years old. What prompts such a young man to ask what will happen to him when he dies?"

Ésh hesitated. The Zizistas believed you should tell no one what you saw in a badger's blood. Since he'd met Clare, Ésh had tried not even to *think* about the prophecy. But he could hardly be a good husband to her if he was dead.

Maybe the prophecy was a lie. The Zizistas could be wrong about things, like the shape of the Earth. White men had travelled all the way around it. And Ésh longed to tell someone. "You said what people say to you is a secret, because you are a Priest."

"Yes." Joseph looked worried now. "But if you are ill, Ésh, you should speak to your grandfather and your brother."

"I am not sick. Will you keep my secret?"

"I will." Joseph sat on a wide metal seat.

Ésh sat beside him but stared at the ground, as if the badger were laid out at his feet. "The Zizistas believe that sometimes, a man sees his own death coming. I have seen mine. I know I will die when I am young."

"You saw a vision that made you think this?"

"Yes."

"Catholics have visions too. They tell a Priest, who helps them interpret the vision."

If telling a Priest was like telling no one, if it remained a secret... "I went on a journey to capture horses. My friend who was with me killed a badger. One by one, we looked at our image in the badger's blood. The badger showed us how we would die. I saw myself as a young man with short hair. I had long hair then. The doctor at Fort Laramie, he cut it. So I will die before my hair grows again."

"Let us say what you saw was the truth. You will be a young man for many years yet, so you may live for many years yet. Your hair may grow long and be cut again."

But a Zizistas would never willingly cut his hair—unless he was in mourning. Was that what the badger had meant? Ésh realized his uncle might be right. The prophecy might not come true till Ésh had been Clare's husband for five, ten, maybe even fifteen years. In a badger's blood, you could not tell if a man was eighteen or thirty. Before Ésh died, he might give Clare children.

When he cut his hair again, would Ésh be mourning one of their children? Or would he be mourning Clare? In making her Zizistas, was he condemning her to die?

Clare *wanted* to be his wife, Ésh reminded himself. She had suggested it, not him. He would not let a murky prophecy ruin their lives. They were happy together, and that was all that mattered.

Ésh would take Clare his grandfather's letter as he had promised. If she read it and still wished to be his wife, Ésh would make her his wife—prophecy or no prophecy.

CHAPTER 37

Love conquers all things; let us too surrender to love!
— Virgil, *Eclogue X* (37 B.C.)

When Ésh returned to Clare's barn, he was carrying his grandfather's letter in a pouch tied at his waist—the same pouch that held the rabbit skin with the words from Independence Rock. René's words might also change their lives. Ésh wanted to give them to Clare as soon as possible—and he never wanted to give them to her. But he had promised his grandfather.

Clare called down to Ésh from the hayloft. "Come up—I have something to show you."

"It is a new book?" Ésh asked as he climbed the ladder.

"No. You'll never guess!"

When Ésh reached the loft, he saw a large hide covered in thick brown hair draped over a mound of hay. He could hardly believe it. "A buffalo robe?"

"I've had it for years," Clare smiled. "It's one of my most prized possessions—but no one else here appreciates it. I've quarrelled with my aunt so many times about this robe. I've had to hide it from her more than once."

Ésh passed his hand over the soft fur. He loved that Clare loved this robe. It was a good sign.

Suddenly, she gasped and looked behind them. "Verily! What is it?"

Instinctively, Ésh turned around. But there was no one else in the hayloft. He frowned and stepped toward the empty ladder. Behind him, he heard rustling and grunts of effort. As he turned back to Clare, she cried:

"No! Not yet!" She was wrestling with the buffalo robe. "Fiddlesticks! I thought I could do this! I *practiced*!"

"What are you trying to do, *nazheem*?"

"Throw it over your head—our heads!" Clare gripped the buffalo robe in both hands, her beautiful face twisted with frustration. "But it's so *heavy*!"

"Why are you trying to throw it over our heads?"

"Isn't that how Indians court?" Again she tried to heave the robe over their heads. She barely raised it to her shoulders. "I read about it. I know it's supposed to be the man who throws the blanket or robe over the woman, but…"

Clare had it wrong in more ways than one. A suitor didn't throw the robe over his beloved's head, only around her shoulders. But Ésh was happy to try Clare's version. He grasped one side of the robe and tossed it upward. "Like this?"

"Yes!" They ducked underneath, till the robe draped them both from their heads to their knees. In the twilight of their tiny lodge, Clare grinned up at him. "I lied, about Verily. I only wanted you to look away."

Ésh chuckled. "I know."

"What do Cheyenne couples do under their courting robes?" Clare's hand stroked the length of his arm.

His fingers danced with hers. He was glad she wasn't wearing gloves. "They speak about the weather and the camp news…"

Clare giggled, and he felt her hurried breaths brush his face as the fresh flowery scent of her surrounded him.

"If the man is brave, he…" Even in the dimness, his mouth found hers without effort.

Clare smiled against his lips but whispered: "I suppose a proper girl pretends to run away?"

She withdrew her hand and her lips and feinted escape—once, twice, three times. Before she darted free of the robe, Ésh always recaptured her. Each embrace became closer, each kiss more fervent. This was his favorite way to communicate. He could tell Clare how much he wanted her without mispronouncing a single word.

In her next play at running, Clare tripped on the edge of the robe, and its weight pulled Ésh with her. They fell together in a cascade of laughter till they were sprawled on the hay. The robe settled over them, shutting out the light. Clare ended up lying mostly on top of him, and the darkness made her bold: she lost little time in rediscovering the taste of his mouth.

Ésh had never heard sounds as wonderful as Clare's soft moans. Beneath the robe, her wordless pleasure caressed him like her mouth and her hands. Whether by the fall or by her fingers, one side of his shirt was pushed up, and she stroked his bare skin.

Yet even as he delighted in her touch, her moans, and her kisses, Ésh twisted uneasily beneath her. Despite Clare's skirt and her leggings, he felt one of her knees hooked in-between his thighs. In her enthusiasm, her knee was climbing dangerously high.

This was hardly the first time Clare had swelled his *véto'ots*, but so far, he'd managed not to press it against her. Now, she risked either kneeing his *véto'ots* or rubbing it with her thigh. Would Clare understand what the bulge meant? Would it frighten her? Just how innocent was she?

In an effort to nudge her leg safely beside him, Ésh's hand slid down from her waist. But when he reached the curve of Clare's ass, he could not help but linger. His fingers wanted to plunge through her skirt. His hand began to tighten, to squeeze.

Clare gasped in surprise, and her mouth broke contact with his. But she made no attempt to slap him or to escape from the robe.

Ésh tried to shift out from under her, but his hand refused to leave her ass.

She must have interpreted his squirming as feigned resistance;

she only pinned his leg more firmly between hers. "*I* will decide when you may rise, sir." Clare held him down with both hands on his chest—one over his shirt and one under it. She teased his lips with kisses like feathers. "For you are *my* captive, to do with as I will."

Did she have *any* idea what she was saying, or what she did to him? Clare's words thrilled through his blood till the throb in his loins became unbearable. All he wanted was to pull her truly on top of him, her hips tight against his *véto'ots*. The warm pressure of her body alone might give him relief.

Why should he stop there? It would be easy to yank up that skirt, rip off those leggings, and bare that soft willing flesh... Clare smiled and sighed so in these furtive kisses—if only she knew the greater pleasures awaiting them, she would never deny him, or herself. She would be grateful. She would wonder why he had waited so long. Beneath this robe, all was possible; it was only them in the world...

First, he would free his *véto'ots* and acquaint her with it. Clare's mouth promised eagerness; she would be proud to feel what she did to him. His hand fumbled in the darkness—and snagged on another shape above and beside his breechcloth. The pouch holding his grandfather's letter.

Ésh shoved Clare away from him and battled with the buffalo robe till he was free. Gasping like a man saved from drowning, he crawled to the edge of the hay and knelt there with his back to her.

Clare must be tossing aside the robe: behind him, he heard a few whimpers, then her unmuffled voice: "Ésh? What's wrong?"

"I could not breathe," he lied.

She crept closer on the hay. He imagined her beautiful honey-brown hair wild around her shoulders. He closed his eyes. He felt her whisper in his ear: "You can breathe now, can't you?"

How he longed to turn around and recapture her mouth—to begin again, to *finish*. Instead, Ésh forced himself to his feet and strode to the edge of the hayloft. He stared down into the emptiness of the barn and waited for his *véto'ots* to give up.

Clare followed him. "Why are we stopping, *na-eham*?"

Because he might never be her husband. Until Clare was certain she wanted to be his wife, Ésh had no right to find pleasure in her body, even if that pleasure was hers. "Because I want to do more than kiss you, *mo'ona*." He tensed but did not turn as Clare slid her arms around his waist and rested her head on his shoulder.

"I want more too, Ésh. I want *all* of you."

He tried to look at her, but he saw only tousled honey-brown hair. "Do you know what happens, when a man joins with a woman?"

Now Clare's body stiffened. Against his back, he felt her draw in a breath that was more like a shudder. "I know it will hurt."

If she thought that, and she still wanted him, she was even braver than he'd thought. Ésh wondered who had told Clare about the pain and what else this person had told her. He suspected that white women did not speak of their bodies and their pleasure as freely as Zizistas women did—especially when they thought no men were listening. He turned to face her.

She kept her hands at his waist and avoided his gaze. "It's true, isn't it? I will bleed?" Slowly, Clare raised her eyes. For the first time, she truly resembled a frightened doe.

"Joining *can* hurt the woman," he admitted, "and the first time, she may bleed."

Clare dropped her gaze again. She was trembling now.

Ésh reached out to touch her face. "But if the man knows what he is doing and he prepares the woman's body, the pain is nothing. She soon forgets it and feels only happiness."

Clare lifted her eyes, and they kindled with hope. "Truly?"

He caressed her cheek with his thumb. "I promise you, *nazheem*."

She frowned. "But why must it hurt at all?"

"It is like…when you began riding the Zizistas way." He slipped his hand around her side to rest on her seat. "Your body ached afterward, didn't it?"

Clare's cheeks began to grow pink, but she did not move his hand. "Yes."

"That is because you were using parts of it you had not used before. When your body becomes stronger, riding will hurt only if you do it wrong or if you do it for too long. Joining with a man is like that—but much, much better." Gently but suggestively, his hand tightened on her seat through her skirt. "I will teach your body to sing, *nazheem.*"

Clare flushed all the way to her collar, and she caught her lower lip between her teeth. "What did you mean, about *preparing* my body?"

He smiled. "I am happy to show you, *nazheem*—as soon and as often as you want." Then he sighed. "But first, you must read this." Ésh reached under his shirt, inside his pouch, and withdrew the letter. "It is from my grandfather."

Clare scowled at him and did not take the paper. "You told Grand-père René about us?"

Ésh's arm sagged, as if the letter had grown as heavy as the buffalo robe. "He guessed that I have been visiting you, and I could not lie to him."

Clare peered at the paper as though it might bite her. "How did he react?"

"He thinks I am 'a scoundrel,'" Ésh muttered.

"How dare he! Your own grandfather! Has he told anyone else about us? Father Joseph or…"

"Not yet." Ésh held out the letter again. "My grandfather made me promise that you would read this, before we…"

"Then I shall read it." Clare snatched the letter and wrestled the folds open—though nothing sealed it. Ésh heard the paper tear.

He wished he knew what it said. He'd recognized only big C's, big E's (both their names?) and several words that began with s.

Clare read the writing for only a few moments before she looked up at him. "What does he mean, about his foot?"

"It is broken. His horse stepped on it."

"Oh!" Clare covered her mouth with her hand. "Poor Grand-père!" Her grip on the letter seemed to soften. She sank onto the hay and continued reading.

GRAND-PÈRE RENÉ had always given her good advice, Clare reminded herself. The least she could do was listen.

Dearest girl,

Esh has told me of your engagement, of your plan to live with him in the West. Before you commit to such a course, I beg you to read this letter through and consider it carefully. I want nothing less than your happiness.

I wish I could say these things in person, but my damned foot will render travel painful and protracted for weeks yet. Even if I did visit Stratford-on-Ashley, even if your family agreed to admit me, I am certain your aunt would insist on hearing every word I say to you. Neither of us wants that.

You are an intelligent young woman, Clare. This is your decision—not your aunt's, not your father's, and not mine. I will do everything I can to help you choose wisely, but I refuse to skulk in your father's back gate as my grandson does.

As for your father, after the way he treated your mother, I say: you owe him nothing. But I also know he will not take kindly to such defiance. Tread cautiously.

I am not so old or so blind that I cannot see how attractive Esh might appear to a romantic young woman. I know you are lonely and unhappy here in South Carolina. I know you long to escape. But please, please reflect: might not your loneliness and unhappiness there be even worse?

There is little romance in the life of an Indian woman. Her life is one of toil, Clare, of danger and violence. Your Grand-mère Anne would be horrified by the thought of a gently bred young woman surrounded by "red devils." I cannot say I blame her.

Slaves have waited upon you since the day you were born. As a Cheyenne wife, nothing would be done for you. You would have to skin and tan and sew all your clothing as well as your husband's. You would prepare all your own meals—but only after you had dug up the turnips, sliced up the buffalo, cut up the firewood, and carved the bowls out of gourds. Every few days, you would dismantle your entire home and strap it to the backs of horses.

The United States Army would consider you an enemy. What if, God forbid, something happens to Esh? You would be left utterly alone with people you hardly understand in a hostile climate. You've never seen snow, let alone tried to wade through it.

Even if you grow old with Esh by your side, you are a reader, Clare. In the middle of the wilderness, where would you obtain new books? You are also a music lover—a music lover who would never play the piano or attend an opera again.

Is there another reason you are entertaining Esh? Do you simply wish to attract David's attention? If David were to run to you right now and beg you to become <u>his</u> wife, would you cast Esh aside?

Esh is my grandson too, and he grows dearer to me every day. I beg you not to use him as a pawn. If you do not wish to spend the rest of your life with Esh, end this now before it goes any farther.

Whatever you choose, dear girl, you will have a home on Archdale Street as long as I am living. Though his collar makes it more difficult for Joseph to welcome you into his household, I know my son will do what he can for you too.

I haven't told Joseph of your intentions yet. Nor will I tell David or Anne. Not until you are certain.

Be certain, Clare. You may have lost your heart. Do not lose your head.

With deepest affection,
Your Grand-père René

He thought she was only toying with Ésh, only trying to make David jealous? How dare René accuse her of such wantonness! He didn't understand her at all!

Even if David burst into this barn and fell on his knees right now—

The thought tingled through her like pleasure.

No! David had made his choice. She must make hers. She *had* made hers. She could not be David's wife. She would be Ésh's. With him, she felt like a powerful woman—beautiful and fierce—not a helpless girl.

"What does my grandfather say?" Ésh asked.

"He's *wrong*, Ésh!"

"About what?"

"He doesn't know me, he doesn't know you—he doesn't know the Cheyenne!" Clare gripped the letter so hard it crumpled in her hand. "I understand that living in a tipi will be very different from my life here—but that is why I want it!"

Clare thought of the men who beat their slaves in the street—of her own suitor who'd raised a hand to Verily when she spilled a few drops of tea. Clare had been able to defend her maid that day, because the man had no power over her—but if Clare became the wife of such a man, if he became Verily's master, he could beat both of them as often as he liked. Ésh had told her that the Cheyenne didn't even beat their children. So much for proper Southerners and savage Indians.

"I don't *want* to own other people!" Clare cried. "I know it isn't right. I may not have prepared an entire meal on my own, but that doesn't mean I can't! I may not have sewn an entire dress or shirt, but that doesn't mean I can't! And it isn't as if I'd have to make *everything*—the Cheyenne obtain things from traders, don't they? Cloth and pots?"

"Yes. Coffee and sugar too."

"Your family will help me, won't they? They'll teach me how to tan hides and roast buffalo? How to pack up our tipi?"

"My mother will be happy to teach you. My sister and Méanév too."

"The Cheyenne have their own stories, their own music. If I don't go with you, I'll never hear them."

Ésh smiled, because he knew her answer before he asked the question. "You are certain, *nazheem*?"

Clare dropped the vile letter and took his beautiful face in her hands. "I am certain, *na-eham*."

He pulled up the bottom of his shirt. Clare's heart leapt—would he join with her right now? Instead, Ésh withdrew something new from the pouch at his waist: a loop of braided black and white strands. The ring he'd made from Mirage's hair. "You will take this, and be my wife for as long as I live?"

"'For better, for worse…until death do us part,'" Clare vowed, holding out her hand so Ésh could slip the ring onto her finger. The band of Mirage's braided hair fit Clare perfectly. But then, Ésh *had* measured her ring finger during their last meeting. Clare smiled at the symbol of their love, more precious than any band of gold. She noticed Ésh still wore her ouroboros bracelet. They were husband and wife—or nearly so. "When— When will we…?"

Instead of grinning, Ésh scowled and lowered his eyes to the floor where René's letter lay crumpled. "First, you must reply to my grandfather. I promised him you would."

Clare released an irritated sigh. "Very well." She rose and strode to the place where she'd hidden paper and a pencil. She sat down again on the hay, using a book for a desk. "I'm sorry I haven't been teaching you to read."

Ésh sat Indian-style at her side, facing her. He smiled. "You will have many years to teach me."

Even as she began her odious task, Clare grinned. "I will, won't I?"

"You can teach me this winter, when we are snug in our tipi."

Clare peered up at him through her lashes. "Won't we be busy doing other things?"

Ésh chuckled. "You are a wonder, *nazheem*. Every man in our camp will envy me such a wife."

"Every woman in our camp will envy me such a husband." Clare dashed off the terse reply that René deserved and offered it to Ésh.

"What does it say?"

She was glad she hadn't mentioned David by name in her note. Fibbing to her husband was no way to begin their life together. Clare read her reply aloud:

"Thank you for your letter, Grand-père. I read every word. But I have not changed my mind. I am resolved to marry Ésh and no one else."

He smiled, folded the note, and tucked it in the pouch at his waist.

Before his shirt dropped back into place, Clare looped her arms around his neck. "Make me your wife, *na-eham.*"

He grinned. "We will start tomorrow."

Clare's heart galloped in her chest. "Do— Do I need to bring anything?"

"Nothing but yourself, *nazheem.*" But he frowned at the skirt of her riding habit. "The cloth you wear on your legs, does it open like a man's trousers?"

"No." Clare blushed. "It's a sort of tie… But I don't have to wear my riding trousers next time. Normally I wear only drawers, and they're already open in the middle. Like your leggings, but without a breechcloth."

"Good." Ésh hesitated, then pulled away from her and stood. "I must return to Mr. Alexander's." When he reached the ladder, he turned back. "It is not the time of the month when your blood comes, is it?"

"No." Clare did feel an ache between her legs, but it was almost like longing—nothing like the coming of her courses. "That won't be for two weeks yet."

"Good." With a parting smile, Ésh disappeared down the ladder.

Clare lay back on the hay and stared at her ring again. She felt weak. She felt giddy. This was really going to happen. She would be Ésh's wife. She would *join* with him. This time tomorrow, or perhaps the day after, she would know what that meant—what it felt like. The pain would be slight, Ésh had said. Soon, she would feel only pleasure.

Wedding Mass or no wedding Mass, vows or no vows—once Clare had endured that pain and discovered that pleasure with Ésh, there would be no question of her becoming another man's wife.

Her father had returned to the plantation late that morning and joined Clare and her aunt for dinner. Aunt Hortense had gloated over how much Clare had learned about running a household, what a good wife she'd make now, and wasn't it time Clare saw suitors again?

Throughout the rest of the meal, her father had stared at her very strangely. First, intent but aloof, like a man assessing a ham at the market, and then seemingly without blinking, as if he could see inside her. Finally, he muttered: "I suppose you are right, sister. It is time."

"I have a list of names," Aunt Hortense enthused. Clare hadn't even been present when her aunt had shown "the list" to her father.

Clare's family might be able to find a suitor who could overlook her indiscretions so far, for the sake of her father's land. But no Southern gentleman would accept a bride who'd lain with a "savage." He'd consider her defiled. As long as she remained a virgin, Clare's future with Ésh remained precarious. Only by surrendering her most precious possession could she free herself from the threat of her father and her aunt.

Tomorrow could not come soon enough.

CHAPTER 38

How long such suspension may linger? Ah, Sweet—
The moment eternal—just that and no more—
When ecstasy's utmost we clutch at the core
While cheeks burn, arms open, eyes shut and lips meet!
— Robert Browning, "Now" (1889)

Clare sat in the hayloft with Mary Eastman's *Dahcotah* open in her lap and attempted to read. She'd discarded her gloves and her hat but not her boots. Beneath the bodice and skirt of her riding habit, she wore no trousers, only stockings, drawers, chemise, and corset, with a chemisette filling the V of her lilac bodice. She felt naked.

Clare worried that Ésh would never come, that they would be separated before he could make her his wife and save her from her father. Her time alone with Ésh became more precarious with every passing hour. Now that her father was back at the plantation, he might become suspicious. Yet Clare had a much better chance of meeting Ésh unobserved here than in the city. Tomorrow was Holy Wednesday. She always spent the Easter Triduum in Charleston in order to attend Mass.

At last Clare sensed another presence in the loft, and she raised her eyes to see Ésh stepping free of the ladder. She grinned.

"Are you ready, *nazheem?*"

She closed her book. "Yes."

He was carrying a canteen over one shoulder. Did he expect them to work up a thirst? "You have not changed your mind?"

"Never, *na-eham.*" Clare touched the folded buffalo robe beside her. "I left it here. I thought…"

"Good." Ésh took up the robe as if it weighed no more than mosquito netting. The proof of his strength sent a shiver of longing through her. He spread out the robe over and below a higher mound of hay, so that it upholstered a kind of seat. Then Ésh sat atop the robe, his back to the higher part of the hay and his legs stretched out before him. "Come."

While he set the canteen on one side of the robe, Clare hesitated. She'd assumed they would lie down. "Where should I…?"

"Start with one of your feet on each side of my knees."

Nervously, Clare obeyed, raising her lilac skirt a little to clear his legs and staring down at him expectantly.

"Good. Now put your knees here." He patted the robe on either side of his hips.

Slowly, feeling wanton, Clare lowered herself over his outstretched legs. Ésh helped her draw up her skirt into a purple pool around her, so that her knees settled on the robe with nothing but her stockings and drawers separating them from the buffalo fur. The weight of her thighs rested on the warmth of his. She felt the nearness of his leggings, mere inches from her most intimate parts; the open middle of her drawers left no other barrier between them. Her gloveless hands perched on his buckskinned shoulders. "Now what?"

"Kiss me."

Clare felt her face growing hotter. She'd encouraged, returned, and continued his kisses, but she'd never initiated one. Gingerly, she parted her lips and leaned forward.

Ésh did not lean to meet her. In fact, he seemed to be bending back a little, against the cushion of the hay and buffalo robe. Yet his green eyes radiated desire. "I want you to choose this, *nazheem*—to choose *me*."

"I do," Clare whispered, pursuing him, brushing her nose beside his as she sought his mouth. "I choose you: Ésh. Ian. Mo'ohtá-wo'neh." She felt Ésh's lips curve into a smile, felt his body tremble with a chuckle all the way to his thighs. She was certain she'd mispronounced his formal Cheyenne name, or forgotten a whole syllable. Still his tongue welcomed hers. *"Na-eham,"* Clare vowed between kisses.

After a few minutes, after an hour, she wasn't sure, Ésh pulled the pins from her hair. He twined his fingers in the locks as they tumbled over his hands. He kissed the two "hailstones" on her cheekbone. For a moment, he fumbled with the velvet ribbon around her collar. She helped him untie it, and he undid the buttons of her chemisette on his own. His mouth explored every inch of exposed flesh: the edges of her collarbones and the base of her throat. "Are you comfortable?" His hot breaths seemed to slide inside her chemise and pool between her breasts. For some reason, her nipples ached.

"Mm," she sighed as she kneaded his arms through the buckskin —half praise and half complaint. She wished she wasn't wearing a corset. She wished he wasn't wearing a shirt.

"What is it, *nazheem*?"

Her fingers tightened and released, tightened and released. She wanted to feel his skin beneath her hands. "Do you think you could take off your shirt?"

Ésh chuckled and obliged.

She drew in an awestruck breath, to see him again, each perfect dip and swell. Her fingers traced his broad shoulders, warm and hard and smooth. Her hands slid lower, caressing the puckered scars above his nipples.

"Do you still choose me, *nazheem*?"

"Yes." She captured his mouth with hers again. "Yes!"

His arms were moving between them, but he wasn't touching her. She broke their contact enough to see he'd unscrewed the lid of his canteen and was wetting a handkerchief. She frowned.

"I am only washing my hands, *nazheem*."

But why should he need to... Her mind began spinning with possibilities, and her body tensed in fear. He sensed it: he renewed his kisses, pressed his warm chest into her hands, stroked her face and her throat.

The sensations calmed and excited her at once. She forgot everything but his mouth and his touch and the restrained strength beneath her hands. His own fingers were so deft—delving into her hair and into her bodice and chemise nearly to her aching breasts— she didn't realize only one of his hands was caressing her. Not until she felt movement under her skirt.

His other hand, seeking the gap at the center of her drawers. Grazing the secret hair at the top of her thighs.

Clare hesitated but whispered again, as much to herself as to Ésh: "I choose you." She assured him with kisses that he had her permission.

While her fingers learned his scars, Ésh stroked her coarse, delicate hair. His cupped hand claimed the mound there, rubbing lazily and then with a gentle force. Her entire body seemed to sway to his motions. His fingertips sank through the curls, beyond them, into—

Mortified, Clare sucked in a breath and broke their kiss.

Ésh frowned and pulled his fingertips away from her flesh, but his palm remained cupped over her mound of hair. "I have hurt you?"

Clare shook her head and hid her face in his neck. "It isn't that. It's..."

"What, *nazheem*?" His fingertips resumed their explorations, every subtle movement making her quiver, making it worse.

"It's not blood—I told you that—and it's not... But I... Sometimes, I...*leak* something..."

Ésh was laughing at her. Instead of recoiling, his fingers dipped into the very substance that shamed and perplexed her, spreading it outwards. "You mean this?"

"Yes!" Clare squeaked in humiliation, still hiding her face.

"This is what I *want*."

"What?" Clare pulled back just enough to meet his eyes. In their green depths, she saw no mockery or disgust, only delight and desire.

His fingers played in the liquid that wasn't quite liquid, painting it over her delicate flesh. "This means you want me, *nazheem*."

"It does?"

"Your body is making itself ready to join with my body." Even as he spoke, his fingers danced through the proof of her wanting, along the edges of hair, across the tender folds. Circling and flicking and diving…

With a gasp, Clare realized Ésh's fingertip had slipped inside her body. Inside the entrance to her vagina, as David had called it.

She mustn't think of David.

Ésh's fingertip worried the little hole he was filling. Clare couldn't breathe, and it wasn't only because she was wearing a corset.

"Does this hurt?"

"No. But it's so…"

"So…?"

Startling. Intimate. She felt the pressure of his finger increasing. Her body *wanted* to accept him, she thought, the way it had gone liquid to ease his entry. Should she push toward his hand? She was afraid to move, so she held perfectly still as Ésh's finger sank deeper: something shifting *inside* her, something she had invited into her body, which had its own texture and its own desires. "So *strange*."

"Good strange?"

"*Strange* strange." She'd had no idea her vagina was so deep. His entire finger must be inside her now.

"Do you want me to stop?"

How could he go any farther? Still Clare answered: "No."

Ésh withdrew his finger so that only the tip was inside her, then filled her again. He repeated the motion but varied it, turning his hand and pressing against each wall of this hidden chamber. With his other fingers, he began stroking her on the outside too. His thumb settled just beneath her mound, but it wasn't resting. It was rubbing and circling.

A longing Clare didn't understand unfurled from the motions of his fingers. She moaned and let her head fall back. It was becoming *good* strange, what he was doing, as his thumb flicked side to side and his finger thrust in and out and—

Then Clare flinched and froze. Something pinched now. She realized he'd inserted the tip of a second finger.

Ésh's hand stilled. He swallowed. "That was too soon, I think. I hurt you?"

She managed to meet his eyes and admitted: "A little."

"I am sorry, *nazheem*." His two fingers motionless, his thumb circling gently, he rested his forehead against hers. "You feel so good. Do you want me to stop now?"

It was discomfort more than pain, Clare decided. "No."

He kissed her again. "It will not always hurt like this, *nazheem*. I promise." Slowly, he slid his second finger alongside the first.

Clare felt her flesh stretching around his, but the discomfort only increased. What had Aunt Hortense said? Something would tear? Was she bleeding right now? Clare's uneasiness sharpened, climbed much higher inside her than Ésh's fingers reached, clamped down on her stomach. Clare tried to ignore the fear and to kiss Ésh back, but he noticed her reluctance.

His fingers slid from her body. "I think that is enough for today."

The ache inside her remained, and new fear roiled. "I disappointed you."

"No, *nazheem*—never." He pulled his hand from under her skirt. Between his first two fingers hung a scarlet webbing. "A bit of blood, you see? That is good. It means the hurt will not be so great next time." Ésh retrieved his damp handkerchief and cleaned his fingers. Then he folded the cloth over and offered it to Clare.

Sheepishly, she pushed the handkerchief under her skirt.

"How is the pain now?"

"It's not bad," she lied as she brushed the cloth against her flesh —flesh that had never been so tender.

"You may hurt for a day or two. But nothing is wrong."

Clare withdrew the handkerchief to reveal another tinge of blood. "Am I not a virgin anymore?"

"That was not joining, *nazheem*."

"I know, but…"

"You are a virgin until my *véto'ots* is inside you."

"Your…*what?*" Both of their gazes dropped between them, to where her thighs still straddled his, to where his buckskin breech-cloth swelled against the lilac pool of her skirt.

"I have heard it called different things in English, and I do not know which one is right. To the Zizistas, it is a *véto'ots*."

Clare couldn't tear her eyes away from that bulge of buckskin. "May—" She couldn't be asking this. But she'd longed to uncover this secret for so many years now. And his fingers had just been *inside* her. Surely it was only fair. "May I see it, your *véto'ots*?"

"You may."

She didn't look up, but she could hear the eagerness in his voice.

"Put your hand here." Ésh guided her fingers to a place at the side of his breechcloth, just under the cord where the wide strip of buckskin folded over. He showed her how to pull the front flap through the cord.

At first, she glimpsed only his hidden hair, dark and curly like hers. Then his astonishing organ sprang free. Clare gasped. Ésh's *véto'ots* was something like a stallion's. Rooted in its tuft of hair, it resembled a brownish-pink mushroom with a particularly thick stalk.

She liked mushrooms.

In the cap of the mushroom, there was a small slit, and from it emerged a bead of clear liquid. Ésh grinned at her, at it. "My body is saying it wants you too, *nazheem*."

But it was so… "You said— You said it goes inside me. You meant…the tip?"

Ésh chuckled, and his *véto'ots* danced with his laughter. "No."

Her eyes widened. "*All* of it?"

"Not my *vé'she'em*." Ésh cupped the globe of flesh from which his *véto'ots* seemed to grow. "But down to here, yes." He circled his fingers around the base of his *véto'ots*.

Clare swallowed. That left a great deal. His organ was both longer and thicker than two of his fingers. "It will fit?"

"Yes, *nazheem*." Ésh smiled. "Your *ma'kesta*, it was made to fit my *véto'ots*. When you are a virgin, your *ma'kesta* is like this." He lifted his hand and made a fist, showing her his fingers curled inside his thumb with only a tiny gap in the middle. "What I did today, I was teaching your *ma'kesta* to open for me." Slowly he loosened his fist, until a larger opening appeared between his thumb and his curled forefinger. "You see?"

She stared at his fingers so she would not stare at his *véto'ots*. "And when I bear a child, my...*ma'kesta* will open even wider?"

"Yes." His brow furrowed. "I wish I could protect you from that pain, *nazheem*. I cannot. But I promise to make you happy every time we join."

So much made sense now. Why the male organ was so long. How a woman could die in childbirth. Clare could scarcely believe her body could accommodate Ésh's *véto'ots*, let alone a baby. Yet she knew these things happened every day, and she was nearly a woman. She had a right to these secrets.

Once again, she was grateful that in spite of their language differences, Ésh always answered her questions—he told her the whole truth about her body, and about his. Unlike David.

She still didn't know the English word for a man's organ, but she no longer cared—to her, it would always be a *véto'ots*. Clare was glad to have another name for her special part besides "vagina." She liked *ma'kesta* much better.

"Miss Clare! Mr. Ésh!"

They both started at Verily's voice shouting from the ground floor of the barn.

"Titus and Quash are coming this way in a wagon! I think they're coming for hay!"

Clare's eyes locked with Ésh's, over his naked *véto'ots*. "Stall them!" Clare cried to her maid.

"I'll try, Miss!"

Frantically Clare rebuttoned her chemisette and Ésh restored his breechcloth. She climbed from his lap and tried to ignore the twinges of irritation between her legs. Her hairpins were scattered all over her skirt and the buffalo robe. She attempted to tidy her locks while Ésh pulled on his shirt and folded the buffalo robe.

"Where did you hide this?"

She showed him the place at the side of the loft where she'd secreted her books and writing supplies. She heard voices and peered down the ladder with her heart thumping in her throat. But Clare knew Titus and Quash would want to stop the wagon outside the front of the barn, below the hay door.

"Hurry!" Clare whispered as if Ésh needed urging. He practically slid down the ladder, then invited her to drop the last few feet into his arms. Together they raced out the back of the barn and climbed one of the paddock fences to Mirage.

Before he leapt onto the mare's back, Ésh kissed Clare one last time and promised: "Tomorrow, *nazheem.*"

CHAPTER 39

Divinity helps those who dare.
— Ovid, *Metamorphoses* (8 A.D.)

The pain was greater the next day. Clare felt little pinches between her legs every time she moved. Verily noticed at once. Clare was terrified her aunt or her father would read the change on her face too. By dinner, sharp-eyed Mr. Cromwell had returned to the plantation, and Clare hoped she had schooled herself not to wince.

The pain would pass, Clare reminded herself. Even if he still hadn't said the words, Ésh loved her—he would do nothing to truly harm her. If she was going to be brave, if she was going to be the wife of a warrior, she couldn't quail at something every woman endured. She must sally forth as if walking didn't hurt at all.

When she arrived at the stallion barn, Ésh was already waiting.

"I must return to Charleston before dusk," he explained, sliding his hands around her waist. "I must give my grandfather your note. Then I can ask him questions."

"What kind of questions?"

"How to make you happy." The wicked look on Ésh's face told her exactly what he meant by that.

Her body still aching, Clare blushed and glanced through the open door of the barn. "You seemed to know what you were doing yesterday."

"I know many things," Ésh acknowledged, his green eyes still glinting with mischief. "But not everything."

"Do you really think René will help us?"

"I think he wants us both to be happy. I must make him see that this is the only way." Yet Ésh's grin vanished, and he dropped his eyes as he spoke.

Clare thought René would become their ally only if they gave him no other choice—only *after* she and Ésh had become husband and wife.

"Your skirt is big today," Ésh observed.

Clare smiled. "It's a cage crinoline. I haven't changed into my riding habit yet." She pulled away from him to retrieve the habit from her phaeton.

Verily stood holding Arthur and scowling at her. Her maid had worn the same glower since Clare admitted she was sore from Ésh's touch.

Clare ignored Verily and turned back to her beloved. "I think I'll let *you* be my maid today, *na-eham.*"

Ésh followed her inside the barn. "What do I do?"

"You help me unfasten things." Clare motioned toward one of the empty stalls. "I've been using these to change." She led Ésh into the stall, and she draped her violet riding habit over one slatted wall. "We could try only removing the petticoat and cage, but I suspect the skirt will still be too full, and I'll have trouble climbing—"

"We have company!" Verily hissed through the door of the barn.

Clare sucked in a breath. "How much time do we have?"

"*None!* Hide him!"

At the front of the barn, Clare heard hoofbeats and a male voice calling out to Verily—not Mr. Tilling's voice or a slave's but Mr. Cromwell's. He wasn't likely to mind his own business, Clare knew:

Mr. Cromwell and her father were as thick as thieves, and he might still have designs on her himself.

But where could Ésh hide in an open barn? His eyes too flitted around them, his body starting to move and thinking better of it. He must be considering and discarding the same escapes: if he dashed out the back or up the ladder, Mr. Cromwell might see him. Should he simply crouch down in the box stall? What if Mr. Cromwell glanced inside?

At the door of the barn, Clare heard footsteps—the heavy, confident tread of a man's boots. Mr. Cromwell was nearly here!

She shoved her riding habit at Ésh. "Take this and get under my skirts."

"What?"

She turned her back to him, where the cage bulged farthest from her body, and pulled up the hoops on one side. "*Now!*"

"If you insist, *nazheem*." Ésh grinned and ducked under her skirts, taking the riding habit with him.

Clare shook the cage, petticoat, and skirt back into place with a couple of hops. As Mr. Cromwell approached up the aisle of the barn, she attempted to brace one gloved hand casually against the doorway of the box stall.

His mouth quirked. Did he suspect something? Had he seen Mirage?

"Good afternoon, Miss Stratford."

"Good afternoon, Mr. Cromwell." Clare tried to ignore the warm bulk of her almost-husband nestled against the backs of her legs. Ésh wasn't actually touching her: chemise, drawers, stockings, and boots covered her from waist to toes.

"I heard you'd been frequenting this old barn." Mr. Cromwell stopped. He was peering behind her into the stall!

Clare willed Ésh not to move.

Mr. Cromwell tapped his riding crop against his boot. "What keeps bringing you back here?"

"It's picturesque, and the light is good." Chemise and drawers or no chemise and drawers, Ésh's face was dangerously close to her buttocks. Where were his hands? He wouldn't *try* anything while he was under there, would he? "I've been thinking of turning part of it into an atelier."

Mr. Cromwell glanced back over his shoulder. "But it's so far from the house."

Dear God, Ésh was pulling up her chemise. "That is the point, Mr. Cromwell. An artist must have absolute quiet."

"You don't worry about your safety, out here all alone?"

Clare worried about her safety right now—about her beloved exposing them both. Ésh seemed to be draping her chemise over his head. His every hot breath tickled the naked skin between her thighs. Her *ma'kesta* grew slick in response. Clare tried desperately to concentrate on the man in front of her and not the one under her skirt. "There's no water nearby—no alligators or snapping turtles."

"I see boars from time to time."

With one hand, Ésh parted the loose back of her drawers, his fingers grazing Clare's right buttock. She quivered and gripped the doorway of the stall tighter. She couldn't move, or she would betray him. "Perhaps you should teach me to shoot, Mr. Cromwell."

"It would be my pleasure, Miss Stratford."

Moist lips seared her buttock, sending a shock of wicked delight through her body. Clare jumped and shrieked.

Mr. Cromwell stepped toward her. "Miss Stratford? What's wrong?"

"I...saw a snake."

He looked behind him. "I thought you liked snakes, Miss Stratford."

While Mr. Cromwell's attention was elsewhere, Clare attempted to kick her beloved with enough force to make him behave himself, but not enough to expel him from his hiding place. "I do, Mr. Cromwell. That's why I was excited."

"Where did you see it?"

"In the stall behind you."

While Mr. Cromwell investigated, Clare both felt and heard laughter stifled between her thighs.

"I don't see anything," Mr. Cromwell reported from the other stall.

"It must have been a shadow."

Mr. Cromwell returned and narrowed his eyes at her. He must be wondering why she hadn't moved from the doorway of this stall. At last, he said: "I'll leave you to your *art*, then, Miss Stratford."

"Thank you, Mr. Cromwell."

He touched his gloved hand to his hat brim in farewell, then strolled from the barn with aggravating slowness. Only after Mr. Cromwell disappeared out the front door did Clare release her breath. "Ésh!" She yanked her skirts around to reveal him still crouching in place.

He'd dropped her riding habit onto the floor of the stall, and there wasn't a trace of remorse on his features. "That was better than the buffalo robe!"

"You nearly gave us away!"

"I *had* to kiss you, *mo'ona*! Your seat is magnificent!" Ésh sprang upwards like a popped champagne cork, and before Clare could get a word in, his hands were cupping her waist, as close to her "magnificent seat" as they could get over the cage. Ésh panted into her neck: "I was drunk on you, on your shape and your scent…"

Clare gulped. "My scent?"

His hands came up to cradle her head, and he whispered hot in her ear: "Your *ma'kesta* is better than any spirits, better than roses. I wanted to kiss you *there*. Can we do that next?"

"You want to kiss my…"

He pulled back to stare into her eyes. He was frowning. "Are you in pain from yesterday?"

Ésh was trembling like a lit firecracker, like he was about to explode. He frightened her a little.

Since she was, in fact, sore, Clare admitted: "I-I am."

Ésh sighed. He released her, and his entire body seemed to droop. "Then we should wait."

He was still her patient, considerate lover—and it hurt her heart to see him dejected like this. Clare swallowed. "If you really want to kiss my—*ma'kesta*…"

"I do. I want to kiss *every* part of you—see and touch every part of you, with none of *this* between us." He grabbed two fistfuls of her pink organdy skirt.

It terrified her, the thought of baring herself so completely—even to Ésh. Especially to Ésh. What if he saw her and changed his mind? What if the shape of her breasts or her belly disappointed him? What if the hairy reality of her *ma'kesta* disgusted him?

But surely if she were naked, Ésh would allow her to undress him too. When she'd straddled his lap, she'd felt the power of his thighs beneath hers, but she'd never seen them. Or more than a glimpse of *his* magnificent seat. Most of all, Clare wanted to know what his *véto'ots* felt like. She also wanted to watch it disappear inside his body the way a stallion's did.

She could disrobe Ésh right now within seconds. Clare's own attire was another matter. With an inexperienced helper like Ésh, it would take a solid twenty minutes merely to remove and restore all her clothing. What if Mr. Cromwell walked in halfway through?

"I will make you so happy, *nazheem*," Ésh promised.

"I don't want anyone to see me but you." Clare frowned at the stable that had been their sanctuary for nearly a fortnight. "We cannot return here—Mr. Cromwell and Mr. Tilling both know I've been visiting this barn. We must find somewhere we can be alone, truly alone, somewhere no one will interrupt us…"

Ésh drew closer again, stroking her neck and whispering in her ear: "Yes—I want you naked all afternoon, all night…"

She wanted that too, not these stolen moments and frantic partings. "I could sneak out at night…"

"Do you know another place we can meet?"

Clare could think of nowhere else on the plantation that provided both comfortable shelter and enough isolation. "Is there anywhere on Mr. Alexander's property?"

Ésh scowled in thought. "I can make a hut big enough for both of us, but anywhere we go, one of the other grooms might hear us. And I do not want to make trouble between Mr. Alexander and your father. Mr. Alexander has been good to me—he trusts me with Mirage."

Clare nodded in understanding. Mr. Alexander might have

dismissed Ésh. Instead, they'd come to an arrangement. Since he was working fewer days, Ésh's wages were reduced, and for now, Mr. Alexander kept those wages as insurance. But in return, Ésh could visit his family and even ride Mirage to the city and back. He could not repay Mr. Alexander with treachery. The life of a free colored man in South Carolina was difficult enough without implicating him in the corruption of a planter's daughter. Clare was, legally, her father's property.

"I will ask my grandfather if you can live with him."

Clare shook her head. Ésh hadn't read his grandfather's letter. Any help René gave them would be grudging, while Grand-mère Anne sobbed over Clare's savage fate in the next room. Father Joseph would surely visit and offer his reproach as well. And David... That was hardly the privacy Clare wanted the first time she gave herself to Ésh, the first time he gave himself to her.

"Then where, *nazheem*?"

Clare wanted somewhere akin to Eden, where she could pretend she and Ésh were alone in the world... Her eyes widened. "Our cottage on Sullivan's Island! No one but the Army is there this early in the season—the ocean is too cold. We'll have the island practically to ourselves."

"How do we get to this island?"

"There's a ferry from Charleston. Oh, Ésh, it's perfect! The ferry dock is only a short walk from our Church Street house, and I'll be in Charleston the day after tomorrow. I always attend the Vigil on Holy Saturday—Father will never suspect. By the time he realizes where I am, I will be your wife—truly your wife. He will have no power over me."

"I have been to Church Street—before I found Mr. Alexander, I lived in a boarding house there."

"Oh, but don't come to the Church Street gate. You'll be seen. Use the gate on Longitude Lane. It's a wooden door with an iron-work window, set in a brick wall covered in white and pink climbing roses."

"Do the roses smell like fruit?"

Clare gaped. "How did you know that?"

Ésh grinned. "Before Christmas, when I was trying to find work and my family in Charleston, I passed your roses many times. I couldn't believe they were blooming in winter."

"That's because they're Noisettes! Ésh, do you realize, you might have looked through that gate and seen me four months ago?"

"I think I heard you singing once. It wasn't English."

"It must have been Irish. You were hearing your future, Ésh! Every time you passed those roses, you were *seeing* your future! We were *always* meant to be together—to meet at that gate."

His face was resplendent with happiness. "Then that is what we will do, *nazheem*."

They fixed their plans. They decided against taking a horse to the island; they'd have to worry about providing the animal with enough hay and water, and they weren't certain how long they'd be away.

"Three days, Ésh. In three days, we will truly be husband and wife."

He scooped Clare into his arms, hoop skirt and all. For a moment, she was weightless—but when he set her down again, the ache between her legs returned.

As she regained her breath, Clare looked up to the hayloft. She remembered Ésh's explanations and the press of his fingers inside her. "Should we... Before you go, should we... I don't know how long we'll have on the island, and I want to be ready. I want my body to be ready."

"I would hurt you now, *nazheem*."

She avoided his eyes. "But I'd rather feel pain now, than..."

"It should not be done fast, and I must go." Ésh squeezed her hand, then strode to the back of the barn to look for Mirage.

Clare followed slowly, worrying about their coming time together and how much pain there would be, if she would enjoy it at all.

Ésh spotted his horse and turned back to kiss Clare good-bye. He saw her distress. He caught her hand again and caressed her gloved palm with his bare thumb. "You know, you can make your-self ready when I am not here. With your own fingers."

Clare's jaw fell open. "Isn't that…wrong?"

Ésh grinned. "Not if you think about me when you do it."

ALL EVENING AFTER HIS DEPARTURE, Ésh's suggestion spun through Clare's head. What had her aunt claimed would happen if Clare ever "violated" herself? *"You will soil yourself. You will start shaking, and you will go mad."* By soiling herself, had Aunt Hortense meant the slickness that had delighted Ésh? Who did Clare trust more, her aunt or her beloved?

"Think about me," Ésh had said. Who else did he expect her to think about?

It was true that ever since she'd seen Ésh's *véto'ots*, she'd wondered about David's—if its shape or color might be different.

No. No! David was the past. Ésh was the present, the future.

With determination, Clare took down the last of David's Parisian drawings from her bedroom wall. The day he'd spurned her for the last time, the day she'd met Ésh, she'd packed up all of them but this one, her favorite of his sketches. The drawing did not depict the view from Montmartre or Héloïse and Abélard's tomb, but two buffalo in the menagerie of the Jardin des Plantes.

Clare no longer needed it. In three months' time, she would be seeing real buffalo with Ésh at her side. She told Verily to place the drawing into the attic trunk with the music box and the rest of David's souvenirs.

She might as well bury them. David might as well be dead, for all he cared about her. There was only one man on Earth who mattered now, and one *véto'ots*. It belonged to Ésh, and she must prepare her body to accept it. Ésh would not have advised her to do something dangerous. She must at least try.

Verily slept in Clare's bedchamber, so she was never alone at night. But Clare told her maid to spend the following afternoon with her sister, before Verily accompanied Clare to Charleston on Good Friday. Clare had two hours alone. She must make use of them. Her body didn't ache any longer. It could withstand a little more prodding.

Her heart thumping in her ears, Clare shut the windows, drew the curtains, and tucked a chair under the handle of her closed door. With a pang of contrition, she stashed her crucifix, rosary, and prayer cards beneath the hinged cushion of her prie-Dieu. She steadied a hand lamp on a book at the end of her bed, then closed the mosquito netting. The netting was transparent, but it was better than empty air protecting her.

She disrobed to her chemise and stockings and tidied her finger-nails. She washed her hands and skimmed the damp cloth between her legs. She slipped inside the mosquito netting, careful not to upset the lamp. Gingerly, she positioned herself against her pillows, drew up the skirt of her chemise, and tilted her hand mirror toward her *ma'kesta*.

The hairy promontory and ruffled flesh looked as ugly to her as they had a few years ago, like something unfinished, like a wound. Yet Ésh wanted to *kiss* this wound. With two fingers buried inside her and another stroking the top of the wound, he'd told her how good she felt. He even liked the scent of her *ma'kesta*. Better than roses, he'd said. The folds of pink flesh did resemble petals.

A rose and a mushroom. Ésh's *véto'ots* was equally startling, but he'd seemed proud of it. Why shouldn't he be? His *véto'ots* was what made him a man.

Her *ma'kesta* was what made her a woman. What would make her a wife, a mother. That was good. That was beautiful.

Her hand inched closer to the glistening gap. Her fingers were slimmer than Ésh's, Clare reminded herself, so she should be able to take two easily. Then, she clamped her eyes shut. She would do this for both their sakes, but she would not make herself watch.

She tried to remember how Ésh's fingers had moved inside her, how he'd pressed against her inner walls. Yet her explorations felt nothing like his—more like an invasion than a caress. That made no sense—how could she invade her own body? The chamber inside her felt shallow now, and she was barely wet. Her tender flesh protested her clumsy reconnaissance.

She recalled how Ésh had concentrated many of his attentions on a small bud at the top of her *ma'kesta*. He'd turned the pad of his thumb against it as if he were unlocking a door. And that was—oh, that was rather nice, even with her own thumb.

Her *ma'kesta* went compliant around her fingers. She was actually starting to enjoy this. It *must* be a sin—but she was obeying her almost-husband… Clare covered her mouth with her left hand, but whimpers and moans reverberated in her throat.

She did not stop till the door handle rattled and nearly stopped her heart. Her jerk of terror and shame pained her insides, shook the mattress, and nearly toppled the hand lamp. She caught it just in time. Clare saw another tinge of blood on her fingers and concluded that she had accomplished enough maneuvers—she would leave the rest to Ésh.

She wondered who had been at the door. One of the slaves, surely.

WHEN CLARE ENTERED the dining room for supper, her father upended his wine glass, slammed it back on the table, and motioned impatiently for Austin to pour him more. But her father didn't eat. Only glared.

Clare attempted to remain calm, but her heart climbed into her throat. Could her father read her guilt on her face? Had he learned about Ésh? Her eyes darted to Mr. Cromwell, who was enjoying his lamb in apparent innocence. Clare dragged her attention back to her father. "I-Is something the matter, Father?"

"You are your mother all over again." It might have been a compliment. But it sounded like an accusation, ground out through clenched teeth.

Clare frowned and looked back to Mr. Cromwell.

He tossed her a smile. "Indeed, Miss Stratford. You look more like your mother every day."

Her father threw his napkin on the table, abandoned his full plate, and strode from the room without an explanation.

The next morning, Clare rode to Charleston in the brougham with her father sitting beside her and Verily on the jump seat across from them. Her father had been in a foul mood all morning.

Clare stared determinedly out the window. Her father grumbled something unintelligible and wiggled around in his seat. Finally, he closed his eyes and seemed to doze.

Clare pretended her father wasn't there. She watched the fence-posts and trees passing by, each one bringing her closer to Charleston, to Sullivan's Island, to her beloved. Yesterday's experiment had left her sore again, but she was glad she'd taken Ésh's advice. In more ways than one, she was going to explore new lands with him. It was only right that she begin with her own territory.

∼

As soon as he returned to Charleston, Ésh tried to give his grandfather Clare's letter. René glanced toward Grandmother Anne, who was on her knees nearby, making a hole in the garden. His foot still in its "cast," Grandfather heaved himself upwards, refusing Ésh's help. With his crutches, René swung himself into his office at the front of the house. Only after he'd collapsed in the chair behind his desk did he accept Clare's note.

Ésh sat down across from his grandfather while he read.

René glared at Ésh over his spectacles—as if Ésh had written the letter himself, when Grandfather knew that was impossible.

"Will you help us?"

"I am not comfortable with this, Ésh. You and Clare have known each other for all of thirteen days. You are an eighteen-year-old boy thinking with your penis, and she isn't thinking at all."

"With my what?"

Grandfather raised his eyebrows till Ésh understood.

"I may be eighteen years and nine months of age, but I am thinking with my head—and my heart. I think your God and my Sacred Powers want Clare and me to be together. How else can you explain my visions of her, my finding work on the property next to hers, the paint horse who brought her to me—or her knowing you, my own lost family?"

Grandfather only scowled and said nothing.

Ésh had believed this man liked him, and he knew René liked

Clare. Did he think she would be happier with his other grandson, the one who had already broken her heart? "When we are together, Clare and I are happy. I thought that would make *you* happy."

Grandfather's attention slid toward the front windows. "It would have, once. But I am anticipating the price of that happiness." His voice had thickened. "Did you know your uncle loved Clare's mother?"

"She told me."

René's weary blue eyes returned to Ésh. "What you have with Clare, it isn't even love yet. It's two aching bodies, not two matching souls. Joseph and Tessa had both. I encouraged them to risk everything for that happiness, regardless of the consequences." Behind his spectacles, Grandfather's eyes shone with tears. "I thought I could save them. Instead, I destroyed Tessa, and I nearly destroyed my son."

While René wiped angrily at his tears, Ésh lowered his eyes. If Grandfather learned about the badger's prophecy... "Clare and I will be different."

Now René's face screwed up as though he smelled something rotten. He grabbed a sharp object from his desk, slipped its point inside his cast, and scratched his toes vigorously, as if Ésh had left the room.

"We will do this without you if we must, Grandfather. But I would prefer to have your help...as a medicine man." In spite of himself, Ésh's confidence faltered at the end. It wasn't easy admitting you were less than a man, especially to your own grandfather.

Without righting himself from his scratching, René glared at Ésh. "Please tell me you don't have a venereal disease."

"A what?"

Grandfather tossed his scratching stick back on his desk. "Does your penis leak pus? Does it burn when you piss?"

"No! I've never— Clare will be my first woman. That is why I need your help."

"Clare will be your *only* woman, remember?"

Ésh clenched his jaw. "I remember."

René let silence settle between them again, then narrowed his eyes. "That you're asking me and not practicing with a prostitute speaks in your favor, I suppose. I'm listening."

Ésh avoided his grandfather's stare. "I *almost* joined with a woman once. But my…penis, um, shot before I wanted it to."

"That is a problem common to young virgins." René's tone was flat, as if he were addressing any patient.

"Do you know how to make it wait?"

"There are a few solutions," Grandfather grumbled.

Ésh felt as if he were chipping away at a mountain with his grandfather's scratching stick. "Will you share them with me?"

René heaved a great sigh, hauled himself onto his crutches, and flung himself toward his case of books. "I am doing this for *Clare*."

"So am I, Grandfather."

CHAPTER 40

A baby is God's opinion that life should go on.
— Carl Sandburg, *Remembrance Rock* (1948)

Easter still hadn't decided which lies were safest or how to save her baby. She couldn't let herself sleep till she found an answer, but she was so exhausted she couldn't think…

Then Cromwell returned to Stratford-on-Ashley ahead of Shadrach. His first days back, Cromwell was occupied with plantation business. But as soon as Miss Clare's bed was cold, as soon as she, Master Edward, and Verily left for Charleston on Good Friday, Cromwell wanted Easter.

He seemed to have returned to his old cocky self, like Shadrach no longer worried him. As Cromwell rutted, Easter gaped up at the canopy of Miss Clare's bed. Had Cromwell *sold* Shadrach? Would he *never* return?

These thoughts distracted her from worrying about what Cromwell might be noticing. He'd left on her chemise, but he must have felt the difference. After he collapsed beside her, he patted her stomach and chuckled as if she were a naughty child. "I think you've been stealing too many ginger cakes in the kitchen, Easter. You're putting on weight." Then realization dawned, and Cromwell bolted up on one arm. With the other, he flung up the skirt of her chemise to expose the barely-visible bump. His glare ricocheted between her belly and her face. "Is it *his*?"

Easter fought the urge to cover herself again. She must remain nonchalant. Maybe she could convince Cromwell it was just ginger cakes, buy herself more time to think. She stammered: "Is what whose?"

"Is it Shadrach's bastard, or mine?"

"Sh-Shadrach's." Her damned voice betrayed her, as jagged as her thoughts.

"You don't know, do you?" Cromwell mocked.

Now her *pride* betrayed her. Pride in Shadrach's patience—or anger at the audacity of Cromwell calling her a whore when *he* had made her one. Because the tone of Cromwell's voice and the scorn on his face screamed *"Whore!"* She couldn't bear it. She wouldn't. Easter propped herself on her elbows and glared back at him. "Of course I know!"

"How could you?" *Whore!*

"I know because Shadrach and I have never..." Tears burst out of her—at the irony and the injustice of losing the man she loved but had never *loved*.

Cromwell sprang from the bed and started pacing, the tail of his shirt flapping around his thighs. "You did this on purpose," he muttered. "You purposefully forgot the vinegar."

"I injected it *twice*." Easter threw the skirt of her chemise back over her legs and sat up. "What possible reason could I have for wanting your child?"

His fists clenched. She feared he might stride back and strike her for the second time. "Then why the Hell didn't you tell me immediately?"

"You were gone! How was I supposed to tell you? Walk up to Tilling and ask him to send you a letter?"

"I returned three days ago! Every single day, that thing digs in its roots…" He stopped pacing. "We must act quickly, or someone will have to *scrape* it out of you. Is that what you want?"

"O-Of course not." She stood up and· approached him cautiously. "But we don't *have* to act. We could do nothing."

"Let it come, you mean?!"

"Would that be so terrible?"

"You said you didn't want it."

"I didn't at first, but…"

Cromwell spread his hands beside his head as if he were trying to block her words. "It doesn't matter. If you have a nearly white baby, the blame will fall on me soon enough. Damn it, Easter! I am *so close* to marrying Clare! She is handing herself to me on a platter —compromising herself so no one else will have her. I can rescue her from ruin and her father will *thank* me! Ten years I have worked for this!" He jabbed a finger at Easter accusingly. "I sure as Hell won't let you destroy it all now!"

I'm not the one who forgot the pessary, she argued in her head. *And I never wanted you to fuck me in the first place. You destroyed yourself, you bastard.* Easter realized she wanted this child in order to spite him, too.

Cromwell yanked on his drawers, then his trousers. "I will bring you an emmenagogue from Charleston, and you will drink it."

Easter swallowed. "A what?"

Cromwell snapped his braces over his shoulders. "A tea that will make you miscarry."

Tears threatened. "And then what am I to do with the child?"

"Throw it in a privy! I don't care!"

Easter sank onto the edge of the bed, and the tears won. But Cromwell was already gone.

In the morning, on Holy Saturday, he left for Charleston.

SHADRACH RETURNED THAT AFTERNOON. He came to the kitchen expecting a welcome. Easter's reluctant greeting told him something was wrong.

Finally, she led him around the back of the kitchen house, closed her eyes, and gathered what strength she had left. "Almost the first time we spoke, the night of Chloe and Cato's wedding, I told you you didn't want me. You should have listened, Shadrach."

"What you talking about, Easter? What happened while I was gone?"

She turned to the wall, braced her forearm against it, and hid her face. "I am with child, Shadrach."

"What? Who done this to you? Did you want him to?"

"No…" Admitting a man had forced her did not mean admitting he was white. It might have been another slave. Not all of them were as kind and patient as Shadrach.

Gently he pulled her away from the wall and placed his hands on her shoulders. "Then I told you, Easter: it don't count. It don't make you any less mine. It don't make this child any less mine."

Tears coursed down her cheeks. "You mean, you would…"

He took her face in both his hands. "It's *your* child. How could I help loving it?" He dropped his gaze to the ground between them. "And maybe…maybe this be a blessing, in the end. Master Dickson, he thought it was Thisbe couldn't have chillun, but what if it's me can't have them?" His eyes returned to Easter. "Just tell me who done this to you."

She shook her head. "He's not important."

"How can I protect you when I don't know who hurt you?"

"If you 'protect me,' you'll get yourself in trouble."

"I know I can't be your child's father if I'm sold off or dead. I'll just scare the man. Let him know worse'll follow if'n he comes after you again. All you got to do is say who."

Dicey approached them, pushing manure in a wheelbarrow for the kitchen garden.

They were too exposed here. Easter didn't want to tell Shadrach the truth. But she knew he would keep pressing her for an answer, and Cromwell might return at any moment. Maybe Shadrach would see a way to save her baby—their baby. She pulled him through the trees to the carriage house. In the shadows behind Miss Clare's phaeton, Easter drew in an uneasy breath and admitted: "I

lied to you, Shadrach. The man who forced me when I was thirteen
—he hasn't stopped. The baby is *his*."

"A white man?" Shadrach whispered.

"He's said *over* and *over* that if I ever tell anyone, or if I ever
disobey him, he'll hurt Verily."

Shadrach cursed.

"I was afraid you wouldn't want me if you knew he still… And I'm
afraid you'll confront him, and I'll lose you…" Easter placed her palms
protectively over her child. "But he wants to kill the baby, and I don't
know how to stop him. He's in Charleston right now, buying poison."

"Master Edward?"

Easter shook her head. "Cr—" Six years of fear choked back
the word.

"Mr. Cromwell?"

Slowly, she nodded.

"All this time?"

"I couldn't tell you. Verily…"

"You tell me any other lies, Easter?"

"No."

"You ever going to lie to me again?"

"Never."

"You love me?"

"Yes."

"You want this child, and Cromwell don't?"

Easter nodded. "I know I should hate it, but I can't. It's a *baby*. I
want to make *him* drink poison—but no slave kills a white man and
survives."

"We'll run. You know I've wanted to for months. I been planning. Every time Master hire me out, I been paying attention,
learning what's out there and who we can trust. We can do it,
Easter. We can get free."

"I won't leave Verily. She isn't safe here."

"We take her with us, soon as she comes back from Charleston.
Miss Clare taught her letters, didn't she? Verily can write us a pass."

"You think that will work?"

"We got to try, Easter." Shadrach gripped the *sankofa* around her neck. "Sometimes, this symbol a bird instead of a heart. It mean: *We are stronger when we remember*. We is free like them birds, Easter. We belong only to ourselves. It's the buckra done forgot, the buckra trying to make *us* forget. We want what's ours, we got to take it."

CHAPTER 41

Our church shall be the starry night,
Our altar the grassy earth outspread,
And our priest the muttering wind.
— Percy Bysshe Shelley, *Rosalind and Helen* (1819)

Clare felt a little guilty about eloping on Holy Saturday. She would miss the Vigil and the Easter Mass. Father Joseph would tell her such delinquency was a mortal sin, wholly apart from her debauchery—in the eyes of the Church, Ésh wasn't even her husband.

After sunset on Good Friday, in her Church Street bedchamber, Clare knelt on her prie-Dieu, her mother's rosary twined around her fingers, and begged God to forgive her. *I haven't forgotten you, Lord. I'll never stop honoring you. I've never been more grateful: you created Ésh and brought him to me, of all people! You gave him a body that delights me, and you gave me a body that delights him. Ésh honors you, too; he only honors you under another name. Please, Lord, bless our union. And protect Verily while I'm gone.*

Clare felt her maid's gaze on her. She opened her eyes to see Verily sitting up on her trundle bed.

"You're leaving in the morning, aren't you, Miss?"

Clare drew in a sharp breath.

"I heard some of what you and Mr. Ésh said in the barn," Verily explained gravely. "I know you're running away, but not where."

"I am so sorry, Verily. I know I promised to help *you* escape. But I expect to return in a few days." After the deed was done, Clare hoped her father would be reasonable and allow her to pack up some of her things for her new life. What use were earrings and chemises to him—or poetry?

"Where will you be?"

"I trust you, Verily, I do. I owe you so much. But if I don't tell you where, you won't have to lie about it. Unless…you want to come with me?"

"Are you going back to the plantation?"

"No."

Verily averted her eyes. "Then I'd better stay. When we go, my sister and I should go together."

"If I *can't* return, you know René and Father Joseph will help you and Easter escape."

Verily nodded and settled under her covers.

Clare stifled her conscience and turned to more material concerns: what should she pack for Sullivan's Island? She raided the kitchen by candlelight, careful not to awake Tilly, who slept in the loft. Fortunately, the cook was already amassing ingredients for their Easter feast. Clare was delighted to find iced oysters, cured ham, and cornbread. She added almonds, dried figs, eggs pickled in vinegar, a bottle of peaches, a bar of chocolate, and benne wafers for luck. She snuck into the garden and filled a large bowl with sweet peas and strawberries.

Clare wanted to bring the buffalo robe, but it was so heavy. Just in case, she disguised it inside an old counterpane and stashed everything in the large myrtle hedge near the gate onto Longitude Lane. *Myrtus communis* was often called bride's myrtle, Clare remembered with a smile, because it was sacred to the goddess of love.

She crept back inside, past her father's dark bedchamber, and stolé the keys to the garden gate and the island cottage from the desk in his office. He didn't bother to lock that drawer. Finally, Clare wrote her father a note:

> Try not to worry about me, and please don't come after me. I am happy. For the first time since Mama died, I am happy.

Then, Clare attempted to sleep. She didn't think Verily slept much either. When Clare wasn't tossing, she heard her maid turning in her own bed.

At dawn, when Clare rose to dress, Verily didn't assist her. As Clare fastened her bonnet ribbon in the near dark, her maid muttered: "I hope you don't regret this, Miss."

"I won't." Clare wished they could part on better terms. She prayed silently that she would still find some way to help Verily and Easter.

Clare slipped down the spiral stairs and through the garden toward the back gate. She liked the way the myrtle-green flounces of her skirt seemed to blend into the bushes and ferns. She would miss this garden—Mama's garden.

On the brick wall along Longitude Lane, the Lamarque and Jaune Desprez roses were just beginning to release their scents of lemonade and passion fruit to the rising sun. As she passed, Clare tugged off one glove and fondled a few satin blossoms. She recalled the Language of Flowers that Mama had taught her. White roses meant "secrecy and silence," and pink roses meant "perfect happiness."

Beside the gate, Clare paused to bury her nose in a Jaune Desprez, and the words of Tennyson's *Maud* bubbled from her lips in a whisper:

> "He is coming, my life, my fate;
> The red rose cries, 'He is near, he is near;'
> And the white rose weeps, 'He is late.'"

"*Nazheem?*"

Clare jumped in surprise like a fool, then whirled to see Ésh's face peering through the claire-voie in the door, his fingertips peeking through the ironwork. "*Na-eham!* You came!" Unlike Maud, Clare's beloved was right on time.

The claire-voie was just large enough that she could tell his shoulders were shrugging beneath his plain brown suit coat. "I wanted to smell the roses."

Clare giggled. For a moment, instead of opening the door, she laced her ungloved fingers through Ésh's and squeezed, transmitting her perfect happiness to him. But he was already grinning. "Are we alone?"

Ésh glanced right and left down Longitude Lane. "Yes."

Clare had hung the purloined keys from a ribbon around her neck. She snatched up the correct one and unlocked the gate. "Did you bring very much?"

"Only this." Ésh patted a saddlebag slung over his shoulder.

Clare looked to her cache in the myrtle hedge. "I want so badly to bring the buffalo robe. Do you think you can carry it?"

Ésh narrowed his eyes as if he were offended. "Yes."

Clare assigned the valise and the portmanteau to herself and transferred them to the other side of the gate. "Could you carry the hamper too?"

Ésh grunted and pretended it was stretching his arm.

"Shh!" Clare reminded him. She could hear her father's slaves stirring in the work yard on the other side of the myrtle hedge. Any moment now, Tilly would discover Clare's thievery.

"Are we going to eat stones?"

"You'll see," she grinned.

Clare locked the gate behind them and took up her burdens, which felt as light as air. She guided Ésh down the cobbles of Longitude Lane and up the sandy thoroughfare of East Bay Street half a block to Adger's Wharf. They saw no one she recognized.

From her reticule, Clare produced two coins for the ferryman. After they'd stowed their baggage, she led Ésh to the bow, as if this would make them arrive sooner. As the ferry steamed across the harbor toward Sullivan's Island, Clare sighed with relief and shared a grin with Ésh. This was really happening! On Easter morning, she would wake in his arms as his wife.

Clare filled her lungs with the sea breeze that ruffled her bonnet ribbons. Gulls called overhead, and a pair of dolphins leapt out of the water alongside the ferry, as if rejoicing with her and Ésh. The creatures were new to him.

When they lost sight of the dolphins, Clare pointed out the pink horseshoe of Castle Pinckney on Shute's Folly, the grey walls of Fort Sumter, and the green oasis of their destination in the distance.

Ésh leaned close and whispered into the shell of her bonnet: "Did you touch yourself when you were alone?"

Clare blushed hot and turned her face away. "Yes."

"Did you enjoy it?"

"No!"

He fell silent.

She glanced over to see that his face was somber now, and Clare wished she'd told him the truth.

"Did you bleed again?"

"A little."

"And now?"

"I am perfectly healed." She smiled at him around the brim of her bonnet and was relieved to see an answering smile. "I am ready, Ésh."

"So am I." He drew her gloved hand over to the front of his trousers. Clare sucked in a breath at the warm ridge she could feel even through his clothing. She thought Ésh was still wearing his breechcloth beneath his trousers.

Clare heard a male chuckle behind them and snatched her hand away. Instead, Ésh interlaced his fingers with hers, squeezing her hand like a promise. She squeezed back.

Sullivan's Island approached with agonizing slowness. Clare told Ésh that it had been named after an Irishman, and that her grand-mother's maiden name was O'Sullivan, which was surely a good omen.

At last they reached the cove and the pier at the edge of Moultrieville. Clare and Ésh carried too much to make running practicable; but as they followed Middle Street to the cottage, anticipation hurried their steps. She was relieved to see all the shuttered houses. They wouldn't have to worry about nosy neighbors. The island was slumbering, awaiting the summer.

Finally she and Ésh were climbing the stairs of the front porch and unlocking the cottage door. They stashed the hamper in the kitchen. This stood beside the cottage, and the back porch connected them. Ésh helped her open the windows to air out the rooms.

As Clare crossed the back porch alone, regret washed over her unbidden and halted her steps. She touched one of the wicker chair arms. How many times had David sat here beside her, David who'd loved her so well as a girl but couldn't love her as a woman, for reasons only he understood?

Then a whiff of ambrosia reached her. "Oh, Ésh! The wisteria is still in bloom!" Clare raced down the back steps to the pergola. She closed her eyes and inhaled the sweet, subtle fragrance.

The vine was a volunteer, a gift from the Heavens. The summer after she turned seven, Clare and her mother had discovered a baby wisteria clinging to the myrtle hedge between the cottage and the beach. Clare's father had wanted to rip the little plant from the ground. "It won't even bloom while we're at the cottage!" he'd argued.

In a neighbor's garden in Charleston, Clare had seen how hummingbirds favored the abundant purple flowers that hung like clusters of grapes. Even if her family wasn't on the island to enjoy the blossoms, the birds and the bees could. After its fragrant flowers had fallen, Clare liked the wisteria's pinnate leaves and long velvet seedpods.

She and her mother had triumphed: they'd persuaded Clare's father to have this pergola erected, to give the vine a permanent home. Now, the wisteria shaded a space the size of a dining room in a corner of the back yard. It was a lovely spot for a picnic, for reading, for napping, secluded from the beach and the neighbors' eyes by the eight-foot-high myrtle hedges. Today, no one would even hear them.

Ésh seemed to like the pergola too. "The Zizistas, they build shades like this out of tree branches."

In the Language of Flowers, wisteria had two meanings: "Welcome, fair stranger" and "I cling to thee." Beneath the pendant purple racemes, Clare brushed a fallen blossom from Ésh's head. The morning sun through the pergola made his golden hair glow like a halo. "I want to do it here, *na-eham.*"

"Do what?" Ésh grinned.

She slid her arms around him and laid her head against his shoulder. "I want you to love me here."

He might have said: *"I love you already."* Or anything of the kind. Instead, he tightened his embrace and asked: "Now, *nazheem?*"

Clare hid her face till she'd swallowed her disappointment. "Not yet. I want to show you something."

They fetched their hats from the cottage. Then Clare looped her arm inside his and took Ésh down the wooden path to the beach, through the gap in the myrtle hedges. Across the harbor to their right, the tiny steeples of Charleston pointed toward the sky.

Clare turned left. Where the tide had wet the sand and retreated, the ground lay firm beneath their feet. Cool but invigorating, the sea breeze carried three pelicans, who soared low over the sparkling water.

Ahead, Ésh spotted the Stars and Stripes flapping atop their pole, then the brick ramparts beneath. He frowned. "Another fort?"

Clare nodded. "Fort Moultrie."

Ésh glanced behind them, toward Fort Sumter and Castle Pinckney. "There are too many forts here," he muttered.

Clare hadn't even told him about Fort Johnson. She took them inland, skirting the sand dunes surrounding Fort Moultrie. They passed beneath palmetto tree after palmetto tree and reached Middle Street again. When she guided him toward Fort Moultrie's gate, Ésh hesitated. He stared up at the blue-coated soldiers on the ramparts, who gazed down at them curiously.

Ésh's green eyes sparked with challenge, as if daring the men to descend. He caught up to Clare and wrapped his arm around her shoulders, though this was awkward over the expanse of her cage crinoline. She slipped her arm around his waist.

She led him to an oblong slab of white marble laid on the ground near the gate.

"Is this a grave?" Ésh asked in a low voice.

Clare nodded. "Do you recognize any of those letters?"

Ésh squinted at the stone. "C and E, like our names."

"It says 'OCEOLA.' He was an Indian war chief." The Army hadn't even spelled his name right.

"There were Indians here?"

"Oh yes. Two hundred years ago, all the people in South Carolina were Indians. There were even buffalo."

Ésh's eyes widened. "What happened to them?"

"White hunters killed the buffalo. Many of the Indians died of disease, and the rest lost their last battles about a century ago. But there are still a few Indians living along the Santee River to the north of us. Osceola, though, he was a Seminole—in Florida to the south of us. He was also part Scottish, like you. Osceola fought very hard to protect his people and keep their lands, but the Army captured him under a flag of truce. That means they lied." Clare too scowled up at the soldiers on the ramparts. "The Army imprisoned Osceola, first in Florida, and then here at Fort Moultrie. Twenty-two years ago, he died within these walls, and then *most* of Osceola's mortal remains were buried here."

"What do you mean, 'most'?"

"Before they laid him in the ground, an Army doctor cut off Osceola's head. It's in a museum in New York now. David has seen it."

Ésh glared at the soldiers on the walls of the fort. His jaw clenched, and his arm tightened around her shoulders. "Why did you bring me here?"

She stared at Osceola's tombstone. "Because there is so much ugliness in the world, Ésh: cruelty and betrayal and loss. I need you to know how precious and rare it is, your beauty." Clare closed her eyes. "I don't mean only your body—though that is exceedingly beautiful—I mean your patience, too. Your gentleness. You have had a dozen opportunities to *take* what you want from me, yet you wait until I am ready."

His grip around her shoulders loosened. Through her sleeve, she felt the tender reassurance of his softly stroking thumb. "I will not hurt you, *nazheem*."

Clare told herself it was something in the sea air irritating her eyes. But her lids were still closed. "I know you don't mean to, and I am so grateful for that."

"If I hurt you, promise me you will tell me?"

Clare nodded and opened her eyes. Ésh withdrew his arm, brushed her tears away, and took her hand.

Under the azure sky, they strolled back along the beach toward the cottage, scattering piping plovers. Usually, Clare delighted in these adorable orange-legged shorebirds. Today, she barely glanced at them. She was more interested in the exotic male beside her.

"We should swim," Ésh suggested.

She'd brought no bathing attire, but they'd seen only a handful of civilians today. Away from the fort, they might as well be Adam and Eve. "The water is too cold."

"I have swam in *ice* water." When they reached the shoreline in front of their cottage, Ésh tossed his hat and his coat on the sand. "Zizistas bathe every morning, and I have not had my bath yet." He sat down to remove his shoes, then sprang up again. "Now you are my wife, you must bathe too." Ésh removed his waistcoat, dropped the braces from his shoulders, and unbuttoned his trousers.

"I-I can't swim," Clare admitted, mesmerized by each new swath of skin. She'd never seen his legs before. They were fascinating sculptures.

"Then I will teach you." Ésh peeled off his socks, then his shirt, till he stood in only his breechcloth, his medicine pouch, and her ouroboros bracelet.

"You can teach me to swim in a mountain lake this summer."

Clare paced a few steps up the beach, aiming for the cottage. "There's an undertow here. If you've never swum in the ocean…" When she looked back, her eyes riveted on the taut curves of Ésh's buttocks. If only his breechcloth weren't ruining the center of her view.

Ésh turned, flexing a delicious array of muscles. "What is an undertow?"

"A current under the water, pulling you out to sea."

"Then I will not go deep. But I refuse to join with a dirty woman. Come!" Ésh lunged toward her.

Clare screamed and ran from his grasping hands, as fast as she could in a cage crinoline. "There's a hip bath in the cottage! I'll bathe there! Ésh! This is my only dress!" It had been a second dress or the buffalo robe. She'd decided on the buffalo robe and a change of underclothes.

The wind was literally against her, pushing at her hoop skirt and slowing her steps. Wearing nothing but his breechcloth, Ésh was more agile. And perhaps she wanted to be caught. He soon scooped her into his arms, cage crinoline and all. Fortunately, there was no one but the shorebirds to see her undergarments as she kicked and surrendered.

Ésh grinned in triumph and carried her toward the surf. "And you thought I could not carry a buffalo robe!" Then, it was his turn to cry out as the first cold wave broke over his bare feet.

"I told you!" Clare giggled.

"This is nothing," Ésh insisted, striding forward. After two more waves smashed against him, he stopped and frowned. "The ground is eating my feet."

Clare laughed. "Sand will do that. I think we'd better turn around."

"Put you down?" Ésh pitched forward as if he were dropping her in the water.

"No!" Clare shrieked, clinging to his neck for dear life.

With only a turn of his head, his mouth crashed tenderly into hers. They kissed and kissed with the ocean shattering against them, dissolving all her doubts. Perhaps Cheyenne warriors never said *"I love you."* Perhaps they thought it unmanned them, like a taboo. Ésh had *shown* her he loved her in a hundred ways. He was showing her right now. She didn't need to hear the words.

When Clare's skirts were soaked with splashes, Ésh pulled himself from the sand. He carried her up the beach, set her down, and gathered his scattered clothing.

"*I* refuse to join with a man coated in sand," she told him as they passed inside the myrtle hedges. "Will you help me shed a few layers and fill the hip bath?"

"I would be happy to, *nazheem.*"

In the hall, she discarded her bonnet and gloves. In her bedchamber, she directed him to the buttons of her bodice, then to the ties of her skirt, petticoat, and cage crinoline.

He reached toward her corset laces, but she caught his hand. "That's enough for now."

Ésh's eyes remained fixed on her corset. She realized he'd never seen one before. "It is like...some kind of shield."

"It feels more like a shell."

"I asked my grandfather about white women's clothing. He said 'If she isn't eager to teach you, you shouldn't be undressing her.'"

Clare smiled and stepped out of the pool of her collapsed crinoline. "Perhaps he hoped you'd get something tangled and we wouldn't get even this far."

She led Ésh to the cistern, feeling brazen for strolling out of doors in nothing but boots, stockings, drawers, chemise, and corset. *Myrtle hedges,* Clare reminded herself as she waited for the first bucket to fill, as she inhaled the soothing fragrance of the wisteria. *The goddess of love is protecting us.* Still she asked Ésh: "Did you tell your family you were here?"

"No. They think I am at Mr. Alexander's." He looked troubled by this deception.

"Where does Mr. Alexander think you are?"

"He thinks I am with my family for Easter."

"Verily doesn't know either. I don't think anyone will find us until Monday, at the earliest. Since tomorrow is a holiday, there won't be any ferries running."

This seemed to brighten Ésh's mood. "Two entire days? I have two entire days alone with you?"

"At least."

Ésh pulled her into a kiss while the cistern overflowed the bucket and puddled around their feet. Then he carried the buckets and hip bath into the kitchen. Ésh filled the tub halfway, and she made a fire in the stove. After her lessons in Phoebe's kitchen, Clare wasn't completely useless. She put on a kettle so they could heat some of the bath water.

"Are you hungry?"

Standing behind her, Ésh slipped his hands around her corseted waist and leaned close. "Very."

"I meant for food, *na-eham*." She eased his hands away and opened the hamper. "I am *famished*. Fortunately, I brought a few provisions, to keep up our strength."

He smiled. "I brought food too." He fetched his saddlebag and pulled out some sort of reddish cake. "This is pemmican. My mother gave it to me."

"It's still good?"

"It is made to last."

Clare accepted his gift and examined it more closely. "Is this buffalo meat?"

"And berries, mixed with fat."

Clare took a bite: hearty, sweet, and satisfying. "It's delicious! Are you sure you don't want some?"

"I saved it for you." He turned to the hamper and frowned. "Now I know why this was so heavy." He lifted out the bottle. "Is this alcohol?"

"It's champagne. We drink it only on special occasions—when we're celebrating something." She grinned.

He was not smiling. He set down the bottle. "Firewater has made many Zizistas crazy. I do not like it."

"We need only take a sip."

"How do you have ice after winter?"

"It's cut in great blocks from northern lakes, packed in sawdust, and brought here on ships. The blocks keep till fall in icehouses."

"'Icehouses'?" Ésh echoed in amazement.

Clare nodded. "Have you had ice cream yet?"

"What is that?"

"Oh, you'll have to try it before you leave Charleston. My favorite is pineapple."

She heard the kettle beginning to boil. But as Ésh turned back to the hamper and continued rummaging, his muscles rippled from his broad shoulders to his delectable buttocks, holding her transfixed. She mustered her courage, reached for the top of his breechcloth, and tugged it loose. Merciful Heavens, his ass was exquisite.

He peered at her over his shoulder. "I thought you were hungry for *food*."

"Your bath is ready." Clare plucked the kettle from the stove and poured its steaming contents into the tub.

Ésh pulled the front of his breechcloth from its rawhide cord, but he did not remove the cord. He stepped into the hip bath and dipped the sponge in the water. Resting one foot on the tub's rim, he washed the sand from his skin. She had an open view of his *véto'ots*. The stalk of the mushroom was limp now, and its cap had disappeared inside a fleshy sleeve. Behind it, his *vé'she'em* hung loose.

Ésh noticed her looking. "Do not fret, *nazheem*—my *véto'ots* will stand up again when we need it." In fact, it seemed to be stirring under her gaze.

Clare busied herself setting out their repast on the slaves' dining table. There was no sense lugging everything to the dining room, and this way she could continue watching Ésh bathe.

He finished, and without any attempt to cover himself, pulled out one of the battered old chairs. Not that Clare minded his glorious nakedness. She did worry, however, that a splinter might lodge itself in some tender part of her beloved. "Wait."

Clare dashed across the porch to the dining room and brought back her father's mahogany chair with its red brocade seat. She took wicked delight in the thought that in two months' time, her father would settle his sagging rump onto this chair, read his newspaper, and drink his coffee, all the while having no idea that Ésh's bare buttocks had preceded him.

Before her beloved sat down, he motioned between his nudity and her undergarments. "We are not even."

Clare knew she was only delaying the inevitable. But the longer she ogled his exquisite body, the more she worried about showing him hers. She drew in a nervous breath. "Very well, you may remove my corset."

His gaze travelled suggestively down her torso to her legs.

"And my boots and stockings," Clare amended. She turned her back and instructed him to loosen her corset laces. She began unhooking the busk in front, but he replaced her hands with his. His fingers grasped and unlocked, grasped and unlocked, brushing her trembling skin through the thin sheath of her chemise, down, down between her tender breasts all the way to the mound of hair at the top of her thighs. Yet Ésh did no more than she'd agreed to before he sat down on her father's fine chair.

Clare placed a tentative boot toe on the edge of the seat, between his naked thighs and very near his *veto'ots*, which communicated its interest in the proceedings. The entire time he'd been naked before her, it had remained outside his body, which must mean his longing for her waxed and waned a little but never disappeared.

After Ésh had slipped off her boots, Clare tugged up the frilly hem of her drawers to show him her right garter. While her stockinged foot rested between his knees, she had the ridiculous urge to slide it across the seat and tickle him, fondle him, with her toes. On the stove, her second kettle began singing.

Ésh peeled off her right stocking, traced his fingers over her shin, and commented: "You *are* hairy here."

"Not as hairy as you," Clare defended. She returned her bare foot to the floor and allowed him to remove her other stocking, then retrieved the kettle. She warmed the bath and stepped in. It gave her an absurd thrill to wash herself with the same water and sponge he had used.

"We're still not even," Ésh complained. She felt him watching each shift of her breasts beneath the linen of her chemise, and her nipples seemed to yearn in his direction.

In her current state, if Clare sat on any chair naked, she was likely to mark the seat with her desire. "Go ahead and start," she instructed, motioning to her feast.

"Are these oysters?"

"Have you eaten them before?"

"No, but I've seen them in the market. How do you open them?"

"There's a trick to it. I'll show you." Clare finished her ablutions. Then she wrapped her fingers around Ésh's and showed him how to insert his blade in just the right spot, how to twist so the shell popped open for him.

Clare had wondered if she'd be eating all the oysters herself. In her experience, outsiders were repelled by the sight of their insides and by the idea of eating them alive. But to her delight, Ésh loved sucking the plump, wet, quivery flesh from its shell. Then, she acquainted him with the pea.

When their stomachs were satisfied, they assessed the chance of rain (none whatsoever) and began building their marriage bed. Ésh noticed her tip-toeing over the garden path, and he laid down rugs between the back steps and the pergola as if she were a queen. The Oriental pile felt luxurious under her bare feet.

They stripped every mattress from the cottage and laid them out side by side beneath the pergola. Over this padding, they draped the buffalo robe, hairy side up. At one end of the pergola, they stashed a counterpane and pillows, including the green bolsters from Mama's old méridienne. Like everything green, they reminded Clare of Ésh's eyes.

He suggested why they might need so many pillows with only a mischievous grin. Ésh also brought out a washstand. Next to the pitcher of water, he placed a small vial. "Almond oil," he explained. "My grandfather gave it to me. Sometimes, no matter how much you want me, your *ma'kesta* does not make enough wetness. It is good to have this just in case, he said."

Clare doubted they would need such an aid, but she appreciated his thoughtfulness—and Grand-père René's. She placed the champagne bottle in the last of the ice and set it next to the washstand.

Lastly, they acquainted themselves with the commode. As Ésh relieved himself into the bowl, Clare was reminded that he urinated from the same organ he was about to push inside her. She drew in a nervous breath to ask: "You will wash yourself afterward, won't you?"

He peered at her from the corner of his eyes as if she had insulted him. "I will if you will."

Clare recalled his desire to kiss her *ma'kesta*, and she was certain to wash herself afterward, too.

Finally, there was nothing left to prepare. They returned to the path of carpet and saw that the buffalo robe was already decorated with fallen wisteria blossoms. Ésh tugged her toward their bed with a glint in his green eyes. His *véto'ots* was standing at attention.

Clare felt the weariness in her bones and caught her lower lip between her teeth. She wanted to, of course she wanted to—but they would do this only once, and she wanted it to be perfect. "Ésh, would you mind terribly if we rested for a little while—only a little while? Last night, I was so excited, I hardly slept."

"Me too," he smiled. "I will wait a bit more"—he demonstrated with his thumb and forefinger a mere half-inch apart—"on two conditions. We take down your hair, and we take off this." He tugged on the side of her chemise.

Clare glanced toward the sheltering myrtle hedges, then swallowed and began removing her hairpins. In the dappled sunshine beside the pergola, Ésh unfurled her hair, and Clare thought: *It does look like honey.*

She reached trembling hands toward the neckline of her chemise. Again he replaced her fingers with his, undoing the two mother-of-pearl buttons in the shape of gardenia blossoms. Then he pulled the linen over her head, leaving her standing in nothing but her drawers, her pearl earrings, and her ring of Mirage's hair.

"*Mo'on-mo*," Ésh breathed. Clare found it very hard to hold still while he lifted his right hand to her left breast. He cupped it gently, letting his thumb hover an inch from her nipple, like a sculptor memorizing his model.

Clare felt and watched her nipple pucker and strain toward his finger. The dusky pink area around it wasn't too large? Women in paintings always had tiny nipples, and they never had a brownish tint. But then, Ésh's nipples were the color of hazelnuts. "I am still beautiful?"

He glanced down at his own straining *véto'ots*. "So beautiful I cannot look at you until we have rested, or this will be over too soon." He squeezed his eyes shut and groped out like a blind man. "Guide me, *nazheem*! Where is the bed?"

Clare giggled and pulled him onto the buffalo robe with her. They lay down as they had that first afternoon in the stable loft, Ésh on his back with Clare cradled at his side and her head on his shoulder. But this time, she was naked except for her drawers—the buffalo robe felt extravagant against her skin—and every inch of his gorgeous body was bared to her view. Clare could not help but marvel.

Ésh sighed and settled. His lips were curved into a little smile, but he kept his eyes closed. She checked. Honest and patient as always, her Cheyenne warrior. Secure in his embrace, Clare traced her fingers over the quillwork on his medicine pouch, then across the rawhide cord he still wore around his waist.

Only one little worm still gnawed at her happiness, no matter how often she'd told herself it didn't matter. For so long now, she'd been terrified that if she admitted her love in words, Ésh would say nothing in reply. Or worse, he'd repeat her words back to her, but she'd detect their insincerity. Then she'd know all of this was a lie. That he wanted only her mouth, breasts, ass, and *ma'kesta*. That he would abandon her as soon as he'd possessed them. How could any man as skilled and patient as Ésh was be a virgin himself?

But surely, if she said those three little words now, he would echo them back from the bottom of his soul. "I love you," Clare confessed from the bottom of her soul.

And Ésh said absolutely nothing.

Clare's face crumpled. She felt tears starting. She raised her head—and realized Ésh was already asleep.

She forgave him.

She returned her head to his shoulder and watched his *véto'ots* sinking into its sleeve. She decided she would wait to sleep herself until it disappeared inside his body. But her eyelids were so heavy, and the rhythm of the surf was so soothing...

CHAPTER 42

You make perfect the present,—condense,
In a rapture…
Thought and feeling and soul and sense—
Merged in a moment which gives me at last
You around me for once, you beneath me, above me…
— Robert Browning, "Now" (1889)

Clare woke to the whirring and squeaking of hummingbirds. Her eyes fluttered open to watch the greedy little creatures darting and dipping through the veils of purple racemes above her head. The afternoon light gleamed on their ruby and emerald feathers.

Clare understood the hummingbirds' enchantment. She loved wisteria too, its glory of contrasts. Its delicate purple blooms preceded most of the leaves, in pleasing juxtaposition to the grey twists of woody vine. It reminded her of Jack's magic beanstalk, though wisteria was in the pea family.

Touched with gold and cream, each individual blossom was a work of art: the scooped banner that reminded Clare of a woman's bonnet, the keels and wings clasped tight like praying hands around the pistils and stamen. These tiny masterpieces united into elegant racemes eight inches long, exploding from the vine in fantastic abundance like pendant fireworks.

Clare loved the way the racemes swayed like gossamer curtains in every breeze. She even liked that wisteria blooms lasted only a few days: their transience made them more precious. But most of all, she loved the scent, potent and soothing, lilac and vanilla yet uniquely its own.

Her warm male pillow shifted beneath her and yawned. Clare sucked in a breath and dropped her eyes to his *véto'ots*. It was halfway alert again! "I missed it!" she pouted.

"Missed what?" Ésh murmured, his voice still slurred with sleep.

"I missed your *véto'ots* disappearing inside your body."

Ésh burst out laughing, his entire chest rumbling against her, shaking off the wisteria blossoms that had settled on his skin. "You have that backward: my *véto'ots* disappears inside *your* body."

"I know; but a stallion's..."

"I am sorry to disappoint you, *nazheem*, but I am not a stallion."

"You *never* carry it inside you? Not even when it's resting?"

"It shrinks when it is resting or cold, but it is always on the outside."

The tip emerging from its fleshy sheath resembled a cautious turtle poking its head from its neck, Clare thought. She liked turtles. And Ésh's *véto'ots* took after a turtle in more ways than one. Slow and steady, it had won her heart. "But it looks so...tender. Is it tender?"

"Do you want to touch it?"

Clare heard the anticipation in his voice. She needed no encouragement, only direction. He kissed her cheek with the moles as if he were thanking her. But she loved to watch him transforming and know she was the cause of it. His *vé'she'em* pulled taut beneath her hand, and his *véto'ots* actually jumped. The way the sheath slid like satin over the stalk entranced her. When a drop of liquid appeared at the tip of his *véto'ots*, Ésh drew away her questing fingers.

"Did I hurt you?"

"I don't want to come until I am inside you, *nazheem*."

"'Come'?"

"That is what my grandfather called it. Also 'ejaculate.'" He enunciated each syllable carefully.

"You're going to curse?"

Ésh frowned. "Maybe I am remembering wrong."

"An ejaculation is a curse or a prayer, something uttered fast and loud."

"When my happiness is greatest, I will utter something fast and wet, here." He touched the glistening slit at the head of his *véto'ots*. "It is my seed, the start of a baby."

"That will happen when you…come, inside me?"

Ésh nodded. "The Zizistas believe that a man's seed is his *exhastoz*, his medicine. When it leaves his body, it should go into his woman, or it is wasted."

Clare's eyes drank in the bead of moisture, the straining tip—all these hours, all these days, it had sought her and she had denied it. But she *wanted* his "medicine." Now. "Come inside me, Ésh."

His breath hitched, and his whole body grew as rigid as his *véto'ots*.

She turned her face to his and touched his cheek. "Come, inside me."

They tore at the ties of her drawers and yanked them down her legs till every inch of her was bare. She wore only her earrings and wedding ring. He wore only her ouroboros bracelet, his medicine pouch, and the cord for his breechcloth.

Clare worried that the sight of her *ma'kesta* might disgust him, so she distracted Ésh with her mouth. He eased her back against the buffalo robe, his medicine pouch brushing her breast as he tucked an emerald pillow under her head. He trailed kisses down her chest while his *véto'ots* tapped hot and urgent against her mound of hair like a fist knocking at a doorway.

Clare moaned as his lips closed around one of her nipples and he sucked as if she had milk. Surely it was savage and wicked to take pleasure in such a thing. Breasts were for feeding babies, not husbands. Surely a gentleman would do only what was necessary to father a child, and a lady would permit only that…

Ésh was a gentle man, but he was no gentleman. She was apparently a wanton.

Her aching, tingling body sank deeper into the chocolate fur that was coarse above but soft below. Ésh rained kisses down her belly, past her navel, into the mound of her secret hair. Her legs tensed protectively, wanting his touch but fearing his rejection. He stroked her thigh and assured her: "*Mo'on-mo.*"

Her legs opened in relief and in welcome. He lay between them, blessing her with his breaths, his words, his fingertips, his—

Clare's body jolted in surprise. When he'd said he wanted to kiss her *ma'kesta*, she'd thought he meant a peck. She'd thought his mouth would be *closed*.

Ésh paused only long enough to grin up at her. "Again?"

Clare's trembling must have looked like nodding. Or perhaps she *was* nodding. Her *ma'kesta* quivered and revelled at each teasing flick, each slow sweep of his tongue. But this *couldn't* be right...

Ésh lingered as if it were. He sucked at her sensitive bud while his forefinger tested her wetness. She was ready. She was very ready. When he slid a second finger inside her, this time it did not pinch at all.

But her insides were shifting wildly: the press of his fingers produced mortifying puffing and slurping noises, audible even over the surf. Clare whimpered from shame instead of pleasure and covered her face with her hair, as if this would muffle the humiliating racket.

Ésh was chuckling; she could feel his mirth against her tender flesh. "Those sounds are *good, nazheem*—they mean your body is opening for me. Your *ma'kesta* changes for our joining as much as my *véto'ots* does—but most of it happens *inside* you."

Clare pulled her hair away from her face. She exhaled her shame and inhaled wisteria and Ésh. "Come inside me," she pleaded.

He knelt upright between her legs and draped her calves over his spread thighs. She felt him stroking her bud with the warm tip of his *véto'ots*, rounded like a satin tulip bulb. Oh, that was lovely. Just when she thought she couldn't become any wetter, new desire bloomed out of her. At last, he slid the tip downwards and found the entrance of her *ma'kesta*. It didn't hurt—not yet.

His eyes had never been more green, more vibrant or glinting with desire. His hair had never been more golden than it was in this moment, framed by the wisteria trembling above him. He was trembling too. "If you want me, open for me."

Clare wanted him. She chose *him*, even if pain would follow. She pulled her legs tighter against her body.

"Not your thighs, *nazheem*. Your *ma'kesta*." His breaths, her breaths, shifted the tip of him just slightly, showing her where to open. "You have muscles here, too."

For a moment, Clare's eyes widened instead. He knew so much about her body. More than she did. And he was always right, always wise. She wished she could kiss him, but his mouth was so far away. Her lying supine and Ésh kneeling concentrated all her sensations in her *ma'kesta*. Perhaps it was better this way.

Open! Clare commanded her newly discovered muscles. But nothing changed; Ésh remained at her door. What were the magic words Ali Baba had used in *One Thousand and One Nights*? *"Open sesame!"* The thought made her giggle, which wasn't what she wanted; but it proved Ésh was right: she had muscles there. Laugh muscles. Joy muscles.

With every fiber in her body, Clare yearned to accept the joy he offered. *Come inside me*, she begged Ésh with her *ma'kesta*. And then, he did. The head of his *véto'ots* peeked inside her claire-voie. She felt twinges of discomfort at his girth, but they dissipated at the sight of Ésh's grin.

Clare grinned back as her body reformed around his *véto'ots*, changing itself to welcome him. She wanted to sit up and throw her arms around Ésh's neck in celebration, but she worried that might disconnect them. The only parts of his body she could reach with her hands were his knees, planted in the buffalo robe. She stroked him there, assuring him that she wanted more.

Slowly, very slowly, Ésh pressed himself deeper: firm and warm and *him*, yet with every breath and every heartbeat the new flesh became hers more completely. She could actually feel his heartbeat inside his *véto'ots*. It was as if he was giving her his heart.

"Am I hurting you, *na-méo?*"

"No, Ésh, no!"

He froze, alarm rippling down his body. "No, you do not want this?"

Clare laughed, and she felt his *véto'ots* even more keenly, wrapped tight inside her. She thought her laughter pulled him a little deeper. "Yes, Ésh, yes! I want this—I want *you*. Your heart."

He peered at her in confusion. "My heart is here, *na-méo*." Ésh placed his hand on his chest, brushing his medicine pouch with the ouroboros around his left wrist.

"I know where your heart is," Clare giggled. "But I can feel your pulse, your heartbeat, *inside* me."

She watched him concentrate for a moment. "I can too. I mean, I feel your heart beating around my *véto'ots*. And I felt your laughter, like squeezes."

Clare drew in a breath. "Did I hurt *you?*"

"No, *na-méo*." He grinned. "Yes, *na-méo*! I want you, *na-méo!*" Even as he spoke, he pressed his *véto'ots* all the way inside her. His *vé'she'em* settled against the base of her *ma'kesta*, and she knew they'd done it. They were no longer virgins. They were husband and wife.

Yet he wasn't calling her "wife" anymore. "You feel so good, *na-méo...*" he rejoiced as he bent forward and took her up in his arms.

She gasped, rendered weightless, clinging to him with her arms and her legs. "What does *na-méo* mean?"

His medicine pouch tickled her chest as he nuzzled her neck, nipping and sucking. "Love. 'My love.'" His words caressed every inch of her skin, outside and in. Her body softened, and the last traces of fear and discomfort literally melted away.

Then Ésh rocked his hips back, pulling out a little. Surely he wasn't—had he already come? Was that it? But no, he pushed deep again.

When he caught her eyes, she knew what he was asking. Clare smiled and touched his face in reassurance. All the while, he retreated and advanced, retreated and advanced. She decided not to worry about the wet slapping noises their bodies were making.

It was soothing, the way he was stroking her inside. Like when Verily combed her hair one hundred times every night. How many times had Ésh stroked her now? Ten? Would he do it a hundred times? She could do this for hours.

Clare sighed in contentment and gazed up at the pergola, at the purple wisteria racemes like a thousand fireworks. *Welcome, fair stranger. I cling to thee.* She'd been so frightened this joining would hurt, but the pain had vanished, just as Ésh had promised. He always kept his promises. It was so pleasant, receiving his body over and over and over like this. It was *pleasing*, to know how much she pleased him.

He kissed down her throat to her breasts, taking one nipple into his mouth. Oh, that was extraordinary: the way each pull on her breast seemed to tug a cord that led straight to her *ma'kesta*. She felt herself going even wetter around him, and the softness was shifting, as if in preparation. Her *ma'kesta* was beginning to pulse like the walls of a heart. She hoped he'd suck on her breasts for a very long—

Ésh let go of her right breast and did not reach the other; he only buried his face halfway between them as he clutched her body against his. He showered praise on her skin till it seemed to pool on her flesh with their sweat. He told her again how good she felt and murmured words in Cheyenne with each thrust: "*Mo'ona. Nazheem. Na-méo.*" She didn't recognize the rest of the words.

She wanted to ask him to suck her breast again, but the words in her head sounded selfish and wanton. She didn't want to interrupt his exertions. His pace was increasing, and he seemed to be fighting for something, or against something. The ejaculations coming out of him weren't even words anymore, only grunts and groans. They should have been silly or revolting, but instead they were endearing, exultant—little war cries she knew he'd made only for her. She did worry he might be hurting himself, but if that were the case she assumed he would stop.

She hoped he never would. Her hands grasped and caressed

every part of him she could reach. She savored the muscles of his arms surging beneath her hands. His scars and the piercings along the rims of his ears that made him Cheyenne. She luxuriated in the pleasure washing over her with every motion, every sound—his pleasure, but rooted, literally rooted, in her body.

She felt so *close* to him—not only his *véto'ots* in her *ma'kesta* but as if his soul were tapping at hers. As if he were scattering all his troubles within her and the moment they reached her, they *changed* into petals, like the wisteria petals falling down on them in a fragrant cascade.

If a vengeful God struck her down at this moment for opening her body to this perfect man instead of attending the Easter Vigil, Clare would die happier than she'd ever been.

Against her, inside her, Ésh's body convulsed with a contained but startling violence. Not so contained: she gasped as she felt him filling her where she thought she was filled already. His medicine, coursing into her. His seed, and the rain to make it grow. Oh, she hoped he was giving her a child.

In the midst of all this glory, Ésh groaned into her neck: "I am sorry, *na-méo.*"

"Sorry? Ésh, you didn't hurt me! It was wonderful!"

"But you didn't— I am sure you didn't—" He was shifting, settling her back against the buffalo robe, withdrawing his body from hers.

Even before he was gone, she ached with his loss.

Ésh crawled from between her legs and continued to berate himself. "Both my grandfathers told me it was almost impossible a woman's first time, that it might take us *months.* I told myself: "'Almost! Might!' I will do it! I will prove them wrong.'" Ésh flopped onto the buffalo robe beside her and hid his face in the fur. "I am vain and I am weak."

"Ésh, why do you think you disappointed me? I *loved* feeling you inside me!"

"But it can be better, *na-méo,*" he muttered into the buffalo hair.

Clare frowned. She couldn't imagine anything better than such closeness: the certainty that he loved her and that he had found pleasure in her body. Even now, the essence of this perfect man was soaking into her core.

"The champagne!" Clare sat up, and she felt his medicine slipping out of her. How long was she supposed to lie still afterwards? She wished she hadn't moved, but it was too late now.

She looked over at Ésh, whose bare ass was as gorgeous as ever. But he still had his face buried in the buffalo hair, as if he were a misbehaving child sent to stare at a corner. Guilt wasn't only the province of Catholics, she thought, though she still didn't understand what he felt guilty about.

Clare leaned over to retrieve a towel, the champagne bottle, and the coupe. She'd brought two, but one had broken on the journey. She stroked Ésh's scarred back to attract his attention. He granted her one eye.

"Supposedly, the first champagne coupe was molded from Marie Antoinette's left breast." Clare placed the mouth of the empty glass around her left nipple and pressed inward, but she overflowed the coupe. "My assets are larger than a queen's!"

Ésh rewarded her antics with a small smile.

Clare unscrewed the muselet and covered the cork with the towel. She'd seen this done, but she'd never done it herself. Fortunately, she remembered to point the bottle away from her husband. The cork exploded toward the nearest myrtle hedge, covering her hand in bubbles. At least Ésh was showing interest now: he was propped on his elbows, watching her.

Clare tipped enough champagne into the coupe to cover the bottom and lifted the glass toward Ésh. "I am no longer a virgin! I am safe from my father forever!" She took a sip, sharp and sparkling. What was it Dom Pérignon had said when he invented champagne? *"Come quickly, I am drinking the stars!"*

Clare settled herself back against the buffalo robe, alongside Ésh with her head on the emerald pillow. "Now it is your turn, my love. Since you don't want enough to get drunk…" Drawing up her knees to make a better bowl, she dribbled champagne into her navel. "What do you think?"

Ésh grinned for the first time since he'd left her body and leaned over her. He kissed her side, licked a few wayward drops above her mound, and sucked the rest from her navel. Pleasure shivered through her. Her *ma'kesta* ached not with pain but with yearning.

"Will you let me try again, *na-méo?*" he whispered against her skin. "To make you happy?"

"I *am* happy, Ésh: my husband loves me and I love him."

His kisses climbed upward. "But what happened to me inside you—I can make you come too. Not in the same way, but we will know when it happens."

He could? They would?

Ésh kissed the breast that was fuller than Marie Antoinette's. "Tell me what you like best, *na-méo.*"

Clare's breath caught. The words in her head sounded so wicked.

He kissed the puckered flesh, but still not the nipple. "Yes? What do you want, *na-méo?*"

Why was he torturing her when he already knew? "I... I liked it when you sucked my nipple."

Ésh obliged. Clare sank her hands into his hair and tried not to pull too hard. Even before he licked and nibbled and sucked at her other breast, her *ma'kesta* was blooming for him. She pushed her hips toward him, but he pulled away to retrieve something from the washstand. The almond oil. "I think a different way this time. Turn on your stomach for me, *na-méo.*"

"But I want you inside me."

"I know what you want," he teased. "Do you trust me?"

"Yes." Still Clare rolled over reluctantly. What was her beautiful husband doing back *there*, where she could see him only from the corner of her eye? At least the buffalo fur felt exciting against her tingling breasts, but all her important parts were turned toward the robe now.

"Lift your hips."

Clare braced her arms and obeyed.

Ésh helped her, kneeling behind her. He drew her hair aside and kissed her left buttock, sucking lightly. "Have I told you how magnificent your seat is?"

"You have."

"And your back is magnificent," he murmured, kissing and sucking at her parts as he named them, bringing his body over hers. "And your shoulder is magnificent..."

"Only the left shoulder?" Clare panted, because he'd stopped to check the wetness between her thighs. They certainly wouldn't need the almond oil. If his fingers could enter her from behind, could his *véto'ots*?

"Mm..." Ésh pretended to consider her question. "This shoulder too." He gave the right one only a peck, concentrating on rubbing his *véto'ots* against her *ma'kesta*. He *could* reach it.

Clare moaned and tilted her hips, straining toward him. She'd been right all along: her *ma'kesta* was unfinished. Only when he filled her again in one glorious glide did she feel complete.

She liked it better, she decided, that men carried their organs outside their bodies. It meant he always had an extra part and she always had a missing part. Now, especially now, with his body aligned with hers from their hands to their heads to their toes, every part locked against its matching part except the sublime center where their differences made them whole.

"Did you know, *na-méo*, your *ma'kesta* can do more than open for my *véto'ots*?" Ésh slid his hand over hers and took her thumb in his curled fingers. "Your muscles can grip me, like this." He tightened his fingers around her thumb. "They can even..." His fingers tightened and released, tightened and released. "Would you try that?"

Tentatively, Clare tried to grip him. She found it worked best when the movements of her *ma'kesta* became part of larger sways, circles, and rocks. Even though his body was covering hers, she felt in control of their joining now, and it thrilled her.

She loved being able to draw him deeper and carry him with her, then tease him by releasing her hold. She not only heard his responses but also felt them rumble along her back. *She* could make a Cheyenne warrior whimper.

As if in recompense, his hand slid around her hip, already slick. It must be the almond oil. His fingertips found the bud at the top of her *ma'kesta*, the spot that controlled all the rest of her. Her entire body trembled in delicious concordance as ripples of joy radiated to the tips of her fingers and toes. She panted into the buffalo robe and the skeins of her own hair.

"Better?" He circled the bud, and she moaned. "Tell me when it is good, *na-méo*, and tell me when it is better. You do not even have to use words. But guide me with your voice and your movements."

She did, making it clear what she liked. If he leaned forward and she turned her head, she could even tell him in kisses. Beneath her skin, her sensitive bud had a little stalk of its own. His slickened fingers flicked it from side to side while she angled her hips and tightened her *ma'kesta* to welcome his thrusts. Around this intimate center, something was building, gathering, coursing... Was this— Was this *supposed* to—

She reminded herself not to panic. Over her own cries, Ésh was shouting encouragement, and she trusted him.

She couldn't have stopped it if she wanted to: her body felt possessed. She ground herself into Ésh's hand and bucked against him, not because she wanted to throw him but because she wanted more contact, more— Then the cataclysm crashed over her: she thrashed and screamed and it terrified her and she cherished every astonishing second.

Her *ma'kesta* pulsed and pulsed, stronger and faster and deeper and wider than she'd been able to do consciously, as if begging Ésh for his medicine. Through her own waning convulsions, she felt him pumping into her, coming after her in a hot rush. She collapsed onto the buffalo robe, hair a tangle, feeble as a shipwreck victim.

When the pulses in her *ma'kesta* faded, he withdrew from her body and lay down close beside her. Through the hair across her face, he grinned at her, looking very pleased with himself. "Better?"

Clare was so stunned and quivery, she could scarcely breathe. Every hair every nail every vein every inch of her flesh hummed in ecstasy.

Ésh waited patiently for her answer, brushing the wet strands from her eyes.

She gulped and panted two words at a time: "I thought I loved you *before*..."

"What was it like for you?"

Not only her loins but her entire body felt like liquid, warm comfortable liquid, as if everything unpleasant were melting away and she were being reformed into something different, something greater. "I feel as if...as if I've perished and come back to life. Like...a current within my own body pulled me somewhere perilous and glorious and then yanked me back again."

"Yes," he smiled.

"I did that for you?"

"Both times. But I think yours was bigger." He gazed at her with admiration, not envy.

She wondered how long her body would keep humming. She would close her eyes every evening and wake every morning with him beside her, with the knowledge that he could transform her at any moment. "How do husbands and wives not do this all day and all night?"

"I don't think they would survive it." Ésh chuckled and tidied more of her hair, his still-slick fingertips tracing her shoulder blade. "This is what I want, *na-méo*: to make you happy."

"Ésh, happiness is a warm fire or a cool glass of lemonade, something expected and fulfilled. *This*... I didn't know my body could *do* that."

"The champagne!" he cried, fetching the bottle. He dribbled it in the curve of her back and sucked it out. Clare wanted to celebrate with him, but she couldn't remember how her muscles worked: she remained tipsy from the fizzing already inside her. Ésh found a solution. He swigged a mouthful straight from the bottle and gave her a champagne kiss. She slurped and swallowed and kissed him back.

The champagne lent her just enough energy to turn on her side, so she was facing him. Each of their hands settled at the top of the other's thighs, playing through the curly hair in languorous possession. Perhaps they were each confirming the wonderland was still there, or perhaps they were priming the pumps.

The stickiness of that hair should disgust Clare. Instead, it delighted her. It was proof of their joining. They had made it together, as they would make a child someday. Ésh's child might be swimming inside her right now.

Yet his face looked troubled again.

"What are you thinking, my love?"

"That I am glad you are my first woman. And I am *very* glad I am your first man." He grasped the hair on her mound. Not tight enough to hurt—in fact, she found it arousing—but enough to emphasize his words. "The thought of another man seeing you like this, hearing you, touching you, *inside* you…"

"Ésh, you need never think about it."

"Do you promise?" The emotions that flickered over his features almost frightened her: not only worry and jealousy but anger and— despair? As if he were certain she'd betray him. "You are mine now? No other man will touch you here?"

Was he thinking of his brother? A vision of David lying sated beside her, *his* fingers slick with her pleasure, flitted before her eyes. Clare's breath hitched with longing, but she forced the vision away. She couldn't have loved David, not the way she loved Ésh. Passion like this must be singular. You felt incomplete without *one* other person, not two. "I chose *you*, Ésh. I want to spend the rest of my life with *you*. As long as…"

"'As long as'?"

"As long as we'll do this again sometime?"

He chuckled, released her mound, and looked down at his *véto'ots*, which hung limp. "As soon as I can, *na-méo*."

Clare teetered inside toward the commode. She noticed the change even then: she carried herself differently. She felt taller, lighter—as if every step were taken on her toes—as if she were always dancing—stronger, absolutely invincible, as if nothing in the world could make her unhappy again.

She caught sight of herself in a mirror. *Is that what a well-loved woman looks like?* she thought. Her hair was a disaster; Ésh's mouth had left a purple imprint on her neck; her face and chest were mottled pink; her skin shone with sweat; his medicine glazed her thighs; and the area in-between was squishy. She had never felt more beautiful.

But she liked her body best when he was touching her. She returned to her husband in a rush, as if he might have vanished. For a moment, she thought he had, and her heart nearly stopped.

In the next instant, he called to her from the kitchen window. They savored the ham, the cornbread, and the peaches. Clare had eaten each of these foods thousands of times before, yet suddenly they seemed richer, sweeter, more satisfying, as if she were tasting the world for the first time.

She took her husband's hand and led him back to the buffalo robe under the wisteria. They experimented and experimented, learning how the positions of their legs and the curves of their bodies altered their sensations.

"Ésh, how many ways can we do this?"

"As many as we want, *na-méo*."

She discovered his nipples were sensitive too, and that it didn't bother him when she dug her fingernails into his buttocks. In fact, he liked it. She loved feeling his tongue thrusting in her mouth while his *véto'ots* thrust in her *ma'kesta*. She loved him sucking her breasts even more, but this left her mouth bereft.

She wished he had two mouths—three—*four*. Her tongue swept greedily over her lips at the thought. She pulled his thumb into her mouth, curving her tongue around it and sucking. He liked this too.

When she came again, the joy was fierce and enduring. He followed her into the glorious depths, and the certainty of his pleasure redoubled her own. Just when she thought the convulsions were releasing her, they grabbed hold again, stronger than before. Her teeth clamped down on the base of Ésh's thumb. She broke the surface of his skin. When she realized what she'd done, tears sprang into her eyes.

But her husband seemed delighted. "I marked you too." He brushed his fingers over the bruise his mouth had left on her neck. "Do you mind it?"

Clare smiled and shook her head. "It's proof I am yours."

He started to withdraw, but she gripped him with her *ma'kesta*. He'd softened only a little. "Can you stay?"

"I will try." He settled deeper again.

The light was fading fast now, and the shadows of the pergola swallowed his beautiful face. But even in darkness, his body was uniquely Cheyenne. She traced her fingers across his shoulder blades, feeling the scars from his vow with the buffalo skulls. To her, the pair of ridges felt like wing buds.

She thought of Eros and Psyche, how the winged god of love visited his mortal wife only at night, fearing his true beauty would stop her heart. If in that moment, Ésh had unfolded above her two great white wings of soft feathers, Clare would not have been surprised.

"Is this normal, Ésh?"

"Biting? I think one of my grandfathers mentioned it."

"No, how much I adore you."

Ésh chuckled, and she felt it inside her. "I do not know. I have never been adored before."

Clare smiled and stroked his wing buds, jealous of the greedy shadows.

"How are they different, love and adore?"

"Adore is more like worship." In contrition, Clare looked up to the rosy heavens beyond the pergola. "I shouldn't adore you." Especially on Holy Saturday. "Adoration is for God." In the western sky, the evening star, the planet named for the goddess of love, winked down at her. "But right now, *you* are the only star in my firmament."

"In your what?"

Clare giggled. "My sky, Ésh!" She caressed his face. "Your name means 'sky,' doesn't it?"

"Yes."

"It might as well be Heaven," she sighed, surrendering to her idolatry.

"Give me my Romeo; and, when he shall die,
Take him and cut him out in little stars,
And he will make the face of heaven so fine
That all the world will be in love with night
And pay no worship to the garish sun."

"Is that a prayer, *na-méo?*"

"It is a kind of prayer." Clare would miss Shakespeare, when she was in the West. But what need did she have for fiction when Ésh was her reality?

He kissed her again, and she thought: *I am drinking the stars!*

When he'd slipped from her body, they tucked the long emerald pillow under their heads, pulled the counterpane over them, and fell asleep on their sides. Her husband curved himself around her back, his nose buried in the hair at the nape of her neck and his legs tucked against hers. He wrapped his arms around her, her arms tight around his. She felt so safe in his embrace, as if nothing would ever harm her again.

She woke in the moonlight aching for him. Perhaps she'd felt the stirring of his own desire. With only a whimper and the press of her hips, she told him what she wanted. Without a word, he made her whole.

This time, their motions were languorous, but their union seemed to last for hours. He did not enter her deeply but stroked her with gentle dips, like a bird skimming a pond with its wings.

Only when he came did her hunger abate. Her crest was softer than an explosion, spreading from her *ma'kesta* in ripples instead of tidal waves. But this climax was sweeter. Sated, still holding him inside her, she slid back into sleep.

CHAPTER 43

And at the last, as everything has ending,
she took her leave, and her way was wending.
— Geoffrey Chaucer, *Troilus and Cressida* (1387)

Ésh was gone when she woke.

Clare sat up in a panic, then spotted her husband kneeling on one of the Oriental rugs beyond the pergola. He remained naked.

Above him, sunrise painted the clouds in shades of peach and rose. Ésh was murmuring in Cheyenne and holding something toward the sky, silver-green stalks that gave off a faint smoke. In spite of his nudity, the sight recalled a Priest elevating the Host at Mass, surrounded by incense, and reminded Clare that today was Easter.

When Ésh finished, he returned to her. "I asked my grandmother for dried sage from her garden."

"You were praying?"

"Yes. I was thanking the Creator and the Sacred Powers for their blessings: for the Sun, the water, the island—and most, for you." He touched her face and then let his hand slip downwards, across her breast and her belly till it came to rest on her thigh. "How do you feel this morning, *na-méo*?"

She knew what he was asking, and she was rather sore. A good soreness, that contained even within the ache the spectacular memories of what had caused it—not enough to keep her from wanting him. If she admitted her soreness, Clare was afraid her husband might issue a moratorium, so she answered honestly: "I have never been better."

"Are you hungry?"

"Still," she grinned, tugging at the cord around his waist to pull him closer.

Ésh chuckled. "I meant for food."

They brought the hamper out to the buffalo robe, which was as much purple blossoms as chocolate fur now. They sat face to face Indian-style, with their knees and their toes brushing. They fed each other figs, pickled eggs, and strawberries. Then Ésh discovered the chocolate bar. He was so entranced, she began to despair.

To bring his attention back to her, Clare tugged at his breechcloth cord again. It hung just below the scar in his right side—inflicted by a Crow horse thief, she remembered. It was the only one of Ésh's wounds that wasn't part of a pair, that he hadn't carved in his own flesh or asked someone else to carve. She wondered if it still ached.

She also recalled that Christ had gained a wound in his right side on the Cross. There was even a prayer "To the Holy Wound of the Sacred Side," written by her own patroness, Saint Clare: *"Adorable wound, I compassionate thee, for the cruel insult thou didst suffer…"*

What wicked thoughts to have on Easter morning.

Clare wondered if her husband had left on his breechcloth cord all this time out of negligence, or if it had a deeper meaning. Somehow this one insubstantial garment increased her arousal, as if there were some secret hidden beneath its tiny compass, some part of him left to discover. The cord also gave her husband a handle. She twirled it around his waist a little, but he only glanced at her. "Could we do it again, Ésh?"

"Do what, *na-méo?*" he asked cluelessly, still nibbling on the chocolate.

She couldn't tell if he was putting on an act or if he had truly lost interest in her. She pouted.

Without letting go of the chocolate bar, he grinned in the way that illuminated his whole face, her whole world—and she knew he'd been bluffing. "I must ask my *véto'ots.*" He looked down to where it stirred rather timidly.

"Is it tired?" she teased him, sliding a fingertip from his cord, down his taut belly...

"I am a bit sore."

Clare jerked her hand away, as if she had burned his skin. "Oh, Ésh! Why didn't you—"

"It is a good sore, *na-méo*—not enough to stop me from wanting you."

At the news of his pain, however slight, Clare should be ashamed. She should pity him, or feel anything else than the pride and *delight* bubbling inside her. What kind of wife delighted in her husband's pain?

Clare did. It was one more cord binding them together, one more proof of his devotion. Of course he was sore. Ésh had been a virgin too—he had also been testing muscles he'd used only with her.

"I *may* have a balm for your soreness, sir. Let me check." Clare wallowed in her own wantonness as she slid her hand into the gap between her tucked legs. "Yes! I've just gotten some in. I have it on good authority that this balm is very soothing on swollen parts..."

Ésh tossed the chocolate bar aside and flung himself at her, toppling her back onto the petalled robe. "Mm, I want to test this 'balm' before I put it somewhere so important..." He parted her thighs and buried his face in her *ma'kesta.*

Clare laughed and sighed and moaned. Above her, two hummingbirds squeaked their outrage and spiralled around each other, each of them furious that the other had invaded his territory. Silly birds. Beneath this pergola, there was a cornucopia for every-one: a profusion of nectar for the birds and for Ésh.

Even if it weren't Easter morning, the way he was licking her *must* be a mortal sin. But it *was* Easter. At this very moment, all across Christendom, Father Joseph and thousands of other Priests were praising God for conquering Death.

While Ésh's tongue was lapping against her, *inside* her, she cared about nothing else. Clare tangled her fingers in his hair and wrapped her legs around his head to bind him to her. Ésh's enthusiasm reverberated all the way to her own throat. Saint Patrick's famous hymn swirled in her thoughts, its repetitions like a pagan incantation:

I bind unto myself today
The strength of Heaven,
The light of the Sun,
The force of Fire,
The power of Lightning…

May Christ be with me, Christ before me…

But in her wickedness, she replaced Christ's name with her husband's:

Ésh beside me, Ésh around me,
Ésh beneath me, Ésh above me,
Ésh behind me, Ésh within me…

Her god was conquering shame, fear, loneliness, loss… With his *véto'ots* nowhere near her *ma'kesta*, the way a proper husband and wife united, Clare was praising her god, her head and hair thrashing in the wisteria petals and buffalo fur. She was obeying her god's every command: she was coming for him, crying out his name and finding Heaven on Earth.

Ésh unhooked her legs and raised his head, his face glistening with her pleasure. It also had four wisteria blossoms stuck to it. "Now, we are even."

"'Even'?" Clare panted.

"I have come four times, and you have come four times."

Clare smiled. She'd woken wondering if she'd dreamt it, the time he'd loved her slow and steady and sweet beneath the counterpane. Either that had been real, or Ésh had had the same dream. She wasn't sure which thought was more delicious. "We're not even," she informed him. "*I'm* ahead now."

"What?"

"When I bit your thumb, I came twice in a row."

He narrowed his eyes in remembrance. "I thought it was just longer."

"I think one stopped and then another started."

"Mm, you are right then." He kissed his way across her mound of hair up her stomach. She was covered in petals and sweat. "We are not even. We must fix that." He circled his tongue around each of her nipples. "But first, it would be a shame to waste this balm of yours." His fingers stirred her wetness as if he were a spoon and she were a pot. "I *wonder* how I might keep it coming and *coming…*"

Instead of entering her, he flipped her over, till he was flat on his back and she was astride him. Clare gasped and braced her arms on his chest. Against her buttocks, his *véto'ots* stood ready for her.

"Come over me," he suggested, "around me—do whatever makes you happy, *na-méo*. I want to *watch* you come. I have never had a good view."

Clare felt suddenly self-conscious, perched atop him with her breasts on display like this. But the sight of her warrior lying seemingly powerless beneath her, as if she had conquered him, with petals falling down on him in celebration of her victory… The sight aroused her tremendously. It made *her* feel powerful.

His expression said *I cannot get enough of you*, and that made her happiest of all. She teased him with the long hair he loved, trailing the honey-brown cascade from the golden crown of his head to the dark, springy curls at his groin. She stroked him with her fingers and watched his reactions. She slid herself side to side, up and down over his *vé'she'em* and *véto'ots*, smudging them with her desire.

Ésh groaned and clenched his hands in the buffalo robe and the petals.

"Do you want more?"

"Don't think about me, *na-méo*."

"Don't think about you?" Clare cried.

"I will enjoy *whatever* you do," he gasped. "I want you to please yourself now."

So she did. She took him slowly inside her, moaning out her pleasure for him. *Ésh beneath me, Ésh within me*... She gloried in her body and his worship. Each rock of his hips, each grasp of his hands, each gaze of his eyes was both praise and pleading. But for her, it still wasn't quite...

Ésh must have seen her clenching her fist against her thigh, reaching toward her mound of hair, and forcing her hand back to her thigh. "Touch yourself, *na-méo*." He snatched up the vial of almond oil, poured it in his navel as if it were a paint pot, and kept pouring. He guided Clare's fingers into the pool of oil and petals. "I want to watch you touch yourself. Show me what you like best."

Clare swallowed. And then, she obeyed. Tentatively at first. Soon, shyness gave way to abandon. Her other hand closed around her own breast. With Ésh urging her on, she kneaded and rubbed and rode. Who would have thought the most profound verse in all of Scripture could be *"And the man and his wife were both naked and were not ashamed"*?

At the climax, she shuddered so violently she imagined shaking every last petal from the wisteria. She screamed so loudly, the soldiers at Fort Moultrie must have turned their heads in alarm. Clutching her hips, his body arching like a bow, Ésh came after her. She gripped his breechcloth cord like a lifeline, cherishing each twitch and pulse of his peak. When he rose up and tugged at her breast with his mouth, the tidal wave ripped through her a second time.

She'd thought she loved him before. Cradling his head against her gasping chest, with his own hot breaths bathing her body in his satisfaction, she'd never felt more fierce or more feminine. She'd never felt more abandoned or more serene. Rapture clung to them like the quivering curtain of her hair.

Then a bizarre sound penetrated the buzz in her ears. Not

hummingbirds whirring or the surf crashing… She realized it was the muffled sound of gloved hands *clapping*. "Bravo, Clare. A mere seventeen years old, and you sound like a practiced professional."

Her eyes flew open to see Mr. Cromwell standing a few yards away, at the top of the back porch steps. "Professional courtesan, not soprano, although that last bit could go either way." He waved his hand in the air like a tipping scale.

Clare and Ésh fell apart, scrambled and slid apart. She groped desperately for the only object within reach: the square emerald pillow from her mother's méridienne. Even with her knees clutched to her chest, the small tasselled bolster proved woefully insufficient. She threw more of her hair forward over her shoulders.

Ésh made no attempt to cover his own nudity. He leapt to his feet and stalked toward her father's steward, his hands fisted at his sides.

Mr. Cromwell remained on the stairs, impeccable in his grey top hat and pale blue suit—such a contrast to Ésh's scarred, sweaty nakedness. "Why, you're only a puppy." Mr. Cromwell's eyes travelled down Ésh's nude body and seemed to pause at his sinking manhood. Mr. Cromwell smirked.

"Who are you?" Ésh demanded.

"Don't you recognize my voice?" Mr. Cromwell drew out his cigarette case and struck a match on the porch railing. For a moment, he was enveloped in smoke. "I'm fairly certain you were hiding in the old stallion barn a few days ago, and I'm *told* I have an accent." Mr. Cromwell stressed his Cambridgeshire pronunciations with particular precision. The man was enjoying this, damn him. Clare couldn't believe she had considered him as a suitor.

She crawled to her chemise and struggled into it. Its neckline was open and it fell barely to her knees, but it was better than nothing.

"Why are you here?" Ésh persisted, still naked.

"*I* am employed by the man who owns this cottage. *You* are the one trespassing in multiple ways simultaneously." Mr. Cromwell exhaled smoke and gestured toward Clare with his cigarette. "Etiquette demands that you introduce yourself first."

Clare searched in vain for her drawers. "Don't tell him, *na-méo!*"

"*Na-méo?*" Mr. Cromwell held the syllables on his tongue, relishing the clue. "And that accent..." He'd leaned his black cane against the railing—how long had he been standing there, watching and listening? Mr. Cromwell caught up the cane again, grasping the gold handle in the shape of a roaring lion's head. With the other end, he motioned toward Ésh's medicine pouch and his breechcloth cord. "What is this? Why are you wearing a string? And where on Earth did you acquire such scars?"

The rest of Clare's clothing was inside the cottage, damn it— she'd either have to run around the front of the house in nothing but her chemise or push past Mr. Cromwell.

He didn't leave the stairs, blocking her path. Like many Southern gentlemen, he carried a cane as an elegant accessory rather than a walking support. Then Mr. Cromwell stuck his cigarette between his lips and lifted the cane across his body, clutching the tapered end and tapping the lion's head handle in his palm as if he might turn the thing into a club.

Nostrils flaring and toes gripping the rug under his feet, Ésh looked ready to charge him anyway. Her husband all but snorted and pawed the ground like a stallion challenging a rival for his mare. "What do you want?"

Clare knew she must be the peacemaker. "However did you hire a boat on Easter Sunday, Mr. Cromwell?"

He tucked his cane under one arm so he could tap the ash from his cigarette. "Your father has deep pockets, Clare, and he instructed me to spare no expense."

She realized for the first time that Mr. Cromwell wasn't addressing her as Miss Stratford anymore. Of course, she wasn't Miss Stratford anymore; she was—Mrs. Lazare?

Cromwell had no right to use her Christian name just because he'd seen her naked!

"It is time to come home and pay the piper now, Clare."

Still covered by only her hair and a slip of damp linen, Clare mustered her courage, strode to Ésh's side, and took his hand. She could feel the fury coiling inside him, but the ring of Mirage's braided hair gave her courage. "My home is no longer with my father—it is with my husband."

"'Husband'?" Trailing smoke, Cromwell motioned between Clare and Ésh. "Did that randy Priest actually sanction this?"

Clare averted her eyes, and Cromwell saw instantly that no such blessing had occurred. The wide neckline of the chemise slipped down one of her shoulders, as if exposing her shame. It loosed a few wisteria petals from her unbound hair.

Cromwell chuckled. "Well, that's a relief—there's still time to rescue you." He took one last puff of his cigarette. "Having seen your puppy at the *height* of his diminutive powers, I feel obligated to tell you, Clare: you can do better. Easily." Cromwell discarded his cigarette on the stairs and ground it beneath his boot.

Ésh's fists clenched while Clare scowled in indignation. She knew Cromwell was insulting her husband, but she didn't understand what he was implying.

Cromwell wallowed in her confusion. "How can I put this delicately?" He pointed the end of his cane toward Ésh's groin and circled it. "Your precious paramour is rather *lacking*. But how is a poor inexperienced lass to know these things? It isn't as if small men come with warning labels."

Ésh lunged for him.

Clare saw a flash of silver, and in the next instant there was a blade pressed against Ésh's belly, forcing him to stop before he even reached the steps. Clare gasped. She'd heard of sword-canes, but she'd never seen one used before. The lion's head was now a hilt. In his other hand, Cromwell brandished the sheath of the cane.

All three of them watched a bright ribbon of blood pulse from Ésh's skin, threading past his navel and into the hair at the top of his thighs.

"Come back to Charleston with me like a good girl, Clare, or I will gut your puppy with a flick of my wrist." Cromwell scraped the blade downward, deep enough to incise Ésh's skin. "Or perhaps I'll just add that warning label, ensure he doesn't curse any sons with his tiny prick…"

Clare was inches away from Ésh; she felt more than saw him

tensing for action. Whether he dodged sideways or shoved the blade away with his bare hands, he risked death or dismemberment. What if Cromwell's next thrust went all the way through him?

Clare grabbed her husband and clung to him with all her might. "Don't, Ésh, please don't!" She couldn't bear to see one more drop of his blood spilled, not if she could prevent it. "I'll go back with him!"

Ésh turned his head to her. "You can't, *na-méo*!"

Clare cupped his beautiful face in her hands. "This is nothing more than a delay, my love."

Ésh glared back at Cromwell. "We will come."

Cromwell's blade remained poised just above Ésh's groin. "*You* are not invited, puppy."

"Then my wife is not coming!"

Cromwell pressed the blade deeper into Ésh's curls. He winced as a new runnel of blood joined the first.

"I will come, alone!" Clare cried.

"I will not abandon you, *na-méo*!"

"You're not abandoning me, Ésh! For one thing, I am the one leaving! Secondly, I am useless to my father now—I am *your wife*, and there is nothing he can do to change that. I will consent to return to his house for *a day*. Perhaps he will see that I am happy and forgive me, when I tell him I don't expect a penny. Perhaps he will stalk off guzzling whiskey and allow me to collect some of my things." She'd wanted that all along: to gather her own little trousseau for their new life together. "Whatever happens, I am yours forever. We saw to that yesterday. We did what we came here to do."

"Very thoroughly," Cromwell commented.

Clare flushed and tried to ignore him. "We've already won, Ésh!"

His brow remained troubled. He seemed to be assessing once again if he could charge Cromwell and get the better of him before he lost something precious. Ésh looked back to Clare. "After you have spoken to your father, you will come to my grandfather's, and stay?"

"Yes, my love, yes! Tomorrow!"

Ésh swallowed and stepped back from the blade.

Cromwell wiped the sword with his handkerchief and sheathed it. He allowed them to enter the cottage, but he stayed uncomfortably close. "Shall I help you bathe, Clare?" Cromwell picked a wisteria blossom from her loose hair.

She gritted her teeth as she rebuttoned her chemise. "That will not be necessary."

"I'll help you dress, then."

"I already have a maid in training, thank you."

Cromwell followed them through the house wherever they went, poking his cane and his nose into everything, trying to determine Ésh's identity. He chuckled and leered at them as Clare and Ésh retrieved their scattered garments from all over the cottage. Cromwell even leaned against the doorframe while Clare relieved herself.

Ésh looked daggers at him. "What is the word, privacy?"

"I can't have the girl climbing out a window while my back is turned."

Clare would have *liked* a bath, but she refused to allow Cromwell the pleasure.

She did her best to tend her husband's injuries, essentially one laceration the length of her hand. Deeper at both ends but not deep enough to truly worry her, thank God. Fortunately, he was already covered in sweet almond oil, which was soothing on rashes—surely it was also soothing on cuts. Clare ended up applying a fresh coat.

Cromwell found Ésh's saddlebag. Ésh yanked it away from him before he could open it, but then Cromwell picked up his breech-cloth from the kitchen floor. The two men had a tug-of-war till Cromwell released his end without warning, nearly toppling Ésh against the stove. Which amused Cromwell to no end.

He let Ésh keep the remaining food, but he reclaimed the hamper. Cromwell even dumped the benne wafers out of their tin onto the kitchen table, sending several of the cookies careening onto the floor. Then, with a smirk, Cromwell dropped the empty tin into the hamper.

Clare pinned up her hair studded with tangles and wisteria blossoms. She left on her sweaty chemise, found her extra drawers, and guided Ésh through her layers. He'd donned only his breechcloth.

She peered at him over her shoulder. "There won't be another boat till tomorrow morning, Ésh, and there's so little food left."

"Then it is a good thing you are going," her husband winked while he tightened her corset laces.

"He seems to be some sort of savage," Cromwell observed. "I'm sure he can spear a fish. Or a seagull."

Clare scowled at him as she stepped into her cage crinoline. She tried to savor this intimacy with her husband and pretend Cromwell wasn't lurking in the corner. One day, Clare told herself, she and Ésh would laugh about this. "Be sure and eat the benne wafers before they go stale—they're good luck."

"I am used to fasting," Ésh assured Clare as he tied on her cage. Then he glanced toward the back of the cottage and the sound of the surf. "I think I will go swimming."

Clare paused to gape at him with her petticoat halfway over her head. "You're injured!"

"I have danced with skewers through my chest—this is nothing, na-méo." He said this even as he tugged the white petticoat down her arms and her corset, leaning close and staining it with almond oil and blood.

"The saltwater will sting!"

He tied the stained petticoat into place over the cage. "I will be fine, na-méo."

"But the undertow!"

"Henpecked already," Cromwell muttered from the corner.

Clare placed her hands on her husband's to make sure he was listening. "Don't go too far, Ésh. If you feel the current pulling you out to sea, swim across it, not against it—*parallel* to the shore till you break free." She demonstrated with her hands. "*Be careful.*"

"I will." Ésh glanced at Cromwell, who was lighting another cigarette, and lowered his voice. "You be careful of him. I think he wants you."

Clare raised her chin. "Well, he cannot have me. I am already taken."

Ésh looked genuinely worried, as if Clare might return Cromwell's attentions, as if some undertow might pull her back to this man and the life he represented. A life of seeming comfort and ease, elegance and wealth. Perhaps her husband sensed that she had once been attracted to Cromwell.

Despite the width of her hoop skirt and petticoat, Clare leaned over and wrapped Ésh in her arms. As long as she kept the embrace brief, she wagered that Cromwell would not be so uncouth as to physically pry them apart. "I belong only to you now, *na-méo*," she whispered in his ear. "You have stamped me with your imprint, repeatedly, and I will open my body for no other man."

Cromwell cleared his throat loudly.

"I love you."

Clare and Ésh spoke the words at exactly the same time. They pulled back and grinned at each other. Oh, it was wonderful to hear: not an endearment in a foreign language but "I love you," soft and bold and proud. It would give her the strength to leave with Cromwell, to face her father, to face anything.

Cromwell rolled his eyes. "Virgins."

Clare's flounced green skirt had been stained by the saltwater, but it was the only dress she'd brought. In the hall, she restored her bonnet and gloves and remembered to give Ésh money for the ferry tomorrow.

"Yes, Clare," Cromwell smirked, "pay your whore for his services."

"I am her *husband*," Ésh reminded him through gritted teeth.

"You'll also need the key, to lock up the cottage when you go." Clare picked up the two keys on their ribbon and offered them to Ésh.

"Wait." Cromwell snatched the ribbon instead and narrowed his eyes at the pair of keys. "What's the other one?"

"Nothing," Clare pretended. Then she simpered. She could be salacious too. "*Everything*. It's the key to my heart, Mr. Cromwell."

He was not amused. "What does this *really* open, Clare?"

She sighed. It wasn't as if Ésh would need to visit the Church Street house again—this time tomorrow, Clare would be at Grand-père René's and in her husband's arms. "It's the key to the garden gate, the one on Longitude Lane."

"*I* will be taking that one, thank you." Cromwell opened his sword-cane just enough to sever the ribbon. "We can't have the puppy entering your 'garden' to remark his territory whenever he wishes." Cromwell slapped the cottage key on the table in the hall, instructing Ésh: "Do try and clean up this little love nest before you leave. Then, if you value your hide, you will disappear. At present, Mr. Stratford considers you beneath his notice—but if you approach his daughter again, I expect he'll change his mind." Cromwell looped the empty hamper through one arm and nudged Clare's back with the lion handle of his cane, urging her toward the back porch. "Why don't we walk along the beach?"

She took up her portmanteau and valise, then looked over her shoulder and found her husband. "Don't forget the buffalo robe."

"I won't, *na-méo*." Ésh smiled weakly and tried to follow them over the threshold.

Cromwell pressed the lion's head into his naked chest.

Ésh stopped in the doorway. But as he peered down at the sheathed sword, at Cromwell's other arm occupied with the hamper, Clare watched Ésh's eyes narrow. She watched the thought rise inside him: *His blade isn't out now—I could get the better of him now.*

Cromwell seemed to read the thought too. "This isn't you against me, puppy. This is you against the entirety of Southern manhood. I'll call in the garrison at Fort Moultrie if I have to. News of a virgin's abduction always gets a soldier's dander up. I'll simply neglect to mention that she's already been deflowered."

"Deflowered"—what a ridiculous term. It was completely backwards. Clare had flowered for the very first time with Ésh, and she would go on flowering as long as he loved her. "I will be all right, *na-méo*," she assured him.

With endearing reluctance, her husband let Cromwell take her. As they stepped from the boardwalk onto the beach, Clare thought: *A stranger seeing Cromwell and me would think WE were the couple returning from holiday—he with his hamper and me with my portmanteau and valise.*

Still wearing only his breechcloth, Ésh strode out after them,

ELIZABETH BELL

past the myrtle hedges to the end of the wooden path. There he stopped.

This was some perverted mirror image of the Orpheus and Eurydice story, Clare thought. Instead of her beloved reclaiming her from Hell, a demon was dragging her from Heaven. Each time Clare looked back along the beach, she saw Ésh standing on the boardwalk, growing smaller and smaller until he was nothing but a distant star.

THE END of *Native Stranger*.
But not the end of the story…

If you enjoyed this novel, pretty please help other readers discover my books by leaving an honest review, even a short one, on Amazon, Goodreads, and/or BookBub. I'd be thrilled if you'd mention the Lazare Family Saga on social media too. Word of mouth, literal or virtual, makes an enormous difference to an indie author like me. Thank you!

Do you want to know what happens next for Clare, Ésh, David, Easter, Shadrach, and Verily? Do you want to know the truth about Tessa's death? *Sweet Medicine*, the fourth and final book of the Lazare Family Saga, is now available for Kindle, in paperback, and in hardcover.